He had the soul of a p
the passion o

In Savage Splendor . . .

His expression turned pensive, as though he were studying her to store her image in his memory. His eyes dropped to her breast, held for a moment, then lifted again to her face.

"Oh, you lovely thing," he murmured. "How you would look in nature's garb lying in some grassy glade hard by Shannon's stream!"

"Who are you?" Charity demanded.

He ended his reverie and swept a graceful bow. "Sean McDougal, at your service, lass."

"What do you want?"

"So little. So very little. Only a kiss, a souvenir to take away with me."

With that he reached boldly forth and took Charity into his arms. Her bemusement lasted until his lips touched hers. Then her basic instincts, held in check till now, burst forth. She drew her mouth downward until it was against his throat. She bit viciously, even as she put her arms around his shoulders.

"Why you savage little vixen!" he snarled. "All right; now you owe me more."

But immediately the flash of anger changed to a look of excitement. His voice dropped to a musical purr. "A kiss is but a fading blossom to die in the press of a memory book. But a souvenir to remember—to stay forever green. . . ."

Even as he spoke he was forcing her to the floor, her crossed wrists held rigidly in a steel grip just below her breast. Then, with his free hand, he swept the skirts of her robe and gown upward. . . .

IN SAVAGE SPLENDOR

Paula Fairman

PINNACLE BOOKS   LOS ANGELES

IN SAVAGE SPLENDOR

Copyright © 1978 by Paul Fairman

An original Pinnacle Books edition, published for the first time anywhere.

ISBN: 0-523-40181-7

First printing, March 1978

Cover illustration by William Maughan

Printed in the United States of America

PINNACLE BOOKS, INC.
One Century Plaza
2029 Century Park East
Los Angeles, California 90067

Part One: *The Laughing Privateer*

1.

Charity was enraged as she watched the four lovely African females who had been led to the block.

Why did they not *resist?* Why did they stand there like dumb beasts and let those brutes examine their bodies as though they were but soulless heifers waiting to be bargained off? Of course they were in shackles and could win no victory, but they could still assert themselves, if only symbolically. They could *declare* themselves.

We are human beings and will not stand passively by and allow lustful men to pry open our mouths and peer in—to lift our skirts and make us stand naked to public gaze while they paw at our breasts and private parts.

They could *fight,* chains or not—claw, bite, scratch—leave marks, however futile, of their defiance before they were subdued, as they of course would be. Their meekness was what stirred Charity's anger as she looked down on the spectacle from the vantage point of her tutor's window.

This was the first slave auction she had ever witnessed; twenty-five chattels fresh off an African slave ship were being put upon the block and the clever auctioneer was now presenting four of the most comely young wenches, with buyers free to examine the merchandise.

A slave auction brought people out; prospective buyers, of course, but also the citizenry both genteel and otherwise. Ladies of quality in their bright crinolines and stylish continental imports strolled about under lacy parasols; children rolled and tumbled at play; men stood about discussing the latest news from Boston and Philadelphia, the two main centers, other than Williamsburg, of colonial unrest. Would anger at injustices to the Colonies flare into armed rebellion? Most thought not, but there *were* the firebrands—Patrick Henry and his ilk—openly stirring the citizenry.

Charity did not consider herself a part of what she beheld—of the people or the town—even though she had been born near neighboring Jamestown of tragic memory, and had spent all of her seventeen maturing years in the surrounding environs.

Her being in Williamsburg at all was the doing of her foster mother, Mistress Mae Varney—"Mad Mae," as the townspeople derisively called her—who insisted that Charity receive some education. So there were the twice-weekly visits to Schoolmaster Jeremy Hicks for private tutoring. Hicks' need of money overshadowed local prejudices against Mad Mae and her foster daughter and closed his ears to the contemptuously spoken falsehoods:

... They live with Indians. ...

4

...They are hardly better than the savages themselves....

No Williamsburg child had ever been allowed to play with that wild young animal named Charity.

This ostracism tended to embolden Hicks in regard to his private pupil. She was remarkably well developed even at an early age; a lissome young beauty calculated to stir any man's blood, and it occurred to Hicks that the sight of that bare bottom would brighten a dull afternoon. So upon this occasion when Charity had not learned her sums, he took his paddle in hand and said, "You must be disciplined, young lady. Bend over your desk and lift your skirt."

Intrigued by what would be a new experience, Charity obeyed, raising her homespun garment as ordered.

"Now your pantalettes. Lower them."

Charity twisted her head about to frown at him. "I'll do no such thing."

"Oh, yes you shall!" Hicks replied as lust overcame him. "I'll vow you lower them often enough for those young Chickahominy bucks!"

The insulting accusation threw Charity into a rage. "Why, you!"

She got no farther because Hicks had snatched her pantalettes down himself, exposing her bare-skinned loveliness to his gaze. He dropped the switch and his hands went intimately to her body.

Charity straightened and spun about and was upon him like God's fury incarnate. Her attack was brief. It lasted only until her teeth sank deep into the flesh between Hicks' thumb and forefin-

5

ger, drawing blood and sending him into snarling retreat.

He stood nursing his wound while Charity pulled up her stripped-down garment and started for the door. That stirred Hicks to even greater anguish, the loss of Mistress Mae's payments for Charity's tutoring.

"Wait," he begged. "Don't go. I am sorry. *Most* sorry."

Charity's temper was mercurial. It could fade as quickly as it flared. She eyed him in frowning judgment. "You are sure? You will never, *never* do such a thing again?"

"Upon my honor."

"Very well," Charity replied primly. "I shall consider forgiving you. Consider it *only*, mind you."

"I beg of you, do not tell Mistress Mae of this incident."

"Perhaps, perhaps not, but I am seventeen years old and quite able to make my own decisions on matters which concern me."

With that, Charity marched out, her pretty little nose in the air. But the dignity of her exit was somewhat marred by the sudden arrival of a visitor to Hicks' chambers—a roughly clad man who flashed her with a quick eye, then shouldered past her.

"Well, I never! . . ." Charity snapped, then went on her way.

Alone with the schoolmaster, the newcomer regarded him as though *he* were the intruder. "All right, Hicks. What have you to say for yourself."

Hicks, pushed from one difficulty into another,

6

sought weakly for words. "I was planning to reach you, Quale. To tell you. . . ."

The man cut in abruptly. "I waited last night," he said. "Like the fool that I am I waited an hour over the appointed time. But no Hicks. No payment."

"I'm sorry, Quale. I truly am. I tried to raise the funds. I was unable."

"So you left me standing about like an idiot!"

"I was *afraid* to face you. I feared your wrath."

Quale advanced in a threatening manner. Hicks, no match for the burly brute, cringed away and perhaps it was that abject reaction that stopped Quale, turning his intent from violence into mere contempt.

"What a miserable creature you are!"

That was unfair! Bitterly so. Any man had a right to better himself; to try to rise from his station. And if Hicks had fancied himself a gambler and found that it was a mistake, his intent had still been a worthy one; so much so that he could not now understand why fate had dealt him such an incredible run of bad cards; or why a lack of simple good sense had permitted him to borrow from a man like Quale, only to lose again and get himself into this perilous mess.

"I'll get the money," he promised. "I assure you. I have a source but it will take a few days."

"How many days?"

"A fortnight."

"You dare to face me with such a lie?"

"It is not a lie! All I need is a little time!"

Quale considered the situation from his per-

7

sonal viewpoint: that of balancing possible payment against the satisfaction of beating Hicks to a bloody pulp. For a man of Quale's ilk there were no other alternatives, what with his aversion to long, drawn out legal pettifogging. However, though Hicks was probably lying, Quale could forego the pleasure of the beating just in case the miserable carrion was telling the truth. And Hicks would not be escaping his clutches in a mere fourteen days.

"I agree," Quale said. "It is against my better judgment and it will go doubly hard with you if you fail. Take that as Gospel, my friend."

"You are most generous," Hicks quavered. "I will not fail you."

"You have that backwards. It is not I you would be failing but yourself."

With that, he strode out leaving Hicks to pray, in his desperation, that something would turn up. Fate owed him that favor after buffeting him about so cruelly. . . .

2.

Wending her way homeward, Charity considered Hicks' apology. Her reaction had not been as it had appeared—entirely from outraged modesty. She had known for some time that her body excited the men of the town, and what Hicks said about the young Indians struck a chord. She'd often seen the hot desire in their eyes and she long since would have been taken had the Indians not feared Mistress Mae's wrath and the mystical powers she possessed; powers strong enough to intimidate even Chahalis, the Chickahominy medicine man. Another reason for pardoning the schoolmaster was Mother Mae's strong faith in the value of education.

Only through learning can you hope to survive when I am gone, my chick. The world is full of hungry wolves and without education they will devour you.

So Charity decided to make peace with the schoolmaster. The lessons would continue. Basically, she was not equipped to think ill of anyone. During the whole of her remembered life she had known only love, kindness, and security. There were no recollections of tomahawks splitting the skulls of her parents; nor the woman, her eyes burning in madness, who snatched her, a newborn bundle, from the arms of a marauding Cherokee. As Mistress Mae explained it to her friend Christopher Leach during one of his visits to the log cabin off the old Ironbound Road from Jamestown to Williamsburg:

"That handful of raiding Cherokees had gone through our place. My husband and child were dead and I was left as such. But the tomahawk blow had been glancing and I arose and followed them and found them at the Sturges place. Tom and Lena were dead and their cabin afire but their babe had not yet been destroyed. My mind

9

had taken flight and I think I probably saw that babe as my own, and snatched it from the monster about to dispatch it."

"A brave act indeed."

"Hardly. Insanity destroys logic and common sense."

Mistress Mae paused; a wry chuckle punctuated her account. "I guess something of value can be found in even the ghastliest horror. At least it was so in my case. When I entered the clearing that day, the half dozen redmen stared at me as though I were something out of hell. They gave up the child without protest and backed away, their eyes upon me, until they disappeared into the forest."

"How strange."

"Not really. When my sanity returned, I recalled the Indian superstition—a madman is touched by the Great Spirit and is favored by the gods. No Indian will harm the insane in any way. As you know, I have courted the mystic all my life. I am skilled with the Tarot cards and know much of the voodoo lore. So I remained mad. I practiced and retained the image and as a result, Charity and I have lived safely in this cabin for all the years, even with some authority in the Chickahominy village yonder."

"You did not move into Williamsburg and seek the protection of the Crown?" Christopher Leach asked.

"They would have taken Charity away from me. They would have called me unfit, a lone female with no husband. So I kept the child away from white society—here in the wilderness be-

10

tween Williamsburg and the Chickahominy villages. We joined with neither. It has been most successful."

"You are to be greatly admired, Madam."

Christopher Leach proffered the compliment even as he noted the change in Mistress Mae's tone; the *most successful* uttered with some doubt and uncertainty, as though some problem were involved. That last was true but the Englishman was not to learn of its nature until two years later.

3.

In the flowering spring of 1775, Christopher was making his last visit to Mistress Mae in the cabin on the Ironbound Road.

He presented an aristocratic figure as he rode his black hunter out of Williamsburg that morning. He wore an expensive blue satin riding jacket, its large pockets and wide lapels highly popular in London and Continental society. Gray fawnskin breeches were molded to his legs, disappearing into black boots polished to a mirror sheen.

Yet, however his appearance marked him, Christopher was not a snob. A handsome young man approaching thirty, he yearned to be accepted on all levels of society and tried to unbend although he seldom succeeded in doing so.

Some took his rigidity as reflecting strength of character, when in truth it was something rather different. Christopher had never been able to escape the domination of his illustrious, steel-willed, elder brother, the Most Reverend Clement Leach, rector of the Church of St. Jude in Kent, southeast of London. Clement, a power in both Parliament and at Canterbury, was some ten years older than Christopher and had exerted his strong influence from childhood. He was a churchman of bleak moral purity with a stern, never-smiling visage that hovered always in the back of Christopher's mind.

The latter had been four years in the Colonies, purportedly on a mission for the Foreign Secretary, but his sojourn was actually a temporary exile, decreed by Clement as being expedient.

The reason was a woman, one Gabrielle Spencer-Dean, daughter of a titled but impoverished English family. Gabrielle, in her mid-twenties, was beautiful, vivacious and, in Clement's judgment, "immoral, notorious, and predatory."

As he summed her up, "Her interest in you, Christopher, is strictly monetary. She resents her poverty and sees you as the key to our family money. It is as simple as that."

"I'm sure you are wrong, Brother Clement. Gaby loves me for myself."

"But consider the ne'er-do-wells she runs with; the woman's reputation!"

"That would all change, I am sure. Once under the influence of a God-fearing family...."

"Bosh! Her course is set. She would never change."

"I think you misjudge her, Brother Clement."

Christopher's stubbornness was disturbing; he did not bow, as he usually did, to Clement's superior judgment. In view of this, Clement spoke to friends in the Colonial Office and Christopher's commission was speedily forthcoming.

"You will investigate French incursions into British territory in the New World," they told him, "and report the strength of their arms and their alliances with the Indian tribes. Your reports must be sent regularly to the Foreign Minister by returning naval ships and packets."

Clement suggested, "The appointment is a great honor to our family name. There are rumors of a knighthood later on."

"The commission extends over four years," Christopher said doubtfully.

Certain of his understanding of Gaby's character, Clement added, "You are thinking of the lass, no doubt, but I have changed my mind on that matter. You may suggest the alliance of our family names and take Gabrielle with you to the Colonies."

"I am delighted at your change of heart," Christopher replied happily.

He hurried to Gabrielle with the news and was distressed when he found her enthusiasm for their marriage sharply diminished.

"Chris dearest—I would positively wilt away in that primitive land! Can you see *me* in drab homespuns, losing my youth and beauty to the rigors of frontier life?"

"But darling, the cities are quite civilized. Williamsburg, Philadelphia, Charleston...."

Gaby laid soft hands on his chest, pouted her pretty lips, and managed a loving gaze. "You will not be gone forever, dearest. I shall wait here and keep myself beautiful for your return. That is, if you *must* go."

"I can hardly do otherwise," Christopher protested ardently.

They parted with a long farewell kiss, Christopher thinking wistfully that Gaby had never looked so lovely.

This was true, but even as he left, her beauty turned feline, her pretty pout became petulant anger. "That bastard, Clement!" she screamed to her maid. "It was his doing. I would dearly love to cut off his manhood and hang it out to dry—if he has one, which I doubt."

Although it appeared that Clement had placed a block in Gaby's path to better fortune, what he did turned out to be a blessing. With Christopher scarcely beyond the breakwater, she began stalking other game. She seduced and married the aging Lord Kirth who obligingly died two years later, leaving her in widowed control of one of England's larger fortunes.

For his part, Christopher served conscientiously and well even though, after getting into his mission, it must have occurred to him that England had no great need to worry over French incursions, or the menace of French-Indian alliances. Since earlier decisive defeats, the French had made little headway toward solidifying their own holdings, let alone usurping those of Britain.

14

Still, Christopher kept making his investigations and sending back regular reports, dull and prosaic though they were.

He considered himself most fortunate in befriending a strange old female who lived off in the wilderness and was in a position to keep him current on the moods and movements of the local Indian tribes. This saved him a great deal of running about and the possible hostility he might have incurred from snooping into their affairs. As time went by he got to know Mistress Mae Varney quite well and considered her a friend; one of the few he would miss upon his departure.

4.

"I shall be leaving for England soon," Christopher said. "One more trip to Philadelphia. Then I shall return, continue on to Charleston, and embark soon afterwards."

"I will be sad to see you go," the old woman said with genuine regret.

"That is most gracious of you."

Mistress Varney was receiving him on the lawn beside her cabin under a magnolia as fragrant as paradise, aglow with virginal white blossoms. She sat on a wicker lounge beside a table from which she offered him rum, she herself sipping a dark liquid he took to be medicinal.

Mae Varney was of fragile cast and perhaps the crueler folk of Williamsburg found some justification in referring to her as "that old crone." Much of her appearance—the unkempt hair, the shapeless black gown, the brittle, eerie laugh—was calculated to support the "mad" image. But the pointed chin, high cheek bones, and piercing black eyes made a fine foundation upon which to build.

"I have come," Christopher said, "to thank you for the help you have given me in my work here."

"You paid me well."

"No more than your services were worth."

They sat quietly for a moment, then the old woman said, "I shall die soon."

The abruptness of the remark, so casually stated, threw Christopher off balance. He could only murmur, "I—I'm sorry," as Mistress Mae placed a hand upon her breast.

"It is here. A great growth against which my herbs and potions are powerless. Soon it will take me off."

"Madam—if there is anything I can do. . . ."

"There is. I have a favor to ask." Her bright black eyes locked into his.

"Whatever I am able to do," he said with sincerity.

"A very great favor. I beg you to take the child, Charity, to England with you."

His answer was a blank stare. Curiously—or perhaps not—the request conjured up a mental image of Clement's stern visage.

"For years," Mae Varney went on, "I have known this time would come. You see, this way of

16

life I chose for the child and myself left a blank in her future—her welfare after I am gone. As things stand she is between two worlds—one which would reject her and the other, the Indian way, which would turn her quickly into a Chickahominy squaw. I have one particular enemy in the tribe, a medicine man named Chahalis. With my arts and skills I have frustrated him for years—stolen his thunder so to speak—and only my living presence protects the child."

Christopher was struggling with his scattered wits. Cutting in, he said, "But Madam, you speak of Charity as a helpless child. She is not that at all. She is a young woman—close to maturity."

"Seventeen years of age. Hardly a woman yet, and completely innocent of the ways of the world." Mistress Mae's eyes burned with fervor as she continued, seeking to sway Christopher's mind.

"I have saved through the years—most of the money you paid me. Also I have done quite well in the sale of herbal medicines to the ailing. All in all, I have some three thousand British pounds. The money came in various forms but it is now in British gold sovereigns . . ." She pointed a clawlike finger, ". . . there—just there beside the tulip tree—buried in the soft earth. So you would be put to no expense. The whole of it is yours."

"But—but what could I do—bringing an unchaperoned young lady back with me from the Colonies?"

Christopher's image of his churchman-brother's granite profile would not go away. He

17

was now imagining Clement's reaction at sight of Charity; the storm of Clement's moral outrage.

"You are a fine gentleman," Mistress Mae pursued, "honest, decent, straightforward. I know Charity would come to no harm from you, and as to what would transpire in England . . ."

She stopped, foundering, no strong argument for her cause offering itself.

"I don't know," she admitted. "I only know of Charity's uncertain future here in the Colonies. But England is a civilized nation and Charity is intelligent and presentable. With you as her sponsor . . ."

Having at last gathered his wits together, Christopher now arose, a frosty figure in his fine attire and stiff formality.

"Madam, I'm sorry—so sorry—but what you ask is out of the question, completely impossible. I am powerless to help you in the way that you ask."

Her plea was silent now; all her anxieties and misgivings radiated from her heart and her magnificent eyes to reflect the intensity of her petition. It was more than Christopher could stand. He was basically a gentle, compassionate man, and when he could no longer face the situation he turned and fled like a felon leaving the scene of a crime. Without looking back he mounted his horse and urged the animal off at high speed until he was again on the Ironbound Road. . . .

5.

The only defense Christopher had against Mistress Mae's forceful plea was to block the whole incident from his mind. This he grimly did, turning his thoughts to the task at hand.

It was a mission to which he was self-appointed. While gathering the comparatively unimportant data on the French and Indian situation, Christopher had become increasingly aware of something he saw as far more important—the growing unrest in the Colonies against British rule.

There was that treasonable organization—the Committee of Correspondence—a loosely knit, but far too effective network of communication through which various nests of traitors kept each other informed. There had already been incidents of open rebellion against the authority of the Crown to levy and collect taxes. In Boston, Philadelphia, Williamsburg, the leaders of the malcontents were blatantly voicing their treasonous sentiments. An entirely just and reasonable tax upon tea had been taken as an issue, much of the tea left unsold and some even hurled into the sea at the Port of Boston.

A perilous situation indeed, and Christopher

could only wonder at the complacency of the Crown in spite of his dispatches over the months. Were they unaware in England of the impending peril? Christopher had to assume so and for that reason he had put a great deal of effort into the *dossier* he was compiling; a sizeable work containing names and locations, with suggestions as to appropriate action if and when the rebellion flared. He verified many of the rumors he had heard in Williamsburg, dug out fresh information of an even more alarming character, and was quite satisfied with the result when his task was completed and he made his quiet exodus from the Pennsylvania hotbed of discontent.

But not quiet enough.

In Philadelphia there existed a central group of men—rebels or patriots depending upon where one stood—who preferred to remain nameless. There was some disagreement among them as to Christopher posing any danger to their cause, but upon his leaving town, William Moultrie, the leader, called the group together.

"I have some late word concerning the Englishman, Leach, which disturbs me. Inquiries at Cowder Inn where he stayed reveal that he has been taking down a wealth of names and details concerning local activities."

"A harmless snoop, I'd say."

"Hardly that, I fear, although I may be misjudging him. At any rate, he troubles me. That report he compiled. A waiter at the inn got a look at it and reported to me. It could well lead the Loyalists straight to all of us if things come to a test of arms."

20

"*When* things come to a test of arms."

"Aye. I fear you speak the truth," Moultrie agreed.

"Then why was something not done before the man left?"

"He has some stature. Obtaining the report from him here in Philadelphia might well have defeated our primary purpose by drawing attention to us. Anyhow, he is now on his way back to Williamsburg from whence he will go immediately to Charleston. His return to England will follow."

"It is too late to overtake him between here and Williamsburg, I fear."

"No doubt. But a brace of pistols should be able to overtake him at some point beyond, before he reaches Charleston."

"Our last resort as things stand."

"But one which should be successful. A lonely road. A single, unsuspecting target. There should be no great difficulty."

There was debate and final agreement after which Moultrie summoned two likely emissaries for the project and instructed them carefully.

"There should be no need for violence if you handle it properly. We want the report, not the Englishman's life. So unless he brings it upon himself, you will take what we are after and send him on his way unharmed."

And thus, a pair of riders were dispatched upon Christopher's trail. Knowing they could not overtake their quarry before Williamsburg, they did not press, saving their mounts for the second leg of his journey. . . .

A long, boring trail, a wearying ride and with his mind now released, Christopher, in spite of himself, found his thoughts turning to the cabin on Ironbound Road and Mistress Mae Varney's desperate plea.

Of course he stood by his original decision. Granting the woman's request was out of the question. Still, he now realized that he could have been a little more gracious in his refusal. He had been brutally abrupt. Instead of turning away without so much as a goodbye, he could have explained the reason for his inability to help her, could have tried to comfort Mistress Mae by assuring her that she need not be so anguished over Charity's future. She was a lovely young lady and there had to be many fine people of good heart who would see that she did not come to harm.

Anxious to atone for his previous lack of feeling, Christopher turned into the cut-off on Ironbound Road toward the cabin in the wilderness.

What he found was incomprehensible; a look of desertion about the cabin so obvious that he reined up abruptly as he entered the clearing. What could have happened? The wicker lounge, the table and chairs had vanished from under the magnolia tree. Blank, uncurtained windows stared blindly back at him.

He approached slowly, dismounted and entered the cabin to find it gutted; furniture gone, dishware missing save that which lay smashed upon the floor. Even the pothook had been wrenched from the stone flanking of the fireplace.

An Indian raid? Had there been death as well

as vandalism and destruction? Christopher
searched about for clues. He found none, whereupon he mounted and rode hard into Williamsburg. . . .

6.

The facts which Christopher went seeking were
cruel ones indeed; he would discover a series of
events, one piled on another, which changed
Charity Sturges' happy life into one of total
disaster.

First, there had been the shock of coming home
to find her foster mother dead. She had known
nothing of Mistress Mae's illness, the latter deem-
ing it a kindness to spare Charity until the last
moment; a well-intentioned mistake as things
turned out, because death does not make appoint-
ments, choosing to arrive unannounced.

Charity sat helpless for a time, holding a
gaunt, lifeless hand in her own. Then by fortunate circumstance a kindly lady arrived at the
cabin for her weekly supply of herbal medicine;
one who could ignore social levels when compassion demanded. The lady invited Charity to return with her to Williamsburg for the night, but
Charity refused. So her benefactor went away
and soon others arrived; three men who were
sent to remove Mistress Mae's body in prepara-

tion for burial. Again Charity stayed where she was, as though the cabin itself had become the only remaining symbol of the safety and security she had known.

The following morning the lady returned in her carriage to take Charity to Bruton Parish Church where a service was held; then to a small cemetery on the outskirts of the town for the burial. A surprising number of people attended and when the interment was completed, the lady looked about for Charity.

She was gone—off and running through the forest—trying to drain the grief from her heart by exhausting her body.

Arriving at the cabin she found the desecration which had been visited upon it in her absence; the whole place looted, no doubt by Chickahominies who had been awaiting the opportunity.

Her emotional well was pretty much drained by this time and she began suffering the deeper hurt which time only would heal. Therefore she was able to contemplate the scene of destruction more calmly; without explosions of grief or defiance. Her own immediate future began pressing upon her mind. Where would she go? What would she do? No immediate answer was forthcoming so, finally overcome by weariness, she curled up in a corner of the cabin floor and went to sleep. . . .

Thus did Mae Varney's extraordinary life end and was her death received by those in the town of Williamsburg; some felt only indifference; others, kindness and compassion.

Only Jeremy Hicks saw Mae's death as a personal advantage.

Hicks, his desperation greater with each passing day, had prayed for a solution to his problem with Quale, and now it seemed that his prayer had been answered. The girl Charity would be alone now and if he acted with sufficient speed—

The thought sent him rushing to Hiram Quale with an idea rather than a plan, Hicks himself being too inexperienced and too cowardly to work out the operation for himself.

". . . A white slave," he told Quale. "Young, beautiful, untouched. You have dealt in slaves and you told me yourself that white virgins are very much in demand."

"True. Such properties are rare. I have buyers."

"This one I have in mind. I am sure the price she would command would be far more than the miserable pittance I owe you."

"White, you say. You must be confusing slaves with bond servants. There is a difference."

"A slave, truly. You saw her when you came to my chambers for your money. She has Indian blood in her but not enough to detect in her appearance. Doesn't that make her a slave?"

"If it is true."

"I assure you it is. She has lived with the Chickahominy all her life and her Indian blood is well known."

"You are offering her to me in payment of your debt?"

"There will be ample money. I demand to be included in the sale," unexpected firmness in his voice.

"I expected you would."

"It is only fair," Hicks said piously.

"Bring the property to me. Finding a buyer would be no problem, if she is what you say."

"There are some details to be worked out. The girl came to me for tutoring so I know a great deal about her. She has no family or friends. Her foster mother died last night—an old crone looked down upon by the whole town."

"Then you do not own her."

"No, but she is free to be taken if we move quickly. There is a Chickahominy who can be persuaded to vouch for her Indian blood. He had an intense hatred for her foster mother and if it is left to him he will turn her over to some young buck to become a squaw. So we would really be doing the girl a favor."

Quale was in no need of such hypocritical mouthings. "How would you persuade the Indian?" he asked contemptuously, "with a flintlock?"

"A few shillings. I could obtain an affidavit."

"You talk like a fool! An Indian's statement has no legal value even if sworn to."

"But you do not understand. I told you nobody *cares* what happens to Charity. The town does not want her. Particularly the good women. They see danger to their husbands if she were cut loose in Williamsburg. They would let the Indians have her and good riddance."

Quale remained dubious as he mulled the matter over. If the schoolmaster's argument had any

26

merit there *was* a tempting profit to be made at the small cost of a few shillings to some Indian or other. Quale did have an avid receiver for such a property—one Orin Cade, a plantation owner living a respectable distance from Williamsburg with a fine appetite for young virgin flesh, and Hicks had said the wench was untouched. Also, for his part, Quale knew he could get the proper legal papers by applying to the right party at the courthouse, again for a mere pittance.

"All right," he said finally. "If you can get the Indian's signed word, we may be able to do business...."

Hicks did have some trouble with Chahalis. The Indian had been savoring the revenge now open to him. But the money he received for signing a simple lie was more desirable than posthumous vengeance on Mistress Mae, now gone and no longer an obstacle.

So the kidnapping was arranged, and the slave trader Quale and the perfidious Jeremy Hicks came to the cabin in the dark of night. They bound, gagged, and blindfolded Charity while she was still only half-awake, tumbled her into a wagon, and took her off to a destiny beyond her imagining.

Orin Cade, waiting at a designated crossroads well out of town, was far from satisfied. "I don't like any of this," he growled. "If this is a legal transaction, why was I directed to this place in the dead of night? It is all very irregular. I regret accommodating you in this fashion. It is not a manner in which I am accustomed to doing business."

27

"I explained that, Cade," Quale replied. "You are not the only one eager to acquire this prize morsel. There are Indians who have been waiting to get their hands on her. So there had to be some precautions taken. She would make some buck a fine squaw."

"But the sale *is* legal?"

"Entirely so. Here is the affidavit attesting to the wench's Indian blood."

Orin Cade inspected the paper by the light of a bright moon. "Walter Chahalis. I never heard of him."

"No reason you should. He has known the girl for years. And here is the bill of sale, stamped and duly recorded. You have made a fine purchase, my friend."

"Perhaps, but it has been on your word, Quale. If she proves to be some ugly slut—white or not. . . ."

Quale replied with unconcerned heartiness. "Then you have recourse. We know each other. We have done business before. You have only to come to me with your complaint."

He spoke with a confidence bolstered by his own investigations. Charity was the prize he'd described. She was an orphan, completely friendless, from a town where she was not wanted; therefore few inquiries would be made. All in all the profit on the deal made the negligible risk well worthwhile.

"Very well," Cade said finally. "You asked for payment in cash. It is here, in this packet. Do you wish to count it?"

"Of course not. There is no mistrust between friends."

"Then move the slave to my wagon and I'll be off. I have a long drive ahead." Cade had come north in a closed vehicle built for transporting rebellious slaves and legally convicted felons. It was a rectangular box on wheels, totally enclosed, with the driver's seat outside. Inside there were facing benches with bolted chains to be used on dangerous prisoners.

As Charity was lifted from one wagon to the other, Cade said, "You can untie her now. Restraints will not be needed."

So, after a brief moment of moonlight and shadow, Charity found herself comparatively free but still a prisoner in a dark, frightening place. And it might have been some comfort to her, however scant, if she could have known the name of her betrayer and what befell him.

As Cade drove away, Quale put the packet of money in an inside pocket and said, "Your debt is paid, Hicks. And some good advice with it. Stop gambling. Your handling of cards is pathetic."

"But that was not the deal!" Hicks protested. "I was to participate in half the return over and above my debt. That would give me. . . ."

"Nothing," Quale snapped. "I was overly generous in allowing you to clear the debt in this fashion. Go back to your schoolroom and profit by the valuable lesson you have learned." With that, Quale climbed into his wagon, adding, "I will not be able to drive you back to town. I am going in the other direction."

So schoolmaster Hicks was left as he had been

before; clear of his debt, true, but with the same bleak hopeless outlook as before. As he trudged back toward Williamsburg, he cursed his fate in high anguish. But this changed his destiny not a whit.

7.

Christopher arrived in Williamsburg and went immediately to the courthouse on Court Street, only to find the magistrate absent. However, there was a fussy little middle-aged clerk to listen to his questions.

"Oh, yes, Mad Mae's death. It came quite suddenly. A woman who went to her cabin for an herbal remedy told us and we saw to it she got a Christian burial."

"She had a daughter, I believe. A girl named Charity."

"A foster daughter. Yes, Charity was sold. The whole matter was handled quickly and efficiently. We thought it best for the town."

"*Sold!* What on earth are you talking about?"

The clerk had a large nose and a pair of narrow rectangular glasses too small for his face. To peer through them he had to almost cross his eyes.

Speaking with bland detachment, he said, "We thought it the best solution—for the town *and* the girl. Otherwise the Indians would have taken her, since there was no place for her here in. . . ."

"You said *sold*. Ridiculous! She was not black!"

"You don't understand. Her Indian blood. . . ."

"Neither was she an Indian."

"On the contrary. A tribesman prominent among his people, a Chickahominy named Chahalis, put his mark on an affidavit stating that her grandfather on the distaff side was a Cherokee. The affidavit was notarized and became an official document."

"This is still madness. Charity had no Indian blood in her. But even granting that, Indians are not sold as slaves."

The clerk paused for a moment as though seeking words to explain a perfectly logical situation to this gentleman. "Not quite true, good sir. Indians are made slaves on occasion, but the practice is not often followed because of the proximity of their people. With the Indian tribes so close, there could be trouble. That is why the African Negroes are ideal for the purpose. They are brought far from their bases of possible retaliation."

"I did not ask you for a lecture on slavery. I am asking about a single individual, a girl whom you tell me has been illegally enslaved. Did no one come to her aid?"

"As I said, sir—she was not wanted. . . ."

"I believe you said there was no place for her here in Williamsburg."

"Exactly," the clerk replied smugly.

"By whose decision?"

"Why, the people—the good citizens. . . ."

"You are an accomplished liar. Under oath I'm certain you would have to admit that the townspeople knew nothing of the situation."

The clerk's face stiffened. "I would suggest, sir, that you weigh your words—"

"Be quiet when your betters are speaking. There may have been some prejudice here in Williamsburg against Mae Varney and her foster daughter, but a public demand to sell the girl into degradation is beyond belief."

The anger in Christopher's eyes overrode the clerk's bravado. "Do you have a personal interest in the girl?" he asked with a new show of concern.

Christopher ignored the question and went on. "I'll vow that the outrageous deed was carried out by a very small clique of scoundrels under a cloak of secrecy. A private sale."

"You are maligning good and worthy men. . . ."

"Who decided in their bigotry what was good for the town. Or was it the greed for money that prompted them?"

"Sir, I refuse to stand here. . . ."

"You will stand where you are and answer my questions. The money. What was the price paid?"

The clerk hesitated. The man before him radiated an aura of authority, but how much was he entitled to know? How extensively into the affairs of others should he be allowed to pry?

Finally, the clerk said, "Some five hundred pounds, I believe."

"Where did it go? Who got it?"

"The Indian was properly recompensed."

"With a handful of beads?"

"I tell you the whole matter was legally handled. It is over and done with. There is no recourse."

"Are you telling me no private citizen can now come forth to right a wrong? What about that false affidavit? Can it not be contested?"

"I suppose it could be. Its validity could be challenged. But I assure you, sir, court action could be long and wearying. Such legal matters move slowly."

"How long?"

"Litigation could drag on for a year, perhaps longer."

Christopher considered that. A bleak prospect indeed. No doubt the blacklegs who had profited from the outrage would be well versed in legal chicanery.

The clerk added, "There would also be the cost, sir. A bond would have to be furnished at the outset."

"For what reason?" Christopher demanded.

"To insure payment of damages and costs in case you failed to win your point in court."

"Then you are saying there is no possible way for me to help the girl?"

"Oh, there is a possible way. It would depend upon how determined you are."

"Let us say that I am most determined."

"You might buy the slave from her present and completely legal owner. Your success would of course depend upon the man's attitude—his idea of the value of his property."

33

"I'll have his name and location."

"Oh, certainly, sir." Anxious to be rid of his tormentor, the clerk turned eagerly to a record book, tore off a strip of scrap paper and wrote with a scratchy pen. He handed the strip to Christopher.

"Orin Cade Plantation," Christopher murmured with a scowl. "Pender's Hook, Brunswick County. Where is it?"

"South of us. Some hundred miles. By the Carolina border."

Christopher smiled coldly. "I understand. You got Charity as far from Williamsburg as possible. How do I get to the place?"

"You ferry across the river. Then you must take the Ironbound to Braddock Road. You will have no trouble from there. If you plan the trip you could make inquiries when you reach Brunswick County. The Cade Plantation is well known."

Christopher regarded the clerk for a few moments, thinking how he would have enjoyed knocking those glasses from his face and reshaping that grotesque nose. He forebore the pleasure, uttered a cold, "Thank you," and left the courthouse.

Outside, he took the black hunter's reins in hand and led him slowly down the street. Christopher was amazed by his spontaneous outrage at the injustice confronting him. Never before had his temper slipped the leash to such an extent.

He found an explanation of sorts. He had never before come face-to-face with such a blatant miscarriage of justice. Previously, his approach had been basically that of his brother Clement, the broader, academic view of human cruelty. Clement harangued against slavery as a great evil, an approach where individual cruelties were lost in the body of the wider aspects. Christopher was sure that if Clement were faced with the Varney matter, his reaction would have been just as explosive.

The thing now was what to do in the short time he had left, a report to high authority appearing to be his only recourse.

With this in mind, he hurried to his boarding house, turned the black over to the landlady's stableman, and entered the house. As he mounted the stairs, he chanced to meet the good lady herself and used the occasion to announce his departure.

"Madam, I will be leaving for Charleston tomorrow. I am due there in a fortnight to embark for England. Let me say that my stay in your establishment has been most pleasant." Then, hurrying on to his rooms, he took foolscap and quill and carefully noted all the details of the Varney matter which had come to his attention. He addressed the memo to Lord Dunmore, Royal Governor of Virginia, and set off briskly on the short walk to the Governor's Palace. There a liveried servant opened the door to announce that the Governor was not available. He was off somewhere on the King's business.

A disappointment. Dunmore was probably in Charleston looking into the embargo of that major port of entry. Christopher had learned in Philadelphia that its failure was a prime source of satisfaction to the more militant element of the colonial rebels.

He handed his missive to the servant. "You will give this to the Governor," he said. Then he departed with some sense of accomplishment. He had done all he possibly could under the circumstances.

There were some final chores and now he set about doing them. He took the black hunter to the Deane Shop and Forge on Prince George Street where he traded the animal along with an additional cash payment for a sturdy closed carriage and a span of bays. He took the new rig back to his boarding house and turned it over to the stableman, after which he went upstairs and packed the sea chest he had used for traveling ever since leaving England. As he locked the chest, he thought of the green fields of Kent. It would be good to go home. He had been too long away from his native soil.

He retired early in preparation for the long day ahead but slept only fitfully. He was up and about well before sunrise, and as he breakfasted he wondered why his mood was so heavy. He now felt an odd reluctance about leaving the Colonies. It was true that he detested the ocean and the long boring voyage, but more important, he was going home. Still, there was no lift of spirit even as he drove off into the cool, green, Virginia morning.

Finally he faced the truth; it was his cowardly attempt at self-justification in the matter of Mae Varney's foster daughter by writing that puny note to the Governor. Dunmore was sitting on a powder keg of rebellion, striving to hold the lid down, so it was utterly foolish to suppose he could find time to help a lone, abused girl. Also, the scoundrels responsible would no doubt have some knowledge of the law—enough to block any legal investigation of their outrageous act. They might well have anticipated some feeble protest such as his own.

This battle with his conscience went on until Christopher reached the cutoff from Ironbound Road into the wilderness surrounding the lonely cabin. There he reined up the bays and sat for a long time listening to nature's morning sounds: the rustling of dew-freshened leaves—the chirping of birds.

Then with an expression of grim purpose he reined the bays about, turned them off the road, and drove into the forest.

The treasure Mistress Mae had so patiently gathered over the years was untouched, exactly where she had indicated, the tended ground so soft that Christopher was able to unearth it with his bare hands. It was in two leather sacks and as heavy as one would expect that much gold to be. He carried the sacks to his rig and threw them into the boot.

There was one more long moment of uncertainty, with Clement's stern accusing face as a backdrop. But when he turned again into Ironbound Road it was with the firmness of a man who had made a final decision; one which would have no doubt greatly pleased Mae Varney....

8.

It was a long, punishing ride which lasted the night. Even freed of her bonds, Charity was painfully bounced about in a wagon not built for the comfort of its passengers. Finally the light of morning seeped in and then the wagon came to a halt.

Orders were given, words Charity could not hear clearly. Then the door was opened and Charity shielded her eyes against the bright glare of a morning sun. Two male slaves awaited her. They gestured toward assisting her down but quickly drew back, confused. Evidently, regardless of their orders, they hesitated to lay hands on a white girl.

The place to which Charity had been brought was pleasant enough by all outward appearances; a most impressive plantation. Across a high hedge and beyond a wide expanse of clipped lawn, Charity saw a stately, pillared mansion gleaming white in the early sun. Off to the west there were cotton fields, bright, crisp, and green, proving that this had been a good year for growing things. The faint sounds of singing touched her ears; slaves at work, finding comfort in the sad, melodic chants they created to fit their sad plight, or had carried with them from Africa.

The man who had brought her to the plantation and given the orders was nowhere in sight as the two slaves escorted her to another, less pleasant area—the slave quarters. There was a row of perhaps twenty cottages along a dusty lane. Many curious eyes watched as she was led to the far end of the cottage row—to a smaller structure which hardly deserved the name. She was gently nudged inside and the door was closed, leaving her in semidarkness. There were no windows in the hut, the only ventilation two narrow slits near the low ceiling on opposite sides of the room. Already picking up the day's heat, the place was stifling. It was furnished with a box bed in one corner, a chair and table, and a large metal bucket in one corner. Charity, grateful for even the smallest favor at this point, found some comfort in the fact that the bucket was clean.

Soon, the door opened and one of her jailers entered to put a jug of water and a tray of food on the table. He left and Charity heard the click of a lock from the outside.

Although she had not eaten for many long hours, the food did not attract her. However, she seized the water jug like one dying of thirst and with no cup at hand gulped desperately from its mouth.

There were no tears, no panic. Her terror and misery seemed to be locked away within. She could not permit herself to see this terrible situation as other than a mistake. It could be nothing else; therefore she had to endure until someone came to rectify the blunder.

She curled up on the bed to wait, turning instinctively toward sleep as an escape for her troubled mind. The heat increased. Sleep would not come. She arose and removed her frock and stripped off her underthings which were now soaked with perspiration. She slipped the frock back on and found that the partial disrobing helped cool her a little—enough to allow sleep to take over. . . .

The unlocking of the door awakened her. Dusk had fallen. A jailer entered with a fresh jug of water and another plate of food. This time there was a gesture of compassion, though a feeble one. The slave said, "You gotta eat, Miss. They's strength in good food."

He left as before and Charity found that her appetite had returned. The food was simple: black-eyed peas with a slab of pork and a dollop of greens in thick pork gravy. Charity would have scorned such fare in Williamsburg, but her hunger was now great enough to make it palatable.

Again, she was left alone, her anguish now beginning to surface. But there were so many questions without answers. How had this terrible situation come about? Who could have done this to her? Why? She went back over the nightmare, trying to sort out her impressions, and remembered that during her transfer from the first wagon to the second, she had heard a voice which sounded like that of her tutor, Jeremy Hicks. But only the voice, and she couldn't be sure. The other of the two kidnappers had cleared her of her bonds. The moon had been bright, but despite the shock of what was happening to her, there was a nagging impression that she had seen him someplace before. But none of that mattered much. She was far more concerned about how soon someone would come to rescue her.

Time wore on. The night dragged by. There were dreams as horrible as her present reality that kept awakening her. She sobbed in her misery and loneliness before, toward dawn, comparatively unbroken sleep came....

9.

The man was of gross proportions; thick chested, florid of face; there was meanness in his thin lips even as he smiled. He wore a blue satin dressing gown, obviously having lately arisen.

"Good morning."

Charity came awake instantly, slipped off the bed and stood pressed against the wall. The man took his time. He inspected the table, looked with distaste at the food left on the plate. He crossed to where Charity had put her underclothing on a corner of the bed, prodded them with a forefinger.

Charity asked, "Where is this place? Why am I being kept in this horrible hut?"

"As a warning. I am Orin Cade and you are my slave, bought and paid for. This filthy sty is a sample of the discipline in store for rebellious

41

slaves on this plantation; only a mild sample. I find that promises of punishment are less effective than a taste of punishment beforehand."

A slave? A master? Charity stared, unable to believe what she had heard.

Cade went on, "But if you serve me well and see to my needs, you will fare much better. You will be given a room in the manor house, good food, and even some pretty dresses to wear." He smiled as though he were the soul of kindness.

Charity was trembling in every fiber. "I am not a slave!" she cried. "Let me out of here! This is all a terrible mistake! No one can buy me or sell me!"

Cade remained undisturbed. The thin smile stayed on his face as he advanced toward Charity. She angled away from the wall to avoid him, coming to a position with the bed pressing against the backs of her knees.

Cade said, "Your innocent pose does not fool me. Actually you have prepared yourself for my visit." He indicated the pile of underclothing, his meaning needing no further words.

Charity said, "I took them off because I was hot. Not because...."

She got no further. Cade stooped and swept the skirt high on her breast, exposing her nakedness below. As he did so, he pushed her backwards onto the bed. Standing so that she could not bring her knees together, he paused to relish the young loveliness now exposed while he swept his robe aside to show his own most unlovely nudity.

There were frozen moments. Up to that time, Charity had desperately nourished a hope, all she had left, that the mistake would be discovered and rectified. But now that hope vanished, the truth glowing in Cade's lustful eyes. He bent to seize her ankles, spreading her and positioning her for his purpose. And like a frightened animal trapped by the hunter, she reacted. As Cade lowered himself over her body, the fearful kitten became a raging cat. One clawed hand went out to rake Cade's face, drawing blood. Then, as his neck pressed against her face, she set her teeth into it, grinding his flesh with all the strength in her jaws.

He came erect with a snarl, his own teeth bared. "Why, you treacherous little bitch!"

Charity's claws arced out again, but Cade had drawn back out of range, one hand on his furrowed cheek. His other hand folded into a fist and a sweeping blow smashed against the side of Charity's head. She collapsed, unconscious, onto the cot.

When she came to, she found that she had been stripped; she lay helpless, her wrists lashed with a rope extending under the cot from one to the other. Cade stood over her, breathing audibly.

"So you want it this way, do you? Then you shall have it!"

Her faculties now functioning, Charity continued to fight. She kicked out with both feet, one heel finding his naked groin, but ineffectually. There was some difficulty now as he sought to grasp her ankles while she churned her legs violently, her face set into a fixed grimace of loathing.

"God! You do have spirit," he muttered as he

captured her ankles and began positioning her for ravishment. He did it slowly and with vengeful zest, pushing her legs upward and over, straightening them at the knees and folding her painfully at the hips—splaying her cruelly until his target was almost a flat surface, the virginity he had bought and paid for now his to enjoy.

Charity continued to struggle and he paused to find pleasure in her helplessness.

"It's time you understood, wench—you are my property to do with as I please."

"I—I'll kill you!" Charity raged.

He laughed and got on with it. The penetration was intentionally vicious. Charity shrieked. It was as though a glowing hot sword had been thrust into her. Then, recognizing the futility of the situation, Charity gritted her mind against the agony.

Pain; it was not totally strange to her. There had been hurts before, though never of this intensity. It came into her mind that Indians never cried. That was the place to go—back into that corridor of memory. Never a single tear from a redman's eye. Never a cry of protest against agony. Only the old women were allowed to wail in grief, and then only at the loss of a loved one.

There was little Charley Short-Bow to remember—a Chickahominy playmate of a mere nine summers—brought by his father to Mother Mae with a forefinger smashed flat up to the second knuckle. Mother Mae examined it: "The finger must be cut off. It is gone and no treatment will keep the flesh from rotting."

Dan Short-Bow nodded, his expression changing not a whit. He drew a large hunting knife from his hip and handed it to Mother Mae who washed it in purple wine. Charley Short-Bow did not look at the knife. His expressionless eyes remained on his father's stern face, not from fear but rather as though he gained courage therefrom. Mother Mae laid the small hand on a white cloth and gave the knife to Dan Short-Bow and pointed. "Just there," she said. Dan Short-Bow poised the knife above the finger, then pressed it quickly down with the heel of his hand. Charley Short-Bow's eyes glazed, but remained open and fixed. His lips twisted and strained. Then his knees melted, his eyes closed, and Mother Mae caught him as he slumped into unconsciousness. She eased him to the floor and tightly bound the finger. Pain beyond words, but never a moan, nor a single tear.

Indians never wept. . . .

Charity returned to the present to find that Orin Cade had finished with her and freed her arms. He lay beside her, breathing heavily. She could smell his sweat.

And even thus defeated, there was still a curious exultation as though she herself had won some sort of victory; a sense of triumph which allowed fresh rage to flood in, and she attacked him with a fury of teeth, clawing nails and driving knees.

Cade took some punishment, his amazement holding him defenseless. But then he reacted, knocking Charity off the cot. There were fresh scratches on his chest and pain in his thighs where Charity's flailing heels had just missed his

45

groin. Lurid curses punctuated his rage as he followed through, lifting Charity and holding her backwards against his chest, thus neutralizing the effectiveness of her struggle. Then he quitted the hut and still clutching her, strode the length of the slave complex. Charity, all semblance of sanity gone, kicked and twisted and screamed. It was as though Cade were carrying a wildcat against his belly.

He reached his objective at the end of the cottage lane and waited for assistance.

"Open the box!" he roared. "Open it!"

The box was a squat, ugly structure about eight feet square, a heavy wooden post supporting it at each corner. The walls were of sheet iron. The roof, forming a five-foot inner ceiling, was of sheet iron also, and heavy, rusted door hinges creaked as two slaves leaped to obey their master's command. Cade literally threw Charity inside onto a dirt floor. The heat was already intense and would rise as the day wore on with the sun baking down on the sheet metal.

Cade slammed and latched the iron door, then drew his flapping robe around him and marched back to the hut where he sat down on the edge of the bed and caught his breath.

His fury abated somewhat, diminishing into cold anger as he muttered, "I'll break that little bitch's spirit or I'll kill her...."

10.

As Christopher approached the Cade plantation, not knowing what he would find, he debated the pose it would be best to assume. The most effective would be to arrive as an officer of the court, but that could bring on problems. If Cade insisted on identification, which he probably would, Christopher was carrying nothing of that nature. A man interested in buying Cade's new purchase? Unsatisfactory also. Cade might not want to sell. The illegality of Cade's action was Christopher's best weapon and there had to be a way to take advantage of it; a better one than merely warning him.

A solicitor-at-law representing unnamed interested parties? That seemed best, so when Christopher drove onto the premises and Cade himself approached—all cordiality and respect what with Christopher's impressive rig—the latter remained aloof and formal, introducing himself according to that plan.

"Some legal matter?" Cade said affably. "Well, just you get down, good sir, and have some refreshment. The road from Williamsburg is long and dusty."

Christopher refused Cade's hospitality, wondering the while if Cade questioned his not having a coachman along with such a fine rig. The man did not seem to.

A slave appeared to mind the team and Christopher relinquished the reins, saying, "I am here on business, Mr. Cade, and I would like to get to it."

"Then let us sit there in the summerhouse and get it over with."

Thus accommodated, Christopher remained formal. "Mr. Cade, I must inform you that you may be in a great deal of trouble. A terrible injustice has been done and I represent some good citizens of Williamsburg who are determined to see it righted."

"An injustice, you say?"

"Unjust and illegal. Do you deny that you kidnapped a girl—a seventeen-year-old citizen of the Colony—and brought her here under duress?"

Cade blinked at the charge. "I certainly do deny it—that is if you are referring to a slave I bought in Williamsburg."

"One Charity Sturges?"

"That is her name."

Christopher studied the man, searching for clues to his reaction. At the moment there seemed to be only surprise and honest confusion. Christopher said, "Mr. Cade, if you truly believe you had a right to purchase the girl as a slave, you have been cruelly deceived."

"I had every right. She is part Indian, which makes her a legal slave. I have a testament to that fact and a legal bill of sale."

"The testament you speak of . . . who made it, may I ask?"

48

"A man named Walter Chahalis."

"Are you acquainted with him?"

"No, but his affidavit is in my possession."

"It is worthless, Mr. Cade. The person you refer to is an Indian. A scoundrelly Chickahominy who would sign anything for a few shillings. And as you no doubt know, an Indian's word has no value in court."

Christopher was happy to see a touch of fear in Cade's eyes along with consternation and rising anger.

"That's can't be true. I dealt with honest men!"

"In our investigation, we did not find them so," Christopher replied, wondering in truth who they were. "Charity Sturges is a white girl of pure background with every right to the protection of the Crown. The blacklegs you dealt with kidnapped her and delivered her to you with callous disregard for either decency or legality.

"I can show you my papers!"

Christopher waved a negligent hand. "That is not necessary. I'm sure you have them. And I suggest you guard them well. They may constitute your only defense at the bar of judgment."

"But dammit, man! I am blameless! I entered into the contract in good faith," Cade protested.

"I have reason to believe that. In our investigation, we found no mark against you. However, kidnapping is a serious crime. In the past it has resulted in hangings. A messy business."

"It isn't fair," Cade cried. "I have always been a good subject of the Crown. I've paid my taxes. . . ."

"Please, Mr. Cade. I think there is little chance

of your hanging. Trial would of course be held in Williamsburg and feeling *is* high there."

"But my word is worth a great deal. . . ."

Christopher appeared not to hear as he went on. "Of course the five hundred pounds you paid. . . ."

"Five hundred! Did those felons say that? I paid eight hundred!"

Christopher allowed some surprise to show. Was this blackguard trying to make a profit? "Hmmm. That complicates matters."

"What does the amount have to do with it?"

"It seems to preclude my ability to help you."

"I do not understand."

"My clients, Mr. Cade, are loath to instigate a court trial and thus air this lamentable scandal. They are convinced of your innocence so far as criminal activity is concerned. So they have instructed me to recompense you for your financial outlay and take the girl with me back to Williamsburg. But I am commissioned to offer you only the five hundred pounds."

A shade of suspicion flared in Cade's expression, causing Christopher to fear that he had overplayed his unaccustomed role.

Cade said, "They would not prosecute? They would let those scoundrels get off scot-free?"

Christopher searched wildly for an answer, then said, "They feel that your resentment against the men would bring quicker justice than they would receive at the bar."

Cade relished the prospect. "If I am given leeway. . . ."

"That is between you and your betrayers."

Christopher arose from his chair. He waited, wishing that he had not been so positive in the matter of money. If Cade insisted on recouping his investment. . . . He said, "Of course I could return to Williamsburg for further instructions, but that would take time and if I did not return with the girl. . . ."

Cade turned sullen. "She is a troublesome wench at best. . . ."

"Then I can only wish you good luck, Mr. Cade."

"Take her and be damned!" he exclaimed. "The loss will not destroy me. And I will find a means of getting it back."

"A wise decision," Christopher said, managing to hide his elation. "And if you don't mind, I'll get started immediately."

"Come with me." And he led Christopher toward the slave quarters.

If Christopher had been congratulating himself on ably playing an unfamiliar role, all that was forgotten a few minutes later after paying Cade his money in gold sovereigns. When he saw the hot box in which Charity was imprisoned, he could only struggle for self-control.

"You imprisoned her in that oven?"

Cade, sure now that he had escaped prosecution, said righteously, "It was no more than she deserved. The tart is paying for these scratches on my face." He motioned to his pair of waiting slaves. "Get the girl."

The box was opened and one of them hunched his way into the torture chamber and brought

Charity out. She hung limp in his arms, filthy from head to toe.

"My God! Is she still alive?" Without waiting for an answer to his question, Christopher took charge. He placed his fingers on the artery in her throat. There was a steady, even beat. Charity's youth and vitality had stood her in good stead.

Christopher's caution struggled with his rage, telling him the wise thing to do was to get away from the place as quickly as possible.

He asked, "Where are the clothes she came in?"

"Thrown away. Too filthy for use. However, there may be some garments in the slave quarters we can spare." He motioned to one of the yard slaves who trotted off.

Christopher took Charity to his rig and put her in as she was. She stirred and moaned faintly. Fairly gritting his teeth in the effort to hold himself in, he accepted two shapeless homespuns from the slave, but at least they were clean.

He climbed into the rig and sat a moment, looking down at Cade. Coldly, he said, "You are a swine, sir. A detestable swine." However, as he drove off, he found the insult of scant satisfaction. . . .

Charity lay limp against Christopher's shoulder as he pushed the rig back onto the main road. He urged the bays along until they came to a section of forest he remembered. There, a creek bubbled over rocks to form a backwater, a pleasant little secluded glade just visible through the trees.

Using one of the frocks as a blanket, he carried

Charity to the creek, laid her on the grass, and bathed her face with his kerchief. She remained pretty much as she had been, hovering on the edge of consciousness. He listened to her heart and was encouraged, but the heat radiating from her body alarmed him. Her temperature was obviously very high.

He threw the frock aside and continued bathing her, washing away the filth of the hot box. But the treatment seemed inadequate; she had to be brought back to consciousness. Desperately worried, it occurred to him that the time had been finely drawn. If he had arrived at the Cade Plantation an hour or so later, they might well have removed a dead body from that horrible oven. But had he still been too late?

Shock; perhaps that was the proper treatment. With that hopefully in mind, he lifted Charity into his arms and literally dipped her into the pond. There was a quick gasp. Her eyelids fluttered. He repeated the dipping process three times, then laid her back on the bank and used the frock as a towel.

She was stirring now, whimpering, and he hurried to the rig and brought back the other dress. With some difficulty, he managed to get her into it despite his inexperience in such matters. He then carried her back to the rig and when they started on, he was encouraged in that, as she sat with her head against his shoulder, she seemed to be in a natural sleep rather than in a coma.

He drove on, his mind now free to consider things as they stood. His first thoughts were a self-examination. This bizarre incident. Had he handled it well? It had been his second experience with the naked body of a woman, but far different than the first with Gaby; nude, maddeningly erotic, and demanding in his arms; her skillful attempt to make herself so sexually important to him that he would want to marry her. And she had succeeded, he thought wryly; he did want to marry her.

But this had been so different, proving that conditions call the turn. At the pool his concern for the girl's welfare blocked out all else; it was a totally sexless anxiety.

Charity was definitely recovering now. Her breathing was even. No more whimpering gasps, and the heat no longer radiated from her body. Christopher brushed a lock of hair off her smooth young face and drove on.

His immediate goal was Carter's Tavern, some fifteen miles down Braddock Road. It was well after dark when they arrived and the golden windows standing out in the gloom of night were a welcome sight.

He pulled up beside the inn, leaving Charity where she was, and approached the door. There was singing and laughter inside and he found the common room quite crowded with local merrymakers. The rum flowed freely.

Christopher paused at the door where the mistress of the tavern saw him and came forward. She was plump, gray-haired under her white cap, motherly looking, and it occurred to Christopher as she approached that tavern mistresses were always plump, gray-haired under their white caps, and motherly looking.

She smiled, quickly gauging Christopher by his attire as a superior gentleman.

"Good evening, sir. May we see to your needs?"

"You do not remember me, do you?"

"I—I am not sure."

"It was some time ago. Four years. I stopped here on my way to Williamsburg."

"Oh, that English gentleman!"

The reply did not necessarily prove recognition, Christopher thought, but it did not matter. He said, "I am on my way back to Charleston and I have my daughter with me. Are your two upper rooms available?"

"Our family suite? It happens to be vacant at the moment."

"Excellent. We shall take it for the night. But there is one more thing. My daughter has been ill and needs rest. Is there a back entrance we could use?"

"Of course."

"Then I will bring her around there and you can have your stableman see to my horses."

Thus an entrance was made without having to traverse the common room. Also, the lady was not permitted to see much of Charity because Christopher bundled her up in his greatcoat and carried her directly into the bedroom of the suite and closed the door when he came out.

"The lass is on the mend?" he was asked.

"Yes, but she is still very weak."

"I did not get your name, good sir. . . ."

"Leach, Christopher Leach. You are Mrs. Carter?"

"Indeed I am. Now let me get this fire going.

You will find a carafe of rum on the sideboard, Mr. Leach, if you care to refresh yourself."

Christopher poured himself a drink and was grateful for the quick heat in his stomach. He watched Mrs. Carter bustle about the fireplace and when a good flame was crackling, he said, "We have had a long drive. Dinner would be most welcome. Is your kitchen closed?"

"We are always ready to serve our guests," he was assured. "Perhaps a thick deer steak, beans and potatoes?"

"That sounds too good to be true. Also a bowl of soup if you have it. . . ."

Half an hour later, a bountiful meal arrived. Mrs. Carter brought it on a huge tray and seemed a little reluctant to leave.

"Anything I can do for the lass. . . ."

"She will sleep, I'm sure. You have been very kind."

Then, responding to a quick urge, Christopher took Mrs. Carter's hand and pressed a gold sovereign into it. "So very, very kind." The lady stared, thanked him, and left, quite overwhelmed by his unexpected generosity, especially at this time. Gratuities, if any, were always given upon departure.

Actually, the gold piece was not for Mrs. Carter alone; rather, it had been a spontaneous gesture of thanks to the fates in general for *their* kindness; a need in Christopher to express gratitude.

Alone, he took the bowl of soup into the bedroom, moved the lamp close to the bed, and gently shook Charity, insisting that she open her eyes.

56

"You must eat," he said. "This soup will give you strength."

Her eyes opened. She regarded him blankly, beyond fear but short of confidence. He lifted her head and brought a spoonful of soup to her lips. They opened. The soup was swallowed. The process was repeated several times—until Charity's eyes closed and she was again asleep.

Christopher tucked the blanket around her and brushed her hair back gently, allowing his hand to pass slowly and lightly over her cheek. He then went into the parlor and attacked his dinner with a zest of hunger he had not experienced in a long time. Then, a leisurely, quiet drink in front of the fireplace after which he fashioned a sleeping arrangement with the sofa and an easy chair, to support his feet.

Once abed, he strove to untrack his mind. This was difficult. Thoughts relative to his new situation kept forming and crossing his consciousness like clouds in a lazy sky.

One of them had interesting aspects. Why had he called Charity his daughter? In order for that to have been true he would have had to sire her before his twelfth birthday.

Why not his wife? Had he told Mrs. Carter they were married he would not have had to literally smuggle Charity in to keep Mrs. Carter from wondering how he had managed to beget so young.

Actually, that aspect did not matter. What Mrs. Carter thought was not important. But his own reluctance to even masquerade as Charity's husband touched deeper chords. It traced back to

Clement, the years of his domination over Christopher; the latter's reluctance to do anything that might clash with Clement's ideas of how life should be lived. A tenuous explanation, but one which hung on like smoke in a still room. Why *not* call Charity his wife as a matter of convenience? Christopher asked himself the question, mulled it over.

All right, he thought sleepily, I'll make her my niece. That should not bother anyone.

The compromise accepted, his mind disconnected itself and allowed sleep to come; this without bringing up the most surprising aspect of all—that of his determination to take Charity with him to England. It had not weakened in the least.

11.

Christopher awoke with a start, coming instantly into complete consciousness. Charity was standing beside his makeshift bed looking down at him. Her eyes were quiet, her manner pensive, her face expressionless.

"Where am I?"

Christopher struggled to a sitting posture. "Charity, we are on the road to Charleston. At a country inn."

"What happened?"

He eased her down onto the lounge and sat op-

58

posite her in the chair holding her hands clasped in both of his. He spoke gently.

"What do you remember, Charity?"

Her look turned deeply thoughtful. Was she trying to remember or silently going over what *had* happened? He could not tell.

"You were taken to the Cade Plantation," he prompted.

"They let me go?"

"I came for you and took you away. Do you know who I am?"

"You used to come to see Mother Mae."

"Yes, we were very good friends. But let's talk about all that later. You must be hungry."

"Why are we going to Charleston?"

"We will meet the ship that will take us to England."

"Why are we going to England?"

"Because Mother Mae put you in my care. And now there is nothing more to be afraid of. No one will hurt you again. You are going to new places. You will see new things, and in time you will be happy again."

Her reaction, or rather the lack of it, he thought, was curious; no fear, no surprise, nor any sign of rebellion. She had only questions, the answers to which she seemed to accept. Christopher could believe only that she was still in a state of shock, although that seemed to be wearing off gradually. He fervently hoped it would not terminate in an explosion of emotion when full realization returned.

She looked down at herself. "This is not my dress."

59

"No. Yours was dirty. We borrowed this one. As soon as we reach Charleston we will buy you some fine new clothes."

"I have no money."

"Yes you have. But let's not worry about that. We must be on our way. We will have breakfast and then we will leave."

She did not object. He took her back into her bedroom and sat her down in a chair. "You sit here. I will order breakfast and we will eat together."

She sat quietly; this bothered Christopher. She was too quiet—too obedient. He would now have welcomed some form of reaction even though he might not know how to deal with it.

He pulled the bell rope and when there was a knock, he expected to see Mrs. Carter. Instead, a girl stood there waiting; a servant of the inn.

Christopher ordered breakfast and the girl brought it quickly, then left in a hurry as though she had been instructed to do so. Either Mrs. Carter was being diplomatic or she was too busy to give service herself.

Christopher stepped into the hall and called down after the girl. "Please tell the stableman to prepare my rig." Her head bobbed and she disappeared.

When they were again on the road, Charity sat quietly beside him, contributing little to the conversation he tried to make—answering in sparse words or not at all. Around midday, he pulled into a grove and laid out the lunch he'd had packed at Carter's Tavern. Charity ate sparingly,

60

nibbling at a pheasant leg, and he did not urge her.

It was in midafternoon that she began emerging from within herself, this coming about in a rather spectacular manner. They were on a road that skirted a large, sylvan pond when Charity sat suddenly upright and said, "I want to swim."

"My dear, I don't think that would be a good idea...."

"I want to swim," she insisted.

Christopher considered the demand and shrugged. Perhaps allowing her to follow her inclination would be her best medicine. He pulled in off the road, behind a grove of trees which provided some privacy. Charity was out of the carriage almost before it stopped, and ran the scant distance to the water's edge. Christopher got out and followed, but before he reached her she had slipped out of her frock, stood for a moment, a slim, naked nymph, and plunged into the pond. Christopher picked up the discarded dress and stared after her. He watched as she sported expertly in the water, above and below the surface like a playful otter. And as he stood on the shore, looking at her in wonder, Christopher had to concede that there was one good aspect of the astonishing performance. Charity was coming alive again. She laughed with pleasure as she frolicked about.

Trying hard to ignore the slim, mature loveliness of his ward, Christopher considered the aspect of what she had gone through. This naked performance spoke eloquently of its violence. The brutality had caused Charity to revert. She had slipped—temporarily, he hoped—back into childhood. God grant there had been no permanent damage! He desperately wished that he had more experience, more knowledge with which to evaluate her condition. He felt so helpless. Then something more personal intruded—her complete lack of modesty, like a small child in the presence of a loving father.

But I am not her father! I am twenty-seven years old and I refuse to see myself as a man in his dotage! The overemphasis was probably a subconscious regret at having lived a comparatively secluded life. Until Gaby came along—he did not finish that thought.

Finally Charity emerged from the pool. He said, "Dry yourself with this frock. I'll go and bring the other one."

"This one is all right. It will dry me when I put it on."

She slipped lithely into the garment and ran barefoot off toward the rig. Christopher followed slowly. When he climbed in behind the reins, Charity snuggled against him and gave him the first true smile of the trip. She murmured, "I'm sleepy. I'll take a nap."

Christopher welcomed this; it would give him time to think, to try and put the events of the past hours and days into some sort of order, events that lay in a heap in his mind.

What on earth was going to evolve out of all this? What would be the next confusing twist in the situation?

He turned his mind away—back to Mae Varney in her wilderness cabin. Poor wretched creature! What greater travail could there be than knowing death would soon snatch her off and leave her beloved Charity at the mercy of villains and scoundrels?

... *only my living presence protects the child.*

He criticized himself harshly for what he had done—striding away and leaving her to suffer with concern for her child right up to the moment of her passing. If only he could tell her how it had worked out; if only he could let her know.

But perhaps she did know. Christopher had never embraced mysticism in any form, but he now discovered that conceding the impossible could be a comfort when it softened one's own guilty feelings.

His thoughts now turned even more deeply inward and he looked at himself in the mirror of his mind. The last four years had changed him; perhaps not for the better, but in England his whole life had been geared to the tenets and precepts of Clement, the highly esteemed rector of St. Jude's in Kent.

"My infallible brother," he mused.

Save in the affair with Gaby he had never questioned Clement's dictates. His way was the right way. All other ways were wrong, at least for a Leach. Thus, Christopher had, over the years, developed a kind of moral snobbery, arbitrarily shutting out much of the world. It had taken four years in the Colonies to broaden his outlook.

His thoughts remained on Clement; the stern,

rocklike fidelity to truth as he saw it. His illustrious brother had missed so much in life.

Of course, Clement was a special person, born to be looked up to. He had remained unmarried and celibate—Christopher was sure of the last. No female ever came intimately into his orbit other than Mrs. Fletcher, his housekeeper at the manse, who blended so perfectly into the gray of the stones and the grim self-assurance of Clement himself. She was female, of course, but it stopped right there.

Taking Mrs. Fletcher into one's arms would be like embracing one of the pillars which supported the venerable old kirk. Christopher caught himself up. Such thoughts were ungracious; snobbery merely turned in the opposite direction.

He became more warmly conscious of Charity snug against his side. The poor child! She would have much to learn in England. That in addition to the healing of the deep wounds inflicted upon her by her savage experience.

She stirred. Without awakening, she reached out and sought his hand. He switched the reins and allowed her hand to slip softly into his. She snuggled down and smiled in her sleep.

12.

After the dust, the mud, and the tooth-jarring bounce over the logs on the corduroy roads, sight of the spires of Charleston were most welcome to Christopher.

However, the town itself surprised him. He'd seen little of it upon his arrival in the Colonies, going north immediately to Williamsburg. Still, he felt that there had been much change. It seemed a busier, more active place. The ways were clogged with wagons and carts; roistering taverns literally spilled out into the street; commerce thrived and it appeared that northern unrest had not reached so far south—a most erroneous impression, as he was soon to learn.

Upon arrival, he went directly to Stern's Hotel on Beck Street near the theater, where he had quartered four years earlier. He obtained two connecting rooms and deposited Charity and his luggage.

After the episode at the pond, Charity seemed to have retrogressed. She remained well above her earlier near-coma condition, but lapsed into a quiet withdrawal, as though all that had gone before was being considered and evaluated in the deep recesses of her mind. She was in no way hostile, automatically obeying Christopher's every directive. He tried to analyze her behavior and found it difficult. He could only wonder again if the horrors through which she had passed had permanently altered her personality, but upon arrival in Charleston there were other things to occupy him.

He went immediately to the Maritime Office in compliance with the orders he had received by official pouch in Williamsburg, that most welcome letter telling him his tour of duty had ended.

He received a shock. The offices were empty. Even the metal sign outside the door had been removed. Puzzling mightily at this turn of events, he took the next logical step, and found his way to the heart of British authority in the town—the Army Barracks. This was a sprawling complex beside the harbor and as he walked along the quays, there was more to disturb him: the unlikely ships moored to the piers. Standing there, big as life, was the *Louis Quinze*, gaudy as a tavern doxie with its gilded carvings arrogantly blatant in the sun. It had been the proud flagship of Louis XV's French fleet and now under the sixteenth Louis it was still a grand French symbol. What was it doing there? Next to it were two lesser Dutch ships, busy little traders looking like shabby drabs beside the royal magnificence of the *Quinze*.

But the most amazing craft was yet to come; one that brought Christopher to a halt. He stared at the slim, low-lying frigate painted black from prow to stern. It flew no flag and had a name completely out of keeping with its sinister appearance:

The Evening Primrose.

Christopher walked on, to be confronted finally by one of the three armed sentries at the barracks gate.

"Please identify yourself, sir."

Christopher marveled. Was the place under siege? He gave his name.

"Your business, sir?"

"I come to see the commandant."

"For what purpose?"

Christopher frowned and produced his letter. "Does this satisfy your curiosity?"

The guard scanned the letter but made no apology. He stepped back, gestured to the other sentries who opened the gate, and said, "You will show this at the guard house just inside." Then he straightened his red tunic and rigidly assumed his post as befit the invincible British soldier.

The red-coated guard inside was more hospitable. A quick look at the paper and he said, "Oh, yes, Mr. Leach, sir. You are expected. They have been waiting for you." He motioned to a second guard. "You will take the gentleman immediately to Commandant Hayes."

Mystery piled upon mystery. Christopher had not expected to be scanned so closely at the gate, nor welcomed as a person of great importance when he finally got inside. It was all very confusing.

Enlightenment came quickly after Commandant Hayes arose from his desk and came forward to cordially shake Christopher's hand. He was a portly man with a plump red face. His bullet head was shaved clean of hair and was streaked with powder from the wig that now lay on his desk.

"Mr. Leach," he enthused in a gravelly voice. "You arrive out of nowhere!"

"Out of nowhere? I came to Charleston from Williamsburg and took rooms at Stern's Hotel on Beck Street as I had planned."

The commandant was pouring two ponies of brandy. "To the King," he intoned, and they drank.

Christopher set down his glass and said, "This confusion as to my arrival is a great surprise. I wasn't aware that. . . ."

"That we were concerned? It is completely logical. Your credentials from the motherland are quite impressive, good sir. Then our intelligence warned of colonial interest in your activities— the pursuit instigated in Philadelphia."

Christopher could not have been more mystified. "Pursuit? You confuse me, sir. I came to Charleston straight away."

"Mr. Leach, our couriers are swift in matters of importance. Word was brought quickly."

"Word of what?"

"A brace of rebels was sent to intercept you after you left Williamsburg. By the grace of God, they failed. Of course we failed also, but here you are and all's well. You were most skillful in eluding your pursuers." He paused to smile. "And also the escort we sent to protect you. Most ingenious."

"But I. . . ."

Christopher broke off, not so much to protest the compliment as to put together the pieces of this puzzle in his own mind. He had made no effort to evade anyone. Then why had trained trackers not intercepted him?

There seemed to be only one possible answer. He had thrown them off by detouring to the Cade plantation in search of Charity. And the reason for the pursuit? If it originated in Philadelphia, there could be only one answer.

The *dossier* he had prepared.

Leaving the rest for further thought, Christopher said, "The situation here in Charleston amazes me, Commandant. The many changes. . . ."

"Sir, this port is close to insurrection. It is a hotbed of treason and treachery. That accursed Committee of Correspondence based up north has spewed its poisonous propaganda down here and found eager listeners. That scoundrel Moultrie should be taken and hung. Would we had the power."

"You must be indeed hamstrung when I come here to find the *Louis Quinze*, a hostile ship, moored in your harbor. Also, the two Dutch traders when there is supposed to be an embargo."

"The *Quinze* is a thorn in our side, sir. The arrogant French bastards! A purported goodwill mission while I am sure they are conferring with rebels for plans to run the embargo. This while the situation between the French and England simmers indecisively in Europe."

"Where are the English ships-of-the-line?"

"Engaged elsewhere. In the Indian Ocean. Facing Boston to the north. Here, we engage in a holding action. We do not even have a British ship we can spare to send you home. However, the Dutch vessel taking tobacco to Portsmouth will be perfectly safe."

"By the way," Christopher said, "there will be a second passenger. A—ah, young lady I am taking to England for schooling."

"Very well," the Commandant said blandly; gentlemen did this all the time. "The Dutch ship, the *Hainaut*, has been awaiting your arrival. No doubt you are anxious to leave as soon as possible."

"Quite."

"You will be completely safe when you are finally asea, but there will still be surveillance here in Charleston."

"When does the *Hainaut* leave?"

"As things stand now, tomorrow evening, if you can be ready to board her the following morning. She will move up the coast and stand to at a designated spot at which you will be delivered. There will be a coach before your hotel at precisely four in the morning. Will that be satisfactory?"

"I suppose so, but with the *dossier* still safe, is all that secrecy quite necessary?"

There was a faint frost on the Commandant's reply. "Mr. Leach, sir, your safety is now my responsibility and you will forgive me if I take precautions. They may not be required, but to fail at this point would be inexcusable."

"I understand," Christopher said hastily, not wishing to offend the man.

"I was sure you would." With that, Commandant Hayes smiled warmly and extended his hand. "Then Godspeed to you, sir, and a pleasant voyage."

"Thank you."

As they parted, Christopher sensed that Hayes was happy to have the problem off his hands so he could get on to more important ones.

Back in the teeming Charleston streets, he could identify neither menace nor the surveillance calculated to protect him, but he was not greatly worried. He was sure that he had inadvertently confounded his pursuers by cutting over the Cade plantation. Had Hayes known only of the chase and not the objective? It really did not matter. The important thing was that Christopher had functioned more expertly than he'd realized. He had gathered important information and had reason to be proud of himself. Now he could only hope that the powers back home would see it in the same light.

His thoughts turned to his new responsibility, to Charity, then to the nonexistent state of her wardrobe. She would certainly need something more suitable for the voyage than a single frock.

With that concern in mind, he caught sight of a sign over a doorway—MADAME FLAVIA—*Modiste.* He entered the establishment and was happy to find no female customers there to wonder at the male intrusion.

A pleasant-faced, middle-aged woman hurried forward to introduce herself. "I am the proprietress, good sir. May I serve you?"

"I am sure you can. I am taking my niece to England and there is a need of shipboard apparel. Three or four very simple frocks, perhaps, and—

71

ah, the underthings which would normally accompany . . ."

"I understand," Madame Flavia assured him. "If you could give me your niece's measurements."

Christopher struggled with the request for a few moments, then said, "She comes to just here," indicating a point about midway on his chest.

"Her bust size?" the *modiste* inquired in a soft tone calculated to be helpful to an embarrassed male.

Christopher made some gestures which indicated that he might be holding a large ostrich egg. "I'd say about—"

"The girl's age?"

"She will soon be eighteen."

"Is she plump—overly slim—normal for her height?"

"Ah—normal. Yes, quite normal."

"I think I can help you. Simple dresses. Nothing elaborate."

"Yes. If you could make up a package for me—the frocks and the rest of it. The time presses."

"Of course."

Relieved at finding such an understanding person, Christopher left the matter entirely to Madame Flavia.

While waiting, an oversight dawned on Christopher's mind. The stalkers Commandant Hayes had referred to. If they had trailed him to his hotel and waited for him to leave, they would think it quite logical that the *dossier* was there to be stolen. And what sort of scalawags would they

72

be? The type who would harm Charity if she resisted their intrusion? Or might harm her for merely the pleasure of it?

The clothing was then quickly packaged and he rushed on to the hotel in all haste, the bulky box under his arm.

Christopher need not have worried. At that precise time, the two frustrated couriers were reporting to William Moultrie at his Sullivan Island headquarters as per instructions before leaving Philadelphia.

"So you failed," the distinguished rebel leader accused.

They glumly admitted that they had. "We did our best but the man must have crawled through underbrush all the way to Charleston."

"Perhaps he did not arrive."

"We are certain that he did. Had he not, we would have intercepted him along the way. He is somewhere in this town."

"Then he will embark for England shortly."

Moultrie dismissed the men and after some thought, called in a lieutenant. "I want you to locate the captain of a frigate moored at the docks. The *Evening Primrose*. Tell him to report to me immediately. Also, stand a watch and let me know what ships leave port during the next twenty-four hours. . . ."

13

"I don't please you!"

That was Charity's greeting upon Christopher's return. He found her in her room curled in a chair, a shabby, rather pathetic little bundle, depressed and unhappy.

Relieved at finding her safe, he now strove to cope with her surprising mood. "Oh, but you do! How can you say a thing like that, Charity?"

"You go off and leave me without a word. You don't care. I didn't think you were ever coming back."

"But I had important business to attend to. And I *am* back."

As he spoke he condemned himself for his shortcomings, his characteristic stiffness; for not being able to unbend and reassure this child who had been through so much. She was not to be blamed for overlooking the things he *had* done for her. In her mind, an amalgam of abuse, shock, and great loss, it no doubt seemed that she had been delivered from one cruel overseer to another; the latter not cruel, perhaps, but certainly stern and disapproving.

Thus he overstated his own guilt as he tried to make amends. And it was quite natural that he overcompensated. He approached Charity, lifted her from her chair, and took her gently into his arms.

"I do have a very high regard for you, my dear."

She remained stiff and unyielding for a time, as though judging his act for sincerity. Then she obviously decided in his favour because her change of mood was like the sun coming out from under a dark cloud. A brilliant smile, a softening, and she seemed to grow warmer in Christopher's arms.

Christopher pushed her away and turned to the box he had dropped on a chair. "My dear, I stopped off and bought you a few things you will certainly need."

Charity brightened even more as he handed her Madame Flavia's package. She now reminded him of a small child at the tree on Christmas morning. She tore off the wrappings and opened the box while Christopher prepared himself for compliments.

They were not forthcoming. Charity's face fell. "Clothes," she murmured in obvious disappointment.

"Yes, clothes," Christopher said, thoroughly confused by her disappointment. "Things young ladies wear."

She pawed through the frocks, pantalettes, and lacy underthings with no enthusiasm whatever. "But they are so bulky! These things ladies wear make them waddle like ducks."

"Good heavens, have you never worn frocks?" he asked in amazement.

"Yes. When I went into Williamsburg."

"What did you wear at other times?"

"Soft deerskins, trousers; not clumsy skirts. If you tried to run in a skirt you would fall down in ten steps."

"But, my dear, leather clothing is not worn in England. You must learn to dress like a lady. It will be expected of you."

"I don't think I am going to like England," she sulked.

"Oh, I am sure you will," Christopher assured her.

Charity investigated further and brought out a filmy nightdress and a lovely pink robe. "These are nice," she conceded.

"And so are the frocks."

Charity brightened. "I shall wear them for you, Mr. Leach," and she was quite suddenly back in his arms.

Alarmed at what her soft warmth was doing to him, Christopher pushed her off and held her at arm's length. "Charity, 'Mr. Leach' is much too formal, don't you think?"

She lowered her eyes. "I don't want to seem forward. . . ."

"But we are getting to know each other. I think you might call me Christopher. Or even Chris." That should make him seem younger, he thought. "My friends all call me Chris."

"Chris," she beamed. "It's a beautiful name."

"And now you must be hungry. I'll order up an early dinner and tell you the news. We are leaving for England immediately."

Charity missed the last part because of her interest in the first. "I *am* hungry. I'd like a big piece of roast venison."

That was good news. She had improved greatly; it was the first time she had evinced an appetite.

"I'll tell them to hurry."

During dinner and afterwards, Charity laughed and chattered and revealed an enchanting side of her nature. There were lapses, momentary descents into retrospective silence, when Christopher believed she was thinking of her foster mother. But these changes of mood were only momentary and Christopher thought he understood that. The shock of the kidnapping, the abuse and the cruelty, had softened the blow of Mae Varney's death.

"We are leaving for England very early tomorrow morning," he said, "so you must go to bed early and get some sleep. We must be up before four o'clock."

Well fed and content now, Charity turned pensive. "England," she mused. "So far away. I can hardly imagine it."

"I will take you to Leach House. It is where my family has lived for generations. I know you will like it."

"Will I stay there?"

"I am sure you will."

Christopher wished that the subject had not come up. He was unclear as to exactly *what* Charity would do in England. There would be the confrontation with Clement. Much remained to be worked out.

One new aspect pleased Christopher greatly. As

77

the conversation progressed, a change took place in his lovely little ward. The erratic, childlike responses, no doubt stemming from the shock of mistreatment, seemed to have vanished. She became more adult, more self-possessed.

She said, "Christopher—I feel most grateful to you. I only hope I can prove worthy of your help."

"Please don't think in those terms."

"But I must. If I cannot find a way to repay you, I shall feel guilty."

"I am amply repaid by seeing you become your normal self so quickly."

"You are most kind. And now, if it is not too much trouble, I would like a bath before I retire."

"Why should it be any trouble, my dear?"

Charity returned to her room. Christopher pulled the bell cord and gave the maid instructions for the bath and heard no more from Charity.

Left to himself, he found that Charity filled his thoughts. There was the vast satisfaction in her improvement, but something else; almost a regret. As a shocked child, she had been close to him, dependent on him, and looking back, he realized it had been a warm and satisfying experience. But now her return to the young woman she had previously been seemed to make her more remote for all her gratitude and need to find ways of repayment.

A selfish attitude, he told himself sternly. Petty and unbecoming of a grown man. If he were not careful, he added wryly, he would become the child and Charity the adult.

As though to deny that implication, he turned his mind to memories of Gaby. Their relationship had been completely on the adult level. The recall was still vivid even after four years and he wondered how she would look upon his return. More beautiful than ever, no doubt.

Late afternoon drifted into evening, and evening into later hours. When the fireplace logs had burned low, Christopher tapped on the door adjoining the rooms. There was no response. He peeped in to find Charity asleep. He retired to his own room and set his watch to chime at three-fifteen.

He slept, but there were dreams. Erotic dreams.

In sleep he became the less inhibited man he yearned to be in real life. He had a model after which to pattern himself, and in dreaming fancy he became Sean, the handsome, laughing rogue he had so envied during his youth.

Sean, the black sheep; and Christopher, melting into his image, was pursuing Gaby through the corridors of Leach House. Her laughter echoed liltingly as the Leach ancestors glared down from the walls. As they ran, Gaby discarded her skirts—so many that he lost count. One skirt after another dropped in his path; a veritable frustration of skirts because her flashing legs were never uncovered.

The dream changed suddenly, and now they were in bed together. There was the scent of lilac and Christopher fought to free himself from the lethargy of sleep.

He succeeded, coming vaguely awake to realize

he was not in his bedroom at Leach House. Where in the devil was he? Oh, yes, the hotel in Charleston. His body had preceded his mind into wakefulness. His manhood awaited his consciousness in full erection and physical demand raced through his blood.

There was a warm, soft body pressed against his back. Arms were about him, hands pressed against his chest, gentle breath on the nape of his neck.

He had left a lighted lamp on the table beside his watch, the wick turned low. Scant light but enough, when he twisted around, to show Charity's lovely face in repose. She had incredibly long lashes and with her eyelids lowered they threw shadows on her high cheek bones. There was a half-smile on her lips which would have been called sensuous under other circumstances.

She was nude and as he turned around to face her and the incredible situation more directly, he strove to collect his sleep-fragmented mind into a functioning whole. It came together slowly.

She awakened; her eyes opened, her smile deepened as her arms tightened around him.

"Charity! For God's sake! What are you doing here?"

"I was frightened in the other room, and I was cold."

"You must go back to your room."

"Why must I? Why can't I stay with you?"

"It's—it's just not. . . ."

"You said you liked me."

"Of course I like you, but. . . ."

Pressing close to him—warmly, fragrantly

sleepy, she felt his rigidity push against her thigh. She opened her eyes and looked questioningly into his face.

Later, Christopher was to agonize over all this; fight his natural guilt by trying to remember each detail, each subtle nuance of what transpired.

There was neither fear nor invitation in Charity's searching look, only a question. What was wanted? she silently asked.

The question coincided with the breaking of the dam inside Christopher. His choked cry was meant as an apology for what he was about to do, but it came out more like the snarl of an animal. Then he went about taking Charity.

This was not difficult to do. There was her eagerness to please, but so different from that which he remembered, the skilled approach of Gaby. The difference between experience and innocence; so marked that even as Christopher's barriers came down, a need for decent restraint prevailed. Cade's previous ravishment had no doubt been as vicious as such a thing could possibly be. Thus there was an added reason to treat this child—this woman?—gently. This even as Charity's eagerness to please was virtually a silent questioning:

Is this how you want me?

Does this help?

Am I doing it right?

Turned now upon her back, she was trying to help while he mounted her. She sensed his restraint and whispered reassurance.

"It doesn't hurt anymore. Honestly. . . ."

81

But the unrestrained joy of pure mating did not really exist for either of them.

Never had a man taken a woman with an anguish such as this. And never had a woman cooperated with such innocent eagerness. And each with the sense of completely failing the other.

As he drove helplessly on, grotesque comparisons flowed through Christopher's fevered mind. Charity's lack of skill was so obvious that this, coupled with her eagerness to serve, made him think in terms of an entirely different appetite—of a neophyte in the kitchen, overly anxious about her first dinner.

Is there too much salt?

Did I put in enough thyme?

Then all else was submerged in climax, but shortly afterward the unavoidable aftermath: guilt; disgust like mud thrown into the gears of his thinking:

My God! What have I done?

From his perch of righteousness he had called Cade despicable. But now did he have the right to judge himself less harshly merely because he had been more gentle in despoiling Charity? Hardly. He was even more the swine because he had violated his position of trust along with his lovely little ward.

Thus his thoughts were leaded whips with which he lashed himself, leaving Charity to her own thoughts—every bit as self-condemning. His restraint, his aloofness, could mean but one thing: she had failed. His silence proved bitter disappointment in her performance.

Another factor added strength to this conviction. She had achieved no physical pleasure, none whatever, from the sexual act. Therefore she was doubly deficient. With all her eagerness to give Christopher joy in repayment for his kindness to her, a dismal fact had become apparent.

Sex, in itself, was a terrible bore.

With this in the forefront, Charity began reshaping girlish dreams into a philosophy of reality. Sex was for the male, who obviously enjoyed it, so the female's function was to make herself available as an instrument for that joy. Charity found solid support for this assumption. A forest creature herself, she had observed much of the forest where she recalled the female of whatever species always reluctant, always fleeing the male, to submit finally through weariness or the persistent demand of the dominant sex.

She considered her own future on the basis of this depressing new awareness. The one-sidedness of the proposition seemed unfair. Why could there not be a sharing? She sighed. Wishful thinking. A waste of time.

Her mind now turned to the miserable failure she had just achieved. With her sense of obligation and gratitude still paramount she had an urge to force herself through the gap which now separated them; to assure him that she had done her best and would improve in the future. But she held back. Would she be able to find the words or would she only make a greater mess of it? He would not bring the matter up himself. He was too kind; too much the gentleman. Of course her own obligation was to learn; to improve. Where, she wondered, could she find a teacher?

She mulled all that over and as she was debating it, Christopher's watch on the bed chimed its melodious warning.

"We must get ready to leave," he said. . . .

14.

With time now pressing upon them, Christopher hurried Charity into her room. He said, "You will find suitable clothing in the box that came from Madame Flavia." He then returned to his own room to prepare for the trip, closing the door after him.

When he was ready, he tapped on the panel, his reserve hardly appropriate after the intimacy of their recent tempestuous interlude.

"Are you ready?" he called.

When there was no response he opened the door to find Charity standing in the middle of the room with a look of anguish on her face. She was still nude from the waist up, wearing only a pair of brand-new pantalettes.

"Mother Mae always helped me with these clumsy things," she wailed.

"You are merely being contrary," Christopher replied sharply. "We have little time, so stop this nonsense and get dressed."

"Oh, very well," Charity pouted, and picked up one of the frocks.

At the stroke of four there was a rapping on the outer door and a man—a mountain of bone and muscle—entered to take up the sea chest and the box as though they had no weight at all. The waiting carriage was drawn by a nervous span champing at their bits, eager to be off. The man-mountain deposited his charges, climbed up beside the driver, and they were off.

Charity seemed to have completely forgotten their recent interlude. She clung to Christopher's arm, her mind still on Madame Flavia's box. "All those clothes!" she murmured. "I suppose I'll get used to them."

Christopher said, "They will do until we get to England. Then you must have a complete new wardrobe."

"You are so good to me I could cry!" But instead, she laughed.

An hour's drive and the rig turned sharply to the left. Soon there were sounds of the ocean, the whisper of waves brushing rocks on a calm night. The luggage was quickly transferred to a waiting jolly boat, the two passengers boarded from an overhanging boulder.

The oarsmen were as stoically silent as the pair who had functioned on land. When Christopher asked, "This ship—does it have accommodations for a lady?" the answer was an uninformative grunt.

As they crossed the chop, Christopher strove to reassure Charity by holding her close, although she showed no sign of fear.

Soon, a great shadow loomed over them, darker

than the dark night. Charity was awed. "It's so *big*," she whispered.

A ladder rattled down the hull as the oarsmen steadied the jolly boat and Christopher said, "Now you must climb up, Charity. I'll be right behind you, so don't be afraid."

Her answer was a little chuckle of excitement and she was out of the boat, up the ladder, and gone.

A crew member awaited Christopher on the deck of the blacked-out ship. He said, "*Mein Herr*, I will take the *mädchen* to her quarters. Captain Meismann will see you in his cabin."

Another hand stood close by. He carried a dark lantern with the slide lifted to provide a sliver of light. Christopher followed it across what he assumed to be the quarterdeck to the poop.

He knew something about ships and from having seen it on the quays he could classify this one. It was a Dutch East Indiaman, used for trading. Wide-beamed, high-pooped, it was built to carry every ounce of cargo nautical engineering would permit. This one, he recalled, had a ridiculous superstructure built aft on the poop, giving the ship the look of a duck with a spread peacock's tail. It would waddle toward England in its own good time.

Christopher's escort tapped on a door, opened it, and Christopher stepped past him into lamplight. It was a roomy, well-furnished cabin, the ports blacked out by curtains.

Captain Meismann stood waiting, hands clasped behind his back. He clicked his heels and bowed. "Good morning, Herr Leach. I see you arrived without incident?" It was more of a question than a statement, but Christopher was not given time to answer. "I am Captain Hans Meismann. You are now aboard the *Hainaut*."

"Thank you, Captain. I understand you will take us to England."

"That is the contract." He had a good, though Teutonically gutteral command of English. He was a heavy-set man of middle age and totally bald, but with a vast wealth of beard which covered the lower half of his face. He wore a neat blue, brass-buttoned uniform as befit his rank.

He turned to the liquor cabinet. "Do you like Dutch gin, Herr Leach?"

"Oh, quite," Christopher replied, although it was the last thing he wanted.

The captain poured two generous beakers and held one forth. "Shall we drink to a pleasant voyage?"

Christopher almost lifted his glass in automatic toast to His Majesty, George the Third, by the grace of God, King of Great Britain, Defender of the Faith, etc.

They drank. The gin was atrocious according to Christopher's standards. They sat down, Meismann behind his desk, and Christopher came right to the point.

"Captain Meismann, while I obeyed my government in the extraordinary manner of this boarding, I am totally in the dark as to the need of it. Obviously there is some peril involved. Now perhaps you can enlighten me as to its exact nature."

The captain sipped his gin and wiped his beard.

"I am afraid not, *Mein Herr*. I only know that you are an important person. I know only that I was approached while ashore on business and asked to take on two passengers. I was told where to put in and at what hour and was cautioned to stand without lights."

"You agreed to that without demanding further information?"

Meismann shrugged. "I was well paid. Generously enough to justify some risk. I saw no peril to my ship or my crew. If the plan for getting you aboard failed I would have left the rendezvous as quietly as I came. But now we see that the plan did not fail. All danger is in the past. Soon we will be safely on the high seas."

"What is your cargo?"

"Tobacco—for London and Amsterdam."

"Is your ship armed?"

"We have no need. There is a two-pounder in the prow and the usual supply of small arms here in my cabin. No need to worry because pirates are not interested in tobacco. They give their attentions to treasure-laden galleons."

Christopher sighed. Still no answers. He arose and said, "Thank you, Captain. I am sure we will have a pleasant voyage. Now if I may retire to my quarters?"

"Certainly. They have been made ready for you...."

The cabin to which he was escorted was comfortably large, that being the purpose of the superstructure built over the poopdeck; comfortable officer's quarters on long boring runs.

The seaman who showed Christopher to his

cabin said, "Your niece is next aft, sir," and
Christopher wondered if there was undue inflection on the *niece*. Perhaps not. A man could certainly travel with a younger female relative and
not be suspected as a roué. . . .

The *Hainaut* was a sturdy ship, as Christopher
discovered after a cursory inspection. The bulkhead between the cabins was plank-thick, no
sound penetrating. Christopher debated looking
in on Charity and decided against it. He certainly
deserved a little time to be alone with his
thoughts. His self-disgust from what had happened at the hotel had worn away somewhat, but
he still cringed at the memory, grimly refusing to
dwell upon its pleasures; or at least making a val-
iant effort in that direction.

Still, recall of that warm, eager young body
kept intruding. So innocent, yet so willing. Obviously, Charity felt that her gratitude had to be
proved physically. He would have to speak with
her frankly about that. He must make her understand that such fervent demonstrations of gratitude were not required; that at times, a single
thank-you would suffice. Of course when he explained it to her she would understand. If only he
had not accepted her thanks with such corresponding warmth.

His mind went back to another occasion, to
Gaby's skilled approach in bed. Her expertise had
not necessarily impressed him as such at the
time. It could only now be appreciated in comparison to Charity's lack of the siren's stock-in-
trade. Beautiful Gaby! He had gotten word of her
marriage and her quick widowhood. Would she

89

have changed much in four years? Had he really been in love with her?

Finally, he drifted off to sleep. . . .

15.

He slept quite late the following morning with daylight streaming in his ports when a knocking on his door awakened him. He arose, donned a robe, and opened it to two visitors; two most surprising visitors: Charity wearing her nightdress beneath the lovely pink robe Madame Flavia had selected, and Captain Meismann holding her firmly by the arm, his whiskers fairly abristle with stiff, Germanic disapproval.

"Herr Leach," he said, "I must ask you to keep a tighter line on this young lady. I must strictly forbid that she wander about among my hands under such circumstances, let alone in this state of *auszichen*."

Even though he got the captain's point, Christopher sprang to Charity's defense.

"Captain, I would say she is hardly undressed."

"Herr Leach, as far as the rules of this ship are concerned, close enough to that state to justify the description. Ladies should not walk about in the presence of strange men while clad for the *Schlafzimmer*." Christopher could hardly disagree with that as Captain Meismann went on. "I am at fault for not advising you when we first spoke. I ask that the young lady remain at all times aft, on the quarterdeck when she takes the air. The forecastle and the forward parts of the ship must be *verboten*. Men at sea on a long voyage...."

He stopped as though feeling that he had said enough and turned to march off up the companionway.

Christopher drew Charity into his cabin and closed the door. "Charity!" he scolded. "You should know better than to go about in your nightclothes."

"I only went to the front of the ship to see the wooden statue they have up there."

"The figurehead," Christopher corrected. "And as to being dragged back here by the arm, I am more to blame than you are. You are in a strange place among strange people. I should have been more constant in my attentions while you are learning new ways and new customs."

"What is *Schlafzimmer*?"

"The German word for *bedroom*. You may feel that Captain Meismann is being harsh but he is responsible for our very lives while we are on this ship and must do what he thinks best."

"I don't care what he thinks. I only care what you think and now you will think even less of me."

"Charity! That is not true! What can I say to convince you?"

Substituting action for words, Charity took two quick steps in his direction. Instantly his

91

hands went out, palms flat, the gesture clearly saying, *Stay away from me*.

"See? You don't really like me. You don't want me near you."

"That doesn't mean I don't care for you. It's just that I have a responsibility. . . ."

"But I'm your slave. You bought me. I belong to you."

"I did not buy you and you are not my slave. That's ridiculous. I ransomed you which is something quite different. I did it because of what Mae Varney told me. . . ."

"See? That proves it. What you did was because of something Mother Mae said before she died."

"Will you stop it?" He stormed back and forth across the cabin. "Charity, things have changed for you. Your life has taken a sharp turn. You are going to England where you will learn to be a lady and live a rich, full life."

"I promise to do that. All I want to do is please you. I am so grateful to you. If you hadn't come after me I would probably be dead now. You don't expect me to be ungrateful for that, do you?"

"You have shown your gratitude so let's just have done with it." He turned away, then turned back quickly. "Charity, listen to me carefully. We are on this ship under false colors. You are my niece and I am your uncle and we must conduct ourselves on that basis. You must remember that we are under the eyes of the crew. . . ."

"But not all the time."

Charity took a forward step. Christopher took

a backward step. "Have you had breakfast?" he asked nervously.

"I'm not hungry," she said sulkily.

"But you must eat."

Charity did not reply. Again, her lower lip was trembling. And now she exhibited the most truly feminine trait of the whole incident by throwing herself into the bunk and bursting into tears.

Christopher approached, his hands extending now in a pleading gesture rather than otherwise. He stepped close and looked down at her; at that lovely young body. She lay with her face hidden in her arms and Christopher's gaze held upon the back of her slim legs, gracefully outlined through the thin material of the robe and nightdress. His eyes traveled up the achingly beautiful thighs, revealed rather than hidden.

No wonder, he told himself, that the morally upright captain of the *Hainaut* had been scandalized.

But that was an unfair, defensive thought. To the devil with Meismann and all the rest of them. Charity was right. The two of them *were* alone now. The erotic urge was great but with a most violent wrenching of his mental faculties, Christopher throttled his rising temperature, turned blindly, and left Charity to her tears.

16

Things now settled into the routine of a sea voyage. Captain Meismann, while he drew the line at nymphs gamboling in the forecastle, still did not run a tight ship. As a matter of fact, Christopher thought him a little sloppy. He remained aloof from his officers, spending most of his time in his cabin with his books. He was a studious man with the good fortune of having officers and a crew who appreciated the comparatively lenient treatment. All in all, a happy ship.

The *Hainaut* had accommodations unfamiliar to Christopher. She carried two galleys and two cooks, one midship for the forecastle hands and one in the forecastle for the officers. Also, there were no set mealtimes aft. The serving was buffet style at all times and Christopher was struck by the variety and richness of the fare. Fresh vegetables, fresh beef, venison and fowl; even fresh fruit. He was sure the menu would deteriorate as the voyage progressed, but at the moment it was little different from shoreside provender.

Charity made an honest effort to develop the ladylike qualities Christopher had outlined. She wore one or the other of the frocks Madame Flavia had selected for her. She obeyed the order from Captain Meismann, relayed through the first mate to Christopher, that she remain on the quarterdeck and the poop and not circulate forward among the crew. This was no great hardship, however, as it left plenty of room for airing and exercise.

While the aft section of the ship was always a point of interest for the crew when Charity was on deck, the officers, gentlemen all, chose to ignore the previous incident and Charity was treated as her new ladylike manner merited.

A week of good weather slipped by. Then conditions changed as the wind grew lazy, the barometer dropped and the fleecy puff balls above turned sullen and laid a gray blanket over the sky. The officers kept close attention on the changes and when Christopher asked, "Are we in for a storm?" Thorson replied, "I don't think so. It looks more like the doldrums. We may be in for fog and dead water."

This was almost an understatement. A short time later, the fog drifted in and began to thicken. Lacy gray fingers formed to take the ship into a huge smothering fist. The sails rippled at times but mainly hung motionless.

As night fell, precautions were taken. Running lights were of little use. Only the sound of a bell, struck at thirty-second intervals, penetrated the blanket of fog, and the ear of the watch was kept sharply attuned for an answering bell.

The air was oppressive, especially in the cabins, and after trying for a time to sleep, Charity arose, donned her robe over her nightdress, and went out on deck in the hope of catching a breeze.

It had been said that shattering events are never forecast; that they usually come unheralded to seize and trap and hold the unwary.

This was the case with Charity. She stood by the rail on the port side of the quarterdeck. The watch officer was on the other side with even the helmsman invisible from the port rail. From that position, Charity sensed rather than saw what took place. It seemed to her that shadows darker than the fog—ghost shadows—were flitting silently about the ship. There were soft sounds as though the ghosts moved about on cat feet. Not yet any cause for alarm, but then a darker shadow loomed close. Another literally arose out of the sea, and even as Charity's lips parted to cry out, a hand was clamped over her mouth. Another hand slipped down her body and there was a soft chuckle in her ear. Then a whisper.

"By Patrick's beard! What have we here?"

The hand on her mouth was in a velvet glove and the breath of the whisper smelled of mint. These aspects of reality snapped Charity out of her momentary daze and she acted instinctively. Her teeth ground down on the hand and she jammed an elbow backward into the body of her captor.

There was a gasp, a soft curse, and she was free. She was never sure why she did not scream, possibly because her anger at being so roughly handled choked out all fear. Still, she sought safety in flight, racing toward the superstructure companionway and the sanctuary of her cabin. This proved futile. Footsteps persisted behind her and when she sought to slam her door a leg was thrust forth to block the closing.

Whatever was transpiring had progressed in almost complete silence. Charity realized this as her attacker again took command. An arm of steel went around her waist, trapping her arms, and that velvet glove now pressed so hard against her face that she could not open her mouth to bite.

While holding her thus, the door partially opened, the man conversed briefly with others in the companionway. A voice informed him, "He's in the next cabin aft." Christopher's quarters, as Charity realized.

"Good," was the reply. "You know what you're after. But gently, gently. Harm a hair on his head and you'll dry in the sun."

A baleful threat but uttered in such pleasant, casual tones as to make drying in the sun a not unpleasant experience.

Then Charity's attacker closed the door and released her. She scurried to the far side of the cabin and was perhaps preparing to scream. But no sound came forth as she clearly saw the man for the first time by the light of her overhead lamp.

He was a totally arresting figure; so much so that she could hardly be blamed for staring in mute wonder. As handsome as Satan's messenger sent to trap innocent maidens; laughing blue eyes, sparkling teeth in a mouth which looked incapable of a scowl; broad shoulders slimming down to narrow hips. As fine a masculine figure as could be imagined.

97

But his dress added more to wonder at. There was nothing of the patch-eyed, bearded creature typifying the accepted buccaneer image. Rather, it was the storybook rascal as visualized by limpid-eyed maidens gazing at the moon through bedroom windows. He was dressed in black; black boots, black trousers clinging to slim, gracefully muscled legs, a gleaming satin sash bound around his middle under a loose silk shirt with flowing sleeves tight at the wrist. A dagger was thrust into a scabbard in his right boot. He stared across the cabin in frank admiration.

"By the saints," he murmured. "You *are* a lovely thing."

Charity pressed her back against the bulkhead and glared.

"Truly. The ultimate beauty of any man's lonely dream," the handsome rascal went on.

Perhaps the compliment, the open admiration, and his unmenacing attitude held Charity speechless; but more likely it was the music in his voice; soft melodious tones with laughter in them; a brogue with which Charity was unfamiliar but could not help being held by the lilt of it.

He was across the cabin now, her hand in his velvet glove. He lifted it and gently kissed her fingers.

He wore a black silk scarf banded about his head, held by a gold clasp at his temple, the rest of the scarf hanging loosely over his shoulder. Charity found her attention drawn to the clasp. It was in the form of a sensuously nude girl.

His look of admiration decreased not a whit. In fact it deepened as he gently cupped Charity's face in soft velvet and held her eyes in his gaze, almost as though his own blue eyes had a tangible power to reach forth and take hold.

His expression turned pensive now, as though he were studying her in order to store her image in his memory. His eyes dropped to her breast, held for a moment, then were again on her face.

And I stand here like a clod doing nothing!

The thought flashed through Charity's mind as his smile again brightened and he murmured, "Oh, you lovely thing! How you would look in nature's garb lying in some grassy glade hard by Shannon's stream!"

"Who are you?" Charity managed to demand.

He ended his reverie and swept a graceful bow. "Sean McDougal at your service, lass."

"Wha—what do you want?"

"So little. So very little. Only a kiss; a souvenir to take away to remember you by."

With that he reached boldly forth and took Charity into his arms. Her bemusement, the spell, or whatever it was, lasted until his lips touched hers. Then her basic instincts, held in check but in no way crippled, burst forth, and Orin Cade had found no more of a wildcat on his hands than did Sean McDougal. Charity drew her mouth downward until it was against his throat. She bit viciously as she put her arms around his shoulders for leverage and sought to drive a knee into his groin.

He jerked away. Quick anger turned his eyes into pits of blue fire.

"Why you savage little vixen!" He backpedalled and held her at arms length while she thrashed and fought and tried to kick him.

"All right," he snarled. "Now you owe me more." But immediately the flash of anger changed to a look of excitement as though this were a friendly game of skill. His voice dropped to a musical purr. "A kiss is but a fading blossom to die in the press of a memory book's pages. But a souvenir to remember—to stay forever green. . . ."

Even as he spoke he was forcing her to the floor, her crossed wrists held rigidly in a steel grip just below her breast. With his free hand he swept the skirts of her robe and gown upward.

Kicking furiously, Charity unwittingly helped, in clearing her lower torso so that he could pry her thighs apart with his knee without the interference of clothing.

The heaped-up material below her breasts kept her from seeing how he partially divested himself of obstructing garments, but when she felt bare flesh against her own, she writhed anew and spoke through gritted teeth.

"You beast! You disgusting animal! You taunted me only to make an excuse to rape me!"

"Easy now, my lass. It was you who did the taunting. You set your teeth into me. I was most gentlemanly."

"You *forced* me to bite you!"

"How strange the logic of the female," he declared; lightly now, without malice. But that scrap of philosophy in no way lessened his intent.

Helpless now, Charity squeezed her eyes shut and awaited the intrusion of his manhood. She expected a savage joining, but it did not come. He accomplished it gently, which brought Charity to a bit of her own philosophy. Approaches varied, still the end result remained the same. Orin Cade's savagery, Christopher's naivete, this buffoon's smiling good cheer—all aimed however deviously at a girl's loins. Even animals had it better. The ram respected the doe's seasonal inclinations. The human male respected nothing.

Sean McDougal went more intently to his work while Charity struggled and cursed him in three languages.

Then she too fell silent. Something was happening; something both shameful and confusing. Then the shame and the confusion were washed away by a rising of sensations she had never before experienced; a stirring of her blood; but more, much more, a hot, surging delight as latent fire so long dormant in her loins suddenly ignited. The flame swept upward, arresting all else within her in its searing wonder.

She heard a soft, coaching voice in her ear: "Love me, lass—love me to the stars and beyond."

And like a rose on a silver catapult, Charity was caught and hurled high into multicolored glory. Instincts far deeper than those of a proper maiden tore her hands from his grasp and found his silky head. Drawing him to her she sought his mouth as though starving for the manna she would find there. Her bite was as savage as before but now in different context; now a consuming tenderness he understood.

Moments later, she was screaming silent surrender into his throat.

Hard upon that first burst of searing flame, there came a second; an explosion in her loins which rocketed Charity into ecstasy close to unbearable.

Exhaustion finally overcame them. For a time, Sean McDougal lay as though he were too weary to arise. When he did, Charity felt no inclination to follow him. Her final lunge into complete womanhood now accomplished, she lay with no sense of shame as he looked down upon her. Rather, there was a surge of satisfaction as she saw the limp state to which he was reduced.

I won. I beat him.

Nor did she miss that which was new in his regard, in his eyes, in his silent reappraisal. A patronizing attitude had been threaded through his early polished gallantry. Now he looked at her with a mixture of emotions she tried to classify. Respect? Wonder? Awe?

As he put his clothing together he said, "You were muttering—strange words in a strange language."

"Indian curses. Chickahominy, Cherokee, maybe Potawatomi."

"You are an Indian?"

"No. I lived near them."

"Where did Christopher get you?"

Recklessly happy, Charity sought to shock him. "He bought me from the man who had bought me from some other men."

"Bought you?"

"Yes, I am his slave," she replied, her voice now pure mockery.

"You are gulling me!"

Charity shrugged, arose from the floor, and smoothed her nightdress down over her body. "Believe it or not," she said airily, "it makes no difference to me."

There was a tapping on the door. Sean McDougal opened it a crack and Charity heard the whispered conversation.

"We got it."

"No trouble?" Sean's lowered voice was crisp and businesslike.

"We had to bind and gag him. He can soon work free."

"What about the rest of them?"

"Trader hands." The tone was contemptuous and no doubt included both officers and men. "We spiked the pop gun up fore and wet down the powder in the captain's cabin. All clear now."

"Good, sound for retreat."

He closed the door. Again he was the gallant, storybook privateer, as he turned back to Charity.

She asked, "Why did you come here?"

He laughed. "To fill my pipe from Captain Meismann's hold."

He swept toward her and took the hand she did not draw back. He led her to the door, bent his head, and kissed her fingers. Then he snatched off his black scarf, put it around his neck, and pressed the gold clasp into her hand.

"To remember me by 'til we meet again."

"Hardly likely," Charity sniffed.

103

"Oh, but we shall," he assured her. "Sooner than you think."

There was another rap on the door. He said, "A moment," then threw Charity a dazzling smile. "Give my love to Cousin Christopher," he said, and was gone.

Cousin Christopher? What did that mean? A great deal or nothing at all.

Still held in thrall by the new world into which she had been so tempestuously thrown, Charity crossed the cabin and opened one of the ports. The fog had begun to thin. Then, as though this were some fantastic play, it lifted, not unlike a curtain on a stage, and Charity saw something as fantastic as the man who had just departed.

A ship; a strange ship; jet black and sleekly lined as though it but waited its master's word to take wings and fly off to some mysterious place over the sea and beyond.

Again the black shadows, now drifting up and over its rail, but just before the fog closed in again, something even more unreal; the name of the ship painted fore near the bow.

The Evening Primrose.

How grotesque! Such a ship should bear a name of sinister portent.

A sharp rap on the door turned her away from the port.

Christopher's urgent voice. "Charity! Are you all right?"

Acting purely from instinct, she rushed to her bunk, slipping off her rumpled robe as she went.

"Charity!"

The door opened.

Charity turned drowsily under the sheet. "Christopher? What's the matter?"

"You are all right, then?" he asked anxiously.

"Of course. Why shouldn't I be?"

"Never mind. Go back to sleep."

"Something must be wrong."

"Nothing. Nothing at all."

He turned and left and it took Charity a few moments to realize what she had done. Through a single, illogical, quick lie, she had cut herself off from ever telling Christopher the truth.

This was a fight between her conscience and her body, and her body quickly won. She would worry about her perfidy tomorrow. Just now, she was held in the sweet aftermath of what had happened there on the floor. Dreamily, she ran her hands lightly over her breasts, still feeling Sean McDougal's lips. Now a woman's breasts, no longer those of a maiden. Her hands slipped lower. Now a woman's body.

Irrationally, she thought of the gold clasp he had snatched from his bandanna. It was still clutched in her hand. *To remember me by 'til we meet again.* . . . She slipped out of her bunk and held it close to the lamp.

It was skillfully executed, a work of art, subtly erotic. The figure of a woman on her knees, hands and face raised as though in supplication. Peering closely, Charity could make out the incredibly fine work which had been done on the face. The lips were slightly open, the tip of a tongue just protruding. But the true work of genius lay in the expression achieved on that tiny face; the smile, sultry and erotic, the yearning etched on it fairly glowing in the gold.

Charity closed her hand tightly over the clasp, her grip doubly symbolical. It would always remind her of her own fierce demand in Sean McDougal's arms. Also, it must be locked away with the secret of what had occurred in her cabin. No one must ever see it except—except the man who had given it to her? Again, she remembered.

Give my love to Cousin Christopher.

Damn him! Damn his black, sadistic heart!

Why had he chosen to propound such riddles and then go laughing on his way? Charity returned to her bunk and though she was neither sad nor depressed, tears came.

In due course they were dried and she faced the most pressing question of all.

Why had she not cried out? Why had she not cried out a warning of what was taking place on the fog-shrouded deck? *There had not been time.* In an instant that silken hand had been over her mouth, the arm restraining her. The excuse sufficed for a moment but then dissolved. After breaking away she could have screamed her heart out between the deck and her cabin. Why had she not? Had the thrall of Sean McDougal fallen upon her from the very first instant? She refused to acknowledge that and went finally to sleep.

17.

Conditions aboard the *Hainaut* changed quickly as the sorry results of Captain Meismann's non-defensive policies brought him to shame. It was not having been boarded; there was no disgrace in that. But to have been taken without a shot being fired on either side; to have been rendered helpless without so much the swing of a marlin-spike!

The pirate crew had drifted silently abaft and come aboard like so many ghosts. They had taken the fore and aft watches like hungry foxes loose in a hen coop, cowed the entire forecastle where most of the hands remained in their bunks, and handled the officers in their cabins like children at play, and all with much good humor. Aside from the pistols and sabers in evidence it could have been a group of jolly companions visiting not-so-jolly friends.

Three of the invaders were in the captain's cabin before he opened an eye. A smiling member of the trio placed a pistol against Meismann's ear and grinned in the friendliest fashion while the other two examined his supply of small arms and then poured a carafe of water into his powder bin.

Of course, with no arms having been distributed, the captain could hardly have expected

107

his crew to rise up in defense with bare fists. However, his roars of frustration penetrated even the thick bulkheads when he assembled his officers in his cabin immediately after the foray.

Given time to analyze the affair the following morning, however, Meismann considered the aspects. He had never been boarded before. But he had never accommodated passengers before, either. So he called Christopher Leach to his office.

"Herr Leach, you are aware of what took place last night?"

"Oh, yes. Two of them entered my cabin with drawn pistols. I discussed the matter with your first mate."

"Did they rob you?"

"No," Christopher lied. "They were very polite. They merely suggested that I remain where I was."

"It is all very strange," the captain said pointedly.

"I understand no harm was done—that nothing was taken from the ship and no one was injured."

"That is the strange part of it."

"Perhaps they found they were on the wrong ship. The fog was heavy, you know," Christopher suggested.

"Perhaps," Captain Meismann growled. "Did the leader of the pack imply that?"

"I did not see him. I saw only the two men. They tied me when they left, but loosely. I soon came free."

"I think we must take mistaken identity as an explanation," the captain said finally. No point in looking for trouble.

It was a lame explanation, however. Valuables lying about in the captain's cabin had remained untouched. Mistake or not, the usual run of pirates would certainly have helped themselves.

The interview over, Christopher retired to his cabin and his own thoughts. He felt no guilt about lying to the captain. That was a matter of diplomacy. Diplomats bent the truth when necessary and he was obliged not to reveal that the raid had been entirely successful. The rascals had gotten what they came for—his *dossier* on the colonial unrest situation.

He viewed this coup with mixed emotions. There was distress at having lost the results of so much hard work; but also a touch of personal pride. The colonial rebels had respected his work and considered it valuable enough to send a ship after it. That proved his time had not been wasted and he thanked God that the privateers had been gentlemen what with a lovely young girl totally defenseless and open to lustful attack. They had apparently allowed Charity to sleep peacefully through the whole incident of the boarding.

For her part, Charity coped with guilt. Trapped into silence by her impetuous denial to Christopher in her cabin, she could only regret that stupidity and continue the pretense that nothing had happened. Her mind kept going back to Sean McDougal, the laughing privateer who had ravished her and in the process plumbed the depths of her emotional well so deeply that there were no words to describe it. Then he had kissed her fingertips and gone on his way.

His promise of another meeting loomed ever larger in her mind. Was it truly possible that they would meet again? And that 'cousin' business. She had to find an opportunity to question Christopher on that without arousing his suspicions. In the privacy of her cabin she pored over the gold clasp. It had become more than an erotic symbol or a mere souvenir of an exceptional event. As she fondled it, she dreamed, transposing herself into the gold and from there into reveries. At such times she shamelessly saw herself as kneeling before Sean McDougal in complete surrender, offering to deliver the erotic pleasure the pose and expression on the face of the little artifact suggested.

At that point, she would stop, not allowing her futile dreams to go farther. The yearning without the reality was not healthy. Her instincts told her that.

18.

The changes decreed by Captain Meismann altered the routine of the voyage from one of pleasant laxity to a far more rigid order of things.

The officers now went about their duties wearing sidearms. The forecastle was no longer a place of lazy contentment. There was no more singing on duty or off. Work became the order of the day. Deck planking took on the patina of fine old wood under repeated scrubbings and brass and metal now glowed brightly in the glare of the sun.

Captain Meismann might well be censured for past mistakes but the new order of things would be meticulously recorded in the log.

But of more concern was the sea-change. It came quickly, as though Poseidon and Neptune had met in hurried conference and decided to hurl their most violent waters at the *Hainaut*. Waves were hurled high against the ship while she nosed bravely forward as befitted an East Indian carrack. She rode the troughs with decks awash and sails furled.

Charity became violently seasick. Having been to sea before, Christopher was relatively immune. He tried to comfort Charity but it did little good. She remained in her cabin and suffered the distress of *mal-de-mer* as the punishing hours dragged relentlessly on.

Finally the week-long storm spent itself and the *Hainaut* returned to an even keel. After a time, Charity ventured on deck with Christopher in sympathetic attendance. Basking there in the sun, she recuperated quickly.

One aspect of her recovery was interesting. Her recall of Sean McDougal dimmed and blurred. His sojourn in her cabin became even more of a dream—a storybook incident without the substance of truth as realities of the moment took their proper places in her mind. High among

111

them was her continuing gratitude to Christopher for rescuing her from lingering death at the hands of Orin Cade.

It also occurred to her that the dreamlike episode with Sean McDougal might well help in giving herself to Christopher more skillfully. *At least,* she told herself, *I am more experienced now. When he is ready I shall be waiting.* Thus it was curious that she saw nothing in herself other than her body as coin of repayment.

The new post-raid regime tended to isolate Christopher and Charity from the now less-friendly officers, drawing them closer together. Charity, soon her old self, approached Christopher with warmth and vivacity. No mention was made as to his moral lapse back in Charleston, but Charity was ready if he chose to repeat his performance.

For his part, there was less difficulty now in practicing restraint even though Charity was as beautiful and desirable a girl as he had ever encountered. He was finding his thoughts turning more and more to Gabrielle Spencer-Dean. No, she would be Gabrielle Kirth now. The breaking of her promise saddened him, but he told himself that he understood; nor did it turn his mind from erotic thoughts about the passionate Gaby. He remembered the heat of their embraces, the sweet, heady release it was her talent to expertly bring about. Thus it was ironic that while memories of Sean McDougal's possessive body drifted at times into Charity's mind, Christopher was thinking of Gaby's hot embrace.

They conversed easily and spontaneously now, with Charity usually the conversational aggressor. At the rail one night under a moon unable to exert romantic influence, Charity went back to an old question:

"Chris, what will happen to me when we get to England?"

"Never fear. You will be taken care of by my family."

"Then if I'm to be a member of your family," Charity went on hopefully, "I should know more about—about my new relatives."

That was jumping ahead a little, but Christopher smiled affectionately. When he spoke it was with pride in his voice. "You will meet my brother Clement. He is a most illustrious man. He followed the way of the church from early boyhood and is now the rector of St. Jude's near our home in Kent."

"Oh?"

"I suppose that does not sound like a great deal—only a rector. But Clement overshadows his position. He is held in high regard in all England as a churchman. He also has great political influence."

"He sounds important. Are your parents living?"

"No. And that is another burden for Clement. As the eldest son, the family is his responsibility. Keeping it together, being father and. . . ." Christopher almost said *and mother,* but that stretched his imagination too far.

"Have you other brothers?"

"No. Only two sisters. There is Mercedes—we call her Mercy." He paused to smile. "We will now have both Charity and Mercy in the family. Mercy is married to Justin Holbrook, a banker. They live in Mayfair, in London. You will meet them when we arrive. Mercy is a fine woman. She fulfilled Clement's every hope."

"Your other sister?"

Christopher's tone saddened. "Margaret—Meg is different. It is almost as though my uncle, Gerold, were her father rather than our own sire, Winston Leach. Meg has wild blood. She has been a great burden to Clement. She ran away and married Dennis Wahl—wealthy enough but a wastrel in many ways. He is not true to Meg, but then Meg herself is. . . ."

What Meg was remained unspoken, keening Charity's curiosity greatly. She said, "You mentioned your uncle in a strange way. . . ."

Christopher was gazing out over the night sea—at the moon now risen and yellow in the sky. His family revelations had turned into a soliloquy and perhaps he was revealing more than he intended.

"Yes, my father's brother. He inherited wild blood from somewhere back in the line. He ran away to Ireland in his youth and married a woman older than himself. They had a son, Sean."

Charity's heart missed a beat. "Sean Leach?"

"Yes but—well, no. Uncle Gerold was killed in a tavern brawl and his wife Daphne remarried. And though he did it for his own reasons, it was a blessing to our family that young Sean took his stepfather's name, McDougal."

Sean McDougal!

Give my love to cousin Christopher. . . .

To remember me by 'til we meet again.

That mystery was solved but it only raised other questions. One of them, why Sean had boarded the *Hainaut* in the first place, nagged Charity like a pesky fly buzzing her ear.

"From what you say, your brother Clement does not approve of Sean—nor do you yourself."

"Approve! Great God! He has turned felon, a criminal, privateer, smuggler . . . I don't know *what* else!"

Seeking to calm Christopher's upset, Charity said, "Your father must have been a fine man." She was surprised when Christopher had to stop and consider, as though weighing that in his mind.

"He was. A dedicated man. He was a peer of the realm but he renounced his title although we did keep our estates."

"He did not want a title?"

"There was a vicious debate in Parliament. It had to do with child labor in coal mines and when my father was balked in his efforts to improve their lot, he gave up his title as a gesture of protest. It is one of Clement's great ambitions that we get it back."

The moon was lowering. It reached the horizon, a romantic, almost erotic setting. That alone should have generated tender thoughts in any man and maid at the rail of a ship at sea.

It did. At least in Charity. She thought of Sean

McDougal and there was a sudden warmth in her loins, a rising of her nipples.

A tightening of her fingers as they gripped the rail. . . .

Part Two: *The Moon Tower*

19.

"Oh, sweeting—have you heard the news?"

Lady Gabrielle Kirth, her lovely eyes filled with mischief, called out the question as she tumbled from her carriage at Camber and hurried across the lawn to where Meg Wahl sat in the summer house doing needlework.

Meg had quietly watched Gaby's approach, the latter coming directly from a sojourn in London. She had noted the horse's lathered state and surmised that Gaby had traveled at her usual breakneck speed. But Gaby's visits were frequent enough not to require any elaborate welcome—or any welcome at all, for that matter—so Meg awaited her approach, admiring her toilette and her selection of dress. It was late afternoon so poor old Lord Kirth's beautiful young widow would have had to start her trip quite early. Yet she looked as though she had just stepped away from her dressing table. She wore a lemon and white striped silk gown, deliciously attractive, which indicated to Meg that there was reason for the visit other than to bring news; that reason of course being Dennis, Meg's husband.

"Gaby darling—how lovely you look!"

That was Meg's greeting, proffered without missing a stitch—as Gaby swept into the summer house and into a chair.

"But darling, have you *heard*?"

Meg's answering smile was close to patronizing, quietly sweet; the reaction of a self-composed woman not given to emotional responses.

"Gaby—gentle down, my pet." Now Meg laid her work aside and poured from a crystal pitcher on the summer house table. "Cool your throat with this lemonade and catch a breath or you'll burst your stays."

That was enough to turn Gaby's mind from the sensational news she had brought. Her reply was tart. "Meg, I have no stays, as you well know. I don't need them."

"Of course not, my dear. I've always admired your handsome figure." *And so does Dennis*, she came close to adding. And in the rapport of their two keen minds, Gaby heard the unspoken addendum.

She hated Meg in a friendly, exasperated way. Meg was always so completely in control. Where she should have been a jealous, unhappy wife, her husband's affairs with Gaby and other available ladies seemed not to bother her. It was all a pose, of course; Gaby told herself that as a matter of personal satisfaction, even though she did not really believe it. She sincerely wished she could see Meg as too utterly stupid to realize what was going on, but Gaby would have had to be stupid herself to believe that.

Gaby smiled as she caught the eye of Durban, the handsome young servant who knelt by a nearby rose bush fussing with a trowel, a ruse to keep him near Meg, as Gaby well knew; nearby to answer Meg's every command, be it to swat a pesky fly or jump into the lake and drown himself. What ridiculous devotion! So the envy and jealousy were actually on Gaby's side. How wonderful it would be to have total domination over such a sexually attractive man; to dictate his every move and action; like a faithful dog trained to obey but never interfere. Gaby had never achieved that sort of a relationship. At the moment, she had to put up with Dennis Wahl's whims and moods; exciting, of course, but so disturbingly uncertain.

Without looking in his direction, her eyes still upon Gaby, Meg lifted the pitcher from the table and called, "Durban, fill this, please." As Durban leaped to obey, Gaby read Meg's smile. It said, *Darling, don't you wish Dennis would jump like that at your command?*

Bitch! Gaby silently replied, then got back to her original subject. "Meg, I came clear out here to give you the news!"

"I've been waiting," Meg replied demurely.

"Christopher!"

"What about Christopher?" Meg asked mildly.

"He is back in England and he brought a trollop with him. A colonial *tart*!"

"No! How devastating!"

"Then you *haven't* heard!" Gaby said smugly.

"Only vaguely," Meg lied. She had been given every detail of the scandal from three sources, but her way was that of a born diplomat. Listen

121

and take in; give out only when it is expedient to do so.

"Well, he arrived in London from Plymouth several days ago and all London is agog. You should hear what's being said in the clubs and coffee houses. Her name is Charity—can you imagine?—and they say she is half Indian."

"How exciting!"

"From what I've heard, Christopher must be flouting her all over London. He has been buying her frocks and shoes—"

"Was she naked and barefoot when they got here?"

"Meg! Be serious. I certainly hope he did not take her to Mayfair."

"I doubt if he would go that far." Meg tried to visualize stiff-backed Justin welcoming an Indian from the Colonies. Poor Mercy, she thought. My poor little sister—tied for life to a man whose heart is on Threadneedle Street and whose mistress is the Bank of England.

"They say she is as beautiful as an April morning," Gaby went on. The statement was close to a pout and Meg knew what was going through Gaby's wicked little mind. The competition. She wanted Christopher now and would not hesitate to destroy anyone who could dispute her claim.

"You have not seen either of them then?" Meg asked.

"No."

Of course not. Gaby would want to size her rival up from a distance and plan a campaign.

Gaby said, "Christopher must be dreading the moment he has to face Clement."

"True. The manse will probably be rocked to its very foundations."

The prediction cheered Gaby. "Do you think it will be that bad?"

"It will certainly be interesting."

Durban had returned with the lemonade and was again kneeling by the rose bush. Gaby, let down by Meg's calm reception of her news, veered away from the subject.

"You seem to be without a husband, Meg."

"Dennis is out riding. He should be back shortly. Will you stay the night?" This was neither an invitation nor a hint to leave; merely an inquiry in a tone of voice which made Gaby writhe inwardly.

Is the woman made of wood? How can she take her husband's infidelity so calmly?

"The ride *was* tiring. If it would not be putting you out?"

"On the contrary. I'm sure Dennis will insist on it."

Before Gaby could reply, there was the sound of approaching hoofbeats. "Speak of the devil," Meg murmured, and Dennis appeared from beyond the stable. He rode his big roan stallion contemptously across the lawn, vaulted a hedge in reckless abandon and brought the animal to a halt a scant foot or two from where Durban knelt by the rose bush.

Dennis Wahl was not of aristocratic mold, yet not unattractive, in a robust, rugged way. He was a dark man with broad shoulders and a stocky body tending heavily toward hairiness; an unkempt black mane flew in the wind. Heavy

123

black eyebrows heightened the illusion of critically penetrating eyes. His frown was semipermanent and he was an exception to the mode in that he kept his face clean-shaven.

Upon his immediate arrival, there was a silence as the two women watched the byplay which ensued. Dennis, bent upon cruelly taunting Durban, used the stallion to that end. He held the nervous animal tightly in check or it might have leaped over both the crouching servant and the rose bush, its front hooves chopping at the sod scarcely a foot from the kneeling man.

Durban remained motionless, giving not an inch. Dennis smiled as he eased the reins a trifle. The stallion's foreleg brushed Durban's back whereupon Durban arose quietly and took the animal by its bridle.

Dennis scowled. "I didn't tell you to rein my mount!"

Durban stepped back, expressionless. "I am sorry, sir. I misunderstood."

Meg smiled with satisfaction at what she saw as her husband's defeat. She said, "Dennis, we have company. Gaby brings news from London."

Gaby looked at Dennis from beneath lowered lashes. She said, "I envy your ability to control that beast. But I fear that someday he will kill you."

"Not likely. Are you staying over?"

"I did bring a small case," Gaby replied blandly, "in the event that there were no other guests."

"Of course you are staying," Meg said. Then to Durban, "See to Lady Kirth's bag." Whimsically

124

she wondered what the reaction would be if she'd said what was in her mind: *On your way, tart*.

"Good," Dennis enthused. "How about a canter?"

"I would be delighted."

"I'll have the hostler take care of your rig."

As Gaby left to change, she passed Durban, the latter returning to again putter with the rose bush. Dennis dismounted, tied his mount, and threw himself into a chair in the summer house. He looked bleakly at the lemonade pitcher.

"Have you nothing except that swill?"

Meg looked up from her needlework. "I can send for whatever you wish."

"Never mind. I'll get it later. What was Gaby's news?"

"Nothing we haven't heard. Christopher's arrival from the Colonies. We know of it, but you paid little attention."

Dennis snorted. "Because I don't give a damn for the comedy your family keeps playing out. I thought you understood that."

"Oh, I do. But you asked for the news; I did not volunteer it, my dear."

"They make their own troubles. If they were not occupied with the current ones they would find others."

Meg changed the subject. "Sibley came by. He would like a new roof on his cottage. The rain comes in and muddies the floor."

"Devil take Sibley! He is always complaining."

"He is a good worker. He always brings us in an excellent crop."

"Then he should have the good sense to fix his

125

own roof instead of sitting there stubbornly getting wet."

Camber, Dennis Wahl's estate, was small when compared with the Leach acres of moor, forest, and seacoast—that or Channel Light, the vast Kirth estate inherited by the fortunate Gaby. There was but a single tenant farmer on Camber—John Sibley, an efficient, industrious man. But he had a stubborn streak and with the roof of his cottage Dennis Wahl's responsibility, he was inclined to let it leak until something was done about it.

Meg knew little about the man but she suspected that he was not above a turn or two at smuggling. This was not an uncommon practice along the wild Channel coast.

Dennis came restlessly to his feet and seized his mount's reins. "Gaby should be ready by now," he said. "I'll go see to her horse."

Meg watched as he led the roan across the lawn. He would probably take Gaby to the south cottage which had been vacant since old Timmons died; a former tenant farmer who grew too feeble to work and was allowed to live out his last months as a pension for faithful service. The cottage was high on a cliff overlooking the Channel; quite a romantic spot.

They would be late for dinner.

Alone with his mistress, Durban moved closer to the summer house and stood waiting like a patient animal. Meg regarded him thoughtfully. He was a handsome, superbly-muscled young man somewhere in his late twenties—Meg had never inquired. He had come first to Camber as a stranger from the Denhigh coal country looking for employment. Dennis put him to work on the estate and Meg began making leisurely investigations as to his potential. Their curious relationship evolved from that point with Durban never presuming, but ever responding to Meg's encouragement. Thus, in time, he became her personal servant.

Meg, for want of a better description, could have been called a sexual adventuress. She found lovers in London and Maidstone and upon occasion had gone to certain notorious places masked, to leave without revealing her identity. She dropped her lovers quickly after testing their wares but did not lack courage, having once visited the famous and infamous Borland Nickelawn to come away with bruises and welts from his sadistic handling of women.

And now, in the summer house, she complimented her faithful man-servant. "I was quite proud of you, Durban—the way you handled that situation."

"It was nothing."

"Still, I was proud of you. And now, I think I would like a bath and some rest."

"I will go and prepare the tub."

Meg followed some ten minutes later, approaching the house from across the wide lawn. It was a sizeable Georgian structure. far too large for two people and a small staff. Meg's suite was on the second floor of the south wing and Dennis never invaded it while Meg stayed away from his digs at the north end. Thus they respected each other's privacy, nor did either of them

127

bring lovers or mistresses into the house. A comfortable arrangement indeed.

By the time Meg reached her suite, the bath was prepared, the water laced with the lilac scent she preferred, and two kettles of hot water in reserve.

Durban stood by, patiently waiting, and when Meg began disrobing, he helped, unhooking and unlacing until she was naked and ready for the huge Persian towel he wrapped around her to keep off drafts on the way to the bath.

Once there, she sank slowly into the tub and laid her head back on the pillow Durban had carefully positioned. Then he rolled up his sleeves, tied an apron around his waist, and knelt beside the tub. Meg closed her eyes and surrendered to his magic fingers as they started their leisurely journey over every inch of her body.

It was a moot question as to whether or not Meg was aware of her cruelty to this man whose adoration was reflected in his every action; in essence, a taunting cruelty in that he was allowed to know her body most intimately, lift her to ecstasy through his loving skill, and yet he was barred from her bed and thus not given the passionate release he so desperately yearned for. She eased her conscience with the knowledge that there were two willing young maids on the domestic staff who were only too happy to be taken by Durban whenever he chose.

The bath-massage now begun, Meg turned her thoughts to Christopher. Four years must have changed him a great deal. The old Christopher, the brother she had known, would never have

128

risked Clement's displeasure by taking a mistress. Then too, Christopher was well aware of his family responsibility. They were of one mind on the matter of family prestige. And with Clement's illness, time was running out. If the title was not retrieved—bestowed on Christopher—the Leach name would come permanently down from the exalted heights of peerage.

Poor Clement! Meg held her mind hard against the rising pleasure of Durban's hands on her breasts and shoulders. She kept it focused on her elder brother. Such a towering figure! A giant in his time; respected by friend and enemy alike; upholding the Leach name single-handed with all those skeletons piled in the closet.

Meg took Durban's wrist and guided him to a point on her thigh close to her groin. "Just there—that muscle . . ."

There was a sudden touch of guilt, rare because Meg seldom felt guilty about anything. If only she had Clement's pride of name and position! Then she could have helped him. But the dullness, the boredom of stilted living was the only thing that ever frightened her. The struggle to get a glowing epitaph carved over one's bones had never seemed worthwhile.

Durban, the clever devil, had left her middle now, and with the embers stirred, was lifting a foot up out of the soapy water. He would work slowly upward, finding every nerve end.

Meg relaxed and allowed her mind to take its own course. She wondered about the colonial lass and what had moved Christopher to bring her back with him. Also, she wondered if half the rumors out of the London clubs and coffee houses were true. Probably not. Had Christopher been anyone but a Leach, the girl would have been ignored. No doubt the pro-slavery forces had been at work, Clement's sermons decrying the trade had been making more converts in Parliament than they cared to admit.

Durban's hand now moved high on Meg's thigh. Her hips jerked in sudden rising pleasure.

With the slave interests seeking to smear Clement, deliberately manufactured rumors spread avidly by the scandal sheets alleged a gaudy situation. "Reliable" sources marked the girl as half-Indian, making her slave material, and inferred that Christopher had bought her in defiance of Clement. Meg discounted all of it, of course, because such conduct on her brother's part was just too ridiculous. However, the rumors certainly honed one's curiosity as to what the lass was really like. She must be invited to Camber—

Meg strained her head backward. Her teeth clenched. Her mouth twisted.

"Oh, Durban! You bastard! You utter *bastard ...!*"

If her reaction and the touch of her body stirred Durban, he gave no sign. He remained wooden, showing the inner restraint which was the basic foundation of the strange relationship between Meg and her remarkable servant....

20

"I think, my dear, that you had better go on to Windward Moors without me," Christopher said.

"Oh?"

"I have business which will hold me in London for several days—an uncertain time. I am to see the Prime Minister and the day he will be able to receive me has not yet been stated."

"If you wish," she said.

There was something new in Christopher's voice Charity could not quite identify but it was in harmony with the changes which had come about in him and her reply conformed to their new relationship. Actually, Christopher's manner reflected a new self-confidence and pride. *I am to see the Prime Minister.*

Upon their arrival in London, Christopher had taken Charity to the Lincoln Inn and obtained lodgings after which he went straight to Downing Street where he gave an account of his colonial investigations to an assistant of Lord North. It was all duly taken down, his findings of revolutionary unrest together with the boarding of the *Hainaut* and the theft of his *dossier*. The report finished, he felt he had done his duty and put the matter from his mind.

However, the following morning there was a

message delivered instructing him to hold himself in readiness for an appointment with the Prime Minister. This was doubly gratifying. The quick interest of the great Lord North himself proved that at least one man in England was concerned with the conditions in the Colonies—also, that his own self-appointed task had not been in vain.

So his time was no longer his own, hence the suggestion that Charity go on alone.

"The drive will be pleasant, I am sure, and I have sent a message on ahead so Mrs. Dylan will be awaiting you."

"You are most thoughtful, Christopher. I'm looking forward to seeing Windward Moors and Leach House."

"I yearn for sight of them myself," he said wistfully.

"Will I meet your brother Clement?"

"Not immediately. He is in Bath taking the waters. Then too, he almost never comes to Leach House."

"Very well, if you think it best, I'll go on ahead."

Obviously, Christopher did, though he did not give Charity his full reason. He had been surprised, then disturbed, by the interest their arrival stirred up in London. Quite odious people had left their cards at the inn and had even hung around the lobby and sought to intercept him with their questions. Hopefully, with Charity out of the city, the interest would fade.

As to Charity herself, she had been inching her way through this civilized forest with the same wariness she would have exhibited in uncharted

Virginia woodlands. She was not in any doubt as to her competence. All confusion had vanished. Maturity had been swift and a new person had emerged. There had been an exact moment of this transition—the morning the *Hainaut* watch called down, "Land Ho," and she saw the cliffs of Dover. Up to that moment, nothing had seemed real, the escape from Virginia and the sea voyage something akin to a fragile bubble ready to burst.

But then the sight of land ahead gave a substance of reality. It was all true. She had come solidly into a new world and a new life and she accepted it without emotional fanfare, with neither fear nor elation; it simply *was*. And much which had been shaping in her confused mind now surfaced in firm resolution. Her future lay with Christopher. He was the man she would marry and her immediate objective was to change her image in his eyes—change it from that of a waif he had befriended to a woman who filled his every need.

The interlude with Sean McDougal remained a thing of joy; a sojourn into rainbow realms; but still the stuff of dreams, though she was more than grateful to him for what he had taught her; for having pointed her toward an important objective, that of becoming the complete woman. And Christopher would profit from the skills to which Sean McDougal had introduced her.

Charity put her new resolves into practice the second night at Lincoln Inn when she entered Christopher's room clad in her filmy nightdress. She was no longer the frightened child seeking paternal warmth and the security of his bed;

133

rather, a seductress come to serve the man she had chosen as her own.

In a sense, this was also Christopher's reeducation into the realities of things as they were. He now enjoyed her without reservation and she found pleasure in being able to fill his needs with skill and efficiency.

There were no emotional testimonials afterward; no pledges of love and undying fidelity; instead, a discussion of practicalities as they lay in his bed side by side.

"You must shop for a wardrobe, Charity. Perhaps we should ask my sister to help. I don't know...."

"Your sister Mercy? The one you told me about who lives in Mayfair?"

"Yes, but she is such a dowdy little thing. Not her fault. It is how Justin wants her to be. He is in finance, you know. Very conservative."

"I think I would be able to make proper selections," she said firmly.

"You have ample funds. I put Mother Mae's three thousand pounds in Barclay's Bank for you. You may draw on it as you choose. It is rather a tidy fortune."

"The money you paid to buy me—to ransom me from Cade...."

"I am assuming that expense myself."

"You needn't...."

"You are well worth it, my dear."

This was an attempt at lightness by a man who had difficulty with humor. A hesitant pat on Charity's breast was a part of it, and she understood even as she recalled Sean McDougal's avid mouth on that breast; the delightful pain of his teeth hard on the nipple.

"There is one thing, Christopher. About the wardrobe . . ."

"Yes?"

"I must of course be properly clad in the gowns of current styles—when in public, that is—but for less exposed times . . ."

"I don't understand."

"I am not used to the restrictions of skirts and stays and in a window this morning I saw a costume I yearn for. Trousers, jacket, and weskit tailored to a lady's requirements."

"The garments are not—ah, transparent. . . .

Charity laughed. "No. No more so than your own trousers and weskit."

"Male attire for the female is most daring in our society."

"True, but the *modiste* told me a half-dozen had already been tailored and sold and there has been much interest." When Christopher remained silent, Charity said, "Of course if you object. . . ."

"No—no. I see no reason why you should not adopt such garb in the privacy of Windward Moors. You have been so used to freedom of movement."

"Thank you, Christopher. . . ."

So Charity did her own wardrobe shopping and with the help of the *modiste*, made several attractive selections. Also, she tried on the trouser outfit and revelled in the freedom. "Make up two," she said. "One in tan and the other in gray with black piping. . . ."

135

Charity had found London most interesting, mainly for the great contrasts apparent on all sides; the ragged, destitute appearance of some, displayed against the opulence of others. Dandies squiring richly-clad ladies moved about in fine carriages while those she had heard contemptuously referred to as the "scum of the city" lay drunk in doorways or extended beggar's hands— mostly ignored.

Still, she was not awed by the size and complexities of the city. The new self-assurance she had acquired stood her in good stead. London was not a place to fear; rather a new aspect of her life to be coped with.

There had been only one incident of true shock. Once, their carriage had passed Newgate and Charity had seen four bodies hanging from scaffold ropes just outside the Debtor's Door of the great prison. If they had all been men, she would still have been shocked, but two of them were skirted, dangling women.

Christopher took but casual note of it. All he said was, "Felons hanged for nonpayment of debt," and dropped the matter.

Thus, another facet of Charity's education. Christopher was a man of good heart, compassionate; this she knew. Yet he could ride past the sight of such inhumanity with scarcely a look. Therefore it was obvious that his life in this society had conditioned him to such an attitude; a society in which compassion and callousness went hand-in-hand, difficult to separate. But good sense told her that London had no monopoly on cruelty. What she had seen was only a part of a world she had never known. No doubt if she had explored Charleston she would have found human carcasses hanging from gibbets too. . . .

21.

Christopher went beyond merely letting Mrs. Dylan know when Charity would arrive. He sent for a carriage from the Leach House stables and with her trunks loaded into the boot, he introduced her to a broad-shouldered man still on the near side of middle age.

"This is Bruce Carton, my dear. Our hostler. He has been in charge of our stables for some years now and you will find him thoroughly reliable. He will drive you to Windward Moors without mishap."

The driver touched his cap politely and looked at Charity through half-closed lids with an expression she neither liked nor could identify. She turned away quickly, attributing her discomfort to the prospect of the long trip facing her. To Christopher, she said, "I'm sure he will. It is my hope that you do not have to tarry long in London."

"At the Prime Minister's pleasure, but I shall hurry to Windward as soon as possible."

Charity wondered if she should offer her lips for a farewell kiss. Was a public show of affec-

137

tion from a mistress permitted? She left it up to Christopher, but he made no gesture in that direction. This she was able to rationalize, to herself at least: *He does not yet understand our relationship. It may take a little time.* . . .

The trip from London to Kent was strenuous but not unpleasant. The time taken in quitting London proper seemed interminable, but once upon the clearer roads of Surrey and on into Kent, Carton made better time, not necessarily breakneck speed, but Charity was bounced around and had to hang on at times.

They had started in early morning and Carton had his route carefully plotted to accommodate a lady's needs. There were appropriate stops at country inns with Carton feeling no need to explain the reason. He merely stood silent by the carriage and waited.

With the sun high, Charity called for a hunger stop, the basket lunch in the boot making an inn stop unnecessary.

Carton came to a halt, got the basket, and handed it into the carriage.

Charity said, "That big oak there. It would be a nice place for lunch."

Carton scowled and shook his head. " 'Twould be a foolhardy thing to do, Miss."

"Are you saying there is danger?"

"Mayhap." He now looked her over boldly, his narrowed eyes resting without apology on the cleft of her breasts held in rounded contour by the tight bodice of her low-cut gown.

"Highwaymen," he added.

"Highwaymen! Do freebooters run loose here?"

"Aye, and not at all respectful of women. You would make a fine morsel for a roaming band bent on carnal mischief."

Charity did not like Carton. The feeling had been instantaneous back in London, but Christopher had spoken highly of him, so that she had consciously tempered it, seeing it then as without just cause. But now the dislike was stronger.

Carton said, "Best I eat the miles between here and Windward if we hope to come in with the sun. You nibble as we go. 'Twill be safer."

Charity could hardly object even though she was now seeing Carton as one who might well be the attacker rather than her protector.

They drove on, and she settled back to endure rather than enjoy. Her thoughts went back to that terrible ride to Orin Cade's plantation, and from there to Christopher's gallant rescue. Then, from that point, curiously enough, to the gold clasp, the only tangible proof she possessed of Sean McDougal's actual existence.

That interlude on the *Hainaut*. The stuff of dreams, and it belonged in the part of her mind where dreams could be stored. Relegating it there had seemed easy enough with Christopher's presence to bolster her sensible resolutions. But somehow, in her solitude, the image of the laughing buccaneer assumed life and reality, to a point of causing her heart to beat a little faster.

She closed her eyes and allowed Sean McDougal's handsome face to stand clear in her recall. It was perhaps through professed loyalty to Christopher that she skipped past the naked embrace—Sean's passion and her response—for

139

contemplation of the aftermath. The touch of his lips on her fingers; the pressing of the gold amulet into her palm.

To remember me by 'til we meet again.

A sudden spine-wrenching gyration of the coach served a useful purpose. It brought Charity back to reality. She settled back in her seat, straightened her gown, and stopped dreaming.

The country through which they passed was not like home; so different from her Virginia forests. There were trees in plenty, but unfamiliar landscapes: rugged areas of brush, rock, and waving grasses; lonely, melancholy, yet beautiful. As they approached their destination, the carriage turned, putting the lowering sun behind a vast stretch of marshland; black reeds against silver water turning pink at its farthest expanse. Charity watched as the panorama changed before her eyes. A cloud darkened the sun to give a new shade of lighting. A lone goose arose from the marsh and honked off toward some rendezvous.

Soon they turned into a road through pine and oak and climbed a steady upgrade to come out on a level plateau; a grassy upland. There, she saw a small herd of sheep busily barbering a lawn of incredible size.

And on the far side was Leach House.

Charity had not known what to expect, but certainly nothing like this. A step backward into England's past. Storybook knights might well have been jousting in the lists; a place ill-named, not a house but a castle with no visible evidence of the warmth and welcome Charity had hoped for after her long day's ride.

Leach House ran the length of ten windows in either wing from a central hall, the whole of it a vast, gray pile of somber masonry with watch towers at both the north and the south ends rearing high over the levels below.

A long, circular driveway brought the coach to a massive front door. They had arrived at last and Charity shook herself mentally. She must not look the country bumpkin. On the contrary, she must appear calm, as though she were quite accustomed to huge medieval estates. After all, she was no wide-eyed child.

Her first impulse was to fling open the carriage door and bounce to the ground, but she contained herself and waited until the now tired and dour Carton got down and performed her service.

"You will see to my luggage," she said haughtily.

"Aye," he grumbled in reply, then touched her arm and led her to where a woman waited by a smaller door cut into the huge one which fronted the house.

The woman had not come forward in any gesture of welcome, remaining where she was until Carton brought Charity to her.

Was this a sign of disapproval? Was the woman another hostile servant to be dealt with? That possibility was in Charity's mind as she remained aloof and sought to give the impression that servants were creatures to be regarded only as attachments to a well-run household.

"This is Mrs. Dylan," Carton said. "She will see to your needs."

The woman was of short stature, a plump, com-

141

pact little person with a round face and graying hair under her white frilled cap. She acknowledged Charity with a curtsey, and the latter could find in her none of Carton's boorishness; an encouraging sign.

But there was definitely something; a holding back, a questioning. There was more doubt than welcome in her voice as she said, "We are happy to have you here, Miss Charity. Please be assured that we will do everything possible to make you comfortable." A tone not uncordial, even friendly; still, to Charity's ear it came out, *Who are you and what are you doing here?* But more in curiosity than hostility.

Carton turned back to the carriage and got busy with the luggage in the boot and Mrs. Dylan's eyes followed him as though she had been put beyond her depth, left alone there with a stranger.

Then Charity sensibly discarded all that she had seen and felt as being unreliable first impression. It had been a long, tiring ride. She was not at her best; a stranger in a strange land and as such too defensive to make good judgments. Thus, her attitude reversed and she saw motherly concern in Mrs. Dylan, who said, "My dear, you must be exhausted after that punishing ride. I am sure you will want a good meal and a bath and a night's rest. Come the morrow, you will see things with a better eye."

Once inside, the wonder of her new surroundings drove all else from Charity's mind. Never in her life had she seen anything to compare. The front door gave into a vast reception hall. Two flares had been lighted on either side of the door and there were lamps on evenly spaced brackets on either wall extending off into the interior, throwing shadows up to an incredibly high ceiling. The harsh grayness of stone all about was softened by long tapestries hung from far above, depicting scenes of colorful medieval times. Two staircases curved upward immediately on the left and the right of the entrance. However, the staircase on the north was evidently not used, a wooden barrier at the foot blocking egress. This gave the upper area on that side a dark and sinister look.

A girl in a black frock, white apron, and white frilled cap awaited inside. Mrs. Dylan said, "This is Dorothy, Miss Charity. She will show you to your rooms while I go and see that food is prepared."

The maid ducked her head in a curtsey and turned toward the right staircase. Charity could only follow the girl as Mrs. Dylan hurried off into the rearward gloom.

The stairway extended to a third level but the maid turned into the second floor corridor. She indicated the first door and said, "These are the Reverend Clement's quarters, but he is seldom if ever here." Further on, past a series of grim family portraits, Charity's guide paused to say, "And this is the door to Master Christopher's chambers."

Dorothy was a bright-faced, pert little housemaid and Charity wondered if she had been instructed to act as castle guide or whether she was naturally voluble. The latter, she decided, and was grateful for the first truly friendly attention she had gotten in Leach House.

"And this is where you will be staying," Dorothy said after opening a third door and stepping aside. She smiled as though proud to have conducted Charity to such an impressive place. "Right next to the Master."

Exactly what did that mean? Were they all assuming she was Christopher's mistress? Charity decided she was reading too much into casually spoken words and turned her attention to the suite. In its way it was as fantastic as what she had seen below. A small reception nook gave privacy to the inner entrance door and beyond was a sitting room with a ceiling not quite as high as the great hall downstairs but still high enough to remain dim to the lamps which had been lit. Again there were tapestries to soften the stone walls and a single, huge oriental carpet covered the floor. The furniture was heavy and dark, but colorful cushions on the chairs and the settee softened the effect.

With Dorothy scurrying ahead, Charity entered the bedroom which was something else entirely. The ceiling was draped in soft blue material, hung from the four corners of the room, giving a tentlike effect. It was obviously there to form a lower ceiling and warm the ambience of the bedroom. The floor was completely covered in thick gray carpeting and the bed was something to behold—a huge, canopied affair, on a platform that lifted it a foot from the floor. Heavy gray silk tasseled curtains waited to be drawn giving the sleeper what Charity saw as a smothering privacy.

Dorothy, her eyes bright as polished blue buttons, was watching Charity with interest. "It's beautiful, is it not?" she said.

"It certainly is."

"This was the bridal chamber."

"Indeed!"

"Yes. But that was a long time ago. The Master would bring his bride here on the first night and the curtains would be drawn while the maids-in-waiting stayed in the room and listened."

"They were allowed to remain?"

Dorothy giggled. If she had been surprised in the beginning, Charity was now amazed. "Then the maids-in-waiting would make wagers on whether there would be an heir in nine months."

"What a strange custom!"

"But if you wagered nine months you were usually wrong. Mostly, the bairn came in seven or eight."

There was something about this merry little lass that made the whole castle less grim; more to the immediate point, she was a fount of information.

"Tell me all about Leach House," Charity said. "Have you been here long?"

"No, only two weeks. But let me show you the bath."

She scurried ahead and was waiting with pride when Charity entered. The bathtub was actually a part of the wall, an extension built out away from it. There was also a stone reservoir above

145

one end with a spigot attached. Dorothy pointed to the reservoir.

"We fill that with hot water and you can let it come down as you choose. Most tubs, you have to pour the water in from a bucket. When you are through you pull that plug and the water drains down into the moat."

"I didn't see a moat when I came in."

"Oh, it's dry now. They haven't needed it to keep off enemies for years."

"How old is this house?" Charity asked.

"Almost two hundred years, I think."

"Why is it so big? I mean there is so much more space than anyone would need."

"They don't use much of it now. The whole other wing is closed off. Nobody ever goes there. That's the Moon Tower."

"The Moon Tower?"

"It's where Randolph Leach killed himself. He was the great-grandfather. Mr. Christopher's father's father's father."

"Why did he kill himself?"

"It was one of the wars. I don't know which one. Mr. Randolph made the King mad by helping the other side, I think. But the King won and so the only honorable thing Sir Randolph could do was kill himself."

A sad resolution, Charity thought. There must have been forgiveness, however, because the Leaches had not been permanently banished from the peerage.

But that was all ancient history. Charity was eager to learn about the here and the now. "Mrs.

Dylan seems a very nice lady. Does she treat you well?"

"Oh, yes. It was Mr. Carton who brought me here from over in Sussex." She paused, her expression turning wistful. "I did have a suitor but there was no dowry and Mr. Carton is a man of substance."

Charity wondered. Nothing had been said about marriage. Had Dorothy been sold to the odious hostler?

"Tell me. . . ."

The question was never asked. There was the sound of a door opening and Dorothy hurried back into the sitting room. Charity followed, to find her luggage had been quietly delivered and Mrs. Dylan had arrived bearing a tray.

"A bite to eat, my dear. I did not know your preferences, heavy or light. so I brought a slice of roasted beef and greens. Also, tea and scones."

"Thank you for your kindness."

Dorothy began laying the food out on a small table. She dimpled at Mrs. Dylan. "I've been telling Miss Charity all about Leach House."

A sudden worry was reflected on the housekeeper's face. She said, "Now I am sure our guest does not want to be annoyed by your prattlings. You just scat yourself back to the kitchen. I'll be there shortly and find some work for you."

Dorothy scurried out. Mrs. Dylan said, "I am so sorry, Miss Charity. There is no call for you to be plagued by a mouthy little filly. Those from Sussex never learn manners."

It seemed to Charity that Mrs. Dylan was perhaps protesting too much. "It was quite all right," she replied.

"Now you eat your dinner, my dear, and I will send Cloris up to attend you."

"Thank you, but that won't be necessary. After this delicious repast, I'll bathe and go to my bed. . . ."

Nonetheless, Cloris arrived shortly thereafter. And if Mrs. Dylan had seen Dorothy as a chambermaid in need of training, this one was the exact opposite. A slim, dark girl, she had an attractive face that showed little expression.

"I have come to be of service to Madam," she said.

"But I told Mrs. Dylan it was not necessary."

Cloris began putting the dishes back on the tray. "I will help Madam with her bath," she replied firmly.

Charity was moved to decline the assistance and send the girl packing, but gave up the idea in favor of remaining passive for the moment. There would be time enough to assert herself after she learned more about the household.

And Cloris' subsequent actions fully supported Charity's first impression of her as a perfectly trained housemaid. There were yes, Madams and no, Madams, uttered in politely firm subservience, this to a point where Charity forebore any personal questions about the Leach family, knowing there would be no informative replies.

Hot water had already been put into the overhead tank and the bath was so deliciously restful that Charity put her inquisitiveness aside for the time being. Cloris anticipated her every move, waiting with a huge towel when she finally emerged, gently helping her to dry herself. She was ready with a nightdress from Charity's luggage which she had opened and started to unpack. Getting into bed was like sinking into a feathery cloud. Cloris smoothed the comforter over her and asked, "Will there be anything else, Madam?"

"No," Charity replied dreamily. "But please do not call me Madam."

"Very well, Miss Charity," Cloris replied and floated from the room—to be placed on a shelf somewhere, Charity fantasized drowsily, until she was again needed. Charity's perfect contentment tempered her reactions to all she had seen and heard.

Leach House was a fine old castle. The retainers were most proper people. Even the distasteful hostler, Bruce Carton, could be tolerated so long as he kept his place. . . .

Later that night at a table in the kitchen, Carton was venting his anger on Mrs. Dylan. "I don't relish your handing my property about. From now on I'll see that Dorothy is kept away from that tippy-nosed bitch! What's she doing here, anyhow?"

Mrs. Dylan replied, "Carton, your trouble is you've been in Windward too long. The Master has given you too much leeway. Now you are afraid someone else is coming in to take over."

"That tart take over? Not hardly."

149

"How can you say that? You have no way of knowing the Master's intent."

"He could have had the decency to come himself and let us know."

"You sound as though *you* were the owner here," Mrs. Dylan said sharply.

"Well, at least I'll stay in charge until I am told otherwise. It is my responsibility."

Though Mrs. Dylan did not remind him, he had arrogantly assumed that responsibility. She herself was presumed by Christopher to be in charge. But she had allowed Carton to shoulder her out because she knew things about him that Christopher had missed. She was afraid of Carton. He was a violent, irreverent man; one who would maim for a penny and kill for a pound, and Mrs. Dylan, a sweet, simple person, was easily dominated. Thus, she never goaded Carton to a point where her instincts told her it would be dangerous.

"Why are you so upset about Dorothy? Do you think Miss Charity plans to possess her in some way?"

"I don't know what she plans. But the little Sussex wench is a chatterbox. Her tongue needs anchoring."

"So? She is a friendly little thing. What could she tell Miss Charity that would harm you?"

"You chatter like a monkey yourself, woman. When I brought Dorothy here I went along with you. I let you have her so she could get used to a strange place. But you've had her long enough."

"You are sending her home?" Mrs. Dylan asked in surprise.

150

"Out of this house—to the stables where she belongs."

"That sweet child," Mrs. Dylan murmured sadly.

"Child, you say? She is eighteen going on. She can see to my quarters and my needs. There are chores she can do."

"Such rude service for her tender nature."

"Be still. If I want to bring in a lass for my convenience it is no affair of yours. You'd best be wondering about the tart I brought from London. She could put us both out of our situations."

"My conscience is clear, Bruce. You'd best look to your own."

Carton growled wordlessly and stalked out of the kitchen, Mrs. Dylan's frustration apparent as her gaze followed him.

22.

Charity awoke with the dawn, the night's rest having revitalized her completely, and it was with a sense of expectancy, even excitement, that she arose and looked forward to the day ahead. She went to the window and gazed out across Windward Moors. On her left she could see the Channel cliffs and the water beyond. The stables were south, and to the right was a great expanse of more or less level, rugged ground sweetly

151

purpled by blossoming growth. There were waving grasses dotted around and about by mounds and hillocks. The moors, Charity assumed, after which the estate had been named. The mire along which she had ridden was not visible from the window; it faced the front of the castle.

Charity hesitated while dressing, then remembered Christopher's words—*in the privacy of Windward Moors*—and chose the brown suit for the day's wear. But then she changed her mind and selected a simple yellow cotton. She hated the clumsiness of women's clothing, bulky restraint she had never suffered in the soft deerskins during her Virginia years. But now it *was* time to start dressing like a lady so she compromised further by putting a petticoat on under the yellow cotton and fared forth to explore.

The interior of Leach House was as ghostly and brooding as before. The oil lamps were still burning in the great hall and no one appeared to be stirring, although in a place of that size there could have been many people moving about in other areas without being evident.

Charity gave some attention to the portraits along the corridor wall; in a sense, introducing herself to the family tree upon which she planned to graft herself. There were no nameplates so she had no idea of the genealogy involved, only that the men were uniformly solemn in their mien. The women, only two of them important enough to be preserved in oil, had obviously been stern, no-nonsense spouses. Charity could only wonder if a Leach ancestor ever smiled.

She hesitated at the front door. To turn inward

and investigate the house itself, or go out into the glorious morning? She decided upon the latter and once outside saw what Dorothy had referred to, the dry remains of what had once been a protective moat. The contour was still there, a ditch running around the house but now overgrown with weeds and partially filled by collapsed earth. Whimsically, as she moved around it, she tried to visualize the time long ago when the moat was necessary as a defense against marauders.

The stable was a long, low building with the roof protruding forward to give a shed effect. There were eight stable doors, four on either side of what was no doubt a tackroom. Charity approached this and looked in, to see Carton seated at a tool table working with a bridle.

"Good morning," Charity said. "You start your day early."

He looked up in surprise, then said, without returning her greeting, "Aye. There is always much to do."

"This is a fine stable. How many animals do you keep?"

"We have two stallions, four geldings, and two mares."

"Would you have a riding mount for me?"

He hesitated. "Are you skilled at horsemanship?"

"I have had a riding horse at my disposal since I was a child."

Turning reluctantly from his work, he said, "Very well. I'll saddle the bay mare. She is most gentle."

"I would prefer a gelding—even one of your stallions."

"They are not well broken to saddle, Miss. Only the Master and I ride them over the estate."

"You may saddle me a gelding then."

Carton went to a row of pegs on the tackroom wall and selected a saddle. When he returned with it, Charity frowned and asked, "That is a *saddle?*"

"Aye, Miss. A side-saddle. Ladies use them."

She touched a curved horn protruding from the seat at an angle. "What is that part for?"

"The lady uses it to support her left limb at the knee with her right foot in the stirrup."

"Do you mean she rides with both legs on the same side of the mount?" Charity asked in wonder.

"Aye. 'Tis the custom."

"And she doesn't fall off?"

"A lady could hardly ride otherwise."

"Well, this lady will. Put a regular saddle on my mount."

Carton glanced down Charity's body, from her bodice to the hem of her skirt. "It would be most immodest. Sitting astride a horse in skirts. Your limbs would be exposed. You will quickly learn to use a lady's saddle."

He was most firm in his refusal and Charity knew that if she expected to assert any authority at Windward Moors, this was the place to start.

"Carton, you will do as you are told. You will put a regular saddle on my mount. And if the sight of a lady's limbs distresses you, I will save you from embarrassment."

With that Charity turned and hurried back to the house, up to her rooms, where she quickly donned the brown trouser suit and marched grimly back to the stable.

Carton stared petulantly as she approached and Charity was glad to see that he had obeyed her. A tall black gelding stood waiting, a standard, hornless saddle cinched into place.

Carton gave no sign of his reaction to her daring male garb. He remained silent, speaking only when Charity prepared to mount.

"I'll help you, Miss."

"You needn't bother. I am quite able to do my own mounting."

With that, she vaulted into the saddle, her foot not touching the stirrup, and started off leaving Carton to mutter, "Whatever else the little tart is, she's a finished horsewoman. . . ."

Flight across the moor on the winged feet of the gelding was a glorious experience for Charity; the first time since leaving her Virginia forests that she felt totally free. The gelding seemed to appreciate the light load on his back and entered into the spirit of pure flight with zest.

Charity urged him on south across the moor, reining him skillfully around obstacles and alongside ravines. She wondered how far the moor stretched and whether it was all Leach property. Then she reined up as she drew close to a line of squat earthen structures. Just beyond were ancient-looking wooden frames built into a low, rocky bluff. . . .

"An old mining venture."

Charity whirled at the sound of the voice to see a man just behind her on a handsome roan. She was suddenly forced to doubt herself. How had he approched so quietly? Were the sharp senses she had developed in colonial forests already turning dull? It was a little frightening.

He was a rugged, shaggy-looking man with a mass of black, curly hair blown by the wind. His clean-shaven face was expressive, not unhandsome, but bearing a moody look; a face one would take to be that of a cynic.

"My name is Wahl—Dennis Wahl. I have the estate farther down—Camber."

"I am Charity Sturges. You—you startled me."

He made no apology whatever, pointing to the huts and saying, "The miners lived in those pigsties. Finally they starved themselves out."

"Is this still the Windward Moors estate?"

"That it is. It goes another bloody mile south. Then you hit Channel Light, another mass of useless acreage. After that my own little plot, Camber. You can cross it in twenty minutes of brisk riding."

"You said your name is Wahl. You are married to Christopher Leach's sister?"

"Yes."

"I am happy to meet you, sir."

"We heard you were coming to Leach House."

"Yes. I arrived yesterday."

"Christopher too?"

"No. He remained in London. He will be here soon."

He eyed Charity speculatively, his heavy black brows giving him a rather satanic look. He said,

"The lass Chris brought from the Colonies. Everyone is wondering. The ladies are all agog."

Charity forced a laugh. "Are newcomers so rare here in Kent?"

"Beautiful ones in men's clothing, yes."

"Oh, this rather masculine suit."

"*Quite* masculine, I'd say."

"Does it offend you?" she asked curiously.

"Hardly. What you wear, young lady, is your own affair. You could go around in a flour sack for all I care."

"I assure you, this mode is becoming quite popular in London."

"I'll say this—it allows you to straddle a horse the way any two-legged creature should." His voice was filled with admiration.

"I am glad you believe in freedom for women."

"To a certain extent. But then the most forward of your sex know their limitations—even the most daring ones who play perilously with freedom."

"*Play* with freedom? I don't understand you."

"It is simple enough. They reach a point where their bravery melts. You, as an example. You can wear those trousers out here in privacy, but you wouldn't dare face Clement Leach so garbed. Nor, I vow, would you appear in them at one of Meg's affairs at Camber."

"You believe that, do you? Well, let me say that I'll go anywhere I please, *dressed* as I please."

"Oh, I'm not challenging you. But I'll wager the opposite."

It certainly sounded like a dare to Charity. In her eyes, Dennis Wahl was beginning to shape up

157

as a person who issued such challenges to amuse himself.

Charity said, "It matters not, since I have not been invited to any of your affairs at Camber."

"You will be—and soon. Before the day is out. Meg will rush to Windward Moors come hell or high tide."

"You make her sound like a determined woman."

"She has a will of her own."

"I look forward to meeting her."

Dennis Wahl did not answer. He was standing up in his stirrups to quiet the restless roan and Charity saw the boldly presented outline of his manhood, formidable even in repose there against the cloth of his riding breeches. The thought came unbidden; it would be truly frightening if extended by passion.

She turned her mind away sharply, and asked, "Is it allowed to ride where one chooses without permission—across the estates? . . ."

He scowled. "I ride where I fancy. Land may be owned but no one has the right to bar another from crossing. Not even the King."

"I think I understand how you feel. Boundaries are new to me. In Virginia I could have ridden clear over into Kentucky and beyond had I wished." Homesickness crept unbidden into her voice.

"I take it that you are at home on a horse."

"I have ridden since I was a child."

"Here you will find fops making a game of it. They wear scarlet coats and charge in mobs against the fox to cut off the brush and wave it like a flag of triumph."

"Then you do not approve of fox hunting?" Charity asked.

Dennis Wahl did not appear to hear the question. Without a goodbye he heeled his mount and went abruptly off in a thunder of hooves. As Charity watched his receding back she decided there was little of which the shaggy man did approve.

But that thought was in passing. Her prime attention was somewhere else; on the erect hardness of her nipples; on the quivering of her thighs as she pressed them hard against the gelding; on those evidences of an exciting revelation.

Dennis Wahl could stir her into a hot urge for mating. . . .

23.

The greeting was most effusive; a touching of cheeks, a seizing of hands, words of warm welcome.

"My dear! You *are* Charity Sturges, aren't you? I am Margaret Wahl, but don't you ever call me Margaret. I would not know how to answer. I am Meg to my friends."

Charity, seated on a bench under a sheltering oak on the north lawn of Leach House, had watched the carriage pull up to the front door. Meg Wahl was handed down by her coachman and had started toward the entrance when she spied Charity under the tree. She turned and hurried in that direction.

She wore a green, watered silk gown with puffed sleeves and the suggestion of a bustle. The broad brim of her flowered hat was angled to set off an attractive face framed in a mass of chestnut brown hair.

Dennis Wahl obviously knew his wife, Charity mused. Come hell or high tide, Meg had arrived as he'd predicted.

Charity rose from her seat and said, "So good of you to call, Meg. Christopher spoke of you glowingly. I have been so eager to meet you."

If Meg believed the lie concerning her brother's regard for her, she gave no sign. She drew Charity down on the bench, still clinging to her hands.

"I hope I am the first to call. I owe it to Christopher to proffer the family welcome."

"The first to call, yes. But by chance I met your husband this morning out on the moor."

Meg did not freeze though there did appear to be a slight chill.

"Oh?"

"I was riding and we came upon each other by the old coal mine."

"I see. Dennis does have a way of coming upon . . ." She almost said *attractive little tarts*. Then she caught herself and finished, ". . . making friends quickly."

"He told me something of the area—where the estates are located."

About his cozy cottage on the bluff?

Aloud, Meg asked, "Will Christopher be arriving soon?"

They were interrupted by Cloris who came from around the rear corner of the house to ask, "Is service wanted?"

"Why, yes," Meg replied. "You may bring us some white wine." To Charity: "You do like wine, do you not?"

Charity assented, allowing her guest to act as hostess. In answer to Meg's question she said, "Christopher? I hope he does come soon. He was forced to stay in London for a time. He is awaiting a call from the Prime Minister."

"The Prime Minister! Clement had better have a care or Christopher will outshine him in value to the Crown."

When the wine arrived, Meg did the pouring and raised her glass. "Charity darling. Here's to a long, pleasant stay at Windward Moors." They sipped, then Meg asked, "How long *do* you plan to stay?"

"I am not really sure." How she wished Christopher were here to get her through this.

"For a long time, I hope. But one thing I came for—I am having some friends at Camber tomorrow afternoon. You *must* come. You will be the guest of honor."

"How kind of you."

"The kindness will be on your side. My friends are dying to meet you and hear all about the Colonies. I understand there are some hotheads over there planning a revolution."

"Christopher is concerned about that. I

presume it is why the Prime Minister wishes to see him. . . . But perhaps you would tell me about some of the people I will meet tomorrow. Then I would not consider myself a total stranger."

"Of course. There will be Gabrielle Kirth. She owns Channel Light, an estate Dennis no doubt mentioned."

"Will your sister Mercedes be present?"

"Oh, heavens no! Her husband, Justin, does not approve of us. I take it you did not meet them while you were in London?"

"No. We did not have time to go to Mayfair."

Of course not. Christopher may have courage but he is not foolhardy.

"Justin is in finance. Very proper," Meg said. "But I am sure Mercy is very happy with him."

Charity considered her next question, then took a deep breath and asked it. "And what about Sean McDougal? Will he be there?"

Meg's pretty mouth came close to going slack. She hesitated, searching for words. "What *about* Sean?"

"I was wondering if I would meet him at your party."

"But he is nowhere around. Not even in England. But even if he were. . . ." She floundered for a moment. "Charity, did Christopher tell you about him?"

"Why, yes," Charity replied innocently. Then she happily pressed her advantage. "Christopher and I have no secrets from each other."

"Then you must know he would not be invited to a family affair."

"I understand he did some smuggling."

"Smuggling—yes."

"I guess we saw things differently in Virginia. I mean, smugglers were considered patriots. We were always in need of the things they brought us."

Meg made a bad job of hiding her distress. "I can only wonder, Charity, which side you are on."

"The mother country, of course," she replied, "now that I am here."

Charity rejected her impish impulse to bait Meg and turned to more pertinent matters. She said, "You mentioned that Sean McDougal is nowhere around. Do you mean that he rarely returns to his native soil?"

"England? It is hardly his native soil. Sean is Irish by environment and inclination."

"Not a loyal Englishman?"

"Oh, I suppose so. Of course, he *is* a Leach, although Clement and Christopher are loath to admit it."

"Do you feel the same way?"

Meg hesitated, then answered with some frankness. "No, not exactly. I admire Sean, but then, everyone does. Such a handsome brute. The man is totally without fear and he respects no laws. He is a fugitive, you know—from both France and Spain. They would love to hang him."

It occurred to Charity that while Meg had come to Windward to size her up as well as welcome her, the name of Sean McDougal had set her mind to drifting.

Meg said, "I think Sean is envied because he does what others would like to do but do not dare.

He flouts all law and roams free. And yet. . . ." She paused, as if searching for words.

Charity waited before urging Meg on. "You were saying? . . ."

"And yet he is not vicious—not cruel."

"I suppose that *is* to his credit."

"I mean freebooters and privateers are cruel and vicious as a class. But Sean—oh, I don't know exactly what I do mean."

Charity was sure *she* knew. Meg was in love with Sean McDougal, and immediately she began estimating Meg as a competitor. Of course she was a married woman, but would that restrain her if Sean turned his flashing smile in her direction? No doubt many women were in love with the phantom privateer.

"You said he comes rarely to Kent?" Charity prodded her.

"Oh, no. He spends quite some time here. He shows up out of nowhere and vanishes as quickly." Meg arose. "But I must run. Arrangements to be made. You *will* honor us at Camber tomorrow?"

"You honor me with the invitation. I shall be there. . . ."

24.

"Did you have a nice visit with Mrs. Wahl, Miss Charity?"

"Quite nice, Mrs. Dylan."

"And now mayhap you would like a snack and tea. I'll have Cloris lay it up in the small dining room."

"No, please. Don't go to that bother. I'll sit here with you."

Charity had wandered into the kitchen from the north lawn where Mrs. Dylan introduced her to Molly, the cook, a small woman not so plump as Mrs. Dylan. Molly wore a white shift under a flowered apron and a large frilled cap, which made her look top-heavy. She acknowledged the introduction with a quick curtsey and returned to her working area at the far end of the kitchen.

Mrs. Dylan now poured tea and Charity said, "You work very hard; this huge house with only Cloris and Dorothy to help."

"No, Miss Charity. The work depends on the size of the family and we never have more than the Master himself and . . ." Here there was a curious pause. "The Master and perhaps a guest or two. With the north wing sealed off, I need little help—only Cloris."

"Dorothy is gone?"

"Not entirely. Carton has found work for her in the stables. She will keep his quarters neat and help about. She comes from a very poor Sussex family."

Did that mean what she thought? Charity wondered as she asked, "How old is Dorothy?"

"All of eighteen, poor child. She has little to look to."

"Why is that? Can she not marry and raise her own family?"

"There is little chance for her to wed. Any man interested would select a prettier one from that litter over in Sussex. Lasses from large families without resources find it hard."

"Perhaps, but I think given a chance Dorothy will make out all right. Tell me—how long has the north wing been sealed off?"

"For many years now. There has been no need of it since the children were young."

"Christopher told me of his father, but not his mother."

"The poor lass died at his birthing. I was much younger myself then, but I remember the sadness. His father rode off over the moor like a maniac and was not seen for days. He was a strange man. He watched the funeral from afar, on a hill overlooking the family vault, and did not come down. When he did return, he had changed."

"You raised the children after their mother's death?"

"Oh, no. I was too young for the task. There was a wet nurse and then the Master hired governesses and tutors. They came and went. Then Clement grew up to where he could take over."

"I'm sure he did a fine job."

"The best he could. But there was wild blood in the Leach line."

"Christopher became a fine man, though. And from what he told me of his sister, Mercedes, she is a sweet, gentle person."

"Aye, but Margaret and Clement fought bitterly. He could in no way control her."

"From what I saw of her today, she has done very well."

"I suppose so. But she married Dennis Wahl not for love, but from spite against Clement and to get free of Windward Moors."

Charity liked Mrs. Dylan a great deal. She was talkative but stated things as they were with hostility toward no one; only sadness for those who had not measured up.

"You were here when the children's mother died. You did not stay?"

"No. I was with my father's company of singers and dancers." She smiled shyly. "You would not now believe that once I was a pretty young thing."

"I certainly do, Mrs. Dylan."

"I danced and sang and we traveled through the English counties."

"You are from Ireland?"

"County Cork. We performed here at Leach House in the great hall and many came to see us."

"That was how you happened to be here when the mother died?"

"Aye. Later, after my father's death, the company broke up and I married and had a daughter. Then I lost them both—Terrance Dylan and my

167

darling." Mrs. Dylan's sadness reflected again; this time for herself. "That was what I call my second life."

"And this is your third? Here at Leach House?"

"For the last fifteen years. I am nigh onto sixty now."

"But how did that come about? That you would return here as housekeeper from your home in Cork?" Had she not been so interested in Mrs. Dylan's accounting, Charity would perhaps have seen her prying as impolite—or at least might have proceeded more gently. As it was, she waited for Mrs. Dylan's answers.

" 'Twas through Carton that I got the situation. He is from Cork also and he knew Gerold Leach, Christopher's uncle, who went there and married an Irish lady. She was older than Gerold but they were happy for a time."

"I was told that Gerold died in Ireland."

"Aye, poor man, and she with a bairn. So she married Gary McDougal whom we knew. You see, all of us went to the same tavern so we kept in touch."

"Did Gary McDougal accept Gerold Leach's son as his own?"

"Indeed. And the boy loved his stepfather. He took the name, Sean McDougal, which shows the depth of his love. Sean was a bonny lad indeed! You would have loved him.

Oh, I did. I did!

Charity silently caught herself up. During all of the questioning had she been seeking to learn more about Sean McDougal? She sternly replied to herself in the negative, then said, "I suppose Sean rarely visits Leach House."

Mrs. Dylan's reaction was curious. She got busy with her teacup, fussed with her cap; acting, Charity decided, quite as an honest, ingenuous person would act when faced with the necessity of telling a lie.

Mrs. Dylan evaded completely. She said, "I do hope the day will come when Clement and Christopher will soften their hearts toward Sean and acknowledge him as the Leach he really is." Then, before Charity could grill her further, she came to her feet and added, "Miss Charity, you must grant me an indulgence. There is much to do and I have been shirking my chores. Have more tea if you wish." With that, she hurried off toward the stairs which took her a half-level up into the great hall.

Charity remained at the table, digesting what she had heard from Meg and Mrs. Dylan. The two accounts. Or rather, the three accounts, those and what Christopher had told her aboard the *Hainaut*.

All in all, she had a pretty complete background of the Leach family and the twists and turns of destiny which had brought it to its present state. As to Sean McDougal—*Damn the man!* Why could she not get him out of her thoughts? And why did Christopher loaf about in London instead of coming to Windward Moors where he belonged?

Charity felt badly let down in spirit. It was this gloomy castle with its cold gray walls! She quickly left the kitchen and hurried out to where there was at least sunshine and fresh air.

She gravitated in the direction of the stable and did not consciously become aware of it until she saw Carton emerge from the stall entrance just to the left of the tackroom. He moved hurriedly and although she was too far away to see his face, his anger at whatever had happened was obvious. He was tugging up his trousers and he strode away without noticing Charity.

Curious as to which horse had roused Carton's ire, Charity moved toward the stable he had just quitted in such haste. When she opened the door she found that the stall within, together with the next one, had been remodeled into living space. She was looking into a bedroom and there on a cot lay Dorothy. The girl was naked, pitifully huddled, and bearing red marks of abuse upon her body. Carton had beyond doubt vented his lust upon her in a most violent and cruel manner.

Charity's eruption of rage was such that if Carton had been present and she had possessed a weapon she might well have killed him. When she entered, Dorothy cringed as though fearful that her tormentor had come back to inflict further abuse. When she saw Charity, she turned away in whimpering shame.

"Please, Miss Charity—go away."

In as gentle a voice as she could muster, Charity said, "No, Dorothy. It is all right. I have come to help you."

"Please go away. No one should see me this way. Not anyone in the world."

"Darling, you've no call to feel that way—not

170

when a friend comes." Charity drew the girl into her arms where, after some hesitation, Dorothy relaxed and clung with her face buried in Charity's breast. Charity remained silent, waiting for the sobbing to run its course—crucifying Carton the while; driving a stake into his rotten heart; hanging him and leaving him to dry on a gibbet!

When Dorothy became comparatively quiet, Charity asked, "Tell me, why do you stand this? Why have you not complained?"

"There is no one to complain to."

"Mrs. Dylan. She would not have allowed you to be abused in this manner."

"If I told her, Mr. Carton might send me away. And I have no place to go."

"Are you telling me that you would rather put up with his abuse than go back where you came from?"

"Back home? There would be no room for me. My father does his best, but there were so many of us."

"Well, my dear, you will have no further worries. You are coming with me. Would you like that? Would you like to be my personal maid and take care of me?"

There was only silence, but Charity interpreted it for what it was—Dorothy was unable to believe such good fortune. Finally she murmured, "Oh, Miss Charity . . .!"

"Then it is decided. Slip on your shift and come with me."

She helped Dorothy get the garment on over her bruises and then led her out of the stable to the house and up to her rooms.

"Now, Dorothy, I am going out for a time. While I am gone, I want you to fill the tub and bathe yourself. Use plenty of hot water and have a care to your bruises. When I come back I'll get some ointments and balms from Mrs. Dylan and attend to you."

Dorothy held back. "Oh, Miss Charity! Use *your* bathtub! I wouldn't dare."

Eager to get to what had to be done, Charity retorted sharply, "Dorothy—stop this nonsense! Do as you are told. When I return, I expect you to be in that tub as I have ordered."

With that, she hurried from the room and down the stairs where she sought out Mrs. Dylan who had gone back into the kitchen. This time there were no friendly overtures.

"Mrs. Dylan, I found Dorothy hurt and abused out in the stables. I have taken her to my room where she will remain until I return. She is not to be approached. She is to be left strictly alone. Do you understand?"

"Oh, Miss Charity. I did not realize. . . ."

"Perhaps not, but that is no longer important. The thing now is that you obey my orders. Is that clear?"

The housekeeper's face was hard to read, it reflected such a mixture of emotions. There was surprise at the sudden change in Charity—from a friendly, pleasant guest in the house, to a cold, grim giver of orders. But Charity thought that fear, even despair, stood out.

However, Charity was not concerned at the moment. She had another task ahead; one she looked forward to eagerly. She left the kitchen

172

and went to see about it, a short search taking her to Carton, whom she found behind the stables shoveling manure—a task, Charity thought, to which he was admirably suited. He straightened and scowled at her.

"Mr. Carton, I just found Dorothy where you left her, raped and abused in your quarters."

"That is none of your affair," he said harshly.

"I am making it so. I am taking her away from you. She is now in my rooms at the house. You are not to touch her—even go near her—is that clear?"

"And what is your authority to put yourself into other people's business?" he asked angrily.

"I shall let you puzzle over that. In due time, Mr. Leach may straighten you out on the matter."

Carton gripped his manure fork, his knuckles white. He was obviously beside himself with fury and Charity felt a touch of fear. Instinct alone told Charity that this was no time to back down. With Carton perhaps ready to spring at her, attack was her only weapon.

She fixed the man with a contemptuous eye and as though she had all the authority in the world, said, "Mr. Carton, you are a rank coward. Any beast who would treat a girl in that fashion could be nothing else."

"You certainly are a wordy little busybody."

"And I have some words to add. If you touch that child again, I shall see that you *hang* for it. Do you understand?"

Carton's show of blazing anger unraveled; slowly, but obvious enough to give Charity a strong sense of victory. The threat had been a telling blow and she sensed this as an opportune moment to retire from the field.

As she moved back toward the house, she tried to further assess the enemy she had just made. Would her warning—a hollow one, in truth—be the end of it? It was difficult to say. Only Carton's doubt as to her authority had saved her from an attack; of that she was sure. Perhaps she had goaded him too sharply.

One thing was true. She had turned Carton's wrath away from helpless little Dorothy. She would now bear its brunt herself. . . .

Left with nothing but his humiliation, Carton sought another target for the wrath boiling white hot within him. He hurried to the kitchen and drew Mrs. Dylan into a far corner.

"That colonial bitch," he snarled. "What do you know about her? Was she sent here to test my authority?"

"What has happened?" Mrs. Dylan asked, as though she did not already know.

"She nosed her way into my digs and found Dorothy."

"Why should that shake you so?"

"Dorothy fought me. I was harsh with her."

"Harsh with her? I can imagine what that means! My allowing you to have her was a sin for the confessional. I should have known that the rottenness in you would come out."

"*You* allowing me? Have a care, woman. You are far too loose with your tongue."

"I should have said no and devil take the loser. What did you do to the poor chick?"

"Enough of your blathering. That impudent slut threatened me with the gallows. Another word from her and I'd have given her the handle of my fork."

"Have a care with your violence, Carton, or you *will* end up with a noose around your neck."

Carton's hands doubled into fists. He advanced a step whereupon Mrs. Dylan, wondering whence she had dredged up the courage, said, "And have a care, my man! Strike me and I vow I'll reach one of the butcher knives on yonder wall before I go down."

Checked again by unexpected defiance, Carton fled the kitchen to wrestle with his frustrations in private. Mrs. Dylan dropped weakly into a chair, her body all atremble.

25.

When Charity returned to her chambers, she found Dorothy sitting obediently in the bathtub awaiting further orders.

"May I get out now?"

"Of course, dear. Dry yourself and I'll comb your hair for you."

With that done, Charity tested her newly-assumed authority by pulling the bell cord. Cloris answered. Charity said, "I want you to go to the stables and bring Dorothy's things back here from Carton's quarters."

Cloris took the order in silence and obeyed, returning with three shifts and some underclothing.

"That will be all," Charity said crisply. Then to Dorothy, after Cloris left, "I guess these will have to do for the time being. Until we can go to the shops for new ones."

"I've always tried to keep my clothes clean," Dorothy said.

"You have done very well. But I'm sure you would like to have some pretty frocks."

Dorothy was silent, as though the very thought of such luxury rendered her mute.

Charity found her new protege amusing in her efforts to be deemed worthy of having been rescued. She rebounded quickly in spirit and body and she bustled about the chambers doing and redoing chores which did not need doing in the first place. She dusted furniture, lifted Charity's frocks from the wardrobe, brushed them gently and reverently, and returned them, while Charity watched and pondered philosophically—how fortune's wheel turns and life repeats itself. Just as Christopher had rescued her from the odious Orin Cade, she had now taken this child from Bruce Carton's brutal clutches.

This child? Mrs. Dylan had marked her as being Charity's own age. Yet Charity regarded Dorothy as being far her junior. Was it a matter of innocence? Charity saw herself as a woman of the world by comparison, even though Dorothy had no doubt been as completely introduced to sexual brutalities as she. Perhaps innocence could be defined as the inability to fight back.

"Dorothy," she cried finally, "for heaven's sake! Sit down and rest yourself. You'll polish all the varnish off of that table."

"Yes, Miss Charity," Dorothy answered, and sat herself demurely down, folded hands in her lap.

Charity used the interlude to quiet her own nerves and try to predict what the future would hold. Up to that point, her actions had sprung from indignation and anger. She had plunged ahead onto uncertain ground and now there was no turning back. She, regretting her harshness with Mrs. Dylan, considered an apology, and decided against it. All in all, there was nothing to do but hold her newly won ground and wait to see if Carton would try to regain his lost prestige through counterattack.

She kept Dorothy close to her for the balance of that day and in a sense, the two of them were ostracized. Orders were given and promptly obeyed, but with the remoteness of servants in a hotel or a wayside inn. Still, Charity braced a chair against the door when she and Dorothy retired for the night. . . .

They spent the following morning roaming the estate on foot. Thus they did not go too far afield, concentrating upon the cliffs which went sharply down to a narrow, rocky beach.

Dorothy had brightened and was almost her old, cheerful self, her youth and vitality recovering her quickly from her cruel ordeal.

"There are smugglers' caves all along the shore

down there," she said, "places where whole ships can hide."

"Smugglers? I'd think that would be very dangerous. Anyone caught at it would be jailed, would they not?"

"Sometimes. But just as often the constable and the King's men take them to London and hang them."

"Do you know any smugglers, Dorothy?"

"Not I, Miss Charity. It would scare me to my death just meeting one."

"Well, let us hope you never do."

A nagging dread had been troubling Charity the whole morning. It was like an itch difficult to find and scratch, and surfaced in her consciousness only as noon approached and she was about to send an order to Carton through Cloris. Then she realized that facing Carton again had been her dread; also that not facing him would be cowardice.

So shortly after lunch, she marched down to the stables, found him in the tackroom, and said, "Carton, I want you to harness a mare to that gig I saw in the carriage yard. You will have it ready and at the door at one o'clock."

She waited. If he refused to obey, where would it leave her? Would the order stiffen his resolve to defy her? Her instinct told her that she must not lose ground with an enemy—and the necessity of harnessing the mare herself would be just that.

Therefore, she was greatly relieved when, after a sullen silence, Carton said, "Aye, Miss. It shall be done."

Thank God he *was* a coward! Now there would be an armed truce between them until Christopher arrived to clarify the situation.

Charity debated taking Dorothy with her to Camber, then decided it was best. She did not yet trust Carton, although she doubted he would be rash enough to harm Dorothy openly. Still, he might arrange an "accident" and thus indirectly avenge himself for the loss of face Charity had brought about. Would he ever try for direct vengeance? Charity doubted it but she remembered the mire she had seen when coming from London. A lethal swamp, surely. And there were many other places on the estate where death or injury could be arranged by a clever mind bent upon mischief. It behooved Charity to remain alert.

It was only an hour's drive to Camber and Charity found the place attractive in a rustic sense, but far less pretentious than vast Windward Moors. As she drew the mare up before the Camber manor she wondered if there had been a mistake. No one was in sight.

Then a man in livery appeared, who approached the gig and said, "If Madam will take that road to the left. It leads to Camber Creek and the picnic grounds where the Mistress awaits."

A few minutes later, Charity came in sight of the colorful gathering. There were rigs and carriages and even a coach-with-six, and twenty or thirty people on a shaded lawn. Beyond was a creek winding its way to the sea.

A hostler was waiting. He saluted and said, "I'll take your gig, Miss."

"Please do. Put the mare in the shade there beside the coach." Turning to Dorothy with some uncertainty she said, "You had better stay with the gig, dear."

The hostler hastened to reassure her. "Miss, there is a stable prepared for the servants."

"Very well."

Although Charity hardly saw Dorothy as a servant, she knew she would be considered as such at this elegant gathering.

As she got out of the gig, a deep voice ordered, "Take my horse also, Cummings," and there he was again, on that fiery roan. Charity wondered if he lived on the beast and dismounted only on rare occasions.

"Mr. Wahl! How nice to see you again. Are you the welcoming committee?"

"Only for special people. Not the likes of those gathered over there."

"I am flattered."

He eyed her with a quirk of a smile. "I see I won my bet."

Charity had lost her courage the last moment and donned the simple yellow cotton she favored as the least restricting of frocks she had purchased in London.

"Yes," she said. "It must give you personal satisfaction even though there was no money at stake."

"I think I would have gotten more satisfaction if I'd lost."

"Never fear. You may get that satisfaction yet," she answered tartly.

"I'll look forward to it."

Dennis Wahl seemed in no hurry to approach the picnic so they stood there, Charity glad of the interlude. She was surprised at the rapport she had felt with this perpetually angry man, and she found this an opportunity to again test her reactions in his presence. They had not changed. Her nipples, eager for attention, had hardened and were pushing against the camisole in which they were imprisoned. Why, she asked herself, did this hairy brute excite her where other men failed to stir her in the least?

Dennis Wahl had turned so that his back was to the gathering at the creek. He pointed off into the woods. "Those oaks," he said, "are centuries old."

A single downward glance told Charity the truth. Dennis was not as bold and forward as he had seemed. He had turned away to hide the erection that was pressing its muscular length against his tight breeches.

Charity, more than able to cope with the situation, laughed softly. "I am beginning to see through you, Dennis Wahl."

"You would be blind not to," he growled. "You have me at a disadvantage."

"Do all women affect you that way?"

"You're a wicked little bitch!"

"But not unsympathetic."

"I have a cottage off the lower cliff," he suggested evenly.

"I'm sure you have. But just now we should join the others or eyebrows will be raised."

"That rabble? They are mostly down from

181

London. Harlots and rakes. My wife's friends. Have a care or they will eat you alive."

"How exciting. If we turn and walk slowly you may be again in control of your passions when we reach the creek."

They proceeded in that manner, conversing on the way. Charity said, "The ladies are most colorfully dressed. Those bright silks and satins. I shall feel shabby."

"No need to."

"The men, too. They are quite gaudy also. Most of them. One might think this was a masqued ball and they are all appearing as peacocks."

"The peacock would be insulted," he laughed.

"That gentleman by the wine table with the absurd wig. It is at least a foot high. Ladies wear exaggerated wigs, I know, but gentlemen . . ."

"Beware of that fop. His name is Borland Nickelawn, a London clubman. He looks amusing and harmless but he is the deadliest swordsman in England—or Europe, too, for that matter."

"Then I shall be most careful if I fence with him."

The pair had been spied and now Meg Wahl came hurrying toward them, while seeking not to spill wine from the glass she carried.

"Charity, darling! You have arrived! And trust my hospitable husband to find you first!"

"He welcomed me most graciously," Charity said ingenuously.

"I am sure he did. But now you must meet the others."

Rather than going from one guest to another, Meg made it a blanket introduction. "Milords and ladies," she called out in a loud voice, "I am honored to present Miss Charity Sturges who has come to visit us from his Majesty's Colony of Virginia. You may return to your revelry when you have greeted her properly."

There were various acknowledgements of the introduction, but no one approached. Still, high interest was obvious from the side glances and whispered comments.

Borland Nickelawn did come mincing up in his brilliant purple jacket, his cream-colored breeches, white silk hose, and high-heeled shoes.

"So this is our little treasure from over the sea. How lovely! Sweeting, we have waited impatiently for your arrival." He took Charity's fingers in a jeweled hand, bent, and kissed each of them in order.

A servant had arrived from the wine table and there were now glasses all around. Nickelawn raised his. "To our colonial queen of beauty."

Charity drank with the rest. The wine had been cooled in the creek, and she found it delicious as it slid smoothly down her throat. As she lowered her glass, she decided that Dennis must have been accurate in his appraisal of Nickelawn's ability with the blade. Without that deadly talent, he would have been the veriest clown. As it was, no one treated him as such.

"I have things to do," Dennis said gruffly, and strode off, his manner a proof to Charity of his sincerity in saying he could not stand these people.

They were conducting themselves variously with Charity finding this, her first true social

183

event on either side of the ocean, a most interesting experience. A musical trio, harpsichord, flute, and violin, was in evidence on a raised platform and two couples were totally engrossed in a graceful minuet. There were others grouped about a smiling dandy who did feats of legerdemain with a silk handkerchief and a number of coins. Others sat at ease or walked about, conversing, laughing, and generally enjoying themselves. Charity's glass was empty. As it was refilled by a passing servant, she wished Dennis had not deserted her, and then wondered how much of the chatter and the whispers concerned her.

A great deal of it, no doubt. This was confirmed by Meg who joined her and said, "They are all talking about you, my dear. They are fascinated, but of course none of them would be so gauche as to admit it."

She was steering Charity toward the creek where there was better shade. And also, though Charity did not realize it, toward Gaby Kirth who was now seated on a bench talking with Borland Nickelawn. The unaccustomed wine had worked quickly on Charity. Meg's guests, whom she had first viewed with some reservation, now seemed most acceptable, a friendly group well worth cultivating. She wondered about Dennis Wahl's hostility. Evidently Dennis was hostile to people in general.

They had arrived at the creek bank and Charity was complimenting Meg on her talents as a hostess when a nearby guest squealed and cried,

"Oh, look there! A fish! A lovely speckled darling! He's come for a glass of wine."

Charity's eyes followed the pointing finger. It was a trout of respectable size, a sudden, keen reminder of her Virginia life. How often during those beautiful days had she come proudly home to Mother Mae with such lush, delicious beauties?

Later, she would ruefully recall her subsequent action, but at the time it seemed a most natural thing to do—she crouched on the creek bank, eyed the lazing trout, judged its depth in the water, and tested an old skill. The test was successful. With a lightning thrust of her arm, she grasped the fish and brought it forth in triumph.

As she held it up, there was a moment of dead silence. Then cheers, laughter, and compliments from all sides; from everyone nearby except Gaby Kirth. The group must have sensed her hostility, because the silence fell again. Gaby smiled icily and said, "My dear! How you dazzle us! Is that the way you caught fish in your native wilderness?"

Her pseudo-friendly manner deceived no one except Charity who arose from her crouch, smiled, and said, "Quite often. It is a skill at which the Virginia Indians excel."

"I see. And what are some of the other customs of those savages? Did you eat the fish raw?"

Charity sobered instantly. She had been a fool, falling into this woman's trap. But how could she have known that it *was* a trap?

Desperately seeking a way out, she tossed the trout back into the stream, maintained her smile, and played the innocent.

185

"Oh, no. We were more civilized than you imagine. But perhaps a little more primitive than we should have been."

As she spoke, she remembered the small cleaver she had seen on the refreshment table. A godsend! It might be her salvation! She went on, "However, you must understand that life was more uncertain there in the wilderness and the skills we developed were those for survival. Perhaps I could demonstrate."

"I am sure we will all be most amused," Gaby replied.

"Then if you will indulge me," Charity said, and crossed to the refreshment table. She picked up the cleaver. "This is quite similar in weight and size to a weapon we primitives used in Virginia. The tomahawk."

The entire group had gathered to watch, avid for whatever excitement was in the offing. Only Meg held back. She had planned the meeting between Charity and Gaby with the idea that it would be amusing. But it had now gone out of her and she regretted her rashness, perhaps sensing what was to come.

Speaking sweetly to Gaby, Charity said, "If you will just stand over there by that tree where you will be well able to see my demonstration, I will be obliged."

Gaby, revelling in what she saw as her triumph, was not as perceptive as she should have been. Otherwise she might have noted the iciness of Charity's smile and the soft, purring tone in her voice. Meg did note this and was uneasily reminded of a preying tigress about to spring. That cleaver! God! Did Charity mean to kill her? Had she gone beyond all bounds of reason?

The guests had gathered in a circle and now Charity faced Gaby, who stood smiling contemptuously with her back to the broad oak tree.

Then, without further ado, Charity raised the cleaver. Her arm came over and down in the flash of an eye. The cleaver streaked end over end toward its target, a spot some six inches above Gaby's head. It sped true, the blade buried deep in the trunk of the oak, neatly skewering Gaby's tall wig.

Gaby screamed and ducked. She went to her knees, the wig remaining cleavered to the tree, with Gaby's natural hair braided into an ugly bun on the top of her head.

Charity broke the silence. "I am so sorry," she apologized sweetly. "I aimed higher, but I am afraid I have lost my skill with the tomahawk."

A concerted gasp went up. There were a few snickers, after which a pause hung in the air. Then Gaby, her fury beyond control, lunged with a scream at Charity. Had she been closer she might have surprised Charity with her attack. As things were, Charity was braced to meet her and enter just as fiercely into the battle.

Gaby's more elaborate gown and her many petticoats proved a burden. Charity, in her less restricting gown, crouched as she had seen Indian youths do in such contests, and caught Gaby low on her thighs, tumbling her head over heels. But Gaby got a hand into Charity's bodice and ripped it down as she went over. Clinging to the torn cloth, she brought Charity to the ground with her and they were a rolling, fighting tangle of bare breasts, pantaletted legs, and flailing arms.

Meg was beside herself. "Stop them!" she cried. "In heaven's name—please! Someone stop them!"

Borland Nickelawn made the first gesture in that direction, but it was a weak one. He stepped forward and poked at the struggling pair with the toe of his shoe.

"Ladies—ladies," he chided. "There are rules for this sort of thing." Obviously he was amused, perhaps even erotically excited by what was taking place on the grass.

But now another guest intervened, one less flamboyantly clad than the other men. His anger was first directed at Nickelawn. He pushed the dandy roughly aside and received a glare of hatred in return.

The man stooped to separate the pair and was then aided by others of the group, men in sympathy with their distraught hostess, and the two female gladiators were pulled to their feet and separated. The attention of the guests was directed mainly at Charity—appreciatively so—as she stood there stripped to the waist, both camisole and frock torn away.

She was a beautiful sight to behold, her hair tumbled over her shoulders, her face flushed with the glory of battle, her lovely, dark-nippled breasts rising and falling with each gasping breath. She was a sight none of the men, nor for that matter, the women, would soon forget. Meg snatched a shawl from the shoulders of one of the guests and flung it about Charity, covering her

188

nakedness. She then led Charity away from the lists, while the others crowded about Gaby.

Charity, her sanity beginning to return, said, "I'm sorry, Meg. I ruined your party. I disgraced myself. Can you ever forgive me?"

Meg's reply was grimly stated. "It was not your fault, my dear. You merely stood up to that slut. And you have not disgraced yourself. Unless I am mistaken you have won the hearts of everyone present."

"You are most kind to say so."

"We will go into the house and tend to your scratches."

"Please, I'd rather leave. I am in no way hurt. I want only to get home and compose myself."

"Very well. If you prefer. I shall call upon you tomorrow."

Dorothy beheld her tattered mistress in stunned wonder as they climbed into the gig and Charity directed the mare toward Windward Moors. They were a good mile out on the road before Dorothy dared speak.

"Did someone hurt you?"

"No. Not really."

"You must feel awful."

Charity drew in a deep breath and straightened her shoulders. "On the contrary, dear, I never felt better in my life. . . ."

Charity braved the stares of two workers on the road into Windward Moors. "Who are those men?" she asked.

If she had not been preoccupied she would probably have noted Dorothy's sudden nervousness. The girl dropped her eyes and murmured,

"Mr. Bruce hires them from outside to work here."

"The outdoor work?"

"Yes, Miss Charity."

One man stared after the gig. The other went stolidly on with his work. The returning pair managed to reach their chambers unobserved otherwise, much to Charity's relief.

26.

Meg was as good as her word. She came to Windward the following afternoon and they talked privately in Charity's sittingroom, Charity having sent Dorothy off to occupy herself elsewhere.

"Oh, darling," Meg lamented, "I shall never forgive myself for not warning you about Gaby Kirth when I invited you to the picnic!"

"But you had no reason to expect what happened."

Meg was unable to tell the whole truth, that she had deliberately arranged the meeting. "At least one good thing came from it," she said. "You will now believe everything I tell you about Gaby. You must know that she will try to get Christopher back."

"Get him *back*! I did not know she ever had him."

"I suppose he was reluctant to tell you about

190

that phase of his life. They were close to marriage when Clement packed him off to the Colonies."

"He certainly did not tell me. I never knew the woman existed until yesterday, except as the owner of Channel Light."

Meg could not restrain a smile of satisfaction over the outcome of the battle even though it had distressed her. She said, "Gaby came with every intention of destroying you in the eyes of others. She planned to mark you as an untutored young savage transported right out of the colonial wilderness. She expected to have everyone laughing at you. Instead, she has put your name on every tongue."

"I am not sure that is to my advantage."

Meg leaned close and took Charity's hand in hers. "Charity, darling. I have a confession to make. Before I met you my mind was one with all the others. I saw you as being a social problem to us. But that is all changed. I feel ashamed and contrite."

"You had no way of knowing what I would or would not be."

"True, but I should have been more loyal to Christopher. I should have trusted his judgment. Anyhow, please believe me now and trust me. I am your friend. You can confide in me."

Would you still be my friend if you knew I intend to bed with your husband?

The thought came as a shock to Charity, bold statement of intent she had not yet admitted to herself.

"Tell me," Meg said in almost a pleading voice,

191

"what is your true relationship with Chris?" When Charity hesitated, Meg added, "What are your intentions toward him?"

"I intend to marry him."

There was no hesitancy in that statement. Spoken as it was, with no mark of reticence, it could have been a sign of trust in Meg's newly stated friendship; that, or a test of it.

"Does that shock you?" she asked.

"On the contrary. I think Chris would be most fortunate."

"Oh, Meg! I am so glad that we met and you are—well, *you*."

"Sweet, you may not feel that way when you truly get to know me," Meg smiled.

"I feel that I know you already."

"Only a part of me." Meg frowned and fell silent, her inner self in conflict. She had never before realized her need of a true friend—one in whom she could totally confide. Perhaps Charity was that person. A fact, or merely a hope? There was but one way to find out. Make the friendship or break it right here.

"Charity, I am more selfish than you know. I have never been true to Dennis, nor he to me. Dennis frequently beds with Gaby Kirth."

"Well, I don't think much of his taste in women. Does he know you are aware of his infidelity?"

"Both of them are. But you see, I don't care. I don't care whose bed Dennis crawls into so long as it is not mine." When Charity did not immediately reply, Meg went on in an attempt to justify herself. "Charity, there are many such marriages.

192

Or rather, they might be called arrangements where both the husband and the wife are satisfied with what they have."

"What you are saying then is that you do not love Dennis."

"Charity! I don't know what love is. It is a word that they throw to the winds. It means everything and it means nothing. Are you in love with Chris?"

"I don't know. I am grateful to him for what he did for me. I plan to marry him, so perhaps that *is* love."

"Not necessarily."

"You are right. I was not being frank. I plan to marry Chris because I see that as best for my own future." Charity, too, was testing friendship.

"Then we do think alike! Oh Charity, darling. I'm sure we shall be great friends!"

There was an urge within each of them to make that true and binding with total revelation. Charity wanted to tell Meg about Sean McDougal—that golden night aboard the *Hainaut*. And Meg yearned to acquaint Charity with more intimate details of her situation.

But Charity held back. She remembered Meg's reaction when she mentioned Sean's name previously. And for Meg's part, she could not bring herself to tell Charity that Durban was—after a fashion—her lover.

So each savored what she had of the other and each warmed her spirit in the glow of the new friendship. The complete testing of it could wait until later.

Charity asked, "Does Dennis know of my dispute with Gaby Kirth?"

"He was told. He laughed. He thought it delightful."

"But he did not take sides?"

"Dennis takes sides with no one. Not ever. He rebuffs all attempts to get close to him."

I do not agree. I could get close to him by merely raising my skirt.

They left the sitting room and walked slowly down the stairs and out to Meg's carriage. Meg said, "One thing you *must* believe, Charity. What I have told you about Gaby. She is vicious and she will never forgive you for what happened. Beware of her. She will get back at you by any means possible."

"I shall remember." She knew Meg spoke the truth.

"Oh, by the way—that man who pushed Borland Nickelawn away yesterday when you and Gaby were fighting. He is dead."

"So suddenly? What happened?"

"Borland considered what he did an insult. The man's name was Henry Squire, a visitor from London. Borland challenged him to a duel. Early this morning, he killed Squire. . . ."

27

With so much to think about, Charity spent a
restless night, nor had the unrest abated on the
following day. The situation at Leach House had
reached a stalemate. The remoteness of those in
charge remained, though Mrs. Dylan and Cloris
were in no way hostile and Charity had no contact with Carton. Feeling there was no need to
face it out with him further, she sent Cloris with
an order to bring the carriage to the door that
morning.

She took Dorothy with her and was directed to
the nearby village of Hempstead. There would
have been greater shopping opportunities in
Maidstone, the closest city of size, but she found
some acceptable frocks for Dorothy and raised
eyebrows when she proffered payment with one
of the gold sovereigns which had lain for so long
in the earth beside Mae Varney's hut.

On the way home, Dorothy, overcome with
gratitude, plagued her until she almost lost her
temper.

"Dorothy," she scolded, "I want you to stop
thanking me. Once or twice is quite proper and
quite enough. An overabundance of gratitude
marks a person as being too negative for any
good. You must learn to think better of yourself.

195

Hold your head high. Whatever fate gives you in this world, you deserve, if it is for the good. If it is not, you look to your courage and at least go down fighting."

"Yes, Miss Charity," Dorothy said, and the advice kept the girl pondering in silence for the rest of the trip.

Once back at Leach House, Charity questioned Dorothy. "How much of the house have you seen?"

"I have been all over the north wing."

"But what about the south wing? It is sealed off, they tell me. Does anyone ever go there?"

"Not really. I almost did but then I got frightened. It's so ghostly over there. The entrances from the hallways are all boarded up."

"Then how do you know it's ghostly."

"There is a way to get in through a door behind the tapestry, next to the kitchen stairs in the great hall. It looks just like the wall but you can see where there is a door. A dark line."

"I'd like you to show me."

"Yes, Miss Charity." Dorothy was standing by the window. Turning away slowly, she said, "I wonder why that man stays out there on the moor?"

"What man, dear?"

"The one on the horse. He just sits on his mount and waits. I wonder what he is waiting for?"

Charity went to the window and looked out over Dorothy's shoulder. There was indeed a horseman sitting motionless to the southeast beyond the stables. He was well away from the house but close enough to be identified.

It was Dennis Wahl on his roan stallion.

Charity knew. She knew instantly; as clearly as though Dennis had ridden up and called, *Come, lass. It must be done.*

He is waiting for me!

How utterly bizarre! This arrogant, silent summons! Charity's reaction was mixed. Indignation, certainly. And surprise. But less of the latter, because deep within, where thoughts fly free, she had known he would come. And she had known from the first that she would go when he called. This in the face of her anger at Dennis Wahl's *knowing* she would obey his peremptory summons.

Such conceit!

No man had the right to such supreme confidence.

Then, finally, the compromise she had to make.

I will go but I will remain in command of myself. Men will not choose me. I will choose them. I will say who shall have me and who shall not. Not for Charity Sturges to stand patiently in the forest awaiting the pleasure of whatever buck strays along.

She reached the stables without being seen, to find Carton away, led out a mare, mounted bareback, and rode off to the southeast.

As she approached him, Dennis Wahl angled in until their paths were one. They remained silent for a time; until he said, "Is that yellow frock the only one you possess?"

"And if it is?"

"I shall have to replenish your wardrobe."

"I am quite capable of doing that myself. Do you not approve of this dress?"

He chuckled. "But I do. You show a fine leg without a lady's saddle."

"How far is the cottage you spoke of?" Charity asked abruptly.

"Twenty minutes along the bluff if we hie ourselves."

Charity put heels into her mare's flank and the animal plunged on ahead. But she was no match for the stallion and soon Dennis Wahl came up beside her, the roan skimming along easily in contrast to the mare's straining effort.

To Charity, now dealing in symbols, that seemed significant, adding to the anger she already felt. The male animal so sure of himself; so supremely confident.

Damn men! Damn all men!...

The cottage on Camber's southward bluff came in sight. Dennis rode on slightly ahead and when Charity arrived he had dismounted and was waiting to take the mare. As he helped Charity down, his hand slid up her leg to her thigh and gripped there for a moment as though it were a promise of the violence she could expect.

Little was said. Charity allowed herself to be carried into the cottage where she hardly noted the accommodations other than to see that they were adequate, a bed the principal piece of furniture. When Dennis tried to lay her down upon the bed, she rebelled, struggled free, and came erect.

He sat down on the edge of the bed and eyed

her with a lazy calculation. "I suppose you must be courted first."

"Where did you get that idea? From Gaby Kirth?"

"Who told you—Meg?"

"I was told."

"Then you do not need the reassurance of undying fidelity?"

"You said, 'Come lass, it must be done.' "

"I do not recall saying any such thing," Dennis said in mild confusion.

"It doesn't matter."

As she spoke, Charity was getting out of the yellow frock as calmly as though she were in her chambers at Leach House. The single petticoat went next, and with no camisole to be removed there were only the pantalettes left. They came off and Charity stood naked.

Her bold act had been clearly a foreplay, but an angry one, her action that of a defiant slave, but a slave to herself. She wanted this man, but on her own terms.

With open appreciation, Dennis savored her lovely, high-breasted body. But he had known how she would be. Her manner, her attitude, were new to him in his experience with women. It brought a murmured response.

"So cold—so grim. . . ."

"Did you expect me to cower in a corner and cover myself with trembling hands?"

He frowned and fumbled at the collar of his shirt, thus giving Charity further opportunity to test her power. Elated by her performance, unplanned and unrehearsed as it was, she said,

"Stand up. I'll do that. It seems you are the one who must be courted."

Dennis ripped off his shirt. Then, in a sort of delayed reaction, he paused and glared down at Charity. She went calmly ahead, on her knees now, undoing the bindings at his waist and lowering his trousers.

He asked, "Is it your aim in life to go about emasculating men?"

"Some I have met do not need my help." She was regarding his exposed manhood. "And in your case I think there is no danger."

She prodded him back onto the bed and quickly finished her work, his boots taking most of the time. Then, if he expected an interlude, he was disappointed. Charity pushed him down onto his back and mounted him. She achieved penetration without his assistance and seized his head to bring his mouth into proximity with her own.

His masculinity quickly reasserted itself. "I will not be raped!" he fairly roared into her face, and lifted her viciously. He turned her about, reversing their positions. His fury was increased by her responding laughter.

"Even the dullest of clods can be awakened," she mocked.

He grated, "You bitch, be still! You would tempt both saint and devil!"

And the byplay was finished. What followed was an explosion of violence stemming from the rage in each of them against self; with Dennis because this lovely slut had caused him to doubt himself even momentarily; with Charity because the physical release of the battle negated her dictum: *I will remain in command.* But she was not doing so. The ravenous demand of her body was dictating the course she took. The brutality of Dennis Wahl's thrust, the savageness of his attack, brought fierce joy, and she returned his viciousness as she clawed at his back and buttocks and sought his flesh with bared teeth. But still room for a wild thought:

Am I seeking vengeance upon this man or upon myself?

Charity screamed elemental hatred into his throat as mutual climax raised them—or lowered them—into the total animal. . . .

There was silence there on the bed, there in the cottage, for an interminable time. Charity spoke first.

"Was Gaby more satisfactory?"

An oblique answer: "So that is what it was?"

"What do you mean?"

"You came only to prove yourself the better wench."

"No. I needed no proof of that. I *am* the better wench, as you well know."

"I know this—you could destroy lesser men than I and you probably have."

"Who speaks with conceit now?"

His passions abated, he regarded her with a clinical intensity. "Are you that way clear through to the bone?"

"I don't understand."

"Is there no shred of tenderness in you? No capacity whatever for love?" He did not understand her; he had never met a woman such as she.

"Love! You *dare* use the word? A man who

hates all things and all people? You should blush and hang your head."

"You go on mocking me. If I asked for a truce, would it be granted?"

Charity now taunted him with her body as well as her words and manner. She lifted her arms and stretched her lovely symmetry like a jungle cat sated by the kill and about to purr.

"I doubt if I would give other than the *beastly* Dennis Wahl a second look. Contrition does not become you."

"Careful, girl. Sex and violence often come separately."

"Very well, I have no relish to be beaten and maimed, so I'll accept your truce."

His look had turned pensive. "What about tomorrow? What about the future?"

"Let that take care of itself. Now tell me—what do you know of Bruce Carton? The hostler at Windward Moors?"

"Why? Has he crossed you?"

"We have our differences. But there is something that makes him wary. He can be frightened by threats. There must be a reason."

Dennis' natural look of cynicism deepened into contempt. "A man of little worth."

"Then why do they keep him on at Windward Moors?"

"I think that Irish woman, Mrs. Dylan, has a great heart or she would send the man packing."

"From what I have been able to see, Mrs. Dylan is afraid of Carton. It appears that he terrorizes her and gets his way in all things."

"Mayhap. They are both from Ireland. Perhaps

they are related. I know not." The subject was clearly of no interest to Dennis.

"Carton brutalized a slip of a girl. I came upon her and took her away from him."

"Best you mind your own business," he said, scowling.

"When I find someone being mistreated, I make it my business," Charity answered firmly.

"Then you must have been very busy among the slaves in the Colonies."

"I would expect just such a senseless remark from you," she answered in annoyance.

"For your own good. Meddlers get into trouble."

"Thank you for the warning. I think it is now time I get back." She bounded out of bed and started to dress.

It was strange indeed, but after they were mounted and riding away from the cottage, Charity realized that Dennis Wahl now held her in greater respect than before the tryst; a hard thing to understand. She did not care about his opinion of her one way or another, having come to him for her own purposes. But to gain his higher opinion by wantonly giving herself to him seemed contrary to what could be normally expected. This made her realize she still had much to learn about men.

He rode with her across Camber and Channel Light to the south boundary of Windward Moors, then pulled up.

"You'll be safe now, lass."

"Are you saying I have been in danger?"

"You can never tell. Those riding across the

land of others could be mistaken for poachers—deliberately mistaken in some cases. And shooting a poacher is not a crime," he warned.

"That does not seem to bother you. You ride everywhere."

"Everywhere I choose. Even on Crown land beyond. I refuse to be hemmed in by man-made boundaries."

"You have courage." Or perhaps, she thought, it was more foolhardiness; a need to maintain his self-image.

"By the way," she said, "if you come again to stand and wait at Leach House, you will wait forever."

"Are you saying we will not go again to the cottage?"

"Perhaps—perhaps not. It will be my decision."

She left him at a gallop, a heady sense of power lifting her spirits. And if any sense of guilt—unfaithfulness to Christopher—tried to intrude, she banished it quickly. What she had done, she told herself, injured him not at all. If anything, it had made her more capable of serving him well as mistress and wife.

More important at the moment were the warnings she had received concerning Bruce Carton and Gabrielle Kirth. Evidently, she had made two dangerous enemies. And given the nature of the country about, no doubt an "accident" to the unwary could easily be arranged.

Thus a curious fact became apparent. One aspect of her life remained in common with the old. The seeming security offered by this civilized mother country was a sham. Windward Moors was no less dangerous a place than the forests of Virginia. Even more so because the perils there had been casual. In Virginia, there had been no individuals who actively sought her scalp while here it was a prize coveted by two vengeful members of the local tribe. Thus it behooved Charity to be ever alert. Common sense alone dictated that course.

But Charity was not fearful. A sense of excitement dominated; an urge to test her wits against adversaries in whatever game was being played. It bolstered her ego to have come to Kent and become a person not to be ignored. Thus she was totally in possession of herself as she handed Carton the reins of her mount. "Cool her off and rub her down," she ordered indifferently.

Carton answered with his habitual scowl.

Charity moved away and then turned back. "By the way, Carton, I notice that things are not quite shipshape here about the stables. Mr. Leach will want to see things cleaner when he returns."

Carton's growl could have been agreement or otherwise.

"Thank you," Charity said and walked on, thinking that Carton's inability to conceal his hatred was perhaps his prime weakness. His foes were never left in doubt.

Still, she had a moment of uneasiness as she all but felt his eyes burn holes in her back. To bait an enemy, especially one of Carton's savagery, was a fool's ploy. She would be a little more careful in the future.

28.

"You can come out now," Carton said.

As he turned back into the tackroom, his scowl changed in quality: less of frustration, more of grim determination.

Gaby Kirth came out of the corner where she had hidden herself and said, "I thought she might wonder about my horse."

"No fear. I got it into a stable before she came around the corner."

"Where do you suppose she has been?" Gaby asked curiously.

"Does it matter?"

"It doesn't really. The important thing is her next trip over the moors." Her voice was flat and hard.

"Not so fast, milady. What you ask takes doing. I'll not be held to a schedule."

"Of course not," she conceded hastily, "but the sooner the better."

Gaby was not taking any great risk in commissioning Carton to do away permanently with Charity—unless he bungled the job, and with all the possibilities of an "accident" on the Windward Moors land there was little chance of that. But even if he failed, she was in no great danger because the word of a lackey would not be taken against one of high station.

Nor was she acting blindly in coming to Carton, as he was known for violence and greed along the coast, to a point where Gaby wondered why the Leaches kept him on; probably because Clement and Christopher paid so little attention to local matters that they knew little of the man's reputation.

So she felt to be in little danger herself; still it was a happy circumstance that Carton also had an issue to settle with the intended victim.

Carton asked, "Do you know why the Master sent that little bawd out here alone? To take over, mayhap?"

"I've no idea. I only know that Christopher has business in London."

"And Clement—when does he return from Bath?"

"I don't know, but I presume before long now. He has been away for some weeks."

"A pox on both. They can stay away forever for all of me."

"That has nothing to do with the matter at hand. How will you proceed? The mire? The cliffs?"

Carton no doubt found pleasure in being able to speak to Gaby as an equal. She forfeited all right to deference by coming to him in the first place.

He said, "Easy now, milady. Be not in such a rush. We have not yet spoken of payment."

"From what you've told me I fancy you would

be happy to do the mischief for your own satisfaction."

"Nay. My complaint is not as great as yours—
whatever it is. I suppose it springs from being
embarrassed at the party."

"Never mind that. Would a hundred pounds be
satisfactory?"

"Nowhere near. I yearn to be away from this
place. Back to Cork and friendlier people, and I
do not intend to go penniless."

"Two hundred?"

"Five."

"You presume on my generosity."

"I think not. Five hundred pounds is nothing to
a woman of your wealth." He grinned wryly.
"And what is it they say? The laborer is worthy
of his hire?"

"Very well. Five hundred it is. When you finish
the job. But do not tarry too long. Now take my
mount behind the stables. I'll leave as I
came. . . ."

29.

Dorothy was waiting outside when Charity arrived at the front door. She was smiling and
there was an engaging little squeak in her voice
as she said, "There is a gentleman to see you,

Miss Charity. I allowed him to wait in your parlor."

Christopher! A quick surge of dread touched Charity's heart. But when she realized he would be waiting in her parlor, in his own home, she was dismayed by her reaction. She had been so anxious for his arrival, hoping he would come quickly. So why the dismay? Had she been lying to herself without knowing it?

She denied that and told herself it was because she felt unworthy. Setting the question aside to be pondered later, she wondered who the visitor could be. She had not thought to ask Dorothy for his name and now she saw the girl following her up the stairs, at some distance behind. Obviously Dorothy did not want to be questioned on the matter.

Charity recognized the young man immediately. She had seen him on the grounds while returning from Meg Wahl's affair at Camber. He was one of the pair whose eyes had followed the gig as it passed.

Closer inspection showed him to be of a healthy, rustic cut; apple-cheeked; blue-eyed. He stood there awkwardly, yet with a masculine grace about him as he twisted his cap in his calloused hands and looked generally miserable. But also grimly determined.

Charity, seeking to put him at ease, smiled and said, "Dorothy told me you were here, but she neglected to give me your name."

"Wilferd Hyde, that's me, Miss Charity."

"I am happy to meet you, Wilferd. Please sit down."

He moved over to a chair and bent himself in the middle to perch stiff-backed on the very edge of the seat.

"And what may I do for you?" Charity asked.

He unhinged and bounced up again, punishing his cap, bending it and tugging at it.

"I have come to ask for Dorothy's hand in marriage."

Charity hid her surprise well, sinking gracefully into a chair and saying, "Do sit down, Wilferd. I don't quite understand. You must explain it to me."

"I have a love for Dorothy."

"I'm sure you do, but I am not the person to come to seeking her hand. You must go to her father."

"Nay. He sold her away. I did ask him over in Sussex and she with no dowry, but I did not care. Then he sold her to a moneyed man...."

"Bruce Carton?"

"Aye. To Carton. And she was gone from my sight." His distress was reflected in his voice.

"So you followed her."

"Aye, I got work here in the yards from that very man."

"But he does not know who you are or why you are here," Charity guessed.

"Nay."

Charity heard the soft opening of the outer door and caught sight of a blue eye peeping around the doorjamb just before the eye was withdrawn.

"Wilferd," Charity said, "I am most flattered that you would come to me with the request, but I am still the wrong person. I think you should see Mrs. Dylan. She is in charge here at Leach House, so it would be proper. . . ."

As she spoke, Charity wondered about local customs, about the law. Carton had paid Dorothy's father. Did that make him the legal owner of Dorothy? Was civilized England no different from primitive Virginia? The idea was too monstrous. Charity rejected it.

Wilferd Hyde was shaking his head. "No, Miss Charity. Dorothy said to come to you. It is your permission she wants."

"I see."

The plea stirred Charity's compassion, but it also touched her ego. Never before had she felt so grown-up, so confident of being able to handle adult affairs.

"Tell me, Wilferd. You said Dorothy has no dowry. Is it not the custom of a man to expect one of his bride?"

"Aye, but it does not matter to me."

Or if Dorothy comes to you with her virginity lost?

Charity did not ask the question. She reviled Carton in her heart and said, "Would you be able to support a wife?"

"Aye, I would. I have offer as tenant-farmer and a cottage at Camber nearby. I would take her there."

Probably the south cottage where old Timmons died, Charity thought; where she and Dennis had clawed ecstasy each from the body of the other. How strange indeed the ways of destiny! Death, passion, and now new and hopeful love all under the same thatched roof.

Charity glanced toward the door. Feeling like a queen, she called, "You may come in now, Dorothy."

The peeking blue eye appeared again, followed this time by the whole of the lovely little bride-to-be. Dorothy was blushing. "I'm sorry, Miss Charity. I did not mean to. . . ."

"No mind, Dorothy. Tell me—do you love Wilferd?"

"Oh, yes! Yes, yes! We were children together. It most broke my heart when . . ."

"I'm glad," Charity cut in, fearful that the girl would reveal the vile ravishment she had undergone. That was a matter between the two of them. Dorothy would tell Wilferd or she would not, and Charity was glad she did not have to make the decision for them.

"There is one thing," she said. "Bruce Carton. He will no doubt be angry. Are you prepared to face his wrath?"

Wilferd's eye flashed contempt. "A putty man! Soft of courage. A skulker. His fear of a broken head will keep him far away."

Charity was happy to have her opinion of Carton supported by this fine young fellow.

"Then Carton has no legal claim on Dorothy."

Wilferd's face remained dark. "A father's greed is not a legal claim."

Wilferd had a jaw which bespoke his feelings on the matter, and Charity could almost feel sorry for Carton if he ever dared come forward with a demand upon Dorothy's person.

212

"One more thing," Charity said. "The marriage. Have you a minister to perform it?"

"Oh, yes! In Sussex. A kindly prelate. He has known us. He has a charitable heart."

"Then if it is my permission you need, you have it. You will leave for Sussex immediately?"

"Aye, before the sun moves an inch."

"Then you have horses."

"Nay. We will walk."

Charity's mind went totally dreamy. How lovely! These two young lovers walking off together through the heather! She tried to fit Christopher and herself into the reverie, Chris holding firmly to her hand with the purple blossoms all about.

It did not work very well.

But then love has many faces, she thought. Her love for Christopher, while not the innocent joy she saw in Dorothy and Wilferd, was still strong, solid, and satisfying.

"Oh," she said, as though in sudden recollection. "You made one mistake. Dorothy does have a dowry."

With that, she went to her dresser and returned with three bright golden sovereigns. Then, after setting Dorothy to packing her new dresses, she put the coins in Wilferd's hand.

"With my blessing," she said. "These and Dorothy's new clothes."

No thanks were spoken but Wilferd, stunned, muttered something. Then at the door, he turned. "If you ever need me. . . ." and was gone.

Alone, Charity walked to the window, glowing from the role of fairy queen she had just finished playing. The purring of her contentment, like a sleek cat stroked and well fed, was almost audible to her ear. Then it all came out in the form of a happy giggle.

The pure joy of giving others the wherewithal of a dream.

In a more practical vein she recalled: *If you ever need me.* For what, she wondered. To kill Carton? Would Wilferd's gratitude carry him that far?

Charity jerked her vagrant mind up sharply. How ridiculous! I really am turning into a blood-thirsty little savage. . . .

But her mind played truant. As she prepared for a bath, the walk-over-the-heather fantasy returned, this time with her hand in that of Sean McDougal.

The reverie lasted for quite some time before she came back to reality and sternly banished it. . . .

30.

Borland Nickelawn, at home in Maidstone, sent his mind seeking its most pleasurable level; the sadoerotic realms where he found life's greatest joys.

Lazing on a crimson satin chaise longue, he gripped, in fancy, a viciously lead-studded whip,

and lashed it sharply down upon the smooth buttocks of a naked nymph who lay helpless in imag-
inary chains. The whip brought a scream from
his lovely victim and left a satisfactory welt
across her smooth skin.

Please—oh, please! she begged as he chose the
words and put them into her mouth.

Again the whip lashed down.

*Have mercy! Pity me! I will serve you as a
slave. Anything! Anything!*

The erotic fantasy went on with the girl finally
unchained, crawling across the room to where he
sat waiting, her fevered tongue doing frantic
penance for the sins he had conjured from imagination and laid upon her soul.

But with the fantasy not yet completed, he
scowled, swept the ghost-nymph back into oblivion, and sprang up from the lounge. It was no
good. Boring. His jaded senses had come to need
more; the reality, not the pale images of his con-
juring. His carnal appetite hungered for substan-
tial food.

But even that had disappointed him in the past
and he well knew the reason. The true victims of
his assaults lacked the innocence needed to make
his gratification complete. There were whores and
jades quite willing to suffer his cruelties for pay,
but they no longer brought him the erection and
the wild savage pleasure which should have
resulted from his sadism. However, there had
been one fortunate aspect of using such women.
The one who had not survived would have caused
him trouble had she not been friendless and
alone. As it was he disposed of her body to a

ghoul who served medical colleges and that was the end of the matter.

And now the progressive rot within him demanded the ultimate innocence it craved, and with a new victim suddenly in mind, he dressed, unstabled a mount, and headed north at a gallop. . . .

Nickelawn, wealthy well beyond his needs, was in essence a law unto himself, because of the customs of the time and his skill with the blade. Men feared him, and with good cause. As a duelist never defeated, he used his "honor" as a device to eliminate any who stood in his way, arrogantly sure of victory on the dueling turf. Thus he was treated with great courtesy at all times because it could mean death to treat him otherwise. That clod Henry Squire learned this truth in short order after the insult at Meg Wahl's picnic, but Nickelawn recalled that incident sourly, with no great feeling of satisfaction, because killing Squire had been no more difficult than sticking a pig. Why, he wondered, did men with no defensive skills allow their tempers to send them to their deaths? Others had done so in the past and there would be more in the future. . . .

Nickelawn arrived at Camber after an hour's hard ride. Meg Wahl, watching through a window in the manor house, saw him dismount, turn his horse, staggering from fatigue, over to the hostler, and come in her direction. She did not go forth to meet him. In that, at least, he could find no insult, nor in the fact that she heartily despised him. Still, he could not be barred by any hostess who valued the life of her husband. Nickelawn had been known to exact vengeance for such slights by forcing insults and thus exacting payment.

The butler announced Nickelawn and Meg received him in her sitting room.

"Borland! What a nice surprise!" she said graciously.

Nickelawn gallantly kissed Meg's hand. "The pleasure is mine," he murmured. "You know you are my favorite hostess."

"How sweet of you to say so. What refreshment would you like?"

"None, dear lady. I am in quite a hurry. I just stopped off to make some inquiries—one of your guests at the picnic the other day."

"Anything I can tell you. . . ." Meg knew instinctively why he had come.

"That little minx, Charity Sturges. She attracts me. Is it true she is half-savage?"

"No. That is only a vicious rumor. But there are other things about Charity that you should know."

"I am all eagerness to be informed, dear lady," he said, bowing again.

Speaking with a boldness which surprised her, Meg said, "The girl is not for you, Borland." Then, even in the face of his sudden iciness, she went on. "Her sponsor is Christopher Leach, therefore she comes under powerful protection."

"You refer of course to your brother, Clement Leach, also Christopher's brother, the darling of Canterbury and the liberal politicians."

"Clement does have much power, and word has

217

it that the Prime Minister, Lord North himself, has taken an interest in Christopher."

"True, but you refer to 'protection' as though I planned to destroy the girl. That hurts me, dear lady."

"I did not mean it in that sense," Meg said hastily. "I only bring the point up to show you how difficult it would be to gain Charity's favor. I am not sure, but I think it possible that she is affianced to Christopher."

Nickelawn allowed his contempt to show. "Ridiculous! Clement allow his brother to wed a colonial savage? Impossible!"

"I only stated what I suspect."

Nickelawn smiled, dropped the subject, and complimented Meg on her picnic. Neither made reference to the Squire tragedy which had evolved from it, and soon Nickelawn arose and took his leave. Tactfully, he had not spoken of Meg's past adventure at his hands.

Meg watched his departure, wishing sincerely that he would go back to his London haunts, quit Maidstone and his country sojourn, and leave the local gentry alone. Already it had cost one life.

But more prevalent was her fear for Charity, that aspect pointing up the fact of her affection for the vivid little colonial. She knew of course that she liked Charity, but fear for her safety made Meg now realize how strong that affection was.

At the very least, Charity had to be warned....

Thus it was, later that afternoon, that Meg sat with Charity under the oak on the Windward lawn and said, "Sweeting, all I seem to bring you is bad news."

Charity smiled warmly and seized Meg's hand. "Darling, it is so nice to see you that whatever news brings you is good."

"Hardly." Meg shook her head in a mild show of despair. "I fear that when I am through giving you warnings you will feel all my friends are roue's and scoundrels.

"I am sure not."

"But I must tell you to have a care with Borland Nickelawn."

"Borland—oh, yes. The gentleman who separated Gaby and me during our disgusting fight. I believe he did it with his foot."

"Quite true, and that pretty well tells you what he is. Thoroughly despicable. I wish I could bar him from my social affairs."

Charity wondered why Meg could not do so if she chose, but did not press the point. "I accept your description of the man, but why should I fear him? Is he going to challenge me to a duel?"

"Hardly that, but he is showing an interest in you. He came to Camber today for the sole purpose of making inquiries."

"I hope you told him that I carry a tomahawk in my skirt and if a man displeases me I aim lower than the wig."

"I am serious, Charity. He wants you in bed. And bed with Borland Nickelawn is a horrible place. He is a sadist of the worst sort. There is a rumor that he actually killed a woman upon whom he was practicing his methods of torture."

"How terrible! Why has he not been arrested?"

219

"The rumor may not be true, but he *is* brutal to his women, beyond all doubt."

"Meg, dearest! You sound as though you expected me to go running into his arms. Of course, you know differently, so you must expect him to abduct me and. . . ."

"Oh, no. Nothing so crude. But the man is not quite sane. I am sure of that. And once he puts his mind to having you. . . ."

"Oh, sweet! I am in no danger. But your worry on that score touches me deeply. I am perfectly safe, so let us drop the odious subject of Nickelawn and speak of pleasanter things. How would you like to see my new wardrobe? Please come. I would value your opinion."

"You flatter me, darling."

They went to Charity's chambers where Meg was soon enthusing over the selections Charity had made in London. "Darling, this blue tulle is divine!"

"But so bulky," Charity pouted. "Meg, I just cannot get used to having myself bundled up the way women dress here in England—or in the colonial towns, for that matter. I have just about worn this yellow frock into a rag because it is the simplest thing I own."

Meg was sorting through the rack. "What are these, Charity?"

"Oh, two trouser suits I bought in London, although I have not had the courage to wear them." She looked wistfully at them.

Meg took down the brown outfit. "So daring!"

"Yes. I understand the style is catching on in London."

"I think it's wonderful! Men's clothing *would* allow so much more freedom." Meg threw her a conspiratorial smile. "Charity, I'll go to London and buy a suit like this one. Then, if you have the nerve, we will appear in public together—lend each other courage, so to speak."

"A beautiful idea, but do you know why I hesitate?"

"I cannot even guess."

"Your brother Clement. Christopher told me about him. He is so proper and—well, a little frightening. If he heard I was dressing like a man . . ."

"Fie on Clement! *I* have always lived my own life."

"You honestly like the suits?"

"I love them."

"Then one of them is yours. I have no use for two of them. I think perhaps that was why I purchased both," she laughed, "in the hope of finding someone to share the shame with me."

"I'll be delighted to share it." Meg's eyes danced. "May I try it on?"

"Do what you like with it. The suit is yours."

Charity helped her friend into the brown suit and when Meg looked into the mirror she clapped her hands like a gay child in her first party gown.

"Why, it makes me a different person!"

"You look marvelous. It fits you so perfectly. I didn't realize we were so alike physically."

"Charity—I'm going to wear it home! Durban will be surprised out of his breeches."

"Sweeting, you look like a London dandy. The ladies will swoon over you!"

221

"I shall give a party very soon. When the two of us appear together the word will get to London."

"It will be a scandal," Charity laughed, banishing any fear of Clement from her mind.

"Charity, we may start a movement. If other women would follow. . . ."

"They will, when they understand the freedom of men's clothing. Meg, have you ever ridden astride a horse?" Meg had, of course, arrived at Windward Moors in a sedate side-saddle. "When Carton showed me a lady's saddle down at the stables it actually frightened me—riding with both legs on one side of a mount. How on earth do you manage it?"

"One does get used to it, but. . . ." Meg seized her newfound friend's hands in her own. "Oh, Charity, I am so grateful to you. I am so happy that you've come to us. It is going to be such great fun." A little embarrassed at her emotional outburst, she added, "You see, I never had a real friend before."

They were in each other's arms. A wonderful warm moment. Then Meg drew back. "I *must* be getting hone, darling. It will soon be dusk."

"Of course. But let me order a carriage for you. Then tomorrow I'll ride your horse back to Camber. . . ."

"No, darling. I can't wait to shock Durban. If you will lend me an appropriate saddle. . . ."

"Certainly, if you wish. We'll go down to the stables and change your mare."

Carton was not about, which pleased Charity.

It had come to a point where she dreaded to look upon the man's face let alone speak with him.

The saddles were changed and Charity held the reins while Meg mounted and sat triumphantly astride her mare.

Charity suddenly felt some trepidation. "Are you sure you can manage it? After all, riding astride is not the same as you have been used to."

"Of course I can."

"Suppose I saddle a horse and ride with you?"

Meg laughed. "But sweeting, then I'd have to ride back with you and we might keep it up all night. Be not nervous about me. I'll go by the shore cut-off. It is shorter than the road and I'll be home in no time."

"Very well, but be careful," Charity said doubtfully.

"I shall. And you must come to me tomorrow...."

"For tea?"

"I'll be waiting...."

As Meg rode off into the dusk, Charity recalled scraps of their conversation.

Durban will be surprised out of his breeches.

I can't wait to shock Durban.

How strange. No reference to Dennis. Could it be that a servant, the unsmiling coachman Charity had seen in Meg's attendance, was more important to her than her own husband? There were Meg's casual references to Durban with no previous explanation. Mayhap that tended to prove Meg's complete confidence in her new friend. Secrets would be imparted later.

This was disturbing. Meg would have the right

223

to expect confidences in return and even though she had accepted that Gaby Kirth was Dennis' mistress, Charity would have difficulty in revealing her own dalliance in the cottage by the cliff.

She sighed as she walked slowly back to the house. How swiftly changes were coming about. And how mistaken she had been in expecting boredom to set in at Leach House. Each day brought new surprises with promise of more to come....

Coincidentally, as she rode through the dusk, Meg was thinking along the same lines, how her life had changed with the coming of Charity. Well, not exactly her life but she herself. Charity had proved to be such a potent force; like a sweep of fresh air blowing in off the sea. Her very presence on the scene, the proximity of her lovely young spirit, had washed some of the cynicism out of Meg's soul. There was no doubt in her mind that they would cling together and provide mutual support in what was to come. Knowing Clement as she did, Meg knew that Charity would face difficulties. But now she would have an ally and Clement might well find them a formidable pair.

Dusk deepened as the mare loped easily along the route she knew so well, Meg hardly noticing the progress. Then, at a point where the bridle path skirted close to the cliff just by the Channel Light boundary, Meg became aware of a presence.

It had approached silently in the near-darkness

of lowering night, moving softly across the thickly sodded heather.

But now there was a rush of pounding hooves, the snort of a charger, the thud of equine weight against the shoulder of her mare.

Then Meg was in open space, thrown free of her mount—falling—falling—falling. . . .

There was a high keening sound—a threadlike scream from the terrorized mare as she fell with Meg toward death on the rocks below.

31.

Durban waited patiently for Meg's return. He had been unhappy with her decision not to use the carriage for her visit to Windward Moors. And when she elected to ride alone, leaving him at Camber, he was even more disturbed. He had learned to accept her absences when she went foraging in Maidstone or London, but at home he had always remained close to her. Thus, he felt cheated.

Durban's acceptance of his restricted role in Meg's life was difficult to explain. No doubt this sprang basically from a hereditary respect for the insurmountable barriers of class. Born and raised in Barstow, a small village in the coal fields of Denhigh, Durban had entered the mines as a child of eight in order to help his widowed mother support his grandfather, long crippled into a wheelchair. An introverted, highly sensitive child, Durban should have been born of other parents in another place. His blind yearning for something of beauty made that shabby land little more than a prison. A gentle person in all respects, he was still of enduring fiber. The years crept by. His grandfather died, followed in time by the mother he adored. There was added tragedy there in the fact that he was never able to express or reveal his love for her. It remained bottled up within him.

A change took place upon his mother's death. He said goodbye to her in Barstow's shabby cemetery and then walked away from the town and the begrimed land without a backward glance. He avoided the urban areas as he plodded on, drawn by the cleaner air and the rustic beauty he had never known.

But the change was in direction only. Essentially, he remained as he had always been, an introvert, a loner, his exterior by no means a mere facade; rather, an impenetrable wall imprisoning the true man inside. Thus he arrived on the Channel coast in his mid-twenties—part man but still part child, no doubt unconsciously searching for someone upon whom to lavish the love he had silently bestowed upon his mother.

He came to Camber and was put to work on the grounds. Then he saw Meg Wahl and thought she was the most beautiful thing he had ever seen; far above him in class, of course, but he would have been content to worship her from across the

226

barrier. It worked out otherwise. Meg, for her part, probably saw nothing more than a fine physical specimen. But he arrived at the right time, when she was in the right mood, and he became her personal servant, allowed intimate association—up to a point.

Meg was not a cruel person by nature, and had she known of the yearning within Durban she might have taken him to her bed out of compassion. So he merely served her a useful purpose. She took what she wished of him, dealing always with the servant, not the man, and Durban was again entrapped, not by environment but by love; and time went on, coming finally to that night when he could wait no longer and went forth to find his goddess.

He backtracked, taking the cliffside route to Channel Light where he pounded upon the door of the dark manor house. This eventually roused the butler who came shuffling to the door in his nightshirt with a lamp in his hand.

He peered through the grated panel and demanded, "Who disturbs honest people at this time of night?"

"I seek my mistress, Margaret of Camber. She left home and did not return. Did she stop off here?"

"We have had no visitors all the day. Why would she be abroad at this time of night?"

"The late hour is what worries me. She left Camber in early afternoon and vowed to return before dark."

Before the butler could comment upon that,

Gaby Kirth called down from the stairs. "Who is there. What is wanted?"

"An inquiry concerning Mistress Margaret Wahl, milady," the butler informed her in less hostile tones.

Gaby came down to investigate. She carried a lamp and had hastily donned a wig in case the caller were someone of importance. Seeing the Camber servant, she did not bother to straighten it.

"Oh, Durban. It is you. You say Meg is missing?"

"Aye. As I told your butler, she left in early afternoon and has not returned."

"Where was she going?"

"To Windward Moors, as she told me."

"Then that is the place to seek her," Gaby replied crossly.

"Your pardon, milady, for disturbing you. I thought mayhap she might have come to you to stay the night."

"And if she had?"

"It is only that she told me she would return to Camber."

"I don't understand. Is Margaret accountable to you, a servant, for her movements?"

"Nay, milady. I am thinking only of her welfare."

"I think she is quite old enough to take care of herself. Now go your way, and cease these night disturbances."

"Very well, milady...."

On the way back to her chambers Gaby wondered about Meg. Was there any cause for

228

worry? Hardly. Her disappearance at this time could only be coincidence. No doubt Meg wallowed in bed somewhere with someone or other. Her whereabouts would come to light in the morning and she would probably not thank Durban for being so concerned. He could well be looking for a new situation come the light of day. . . .

Durban rode on to the stables at Windward Moors and routed Carton out. "My mistress, Margaret Wahl. I am seeking her. Did she come here?"

Carton pawed at his sleep-filled eyes and replied, "Aye. She visited at the manor."

"She is still there?" he asked anxiously.

"I don't know. I think not. Her mare is gone."

"Then you saw her leave?"

"I did not. I was busy elsewhere late in the day. When I returned, her mount was gone."

Durban had pushed on into the tackroom with no fear whatever of the surly Windward hostler. A lamp was still lit and Durban turned it up. A golden glitter reflected from the saddle rack and he strode over to investigate.

"This is milady's saddle. See? Her initials in gold on the cantle. Why is the saddle here and not her mare?"

Carton's scowl deepened. "I know not, but I warn you. Get out of this stable. Off these premises or you'll get a beating you will not forget!"

Charity did not know why she was so restless that night. Worry over Meg, perhaps? But she really had no reason. Meg was an accomplished horsewoman and knew the land thoroughly. But sleep eluded Charity and for that reason she was at the window when Durban rode up. The moon revealed the figures of horse and rider and then lamplight from the open door verified the arrival. Quickly, Charity slipped on a robe, hurried out, and was at the door of the tackroom when Carton made his threat. Both men turned.

Durban said, "Miss Charity. I apologize for my intrusion. . . ."

"That's quite all right, Durban. Is anything wrong?"

"I am quite worried about Mistress Margaret's safety and I came seeking her."

"She did not return to Camber?" she asked in amazement.

"Nay, and here I find her saddle but not her mare or my mistress."

"I can explain about the saddle, Durban. Come with me." She led him out of the tackroom, deliberately ignoring Carton.

As she and Durban walked together toward his mount, Charity said, "Meg left here just before sundown. She was using a gentleman's saddle. That is why hers is still in the tackroom. Meg is an excellent horsewoman, is she not?"

"That she is."

"Perhaps she stopped off at Channel Light on her way home."

"I inquired there. They have not seen her."

"Then somewhere else. She has other friends, I'm sure."

"Aye."

The man interested Charity. While he conducted himself like an ideal servant, he seemed somehow unsuited for the calling. She sensed that there was far more to Durban than stood revealed.

As he prepared to mount, Charity said, "You are most devoted to Meg. I am sure you have a very deep affection for her."

He turned his eyes away in embarrassment. For some reason, that annoyed Charity. She snapped, "Durban! For heaven's sake! You can be a human being in my presence. I am not one of your fine English ladies. I come from Virginia where people are equal and we pay no attention to class. I shall treat you as an equal and I hope you will treat me the same way."

"That is most gracious of you. I have heard that the Colonies give a man opportunities we do not have in England."

"Of course there is slavery over there but, in a way, that makes my point. Any man with the money to buy, can own a slave. Pedigrees count for nothing."

Why, Charity asked herself, was she being so informal? Was it an attempt to loosen Durban's tongue in order to pry through him into Meg's life? If so, it was a dishonorable thing to do.

As he searched for words, Charity said, "Durban, I am also concerned about your mistress. So if she does not return to Camber tonight, come to me tomorrow and we will search for her together."

"I am most grateful for your concern."

He mounted and rode away. Charity watched

until the night covered him. How very odd! Durban prowling the darkness when Meg's own husband apparently showed no concern.

As she walked toward the house, Charity truly shared the servant's concern. This *was* the first time Meg had ever forked a horse. But her animal had seemed gentle enough. Charity brushed the worry from her mind. There was no need of it. Meg was a person well able to take care of herself.

32.

Carton watched tensely from the darkened tackroom as Charity and Durban parted. He had come straight from fulfilling his agreement with Gaby Kirth—returned to the stable where he awaited an inquiry from the house as to Charity's absence. While waiting, he rehearsed the words and manner which would show him completely innocent of knowledge as to her whereabouts. Probably Mrs. Dylan would come and she would not be difficult to convince.

Then, the expected knock on his door, but by an unexpected visitor, asking about Margaret Wahl. Why the devil should he know anything about the Mistress of Camber? But then when Durban discovered her saddle in the tackroom—something Carton had overlooked—fear began crawling through Carton's veins; vague fear he quickly put down. There was no reason for it other than a natural apprehension; no reason at all to connect it with his having stalked and done away with his prey.

He berated himself for not checking the horses upon his return. But that would still have proved nothing but the fact that the Mistress of Camber had come visiting.

Then, when Charity appeared like a ghost in the doorway, Carton almost swallowed his tongue. God in heaven! Had she come to point a phantom finger and send him to the gallows? For a moment, Carton knew the taste of pure terror; until he saw that Charity was not a ghost. This brought a relief of sorts; time to puzzle things out.

The truth was now self-apparent. He had made a terrible mistake, and the mistake had been the colonial bitch's doing! Carton's victim in the dusky gloom cliffside had been wearing male clothing and was riding astride her horse. Physically, the two women looked alike—enough to be taken for one another in the lowering darkness. The error in identity was quite natural. It could have happened to anyone. God in heaven! That arrogant little tart from Virginia would be the death of him yet!

Carton downed a half-beaker of whiskey to steady his nerves and forced himself to think logically. The act was the thing, not the victim. So long as the act had gone undetected the situation remained as before. Of course, Charity Sturges would now be as safe as in church so far as he was concerned. A second death piled on the first was out of the question. That left him with the problem of Gabrielle Kirth; whether or not she would consider the contract fulfilled and pay him his fee. Like as not the murderous wench would do the opposite, leaving him no better off than before.

But then a hope dawned. Mayhap all was not lost. The body of his mistaken victim had not yet been discovered and along that wild coast it could remain undetected until a thorough search was undertaken. Therefore it behooved him to contact the mistress of Channel Light immediately, tell her the job had been done and demand his five hundred pounds. A second dollop of whiskey warmed his blood and told him the ploy was brilliant and that it would work. With this encouragement, he saddled a mount and rode off to the north. . . .

For the second time that night, Gaby Kirth's butler was awakened by a pounding on the front door. Grumping as before, he left his bed to peer out through the grating to demand, "Who may you be? What do you want?"

Carton called out, "I come seeking a visitor to Windward—one Charity Sturges. When she did not return from a ride on the moors our housekeeper became worried and sent me out searching."

Confusion was added to the butler's annoyance. What manner of business was this? Everyone disappearing and searchers expecting to find them all at Channel Light. And this one shouting

234

his lament in a voice loud enough to wake the dead.

"Be calm," the harassed butler suggested. "I am not deaf, you know."

Carton said, "My apologies," but his shouts did awaken the mistress of Channel Light as he'd planned, and brought her down from her chamber, as he'd hoped.

Gaby, sans wig this time, opened the door and when she saw Carton, she told the butler, "Return to your bed, Soames. I'll handle this." Then, alone with Carton, she demanded, "What are you doing here? Have you lost your wits?"

"Nay, Madam," Carton said in less of a roaring voice. "I have come to report a successful end to our arrangement."

Gaby was suspicious. "So soon?"

"The opportunity came. I took advantage of it."

"How?"

"Over a cliff on Windward Moors. At dusk this day. And you should agree that it is best I leave Kent on the instant."

"Were there witnesses to the accident?" Gaby whispered.

"None."

"Will the death soon be discovered?"

"There is little chance until a thorough search is made."

The idea of Carton leaving immediately appealed to Gaby. If there were any questions, the simultaneous disappearance of both the murdered woman and the Windward Moors hostler would be indicative.

235

"You are sure you will never be seen in these parts again?"

"I am no fool, Madam. Even though I could not be charged, I will not tempt fate."

"Very well, wait here."

Gaby had not really expected to pay the stipulated fee at all. With Carton enmeshed in the crime, he would have been in no position to complain about nonpayment. But as things stood, payment would be wise, she decided; money to get him off and away, his guilt confirmed by his flight.

She returned with the funds. "Now; you will leave? Tonight?"

"Before dawn, milady."

"Good. And never let me hear your name again."

As she returned to bed, Gaby recalled the earlier inquiry about Meg Wahl. This stirred a germ of uneasiness in her mind, but as there was no way to associate that with the night's dark deed, she dozed off with a clear conscience.

33.

Heartened by Charity's promise of cooperation, Durban came again to Windward Moors the following morning. He waited outside the great hall

236

and when Charity emerged she stated the obvious.

"Margaret has not returned."

"Nay. I waited the night."

"I presume her husband is out seeking her."

Durban shook his head in the negative. "The Master believes she is off on business of her own. She has been away before."

"But you do not agree."

"He may be right." But Durban's voice implied he did not think so.

"Let us hope he is."

Leading his mount, Durban went with Charity to the stable where a knock brought Carton, sleepy-eyed, to his door. Exhaustion produced by the activity of the previous hours had negated his promise to Gaby Kirth to leave those parts immediately.

Peering around the doorjamb as a concession to modesty, he demanded, "What's wanted?"

Charity said, "I need a mount, Carton. Is laziness another of your virtues?"

"A pox on your needs," Carton growled, and slammed the door.

Durban moved forward, his fists doubled, but Charity held him off. "Pay no mind," she said. "A dispute would not be worth the trouble."

Whereupon Durban saddled a mare and he and Charity were off across the moors.

Riding beside him, Charity said, "You told me that you thought your master might be right— that Margaret was attending to her own business."

"Aye. It could be."

"But you have no idea what that business is?"

"I have an idea. Sean McDougal's frigate is anchored in a cove off Leach House. Milady might be with him."

He spoke in such a quiet manner that Charity was slow in comprehending what he said. This was to her advantage, however, because it gave her time to adjust to the news and frame a quiet reply. "I see. Then Margaret and Sean McDougal are good friends?"

"Sean McDougal has many friends."

"Then his coming to Kent puts him in no danger?" Charity spoke calmly, the relief she felt not evident in her voice.

"There is no reason for danger."

"But he is a smuggler and a freebooter. A man against the law."

"He has done no smuggling for a long time and no one in all of Kent would testify against him. As a privateer he is wanted by France and Spain, but he has the blessing of England. He does not touch English ships—only those of the King's enemies."

"Is Holland an enemy of England?"

"I think not."

Charity did not pursue that aspect of the situation. She had enough to occupy her mind as it was. Then, without prodding, Durban continued.

"There is hostility between Sean McDougal and his cousins, Christopher Leach and the Most Reverend Clement Leach. So he does not affront them by coming boldly into their presence."

"He fears them?"

"Oh, no. Sean McDougal fears neither God or

devil. He simply does not wish to embarrass his cousins."

Although Charity had been hanging on to Durban's every word concerning Sean, she now backtracked.

"But Durban, if you suspect Margaret is with Sean, why do you not visit the ship and find out."

"That would be unseemly of a servant, Miss Charity. If she is with him, then all is right with her and it is not my place to follow after her."

"But if she is not . . .?"

"That is why I must search the moors."

Charity reined her mare up. "Durban, there is no point in our riding together and both of us covering the same area. We should separate and go in opposite directions."

"But Miss Charity, the moors are dangerous for one not used to them," the man protested.

"Durban, have no fear. I have ridden over rough country most of my life. I have coped with danger before."

"Very well, Miss Charity. If you insist."

"I'll cut over toward the cliffs and I'd suggest that you explore around the old mines. And let us hope," Charity added, "that we have no success."

With that, the two searchers went off in opposite directions. . . .

Carton was annoyed with himself at having overslept. He was as eager to get out of Kent and back to Ireland as was Gaby Kirth to see him go. As he dressed he made his plans. He would take the best of the Windward stallions and ride west. Before any investigation could be made he would reach an Atlantic port and sell the animal. Then he would cross to Ireland, avoid his old haunts, and lose himself in the fastnesses of the Emerald Isle. A man with a reasonable fortune could do well in that favored land.

He was taking a final look about his quarters, his mount saddled, when there was a sharp rap on his door. His guilt-charged nerves tightened on the instant. Then he took command and told himself nothing could be amiss.

"What is wanted?" he called out.

"A word with you, Carton."

Carton opened the door to John Sibley. He knew the man casually, the tenant farmer at Camber, but had had no dealings with him. Had he come with an accusation? Fearing this, Carton stayed wary, standing ready to strike out at the man if necessary.

But Sibley was hostile in neither word nor manner. He said, "I bring you a proposition, Carton. One which would be of good profit to you."

"I would not be interested," Carton replied.

"But how do you know that, man? You have not yet heard it."

"I have matters to attend to."

"You could give me the courtesy of a few moments. The decent thing to do."

"Very well. Let's have it," Carton said impatiently.

Sibley entered, closed the door, and sat down. "I come as a middleman, not the principal in this proposition, but with a generous offer of payment for a task of small risk and little effort."

"Little effort, you say, but there *is* risk."

"Yes, a small risk and a generous payment to make the risk worth taking."

"What is the payment?" Carton's greed overcame his caution.

"Three hundred pounds."

"And what task? To purloin the Crown jewels?"

"Hardly. Half down and half on completion."

"The task, man! Tell me and have done with it!"

"To act as drayman for no longer than the length of a day. You will take an empty cart to Lynch Mill Crossing. Do you know the location?"

"North of here. Inland from the coast. Hard by the West Hill Armory."

"Aye. A drive of some three hours, no more. There you will be met and your cart will be loaded with six coffins."

"Six coffins! Am I some sort of ghoul?"

"A device to lessen the risk," Sibley explained.

"What will the coffins contain?"

"That is not your concern. They will be well sealed."

"It sounds hare-brained and far from safe."

Sibley arose from his chair. He had already taken a sheaf of pound notes from his pocket. Carton watched as he put them back.

The farmer said, "Very well, Carton. If you are not interested, I've been wasting my time."

He had grasped the door knob before Carton said, "Not so fast. I have not refused. But I think the trick is worth more. Say four hundred?"

Sibley was not as agreeable as Gaby Kirth had been. He opened the door. "The fee is ample."

"Half down you said. The rest? . . ." Carton knew there had to be more to it.

"When you deliver the coffins to Gallant's Cove."

"That is on Windward property," he said in surprise.

"Aye. Time yourself so that you arrive after dark. A shore boat will be waiting and you will be paid the balance."

Carton was thinking swiftly. His greed tended to offset his fear of trouble. And after all, why should he rush away to Ireland? A day or two would make no difference and it would be a matter of life-long regret to leave those easy pounds behind.

"All right," he said. "I am your man."

Sibley delivered the half-payment, but with a warning. "Remember this, Carton. If you cross us up in any manner, it will go hard with you."

The thought had come to Carton's mind, but he'd rejected it. He did not care to have dangerous men on his trail during his retreat to the western coast. No need to cross Sibley, really. His luck was in and would carry him through.

He asked, "What day? Tomorrow? The next?"

"Thursday. Two days hence."

"As good as done," Carton said, pocketing the added revenue.

34.

Charity was as anguished as a reformed drunk-
ard confronted by an endless supply of rum.
When not directly faced by the temptation she'd
found it quite easy to chart her best course—
marriage to Christopher—and relegate Sean
McDougal to the realm of dreams.

But now he was back in her sphere, in the vi-
cinity of Windward Moors—reachable—and
again he filled her mind, potent with all the trap-
pings that made forbidden pleasures so attractive. He bloomed more than life-size in her mind,
the image haloed by a kind of savage splendor in
a glow of her own making.

The thought of Meg Wahl being with him ate
at her pride and jealousy even though she considered Meg her best friend. Best friends, she
now realized, could easily fall out when love was
at stake.

Love? She snapped that up indignantly. She
was *not* in love with the swashbuckling vagabond
who had boarded the *Hainaut*, casually raped her,
then went laughing on his way.

Therefore, as she angled toward the Windward
cliffs she did not think of Meg as the victim of an
accident, lying dead or injured; rather, she saw
her as a siren, luring Sean McDougal into her

arms. She reached the cliffs and rode northward, coming finally to a place where the heather thinned and there were hoofprints in profusion. A rendezvous had taken place at that spot hard by the overlip of the cliff. Sean and Meg meeting there on the moor?

Somewhere below, the *Evening Primrose* was moored in a cove. *Evening Primrose!* What an absurd name for a ship! And what an absurd ship, for that matter. Somewhere down there Sean would be in Meg's arms.

But mayhap not. Sean was not one to linger in his cabin after a long sea voyage. He would come boldly ashore.

Then it dawned.

The Moon Tower.

Of course! Boarded off from the rest of Windward Moors, it would be an ideal place for someone of Sean's arrogance to sit, high above them all, and laugh at the doughty Leaches.

Sean was in the Moon Tower!

Absolutely.

Well, perhaps not of a supreme certainty but it was clearly worth looking into.

The search for Meg pushed from her mind, Charity returned to the stables. She turned her mount over to Carton, her mind too full of other things to note the radical change in his attitude toward her. He actually smiled as he took the reins, as Charity hurried off toward the house.

She entered the great hall and went directly to the tapestry Dorothy had previously indicated, and sure enough, it hid the door to which she had referred—the outline easily seen by anyone informed of its existence in the gray stone wall.

Now a difficulty arose. There was no indentation, no knob or handle to grasp, but doors were made to be opened and Charity was determined. Long impatient minutes later, she found a small loose stone close to the floor at the perimeter of the stubborn rectangle. She pressed with all her strength and the panel responded to this *open sesame* and swung silently inward. Charity stepped through. The panel closed behind her.

She knew instantly that the tower was occupied; there was faint laughter from above as she peered skyward. Slits in the circular stonework just below the turret high above gave enough light to reveal a wrought iron staircase circling along the inner surface of the wall.

Charity began to climb, her ears straining for other sounds. With Meg's lovely face in her mind, she listened for sounds of passion, the moans of delight she had conjured up in her fancy and now strained to hear in reality. Meg in Sean McDougal's arms. The thought ate at her vitals.

She climbed.

To come finally to the floor of the turret and a trapdoor at the top of the stairway. It gave easily. She pushed it aside and lifted herself until she was half inside the turret room and half below it.

The circular space was partially filled with armament: muskets, pistols, bayonetted flintlocks scattered about. But Charity's attention was directed beyond—to the bed on the far side of the turret opposite the trap door, occupied by two naked bodies; a man and a woman. The pair raised their heads in unison.

Cloris, the chambermaid, remained blank of expression. The man, Sean McDougal, braced on one arm, was scowling in anger.

He demanded, "Who in the devil are you and what do you want?"

Charity froze, unable to move, unable to think. Then she was pelting back down the stairs at the risk of life and limb.

Back in her chambers, her cheeks still flaming, Charity sought to gather herself together. She paced the floor, then forced herself to sit down and quiet the pounding of her heart and the trembling of her whole being.

You have been a complete and utter fool, she told herself. *He did not even recognize you!*

That helped, making way for a less disjointed train of thought and the realization that she had only herself to blame for what had happened. She'd had no right to intrude on Sean McDougal nor question his actions in any way. However, it was painful to find that he had completely forgotten what had taken place on the *Hainaut.*

But mainly, she was dismayed at her own lack of control. This was a weakness in herself that she would not have believed until that moment. It had been of a different nature than the flare of rage brought on by Gaby Kirth's baiting at Meg's picnic. That had been justified. Anyone who did not stand up for his rights was a coward. But to erupt into a wild fit of jealousy without reason! Humiliating! It would never happen again.

But then Charity found some justification for

246

the anger, apart from jealousy. *She* was in charge at Windward Moors. *She* had been sent there by Christopher, so it followed that he expected her to protect the interests of the family if such protection were needed. So she had every right to resent Sean McDougal sneaking onto the Leach premises and corrupting the chambermaid while he laughed at his absent hosts. And all those guns—what were they for? Did he plan to withstand a seige if he were discovered?

Quite obviously, there was a conspiracy in Leach House that wanted looking into and with that in mind, Charity marched off to find Mrs. Dylan.

The housekeeper was drinking a cup of tea at the table in the kitchen. She came to her feet as Charity approached. Since the Dorothy episode, the housekeeper's attitude had become more that of a servant and less of a friend.

"Miss Charity," she said, "is something needed?"

"Yes. Some information, Mrs. Dylan. Sit down, please."

"Tea?"

"No, thank you."

Mrs. Dylan sat down and Charity took a chair opposite her. She spoke crisply. "I want to know all you can tell me about Sean McDougal."

"There is not a great deal. . . ."

"Oh, come now. I know he is staying in the Moon Tower. I saw him there."

"You spoke with him?"

"No. He was—he was occupied."

Mrs. Dylan's eyes narrowed questioningly.

"How did you know it was Sean? Have you two met before?"

"We—Mrs. Dylan, that is neither here nor there. I want to know what he is doing in the tower. And don't tell me you were not aware of his presence. I want no more lies."

"Miss Charity! I have not lied to you."

"No, you have not. I'm sorry I put it in those words. What I mean is that there will be no more secrecy in Leach House. Mrs. Dylan! I am not your enemy! I know you are a very good person doing the very best you can. There is no reason why you should not confide in me."

"But when the Master comes you will be obliged to tell him about Sean."

"I am not at all sure of that. It depends upon Sean's reason for being here; whether or not it is to show his contempt for Christopher and Clement."

"Quite the contrary. Sean is contemptuous of no one."

"He certainly knows of their low regard for him."

"That bothers him not a whit. It is just that the tower is convenient for him. Perhaps he does feel that he has a blood right to visit Leach House."

"He has no other place to go?"

"No, no! He would be welcome in any hut, cottage, or house for miles around. His presence would be considered an honor."

Charity shook her head. "I just don't understand! Christopher called him a felon. But most people *are* inclined to admire wild, reckless men."

248

"He is not only admired. He is loved. The men who go to sea with him to take the ships of England's enemies are all from Kent. They are a special class of men, Miss Charity, and he has shared with them—made them better able to take care of their wives and bairn. They are not the ruthless cutthroats who crew the pirate ships with their death's head banners and slaughterous ways." She paused, as though no words she could find would fit. "There is a magic in Sean."

"Then why are Christopher and Clement so against him? He must be breaking English laws."

"Oh, he does when he feels they are unjust. He smuggles without the least twinge of conscience."

"Smuggling can be a hanging offense, I understand."

"Aye, but the people of Kent would die on the scaffold themselves before they would speak out against him."

Another question occurred to Charity. "McDougal," she said, "is a Scotch name, is it not? And Sean is of English blood. Yet he is more like you in speech and manner. Irish."

"Gerold married an Irish colleen. She was as fair as ever breathed the pure air of Ireland. She was Sean's mother and he inherited from her only." Mrs. Dylan paused to dream for a moment. "I see her so clearly in Sean. It was as if she did not die; as though she became a part of him and lived on."

Charity had quite a different vision of the ubiquitous freebooter up in the tower with Cloris in his arms. But curiously, this did not greatly bother her now, and she had to admit, ruefully, that she had become class conscious. Thinking of Meg and Sean together had sent her into jealous spasms. But with Cloris, a housemaid. . . .

Charity rejected the thought and began forming a more practical image of Sean McDougal. He was a rank opportunist who rode roughshod over people too stupid to see through his Irish smile. He was a conceited mountebank who needed deflating, and she would enjoy the task. It would, in fact, be a pleasure to wipe that smile from his face.

She said, "Mrs. Dylan, when I looked in at the tower I saw a surprising number of guns up there. All shapes and sizes. What do you know about them?"

"Nothing, Miss Charity. Sean has not told me and I have not asked him. They were brought in through the tunnel."

"The tunnel?"

"Aye. There is a tunnel from one of the coves below the cliffs. It leads to the base of the tower. It was used in other days when war made coming and going dangerous."

"And it is still being used," Charity murmured.

"Sean and two of his men brought all those weapons to the tower shortly after he moored his ship."

"I wonder why?"

One thing was certain. His confidence was overweening. He was obviously sure that no one would reveal his presence in Leach House. He would soon learn, Charity decided grimly, that he was mistaken.

She considered telling Mrs. Dylan of Cloris'

fall from virtue, then decided against it. The housekeeper, completely under Sean McDougal's thrall, probably knew about it and bringing it up would only embarrass her. Then, too, if the girl wanted to become a tool for the gratification of Sean's carnal appetite, it was her own affair. Cloris was of age and perhaps the thrill of Sean's lovemaking would be sufficient reward for later disillusionment.

Charity said, "I think I shall now have that cup of tea you offered me, Mrs. Dylan."

35.

Charity returned to her quarters to think about Sean McDougal. She went back over her conversation with Mrs. Dylan; listening again to the confidences and explanations; this while planning to confront the man and demand some more satisfactory explanations of his outrageous conduct.

She considered returning to the tower for the confrontation, but decided that would not be wise. Heaven only knew how long he would wallow about on that lustful bed. And even though he had finished with Cloris, it would be better if Charity met him on neutral ground.

There was a diversion late in the afternoon when a messenger from the post brought a letter. It was from Christopher, his precise hand on the envelope indicating that it had been sent from London.

Charity felt a surge of elation. So her solitary watch at Leach House would soon be over! Christopher himself would come home and send Sean McDougal scurrying.

Her mind raced as she hurried to her chambers to read the missive in complete privacy. There were decisions to be made. How much of what she had learned should she tell Christopher? About Sean, of course, and he should certainly be informed as to the true character of Bruce Carton. But then again, should she warn Sean away in advance to prevent an unpleasant confrontation?

With no decision clearly made, Charity opened the letter and began to read:

Dearest Charity:

I am desolated by the circumstances which have forced me to remain away from you. Yet, in many ways, they are most fortuitous. I have had two audiences with the Prime Minister, and his evident high regard for my poor capabilities is most complimentary and gratifying indeed. He has given me the assignment of putting down my day-to-day, nay, minute-by-minute, contacts with certain prominent colonists whom I met while on my mission there. An exhaustively detailed dossier to be used when the malcontents are defeated and forced to accept the King's justice.

The Prime Minister also expressed his faith in my abilities by suggesting that there

252

are other areas of diplomatic endeavor in
which I may be of great value to him. This
unexpected development augers well for us
as it possibly opens doors hitherto tightly
closed. How long I am to remain in London, I
do not know but in any event I will be com-
ing soon to Windward to confer with brother
Clement. Until that time, dearest Charity,
keep me in your memory and in your heart.

Most devotedly,
Your obedient servant,
Christopher Leach.

Charity went through the letter three times,
searching for subtle meanings.

... which forces me to remain away from you.

That, she decided, was certainly an expression
of love and longing. Christopher missed her and
wanted to be by her side.

She was proud of the recognition he had received since arriving back in London even if it
meant that they must remain apart for a while
longer. With the Prime Minister himself as a
sponsor there was no limit to the heights he could
climb—the heights they could climb together.

The latter part of the letter was somewhat disappointing. Christopher would come to Windward
Moors in due time to confer with Clement. That
seemed to imply that seeing her would be inciden-
tal to the prime reason.

She became annoyed with herself. Analyzing a
letter word for word, phrase by phrase, was a
lovelorn maid's pastime. Charity was beyond that
stage, a practical person aware of true values.

Then too, the final lines really made up for the rest and cancelled all doubts.

. . . *dearest Charity, keep me in your memory and in your heart.*

Those were the words of a man in love!

Charity was swept with a sudden wave of relief. Coming unbidden, it confused her and sent her searching for a reason. Because Christopher was not coming home? Ridiculous! Because she feared she had not handled things properly at Leach House and he would be disappointed in her?

She was not called upon to struggle with that. The arrival of the letter was followed by a visit from Dennis Wahl.

This time Dennis did not come as a lover. His mien was deadly serious and Charity could see from his appearance that he had not slept.

He said, "Meg has not been seen or heard of since she rode away to visit you, Charity. I think I must face the truth—something has happened to her."

"Oh, Dennis! You must be wrong. Meg is an able person. She rode well. There would be no reason for an accident."

"Accidents happen without reason. Tell me, was she in good spirits when she left Windward that evening?"

"Excellent. I offered to ride back with her but she refused."

"I am gathering a search party. We will comb the country around."

"Durban and I went over the moors very thoroughly. At least Durban did." Charity waited to

254

see what response Dennis would make to mention of the servant's name. There was none. Obviously the man was too concerned to harbor petty jealousies. Nor did he wince at the suggestion that Durban had been more concerned than he. None of that mattered anymore.

Charity asked, "Where will you begin your search?"

"The cliffs."

"What about that horrible swamp along the road?"

"There is no point in searching there. If she got into the bog all God's angels would never find her. Besides, when she rides she never takes the outer road. She uses the cliff paths."

Charity said, "Dennis . . ." then hesitated.

"Was there something?"

"Yes. Sean McDougal is here. His ship is moored in some cove below the cliffs. Perhaps . . ." Again she fumbled. "I understand that Sean and Meg were friends."

"She is not with him," Dennis growled. "I have already talked to him. He knows nothing of her whereabouts."

Charity laid a hand on his. "Dennis, I am sure it will all work out. As I said . . ."

He cut her off. "The reason I came was to ask you if you could tell me anything that might help, you being the last person to see her."

"I wish to heaven there were."

"Thank you. I'll be off now. The search will begin immediately."

They had talked on the ramp outside the castle and Charity watched as he mounted his stallion and thundered off toward the moors in the direction of Camber.

So Dennis knew of Sean McDougal's presence at Windward Moors. It seemed that everybody had known but the stranger from Virginia who could not be trusted!

Charity moved toward the front door, then turned decisively and walked off toward the cliffs. It was a twenty-minute hike through the lush, purple heather and when she arrived at the high, vertical embankments a sense of great loneliness fell upon her. Below, a line of white froth washed at the narrow beach beyond the rocks hard by the cliff. There was a sadness in the murmur of the surf and the whispering of the heather in the wind, and a corresponding mood of depression settled over Charity. Was Meg's broken body somewhere down there on those rocks? It was hard to visualize. She had been so vitally alive; so warm; such a wonderful new-found friend.

Charity went back over her tenure at Windward Moors, and as she looked out across the channel, the whole swift transition from Virginia seemed mad, unreal. Such a short time and yet the cabin off Ironbound Road was now so far away in both distance and in the immediacy of her mind.

As she meditated it came to her finally that she was forcing those images in order to deny that which drew her mind and her thoughts. Somewhere down there in a hidden cove was a black frigate; also a tunnel mouth through which Sean McDougal gained entrance to Leach House and the Moon Tower. She could see no path down the face of the cliff. Had she found one, Charity would have been sorely tempted to go down and search.

To satisfy my curiosity, she told herself even as she knew that was a lie. It would be to find Sean McDougal. A man who did not want her, who did not even remember her.

Cheap! Shallow! Weak!

Those spontaneous accusations against herself brought her sharply out of her mood of self-pity. Ridiculous! What was she doing there on the cliffs in the first place?

Quite herself again, she turned back toward Leach House. She walked briskly, drawing in deep breaths of the keen salt air. Life *was* good! Fortune had smiled on her. The future held great promise. As Christopher's wife she would be respected and would move in circles even now beyond her imagination.

Thinking along those lines, she had lifted herself high—by her mental bootstraps, so to speak—by the time she was again in her chambers.

Entering her bedroom, she froze—to stare at the canopied bed.

A freshly plucked evening primrose lay on her pillow.

Then from a chair by the corner table there came a soft, musical voice.

"I have come to apologize to my sweet colleen. . ."

36.

At that very moment, Bruce Carton, in a fit of anger, was slamming his fist against the wall in his stable living quarters.

Damn it to all hell! That snooper had been back!

Carton had been off in the village and returned to find clear signs of intrusion. Two of the stable doors were ajar after he had left them closed. The horses were nervous, and now in his quarters, he found things moved; the drawer to his chest half-open.

It was as though his tormenter had left deliberate marks of intrusion into places where he had no business. What did it mean?

He would question Mrs. Dylan as to whether anyone had been seen sneaking about the stables. He doubted if she would have noticed, however. The blackleg had certainly come on a mount, so Carton went outside and checked about for suggestive prints. He expected little success and found less. Then an approaching horseman made him forget his quest.

John Sibley pulled up and dismounted. Carton said, "Sibley—I've been expecting you," substituting that for the mere hope that the smuggler would visit him again.

Sibley entered Carton's quarters without being invited and closed the door after Carton followed him.

"The little chore I did for you," Carton asked. "It was satisfactory?"

"It worked out well. Would you like to accommodate us again?"

"I might consider it—for a more respectable payment."

"For less. You were overpaid the first time. We are not made of money."

"Ho! What sort of a mark do you think I am? Risking my safety for paltry sums."

"Two hundred pounds is quite enough for less than a day's effort."

"If that is your belief, you'd better seek elsewhere."

"Very well. As a matter of fact, our confidence in you is not the greatest." With that, Sibley turned decisively toward the door. Carton followed him.

"That is deceitful talk! You know well that you come to me rather than using one of your own men because moving the goods across to the channel is the most dangerous part of it. And now you offer me a third less."

"Think as you will, there are still plenty of men who would be happy to earn two hundred pounds, whatever the danger."

"There is something else to think about," Carton said. "If you treat me badly I might just speak with the constable. There would be a reward for turning up your operation."

"I am sure there would be, but what makes you think you would live long enough to collect it?"

The cold light in Sibley's eyes made Carton regret his threat. "Man, you know I would not really do a thing like that. But you cannot blame me for trying to get a fair price."

"A dangerous way to do it, Carton. Even as I ride away you could be doomed for such words."

"Forget I said them," Carton said quickly. "To prove my good will I shall take your offer. When must I go?"

"Tomorrow, the same hours as before. Do you remember them?"

"Of course I remember them."

"Then we have an agreement."

After giving Carton his advance payment, Sibley rode away, leaving the hostler of two minds. He was happy to get paid good money for what had proved to be easy work. But then Sibley did not have to openly show his contempt while making the deal. Sibley, a smuggler himself, had no right to look down upon others.

However, on balance, Carton was satisfied. He thought of Gaby Kirth and grinned to himself at the discomfort he saw as being her lot. He sensed the confusion, even the fear she must be experiencing. With Margaret Wahl missing and the new tart still very much on the scene, Lady Kirth would not know what to think. What had transpired should be a lesson to her, he thought. It would teach her not to deal contemptuously with those she looked down upon. And if she expected him to complete the commission she was stupid indeed. Doing away with Charity Sturges in whatever manner, as things now stood, would be the rankest kind of folly. He was now a darling of good fortune with a profitable enterprise laid on his doorsteps; one which should continue for a time with enough return to set him up in Ireland as a true country gentleman. Two carloads of goods came far short of loading a sea-going frigate. There should be many more. Then too, when the ship was finally at sea, a word to the constable might still be a sensible risk. If he decided to peach, Sibley would find him a hard man to kill.

All in all, Carton was satisfied....

He was right in his thoughts on Gaby Kirth's state of mind. With that insufferable colonial bitch still on her two legs and hope vanishing for Meg Wahl's safety, Gaby could not doubt that something had gone wrong. The timing of Meg's disappearance could not be swallowed as a coincidence. That buffoon Carton had blundered. But how? How could he possibly have destroyed one in place of the other? Could it have been possible that his mental capacity was so limited that he put the wrong name to the target of her wrath? As things stood, it did seem a possibility. Her regret at trusting Carton with so delicate a task was now monumental. How could she have been so stupid when there were others of higher mentality to whom she could have appealed? Borland Nickelawn, for instance. That deadly dandy would probably have accepted the assignment as a lark and executed it with smooth dispatch. And so sincerely did Gaby wish Charity out of the way that she would have gladly paid with a session in Nickelawn's rooms under his whips.

She did not dare contact Carton for an explanation. With the alarm out for Meg Wahl and all eyes watching, a visit to the Windward stables would be pure folly.

Gaby could only wait, evince her concern over the fate of poor Meg, and hope for the best. . . .

37.

Charity's anger at seeing Sean McDougal lolling casually in her bedroom chair was not a spontaneous outburst; rather it was a sanctuary into which she retreated; a curtain behind which she hid as though he were able to look into her mind and see how completely he had occupied it.

"What are you doing here?" she demanded. "Is it your custom to come uninvited into bedroom both at sea and on land?"

He smiled gently. "Then you do remember. I thought our previous meeting had been forgotten as just another interlude in your busy life."

"You are insufferable! Get out this instant!"

He arose from the chair and for a moment Charity feared that he might obey her. But then he sauntered toward the bed, picked up the evening primrose, and eyed it pensively.

"You did not appreciate my small peace offering."

"There is a whole planting of them out on the lawn. Besides, I don't know what you mean by peace offering. I was not aware that we were at war."

"I thought mayhap you were angry at me for bestowing a few happy moments upon a lonely chambermaid," he said mildly.

"Then you did recognize me!"

Charity could have bitten off her tongue the instant the words were out of her mouth. This clever cad had tricked her into admitting a concern she would not have revealed under torture.

He said, "This is my apology, sweet one. You caught me unawares. I had been busy and my attentions were elsewhere."

"I don't care where your attentions were, so don't misunderstand me. Your actions are of no concern to me!"

"Then why are you so angry?" he asked with the maddening gentleness that grated on her. It was almost as though *he* were forgiving *her* rather than seeking her pardon.

"I do have a concern," Charity said. "I want to know why you are hiding in that tower where you have no right to be."

"But I do not hide, my love. . . ."

"Don't call me your love!" she said furiously.

"I do not hide," he repeated. "it is a convenient place for me to await my next sailing."

"You will leave soon?"

"In time. Does that distress you?"

"Why should it?"

"I had dared hope you would shed a loving tear at the loss of me."

Was he baiting her? Charity could not decide. There was a different atmosphere in Leach House than in her cabin on the *Hainaut*. Nor was Sean McDougal the same dashing adventurer she remembered. He was now clad as the veriest peasant farmer. Heavy clog shoes below loose shapeless ankle-length trousers. A red shirt and a washworn unbuttoned weskit completed his garb. Still, the aura of the laughing freebooter gleamed through. The magic to which Mrs. Dylan referred? The thought came even as Charity rejected it.

She had unconsciously dropped to the edge of the platform upon which the bed rested, her legs tucked sideways on the narrow perch. Sean came forward, folded himself gracefully down before her and looked pensively into her face. He still held the evening primrose and now he reached out and placed it gently in her hair.

He murmured, "Your beauty shames this little blossom."

"Will you stop such silly talk and be sensible? I would like some sane answers to some sane questions."

"Your adoring servant, sweet one. Ask on."

"All those weapons in the turret. What are they for? Why have you brought them here?"

"They are samples of my next cargo," he answered without hesitating.

"You are transporting armament?"

264

"That I am. And I must have a care that what I take on is of the best quality."

He had a disconcerting way of replying to her queries: giving direct, simple answers while the bulk of his attention remained upon her face—studying her pensively as though wishing to imbed the very arrangement of her pores into his memory.

Charity tried desperately to disregard the fact that her blood was racing even as she feared he would hear the pounding of her heart.

"Where are you taking them?" she asked.

"To the Colonies, where they will be put to good use."

"And of course you are richly paid for your treason."

"Paid? Only the cost of the wares. Treason? You yourself come from those lovely green shores. Why do you call it treason?"

"Why shouldn't I? I am now in England, a loyal subject of His Majesty."

"Then you believe that George's tyranny is a God-given right?"

"I—I believe in the established order of things," Charity replied, the words coming out for want of better ones, with no great meaning behind them.

His reply was quietly understated, as though his mind remained with his eyes—on her face. "George is a royal buffoon. The angels would laugh at him were he not so pathetic in his stupidity. His throne is not God-given. God turns from His lesser creations to enjoy His masterpieces of beauty. The earth, the seas, the valleys and mountains, the rising of the sun and its glorious settings."

Charity did not want to listen to words which would have outraged Christopher. Still, she could not champion his cause nor draw back from Sean McDougal. She did not *want* to draw back from Sean. A grotesque thought wormed its way into her conscious mind even as she cringed from it. What if Sean suddenly arose and left her chambers?

With a violent wrenching of her mind, she changed directions. Aware of what would take place—what she *wanted* to transpire—she told herself how it would be.

I will not come whimpering into surrender. It will be my way, on my terms.

That had been so simple with Dennis Wahl. So why not with Sean?

They arose together and she reached forth to slip his weskit from his shoulders. Speaking with a forced calm, she said, "We are wasting time, are we not?"

"Then you do remember."

"Did you expect me to forget?"

Soon, she was in bed, her naked body pressed close to his; the heady opiate of his presence saturating her being. This was different from the battle with Dennis Wahl at the cliff hut. Charity wanted to attack, but she could not. She could only wait, knowing the attack, mutually mounted, would come in due time. At the moment there was triumph of sorts for her in Sean's manner. This was not an unfeeling, unemotional rape, as it had been before. He was subdued, curiously

266

thoughtful in his approach—as though there was
something he did not quite understand, something
new in his experience that gave him pause on the
threshold of passion.

His whispered plea, "Love me, my darling,"
brought her a fierce happiness. He had made the
plea before, on the *Hainaut*. But this time the
tone was different. There was a substance in his
manner which had not been there before.

Then, as though through mutual knowledge of
each other, the violence of complete and ecstatic
love left all else in abeyance. While just as car-
nally fierce, it was more satisfying to Charity because it was not a ruthless wrenching of pleasure,
each from the body of the other. Each eager to
give as well as recieve, their mouths searching
shamelessly. Charity hunted for the most sensitive
nerve ends of her lover's manhood while he in a
sense put her naked loveliness on an altar and
worshipped it in pagan abandon until she could
hardly keep from screaming. Then, when he
mounted her and she joyously opened to him, it
was as though she were receiving a special gift
from gods who were not offended by animal de-
lights. . . .

Finally, Charity lay exhausted in Sean's arms
and there was silence for a time. When he spoke
again, he was more the gay freebooter she had
known.

He said, "There are islands in the south seas,
my bonny darling, that would break your heart.
Warm beaches, waving palms, sunsets to drench
you with glory. Happy children of innocence

wearing only what God gave them, a delight to His eye, the comfort of His heart."

"Sean, you speak of God while you seem to flout your Christian heritage. How is that when you have Clement as an example?"

Sean laughed. "I am most religious, my darling. It is just that old ones misread the ancient precepts. They tell us that God was angry and hurled Adam and Eve out of Eden. Not true."

"Are you telling me He allowed them to stay?"

"He understood and forgave them, and all their trouble since has been their own doing. In a short time through guilt and greed and all manner of mistakes, they made Eden look like a place into which exiles would be packed off. That was the old theologians' great mistake. They could not imagine how so few could vandalize so much so quickly, so they called it the land of Nod, I believe, and said Eden was forever closed to mankind."

Charity laughed. "You are mad! Absolutely mad! You are saying that we are in Eden right now."

"And a beautiful place it is for those who open their eyes." He stopped for a quick kiss before going on. "That is what I shall do for you, my loved one. I shall open your eyes. After delivering the arms to the Colonies, we will round Cape Horn and live out our days in tropical splendor."

Charity ran idle fingers through his hair. "We will do no such thing, lover. I shall remain where I am and lead a proper life among proper people." Charity had never felt so competent, so complete. Delightfully sated, her physical passion drained away like champagne running out of a crystal bowl, she was in total command of herself—and to a great extent of Sean McDougal. She was beginning to understand the magic of which Mrs. Dylan had spoken. Sean was a classic combination of the dreamer and the doer. His charm reached into others to find and color their fantasies with rainbow shades. And though he had grown into a man of fearless action, he still retained the heart of a child.

Her disclaimer did not bother him in the least. He used a fingertip to toy with a still-distended nipple and said, "You are naturally timid, my love. The joys of which I tell you are frightening in their beauty. But you will change."

Then, before she could straighten him out on that matter, he looked at her with sudden distaste and said, "Charity—Charity. It has too pious a sound. We will change it." He pondered for a few moments before a smile lit his face.

"Mavourneen! Yes! I have it! Mavourneen! There is music in the name and it fits you. Say it!"

"Mavourneen." Charity tasted it in her mind like an unfamiliar morsel on the tip of her tongue.

"No, no! Not as though you were grating turnips! Allow the sound to roll from your throat as though it were falling off velvet."

Charity laughed. "Sean! Stop this nonsense! My name is Charity and it will remain so."

"No. It is changed. Charity is laid away in the oblivion she deserves. Mavourneen now rises out of the sea, as beautiful as the blue waters that gave her birth."

"With a sea shell to ride on, no doubt."

"On the wings of morning." He bounced up off the bed. "I must go. I have many tasks and the colonials watch the horizon for my arrival."

Charity watched him dress and it occurred to her that even in the peasant togs, he was still the handsomest man she had ever seen.

Alone with her thoughts, she marveled at her display of good sense even while in the arms of a dreamer whose spell was so potent that she could almost see those faraway islands under a tropic moon. That was good. It bolstered her confidence. She was strong. She could take the joy of Sean McDougal and reject the fallacy of his romantic promises. . . .

Part Three: *The Clouded Dream*

38.

For the next few days, Charity lived in a world made possible by circumstance; Sean McDougal was at Leach House; Christopher was off somewhere on the Prime Minister's business. She saw much of Sean. They made love; they walked through the heather and she enjoyed his nearness, his buoyant personality, and his talent for turning the most ordinary situations into ladders up which to climb into realms of starlit fantasy.

Charity had no fear whatever for her own emotional safety. She was like the opium eater who indulged in his vice but always with the certainty that he could turn away from it forever at a moment's notice. In her case, it was an easy assumption, not having yet been tested.

As to a troublesome conscience, she trapped it behind a nimbly constructed barrier of reasoning. Until she and Christopher were married, they owed each other no fidelity. She told herself in more or less honesty that if he sought women in London, she understood and accepted it; an easy sacrifice because she knew very well he would not. And if it was fair for him, it was fair for her. After all, she had opened the way with Dennis Wahl while suffering no qualms, so why should she feel differently about Sean McDougal?

She learned other things about her gay freebooter. He was not all laughter and charm. She visited the *Evening Primrose,* hidden cleverly under greenery in a deep channel cove, and found him to be an efficient aide in seeing to the loading of the arms and ammunition for the Colonies. Mrs. Dylan had been right concerning the caliber of the crew who served on the ship. They were in no way of pirate cut. They had been carefully selected by Sean from the local gentry and were high in dedication to whatever cause he furthered, were intensely loyal, and while of possible low birth, were of high individual intelligence. She got the impression that all the men who worked with him did not necessarily serve at sea. He seemed to have an extensive landside organization working silently, smoothly, and efficiently.

The days were idyllic. Then, after all too brief a time, they came to an end.

On the fifth day after Dennis Wahl's visit to Windward Moors to question Charity, the bodies of Meg Wahl and her mount were found amid the rocks at the foot of the cliff over which she had gone. They had both fallen into a pocket of heavy underbrush behind a boulder, most difficult to find.

Word spread over the countryside and an inquest was called. It convened close by, in Hempstead, where the village hall was used, spectators spilling out into the street. The inquiry was held the day following discovery of the tragedy because the coroner, a doughty little physician of the area, wanted it completed before Clement Leach arrived on the scene to overshadow him in importance. Or such was general opinion. Also, it was believed that the observers came mainly to see the sensational young newcomer from the Colonies. Accounts of Charity's battle with Gaby Kirth had been told and retold.

The questioning was inept at best, leaving many pertinent aspects unrevealed. Charity, in answering only the questions put to her, set the time of Meg's arrival at Windward, and that of her departure. The coroner seemed determined upon a finding of either accident or suicide. Thus Charity was questioned only as to Meg's state of mind. She stated truthfully that Meg had left in high spirits.

Carton's testimony did him no harm, even with Gaby Kirth's eyes upon him. Gaby had secured a chair at a good vantage point and a keenly observant spectator might have noticed the intensity of her attitude while Carton sat in the witness chair. He stated that he had not seen the deceased on the day of the tragedy other than to assist her from her mount upon her arrival at Windward Moors. He had then gone off to patrol the estate against poachers who had been quite active at the time. When he returned, the lady's mount was gone, so he assumed she had left. Nothing was asked or given relative to the switching of saddles, or any other facts most pertinent to the situation. As he left, Carton threw a bold grin in Gaby's direction, reflecting his overweening self-confidence.

Durban testified quietly and clearly as to his movements on the night in question, his search for his mistress and his lack of success in finding her. No corroborating witnesses were called to support his testimony.

Dennis Wahl's testimony was possibly the most interesting to the spectators. It was somewhat more penetrating as the coroner sought to unearth any hostility between Dennis and Meg. It was his sole allusion, though most indirect, to the possibility of foul play. He seemed of the opinion that if Meg had been murdered, only her husband could have been responsible. Dennis' testimony that he thought Meg was visiting somewhere and thus did not hurry off in search of her was accepted. The contrast of his seeming disinterest to Durban's obvious anxiety was left unexplained, though it must have piqued the interest of the spectators.

The testimony of the search party members—how the deceased was found, the condition of the body—was routine and the verdict came with the corner's jury not leaving their chairs.

Accidental death while riding too close to the Channel cliffs in uncertain light.

As the hearing broke up, Gaby Kirth looked about hoping to see Carton and, if possible, to have a few quiet words with him.

But Carton was nowhere to be found.

The scaly bastard is avoiding me, she told herself, and returned home no less frustrated than before. . . .

39.

Clement Leach, speaking to his brother Christopher, said, "I read the report of the coroner's hearing. A miserable, amateurish performance. Too quickly called. Most clumsily handled."

"I agree," Christopher replied. "But I do think they arrived at the truth. Meg's tragic death could only have been an accident."

Christopher had arrived at Windward Moors from London with all possible speed, but such was the situation that the reunion with Charity was hardly what it would have been under normal circumstances. He had kissed her quickly and lightly even as she saw his gloom and distress.

But she saw more, or thought she did. Christopher's sojourn in London's high political circles had brought subtle changes. He was somehow a more positive person. It was too soon for Charity to be sure, but the uncertainties, the self-doubts she had sensed in him, were gone.

Then, when Charity had had hardly time to console him for the grievous loss of his sister, a mounted messenger came from St. Jude's to say that Clement was back at the church and wished to see Christopher immediately upon his arrival.

With that, Christopher practically turned on

his heel and left. His almost rude departure hurt Charity, but she could make allowances. Christopher was tired from his long ride into Kent. He was under stress. Those were the reasons for his abruptness, she told herself, not lack of consideration for her.

Arriving at the church, Christopher entered and went to the altar in front of which Meg was now resting, the casket understandably closed. There would be no viewing of the remains.

Christopher went to his knees and said a prayer for the soul of his beloved sister, the term *beloved* in no way out of place. Christopher *had* loved Meg dearly, his distress at her wild ways notwithstanding. And as it always is when opportunities vanish to return no more, he wished that he had been more demonstrative of his affection. He should not have allowed Meg to stand alone against Clement's harsh opinions and criticisms, justified as they no doubt were. Had she been given his support she might not have rushed off into an undesirable marriage and this tragic ending might not have come about.

These were bad moments for Christopher. He ate the bitter fruit of personal failure now acknowledged, then arose and went on into the manse where Clement awaited him. The elder brother lay pallid and worn on a chaise longue in his sitting room.

Christopher hurried forward, pressed Clement's hand in his own, and spoke with alarm. "Clement—you are ill!"

Clement brushed the observation aside with a weary gesture. "It was a tiresome ride over from

278

Bath. However, I was glad enough to leave the place."

"The waters did you no good?"

"Mayhap—mayhap not." Clement's eyes had not changed. They were still of piercing quality as he looked up into Christopher's face. "Brother," he mumured, "we meet under tragic circumstances."

"True. I wish you could be spared the sorrow."

"Draw up a chair. We must talk." With Christopher seated beside him, he went on. "Tragic, but I am sure that Meg has already made her peace with God and He has forgiven her transgressions."

"I am sure He has."

"But we must now speak of the living, Christopher. Life goes on."

At this point Clement made his observations as to the ineptness of the coroner's inquiry. It was discussed for a few moments with agreement that accidental death had been a true finding.

Then Clement said, "Word came to me, Christopher, of your contacts with the Prime Minister. I am most gratified. You have become a person of importance—or at least you now have the opportunity."

Christopher was surprised that his London success had been relayed to Bath so quickly. But then he realized that Clement, however ill, would not remain out of touch with current affairs. He had powerful friends and many of the politically ambitious were happy to keep him informed.

"I am afraid," Christopher replied, "that the opportunity is still greater than the success."

"But are you aware of how tenuous your position is?"

"I don't quite understand you."

"That girl you brought from the Colonies," Clement said flatly.

If Clement noted the stiffening in Christopher's manner, he gave no sign. "Yes," the latter replied. "Her name is Charity Sturges. I found her in the hands of an utter scoundrel and I would have been unchristian had I not rescued her."

"But was it wise to bring her with you to England?"

"It was my decision," Christopher replied with even greater stiffness.

"Have you gotten word of your ward's activities at Windward while you were in London?"

"There has scarcely been time."

"She attended an affair given by Meg at Camber. While there, she viciously attacked Lady Kirth with a meat cleaver. It seems that only through the grace of God did she avoid becoming a murderess."

Christopher gasped. "Clement! I am sure you were misinformed!"

"There is little likelihood of that. I am sure your Charity Sturges is in need of firm discipline. If her wild ways are not curbed, the results could be tragic."

"Clement, until I look into the matter, I can render no opinion."

The door opened and the male nurse who accompanied Clement came forward anxiously. He said, "Your pardon, but the Reverend's health is

280

not of the best. He should not overstrain himself."

Clement waved the man away with some annoyance. "I am quite all right. However, you might instruct my housekeeper, Mrs. Cutts, to brew us some tea."

The nurse made his reluctant exit and Clement said, "I have wondered, Christopher, if there is any significance in the fact that Lady Kirth was the object of the girl's attack."

"Why should there have been?" Christopher's confusion was obvious.

"Christopher! Do not be intentionally obtuse. You and Lady Kirth were romantically inclined when you left for the Colonies."

"And is that pertinent?"

"It certainly would seem pertinent if your Charity Sturges knew of it and has romantic feeling for you of her own."

Clement waited while Christopher considered his reply. In Christopher's mind this was an important moment if he chose to make it so. Was it the time, with Clement ill? He decided that it was, regardless, and said, "Brother Clement, I have made a decision. I intend to marry Charity. She is a lovely, unspoiled, honest girl and I want her for my wife."

Christopher waited for the explosion that he felt was sure to follow such a declaration of independence.

But Clement did not flare out in the expected blaze of anger; this, more than anything else, indicating the seriousness of Clement's illness. More pointedly than ever now, Christopher realized he was looking at a tired old man. The fire-eating reformer of other days was gone.

This brought a surge of guilt; as though he were taking advantage of a crippled opponent. He would have much rather come head-to-head with the old Clement.

"Perhaps," Clement said, "there should be further discussion."

Christopher wished he could retract his words. This was no time to bear down on the brother he knew so well. But defeat for any reason was still defeat. This was something he had learned in the preceding four years.

"Clement," he said, "your advice and guidance over the years has been wise and of great value to me. I will listen to your counsel in this matter. But you must get to know Charity. When you do, I am sure you will come to my way of thinking."

"But your career . . ."

"If it balances on so abitrary a peg as whom I decide to marry, then it is bound to fall in any event."

The tea arrived, but Clement ignored it. He said, "We argue our differences, Christopher, while our sister lies dead before God's altar."

Thus he reversed his earlier declaration, that the living rated attention over the dead. Christopher arose from his chair.

"Clement, you must rest. Your strength will be needed. The funeral . . ."

"Never fear, Christopher. I will not fail Margaret. . . ."

Christopher left soon afterwards. As he rode back to Windward Moors, he felt in no way elated by his victory over his brother. He was pondering this when his attention was caught elsewhere.

An empty cart was standing in the outer road hard by the mire which skirted it; a span of horses hitched to it waited patiently.

Christopher's own rig had been hired in London, and with the sudden call to St. Jude's he had not dismissed it. His driver, forced to stop, got down to move the cart from his path. But then Christopher, frowning in puzzlement, got down also. "Wait a moment," he said.

The cart looked familiar, but there were several of them at Windward and he could not be sure. However, the horses were another matter. He quickly recognized them.

"This is my cart," he said. "These are my animals."

The driver replied, "Strange, is it not, sir? Out here abandoned on the road with no one in sight. Where is your man?"

"I have no idea, but I certainly own what you see here. You had better take the cart back to my house. I will drive your rig and follow along."

The driver shrugged and obeyed. Christopher followed him, wondering what sort of laxity had been involved. Bruce Carton had the responsibility of the stables. Why had he abandoned the cart on this lonely road . . . ?

40.

The answer was a savage one indeed. Had Christopher come along a scant hour earlier he would have been a witness.

Carton had left the Windward stables in high spirits. It was his third smuggling assignment and the rewards were piling up. One more trip, he thought, and he might possibly depart Kent for Ireland and a new life. He was also most happy at the coroner's verdict, arrived at without the least suspicion of his complicity or guilt. The gods, he felt sure, were favoring him to make up for all the years he had been neglected.

As he came to the point where Christopher found the cart, there was someone waiting for him, a man he recognized as Meg Wahl's servant. When Durban did not get out of his way he was forced to stop.

"What do you want?" he demanded. "If it's a favor now that you lost your soft berth at Camber, you may look elsewhere."

"I ask no favor," Durban replied. "I have stopped you here for an accounting."

"An accounting of what?"

"After my mistress disappeared, I went over the path she would have taken when returning to Camber from Windward. I found a place where

284

the tracks of horses were marked in the bare ground hard by the cliff face. Two horses came together there and I found shoe prints clearly outlined. So I made further investigations at the Windward stables."

"So you were the sneak thief who came nosing about in my quarters. What did you steal?" Carton sneered.

"I stole nothing. I spent most of my time in the stables checking shoes."

Carton got down from the cart. "And now you will pay, you scoundrel. First a good trouncing. Then I shall drag you before the magistrate."

Durban was undisturbed. Nor did his manner show open hostility to Carton; he displayed a dogged, emotionless approach to what he intended to accomplish.

As Carton hesitated, his fists doubled, Durban pointed to the near stallion hitched to the cart. "This is the mount you used. He wears a bent shoe that you have been too lazy to replace. He is the horse you rode that night when you pushed my mistress over the cliff. I suspected it before, but when her body was found down there, you stood condemned in my mind."

"You're mad, Durban," Carton blustered. "And you do not really mean what you say or you would have gone to the authorities. Now you come to blackmail me."

"At the inquest you were found to be without guilt."

"That alone should convince you that you would have no chance to involve me. However, you might try and I do not wish to be incon-

venienced, so I might submit to your blackmail—
a reasonable payment, that is. A few pounds to
help you on your way to a new situation."

Durban ignored the offer, nor did he further
enlighten Carton as to his intent. Instead, he
moved forward and when Carton saw his approach as menacing, he lashed out a fist in defense. Durban crouched, went under the arc of
the blow, and wrapped Carton in a bear hug. He
had his foe at a disadvantageous angle, but a
quick, hard squeeze threw Carton offguard and
Durban was able to better his hold by slipping behind to apply more direct pressure.

Muscles toughened and hardened by long years
in the coal mines now came to bear. Crushing
strength applied to Carton's rib cage brought a
gasp of pain.

Carton now came violently alive, fighting the
hold, lashing with arms, elbows, and heels. The
blows were painful to Durban, but he did not
flinch. He took the punishment stolidly, depending on his great strength to gain his objective,
which Carton recognized when, inch by stubbornly stepped-off inch, Durban edged him closer
to the swamp.

Still, Carton refused to believe it. He dared not
believe it. He cried, "All right, man! I realize you
are worked up. I will humor you. We will go to
the magistrate together." His words turned into a
cry of pain as his rib cage bent inward. Good
God! This madman had the strength of devils.
Who would have suspected? But he was no
stripling himself. Durban could not hold that iron

grip indefinitely. Carton had only to keep fighting.

This he did until they were boot-top deep in the lip of the swamp. Then terror took over.

"I know what you want," Carton babbled. "You want a confession! You have it, man! It was I, but I was driven to it. That titled wench Gabrielle Kirth came to me with dire threats. If I did not do as she ordered, she would see me hanged for a trumped-up crime I did not commit. I was beside myself! I went to your mistress there on the cliff to warn her, but there was an accident. A pure accident." Carton screamed in pain. "Have mercy, man! You are breaking my ribs!"

They were now deep in the swamp.

"You cannot do this! You are murdering an innocent man! Have you no conscience?"

He babbled on as they went deeper into the swamp; slower now because the ooze on the bottom caught and sucked at Durban's feet.

By the time the marsh water had risen to their chests, terror had driven Carton beyond reason. The sounds he emitted were no longer human.

Further progress into the marsh was no longer necessary. The quicksand had taken over, sucking them down. Durban realized that unless he released Carton quickly and struggled back to the shore, he too would go down. Still he hung on. Consciously he had not contemplated suicide. But now it did not matter. The quicksand took its lethal grip and it was too late.

The water reached their shoulders, their necks. When it passed Carton's chin, his mouth was open, animal sounds coming out. The roiled-up slime and filth from below flowed in. Durban watched Carton's eyes roll upward. Then his head disappeared.

The end came quickly for Durban. As the quicksand pulled him down he closed his eyes, took a last deep breath, and faced death as he had faced life—with animal stolidity.

For a time, the surface of the marsh was disturbed by the struggles below. Then the mud and the slime settled back down to the bottom and the surface was again serene.

Only the empty cart and the patient team were left to mark the scene of violence and death.

41.

Circumstances sharply altered the second reunion of Charity and Christopher. There was the puzzling matter of the abandoned cart and the disappearance of Bruce Carton, a mystery which of course would never be solved. Conversely, Durban vanishing caused scarcely a ripple at Camber. It was assumed that with his mistress dead and no longer in need of him, he had wandered on.

But at Windward, the loss of a sister and the coming funeral eclipsed all else. Christopher, upon his return from St. Jude's, was remote in his attitude but did not seem in any way critical of Charity; he was, rather, occupied with his own personal thoughts. He had no questions for Charity and she proffered none of the information she had gathered at Windward prior to his arrival. In essence it was a time of mourning with nothing more currently important.

There was an indication of Christopher's unshaken regard for Charity when he took her for a walk in a direction she had not previously gone—northward to a grove of trees a half mile from the house. Partially hidden there at the end of an overgrown path stood a squat, gray-stone structure of melancholy mien. Above its rock-pillared entrance was carved the name, *Leach*.

Christopher said, "She will rest here. In time, we will all join her."

"Are all the Leaches brought here?" Charity asked, shivering.

"The family vault. It dates far back."

Christopher had said, *we*. Clinging to his arm, reassured by his presence and his quiet strength, Charity dwelt upon that word. It included her. She was sure of that. She pressed close to him. "Christopher—I *do* love you."

He smiled and squeezed her arm but remained silent.

Charity made no effort to contact Sean McDougal nor was he greatly in her mind. She assumed that he had quitted the tower upon Christopher's arrival, but made no effort to find out.

She mourned Meg's death, her grief sincere even though she had known her for such a short time. There was another aspect also; the tragedy somehow brought her closer to the Leaches as a family, and regardless of his preoccupation, closer to Christopher. She was doubly certain now that she wanted nothing other than to cling to him, to be his wife and share his future.

The stern attitude of Justin Penrose, Mercedes' husband, was brought clearly to light when he refused to come to Windward Moors prior to the day of the funeral. No doubt his Mercy longed to be with her family at such a time, but Justin's word was law.

The funeral was set for ten o'clock the following morning and Clement drew on his reserve strength to serve at the altar. The priestly robes of his office hid much of his inner weakness and he was an impressive figure, his voice strong and resonant through the eulogy.

Many people came to St. Jude's, some to occupy rear pews, leaving the family to their privacy closer to the altar. Many others waited outside for the casket to appear, standing about in silent sympathy.

One unwanted mourner intruded arrogantly upon the privacy of the family. Borland Nickelawn. In all his foppish finery, he minced his way forward and took a seat hard by the bier.

Clement's eyes flicked in his direction, but he pointedly ignored him, going on with the service. Christopher and Dennis Wahl had a more difficult time restraining themselves. Dennis seemed on the verge of lunging at Nickelawn and hauling him out by his heels. Christopher, his face a mask of anger, turned his eyes away as though resisting the same temptation.

The services ended, the casket was carried

forth on the shoulders of six workers from the two estates, men carefully selected for the honor. It was placed on a cart draped with a flag bearing the Leach crest and drawn by a single black stallion led by another honored estate workman. Then the family emerged, Christopher and Dennis glancing about, hoping Nickelawn's intrusion was at an end.

Then, the long, slow journey to Windward, the family walking behind the catafalque. Farther back was a contingent of those who had waited at the church, a space separating them from the family.

But between the groups, just behind the close mourners, Borland Nickelawn strutted along like a king's jester in a medieval procession. Perhaps the fop could not be blamed for his affected manner of walking; perhaps he knew no other way. But he had to know that his presence was offensive. Doubtless, it was a deliberate act of defiance; a deliberate baiting of those who despised him.

Ironically, the procession moved along the marsh road, passing close to the lonely place where Meg's murderer and her avenger stood deep in swamp quicksand, their arms forever entwined in death.

When the cortege reached the Windward Moors road, only the family continued on, they and the honored workers who attended the casket. Also, Borland Nickelawn, keeping his position behind Justin and Mercedes Penrose. Justin turned and said, "The interment is private."

"But I am a dear friend," Nickelawn protested.

Justin looked uncertainly ahead to where Charity walked beside Christopher and Gaby Kirth followed the catafalque. He hesitated, thinking that if those trollops were not excluded, Nickelawn had a right to remain.

Christopher had not looked back nor had Dennis, their attention on the cortege and upon Clement, concerned as to whether the long march would be too much for him. Thus, Christopher did not see the intruder until they reached the house, made the northward turn, and were halfway to the vault.

Christopher doubled his fists in anger, a man trapped between rage at Nickelawn's impudence and respect for the occasion of his sister's funeral. His decision was to do nothing. It was too late. Disrupting the procession to order the buffoon away would have destroyed all dignity.

The final rites at the vault were completed with the bearers of the casket carrying it inside, followed by Clement who said a prayer before emerging. Then the six sturdy men closed the heavy door which had been previously opened to await them. The procession now retreated to the house where, at the turn in the road leading out, Christopher advanced upon Borland Nickelawn.

Speaking from between stiffened lips, he said, "You will leave, sir. You will leave immediately."

Nickelawn shrugged. "But my rig is back at the church. I have no means of getting there."

"You have your legs or you may crawl, for all of me. You have desecrated this occasion with your buffoonery and you will leave before I have you carried away bodily."

Nickelawn lifted his head in haughty disdain. "I was a dear friend of the deceased and I consider what you say an insult. One you shall answer for, sir."

With that, he removed the purple glove from his right hand and slapped it across Christopher's face.

"You may name the time and the place," he said.

Christopher remained rigid, restraining himself admirably. And in doing so, he made a mistake. He would have been entirely justified and supported had he attacked Nickelawn on the spot. But instead he remained a gentleman, saying, "I am due in London immediately. It is imperative that I go. But I shall return before too long. Would five days hence be satisfactory? At a place of *your* choosing?"

"Quite. At the Dueling Oak on the Camber estate?"

"I shall be there. At dawn?"

"It is customary. You have a choice of weapons."

"Blades, as you probably prefer," Christopher said coldly.

"Perhaps, also, we could do away with certain formalities. The visits of our seconds. They could accompany us to the dueling ground without making formal calls?"

"I agree. Now you will leave these premises."

The witnesses of the challenge and the acceptance stood in stunned silence. It was only after Nickelawn had gone some distance toward the outer road that Dennis Wahl found his voice.

"Christopher! You fool! You have just committed suicide!"

"I think not."

"Face facts! That fop kills indiscriminately! He glories in sending good men to their deaths."

"Be that as it may. Do you suggest that I should have let him desecrete Meg's funeral with his clownish presence and make no objection?"

"I am saying that something must now be done. In challenging you he has gone too far. The Prime Minister would intercede. He can be put down."

"There will be no intercession. I will not be marked publicly as a coward."

Justin, as gravely concerned, spoke out. "The dueling ground. On your estate, Dennis. You could forbid it."

"That would do no good. Another place would be arranged. Better it does take place at Camber. Then we can at least . . ." Dennis stopped, unable to find encouraging words.

Clement, drawn and pale from the ordeal of the funeral, and no longer the dominant leader who would once have taken charge and directed a sensible course, could only murmur, "May God defend the right!"

Christopher turned to Charity, his manner softening. "My dear, I neglected to tell you that I am required to hurry back to London for a time. I shall return as soon as possible."

Justin squinted up at the sun. "We must leave," he urged. "I too have affairs which must be attended to."

That was the only farewell Charity received,

and she stood watching as Christopher, who had dismissed his London rig, climbed into Justin's carriage. Mercedes waved sadly as it pulled away.

Dennis Wahl turned to Charity. "You have had a difficult time," he said.

"No more so than you—than the others."

"May I escort you back to the house?"

His manner was so highly respectful that Charity had difficulty in envisioning the two of them as it had been—tearing at each other in pursuit of erotic satisfaction. The loss of Meg had evidently hit Dennis very hard.

As they walked, Charity asked, "The duel—is it as bad as you made it sound?"

"It could not be worse. That damnable dueling custom! It must be done away with. It is in disfavor now, but that is not enough. Old barbarities die hard."

Even in her distress, Charity could not help noticing that Clement, along with Mercedes, had been handed into his carriage and driven away; that he had made no gesture of recognition, ignoring her pointedly, or so it seemed.

"Something *must* be done," Charity said. "Christopher cannot be allowed to throw his life away."

"The Prime Minister could forbid the duel, but with Chris's stubborn pride, he would probably go ahead with it anyhow."

"Perhaps they will persuade him in London."

"We can only hope so. . . ."

42.

Alone in her chambers, Charity felt like a soul deserted, truly a stranger in a strange land. Never had she felt more useless, more helpless. There was her keen disappointment in the failure of her reunion with Christopher. She was now forced to call it a failure even though ample reason for his remoteness existed. But overshadowing that was the fear that he would be taken from her before she ever saw him again. The end of it all. Loss of the man she had chosen before she had made him her own.

Something had to be done. There *had* to be a way!

And without further consideration, Charity hurried off to her only sanctuary in this time of trouble.

Sean McDougal.

She climbed to the turret room, arriving breathless, to find it empty of the armament and deserted. Sean had moved out; a room now tenanted by only the ghosts of those who had used it before. An achingly lonely place.

Fairly tumbling back down the circular stairway Charity searched anew and found Mrs. Dylan seated in the kitchen with a cup of tea. She too looked lonely and pathetic in her black mourning frock.

"That lovely lass with us no more," she murmured. "We will be the less for her passing."

"Mrs. Dylan," Charity said, "I *must* see Sean McDougal. He is not in the tower. Where could he possibly be?"

The housekeeper reacted slowly, and finally said, "It is hard to tell. On his ship, mayhap—in the cove. Have you been there?"

"Yes, but the path down the cliff. It is steep and treacherous. I fear I would fall without Sean's help."

"You have not been through the tunnel?"

"No. You must show me where it is," she said urgently.

"The going there is not difficult. But you will need a torch."

Mrs. Dylan took a pitchblend flare from a socket on the kitchen wall and lit it at the stove. "This way," she said.

She led Charity to a door at the far end of the kitchen which Charity had previously seen as leading out into the overgrown moat. But just beyond the door was a closet-like enclosure which opened to the top of a narrow stairway.

"Down there," Mrs. Dylan said. "You will have no trouble. When you come out of the tunnel, the cove is on your left. You must step carefully there. The going is difficult."

"Thank you, Mrs. Dylan. You are very kind."

"Please warn Sean of the Master's arrival if he is not already aware. I have not seen him for days."

"I shall do so, although I am sure he knows."

The tunnel was not difficult. Its floor had been worn smooth by many trips. But as Mrs. Dylan had said, the going on the Channel shore was not of the best. Charity struggled over rocks and through underbrush deliberately left untouched in order to hide the tunnel mouth.

Then she was on familiar ground and made her way to the ladder at the prow of the camouflaged *Evening Primrose*. One of the ship's hands was lounging by the rail to watch for intruders and was quite surprised when one appeared.

Charity came nimbly up the ladder. She had seen the man before so they were not strangers. "I must see Captain McDougal immediately," she said. "Is he aboard?"

"Aye," the man replied, touching his cap. "I'll take you."

"That will not be necessary. I have been in his cabin."

She hurried astern and along the rear companionway, but paused at the door to Sean's cabin. The forward hand had not mentioned the fact that Sean was occupied.

A man with a heavy voice was saying, "We have no idea what happened to him. If he ran away, why was the cart on the road by the swamp?"

Sean's reply: "Maybe he had nothing to do with the cart."

"That is possible, but it no longer matters. New arrangements must be made."

"Will you have trouble?"

"I think not. There are men of more decency

298

who would be happy to take the generous payment."

"All right, Sibley. I leave it in your good hands."

Unreasonably annoyed at the delay, Charity rapped sharply on the door. Sibley, whom she had never seen, opened it, frowned at her, and went quickly on his way. She entered the cabin and closed the door behind her.

Sean stared in surprise before exclaiming, "Mavourneen, my love. You are a mess! Have you been fleeing the devil's hosts? You have torn your skirt in two places. And there is a rent in the bodice. Remove the miserable gown."

Charity ignored that in turn and said, "You were not at Meg's funeral."

He sobered. "Not in the procession. But I was there in spirit and bade her farewell in my own fashion. I am sure she would not have wanted me to embarrass Christopher and the Reverend with my presence. There will be other times and other places."

"Then you do not know what happened."

Before Sean could answer, the high-blown courage upon which Charity had been riding lost its buoyancy and she plummeted into despair. Rushing forward, she threw herself into Sean's waiting arms.

"Oh, darling! I'm so miserable!" she cried.

He held her close, smoothed back her disheveled hair, and brushed his lips lightly across her now tear-stained cheek.

"Gently, lass, gently. Be not so disturbed. The world when I last looked was still in place."

299

"You don't know what happened at the funeral!"

"Then tell me, sweeting," he said calmly.

"That horrible Borland Nickelawn. He attended!"

"That fop! Why did they not throw him to the dogs?"

"He followed the procession, clear to the burial vault. Then Christopher ordered him off. There were words and he challenged Christopher to a duel."

Sean drew back and held Charity at arm's length, his face now grave. "Chris refused, of course."

"He did not! They will duel five days from now at the Dueling Oak at Camber. Christopher will be in London until then."

Sean chewed reflectively on his lip. "Chris had the right to declare the weapons. Of course he selected pistols."

"He did not. He is so stiff-necked. He said blades would do very well."

Sean turned away, frowning. "By Patrick's beard, what a fool!"

"He is very proud," she said defensively.

"And his silly pride will be the death of him."

As he pondered the situation, Sean took a dueling pistol from a brace bracketed on the bulkhead. He studied it, but the action gave little indication of his thoughts.

Charity said, "Darling, perhaps you could talk to Nickelawn and dissuade him. If you spoke out he would know all others were against him."

"That would do no good," Sean replied. Then he appeared to change his mind. "I *could* speak with him. In fact, I shall. The buffoon will no doubt be playing whist at the Domino Club in Maidstone. Either there, or he will be in his quarters. He owns a small house in Maidstone on Goose Lane, hard by Conover Square." With a contemptuous twist of his lips, he added, "Just next door to that pink-fronted brothel. So convenient for the scum."

He again drew Charity close. "I must hurry to reach Maidstone by early evening. I will send you back to Leach House with an escort."

Charity objected. "It will not be necessary. I will return as I came, through the tunnel. I left my torch at the entrance still burning."

Sean demurred, but Charity insisted. Bestowing a long, grateful kiss upon him, she hurried out, saying, "I will wait for you. Come to my chambers when you return." With that, she left, clambering over rocks and through underbrush as she had come. As she moved through the tunnel she prayed that Sean's word would have influence with the deadly swordsman who contemplated Christopher's death. . . .

43

Borland Nickelawn had not given up his sadistic
dreams of Charity Sturges. On the contrary, they
increased as he found pleasure in envisioning
that lovely body lying naked and helpless before
him. No concrete plan for achieving this reality
had occurred to him, not even as he attended Meg
Wahl's funeral. He had decided upon that as a
whim. He enjoyed flaunting himself in the
presence of those who held him in contempt. That
was his conscious thought, but perhaps there was
a subconscious urge to put himself into Charity's
proximity after the manner of a hunter stalking
prey for which a trap had not yet been devised.

During the whole of the funeral he had his eyes
upon Charity, who clung through it all to Christopher Leach. Therefore it was logical that he
saw Christopher as a block to his ever possessing
the girl. Thus he considered the challenge a piece
of good fortune, drawing Christopher into a situation where he could safely eliminate him. He no
doubt realized that he would be tempting reprisal
from powerful, highly placed people, but dueling
was not illegal. The duel would be fair and im-
partially supervised. Therefore even the King
would have no legal redress.

These were his conclusions on the night he

played whist at the Domino Club. Deep in his game, playing to win as he dueled to kill, he became aware that an unnatural silence had fallen over the room. He looked up to see Sean McDougal, the legendary freebooter whose name was a byword in England and a curse in France and Spain.

Sean's arrival had caused a stir at the tables nearest the door, but such was the control of the English gentleman that widened eyes and pursed lips were the only reactions.

The proprietor of the club, a rotund ball of a man with a ruddy face, came forward with a smile and a bow.

"Welcome, good sir," he said quietly, so as not to disturb the already distracted players. "Would it be your pleasure to take a hand?"

"No, thank you. Not this evening. If I may, I shall wander about and amuse myself as an observer. Perhaps I shall join in a game at some later day."

"You will always be welcome, sir," The man bobbed his head and as he started his retreat Sean murmured, "Thank you."

With the attention of the players covertly upon him, Sean gradually made his way to the table where Borland Nickelawn was playing. The celebrated duelist, instinctively on guard, could only wonder. Was McDougal's arrival a mere coincidence? True, he had long since severed his fortunes from those of the Leaches; still, he was of their blood and could have come with a purpose.

That Sean did have a purpose was indicated

when he stood for a few moments at Nickelawn's elbow, then commented, "You seem to be playing very badly." He did not use a name, but left no doubt as to whom he was addressing.

Nickelawn looked up with a jerk, doubly wary now. What was in the wind?

Sean continued to watch his play. Then he addressed the player opposite. "It would seem, sir, that you have drawn a miserably inept partner."

The tension increased as Sean's intent, that of rasping Nickelawn, became obvious. Nickelawn's mind raced. What did this mean? What was McDougal's objective in baiting him? He considered the man's reputation. Sean was known on several oceans and two continents as a bucko who feared neither man nor devil.

Deep-seated cowardice, held long dormant by the assurance his blade had given him, began to surface in Nickelawn's mind. Was there a way to retire from the table without losing face?

Hope of that vanished when Sean stepped closer, regarded him with even more open contempt, and asked casually, "Where did you get that absurd wig—out of some whore's closet?"

At this point Nickelawn choked back his fear even though this wild freebooter might well be ready to kill him on the spot. One could never tell which way a cat of his sort would jump, but honor demanded that Nickelawn face up.

He arose from his chair whereupon Sean took a glove from his pocket and lashed it viciously across Nickelawn's face.

Immediately, the duelist lost all fear. To his

mind, McDougal, in his arrogance, had made a mistake in playing by the rules. Nickelawn said, "I accept your challenge."

"At the Dueling Oak at chamber? In two days, at dawn?"

"Agreed. I choose rapiers."

"Excellent. And be sure to show up. Do not sneak away like the dog that you are."

With that, Sean smiled, said, "Good evening, gentlemen. I apologize for the intrusion," and left the club. . . .

44.

Charity waited at Windward Moors, sleep as far from her as the stars. Hours passed; she quitted her rooms when the walls began closing in on her and left the house to walk about the lawn under a sickle moon. She saw no romance in the icy crescent, only menace; nothing of medieval beauty in the great castle-house looming darkly above her, only shades of those who had died there, attacking it and defending it.

Finally, she returned to her chambers and spent another unhappy hour, after which she could stand it no longer. Perhaps a cup of tea would help. She hurried to the kitchen which she expected to find deserted. It was not. Mrs. Dylan sat at the table looking even more forlorn than when Charity had previously seen her. There were used dishes on the table indicating that she had just eaten or given someone a meal.

"Mrs. Dylan," Charity said, "I have been expecting Sean McDougal to come. But it has grown so late . . ."

The housekeeper looked up dully. "He was here—the fool!"

"The fool? Why do you say that?"

"He committed himself to his grave."

"I don't understand."

"He went to Maidstone this night and challenged Borland Nickelawn to a duel."

Charity gasped. So that was what Sean had in mind back there in the cabin of the *Evening Primrose!* If only she had suspected!

Unable to accept Mrs. Dylan's verdict of death, she said, "But perhaps he can win over Nickelawn."

"You should know better than that," Mrs. Dylan replied with a show of anger. "Sean is able and competent, yes, but he is no match for Nickelawn. He has never made an art of killing for the sheer joy of it as has that blackguard whom he must face. In twenty-four hours he will be a dead man as surely as the sun will rise."

So that was why Sean had not come to her as she had expected. In blind desperation, she returned to her rooms and flung herself upon the bed. Between sobs, she wailed aloud, "What have I done? What have I done? I have now doomed *both* men I love!"

That was the first time she had openly admitted that her feeling for Sean was love, but the declaration passed through her mind without note. She dried her useless tears after a time and sat up, forcing herself to think sanely. Return to the ship and beg Sean to abandon his mad course? That would be useless. Sean, no more than Christopher, would never back away where honor was at stake. If anything was to be done, she must do it herself. But what? The answer came and she stated it aloud, this time as though she had to hear the words in order to make it a firm resolve.

"I must kill Borland Nickelawn myself."

At first, the decision seemed monstrous. But then that feeling passed. It would not be murder; rather, the stamping out of a venomous bug not worthy of living. There was a way to do it; there *had* to be a way.

The resolution gradually brought comfort to Charity. It revived the confidence in herself that had always been a mainstay of her character. It calmed her nerves and set her quietly thinking, searching for the plan she was certain would evolve.

It came into being with surprising speed, not fullblown, with some details still to be worked out. And she was so sure that the whole plan could be quickly shaped that she put it off until the following day.

Thus she allowed the strain of long hours to take over and retired, going calmly to sleep....

45.

By dawn, it was obvious that Charity's subconscious had been working furiously through the night because when she awoke the thought was clear in her mind.

Today I kill Borland Nickelawn. Today I smash a bug.

And with what she considered complete justification for murder, the prospect was exciting.

She took a cold bath, put on her faithful yellow-striped frock, and went to the deserted kitchen where she made a cup of tea and ate a scone. Then to the stables, alert in case Carton had returned, where she hitched up a gig and drove to Hempstead.

On her previous visit, she had seen a small apothecary shop next to where she had bought Dorothy's clothes. It had not yet opened and she rapped sharply on the door.

After a time, the proprietor, a nightshirted grayhead, heavy with sleep and short of temper, opened the door a crack.

"What is wanted at this hour?" he demanded.

"I am in need of a drug," Charity said.

"But milady, it is not yet six o'clock!"

"Quite true and I beg your pardon. I have not

308

slept and I must have some laudanum or I shall perish from wakefulness."

"Come back when I have dressed and had my tea."

"Much better you get me the drug and go back to your bed."

The proprietor gave grumbling assent and allowed Charity to follow him into his establishment, from which she departed a short time later with a vial of the drug safely in her possession. On the way home she regretted, along with the apothecary, her early start, and looked forward with dread to the long hours of the day.

Back at Leach House, she found Mrs. Dylan astir, with tempting odors of breakfast filling the kitchen. Charity said, "Those eggs are a welcome sight, Mrs. Dylan."

The good lady sighed. "Preparing food is a habit I find hard to break. Would that there were those in the house to eat it."

"I will do my best," Charity assured her.

Conversation fell off, but with Charity well aware of the dread that filled the housekeeper's mind, she finally said, "You love that mad fool who is throwing himself away so needlessly."

"It would be difficult not to." She picked at her food. "What is it the Scriptures say? The good die young?"

"That may be written but it is not necessarily true. Be of better cheer, Mrs. Dylan. Sean has not yet been run through by that odious clown."

The housekeeper shook her head. "True, but hope is hard come by as things stand."

"Did Sean tell you why he challenged Nick-elawn?"

"No. I presume they came upon each other and Nickelawn made himself too obnoxious to be tolerated."

That was like Sean, Charity thought, keeping secret the fact that he had placed himself between Christopher and death. "I think," she said, "that things may yet turn out well."

"I pray so."

"By the way, Mrs. Dylan, do you have any oil of the olive here in the kitchen?"

"Aye. We use it in cooking."

"I would like a cruet if you could spare it. In Virginia we found it a balm for rough skin."

"You are quite welcome to as much as you need. . . ."

The day dragged on, but fortunately there were still things to be done and the sun was well up when Charity saddled a mare and rode off to Camber where she was happy to find Dorothy and Wilferd established in the hut they would occupy as tenant farmers on the Camber acres. There were now curtains in the windows and weeds cut away from the door.

Dorothy saw Charity coming and rushed forth, her eyes sparkling as she waited for her benefactor to dismount. The instant Charity was afoot, Dorothy seized Charity's hand and kissed it.

Charity snatched it away. "Dorothy! I taught you better than that!" She looked into the girl's face. "You are very happy here, aren't you?"

"Oh, Miss Charity, it is like heaven!" Then she

310

said, "It was so terrible about Miss Margaret. I cried when I heard. She was your friend."

"Yes, my very dear friend."

"We went to the church and followed along, but we stopped with the others at the marsh road."

"You should have let me know. You would have been welcome at Leach House."

"We did not want to intrude."

"Dorothy, I would like to see Wilferd. Is he about?"

"Yes. He is over clearing brush from around the duck pond." She lowered her voice. "It has been very difficult for him."

"Why difficult?"

"We were given the cottage but he does not know what to do. Mr. Wahl, because of his great loss, has not had time to tell Wilferd his duties. So Wilferd finds things to do by himself."

"I am sure Mr. Wahl will get to him in due time. Where is the duck pond?"

Dorothy pointed. "Over beyond the pine ridge. There were fowl coops there once but they are gone. . . ."

As Charity rode off in the direction Dorothy indicated, she realized how badly rundown Camber had become. And now, with Meg gone, would Dennis allow it to go to complete ruin? It was sad indeed.

Wilferd saw her coming and ran to meet her. He helped her down. "Miss Charity, I'm glad that you came!"

Charity laughed. "You seem quite overcome. Why are you so eager to see me?"

"I mean that something must have brought you; some way I can help. We have been hoping for a chance to repay you even in some small way."

Charity felt guilty—that they would expect a visit only if she needed them. She said, "I am delighted to see both of you, Wilferd, and there *is* a favor you can do me."

"I am ready, Miss Charity."

"Not until this evening. As you may know, Carton is no longer at Windward Moors, so we have no hostler. I need someone to drive me into Maidstone this evening."

"At what time?"

"If you would come to Windward and harness a team to the carriage and have it at the door around six o'clock, I would be grateful."

"I shall be there."

"I would also like you to wait for me, although I don't know how long I will be engaged at Maidstone."

"That does not matter. I will wait all the night or longer."

"Thank you. I will see you then at Leach House this evening...."

Riding back as she had come, Charity felt let down, not from the task she had set for herself but because of the wait which must now ensue. The slow hours. Without realizing it, she veered the mare off the direct course to Windward and reined up at the path leading down to the cove where the *Evening Primrose* was hidden. It was only then that she realized how she yearned to feel Sean's arms around her, his strong body

312

pressed hard upon her own, the ecstatic struggle she remembered so clearly.

She turned away, reining her mount in the direction of Leach House. She rode slowly through the heather, thinking how there was the breadth of a hair between sex and violence; not even that, at times. Perhaps, she thought, they were not separate at all, and she wondered if the violence she planned, the murderous intent saturating her mind, had caused the sexual stirring of her blood. How little we know of ourselves, she thought; how ignorant of our weaknesses and strengths until circumstance forces us to test them!

Arriving back at Windward, she went about the last of her preparations for the task ahead; this when she went to the kitchen, to the butcher's board on the wall, and selected her weapon. She chose a bone-handled knife with a six-inch blade. She tested the cutting edge on a stone-hard turnip. It was like a razor. Mrs. Dylan sharpened the knives with as much care as she polished the silver.

The clock finally crept its way to the hour of six. The carriage wheels grated upon the drive. Charity, clad in her remaining trouser suit, hurried down the stairs. She clutched a purse in which were the drug, the oil, and the knife with which she could cut the life out of Borland Nickelawn. . . .

313

46.

With all her preparation, there was one chancy aspect to Charity's plan. Would Nickelawn be at home that evening? Of course she had no way of knowing, but she felt that with the duel scheduled for the following morning he would hardly be out roistering.

That proved to be true. Charity passed a nervous few moments after knocking on his door, but then there was an eye at the peephole and the door was opened.

There was no effusive welcome; rather, a look of suspicion. Without a wig and no powder or paint on his lips, Charity saw the man as rather handsome. Touseled blond hair fell over his forehead and there was a look of youth about him; an incongruously innocent appearance when compared with the clown who strutted in public. He was wearing an elegant cerise lounging robe and looked like a man-of-the-world spending a quiet evening at home.

Charity forced a smile. "Am I not welcome?"

He stepped back, opened the door wider, and permitted her to enter, his puzzled look remaining. "I must assume that you did not expect me," Charity said.

"Nor did I," he answered.

"Then I am afraid you misjudged me, Mr. Nickelawn. What did you see? A shrinking violet who cringed at the touch of a man's hand?"

He smiled in spite of himself. "Hardly that, after your set-to with Gaby Kirth."

"La! That was delightful!"

With his attention now on the mannish suit, Charity posed gracefully and asked, "Do you like it?"

"I'd say it is quite daring. Do the Leaches allow you to wear such attire?"

"Again you midjudge me. I wear what I please when I please. Does that not make us kindred souls, Mr. Nickelawn?"

He rubbed a slow hand across his chin and got to the question uppermost in his mind. "Miss Sturges, why are you here?"

"Well, so long as I am here, you might ask me to sit down."

"Please do." Nickelawn remembered his manners and took Charity's hat after she removed it.

"Why am I here? I will speak plainly, sir. I have heard stories of exciting times here in your house. I am someone who loves excitement and I would be disappointed if I were unable to learn of them personally. So with the time very short...."

"What do you mean by that? The time very short."

"Why everyone knows, sir, that Sean McDougal is going to kill you at dawn."

Nickelawn laughed. "I am afraid you have been misinformed. I have no intention of dying tomorrow."

"Then later, five days hence. You probably do not know that Christopher Leach is most expert with the rapier."

He passed that over as not worthy of comment. Studying her keenly, he said, "Am I to believe that you actually came here for pleasure?"

"Is that too hard to believe? Meg Wahl stirred my curiosity greatly by her account of your skills."

"You do not seem much disturbed by her death."

"In truth, I hardly knew the woman. She was a sweet person and I was attracted to her." Another smile, more wicked now. "Especially to her way of life."

Nickelawn said, "I have been most inhospitable. Might I offer you a drink?"

"Thank you. I prefer brandy if you have it."

"Of course."

"And if I may, I'll use your bath chamber."

"Just to the right—through the bedroom."

Gaining the privacy, Charity removed the cruet of olive oil from her purse. She had brought it along because she remembered, in those long-ago days in the cabin off Ironbound Road, when Mother Mae's advice to those who tended to overindulge was to coat the stomach with olive oil before drinking, thus staving off the effects of strong liquor. She could only hope this would help in her case, and after she had valiantly poured the stuff down her throat, fighting nausea the while, she felt that she had earned the protection.

When she returned, Nickelawn was standing at his liquor cabinet. He brought two brandies to

316

her chair and they saluted each other. "To an exciting night," Charity murmured, then fought hard as she downed the drink, trying to make it appear that sluicing fire into her stomach was a habit rather than an excruciating ordeal.

Nickelawn's tension had vanished. Perhaps he still did not have sufficient reason to trust this little trollop, but visions of what lay in store for her cancelled out all else. As his robe fell carelessly open Charity saw that he was totally nude underneath. At the risk of overplaying her hand, Charity ran her eyes over his body and said, "You have an attractive physique."

His wariness had vanished completely. Drawing the robe aside, he posed in the classic Greek manner. "I am quite proud of it. And I am sure that yours will compare favorably."

"I can only hope so," she answered modestly.

"Did Meg tell you about my guest room?"

"She told me of a room where you—entertain—your guests, yes."

"Would you like to see it?"

"That was my main reason for coming to you. But I would like to be in a more mellow mood. A single glass of brandy hardly. . . ."

"Of course," Nickelawn interrupted, and reached for Charity's glass. However, she was quicker and took his, saying, "Allow me. Who knows—someday I may become a housemaid and shall need the practice."

With that, she went to the liquor cabinet, her knitted bag dangling from her wrist. Shielding the act with her body, she poured the brandy and then emptied her supply of laudanum into Nicklelawn's glass. It was a touchy moment. He stayed where he was and did not see what she was doing, but there was uncertainty in her own mind. She'd had no experience whatever with the drug. Did it have a strong taste? Would Nickelawn detect it in his brandy? Perhaps it should have been administered a little at a time, but Charity was not sure of getting another opportunity.

The idea came to her of abandoning her plan; of simply taking the knife and lunging at Nickelawn with the hope of success. But that was too risky. She could so easily fail.

One point was significant. Not for a single moment since she had arrived in this monster's den had she wavered in her objective. She was still determined to save two lives by taking that of a man who was not fit to live.

The laudanum successfully transferred, Charity put the vial back in her purse and returned with the drinks. Nickelawn's was full to the brim, while she hid her own less generous portion by closing her fingers over the length of the glass. Then, lifting it again in salute, she gulped it down and was gratified when Nickelawn followed suit.

So far, things were going well, but Charity could no longer delay the proceedings. Nickelawn said, "I am sure you are sufficiently mellow by this time. Come with me. I have a surprise for you."

"Wonderful. I am ready. But we should not go like camels to an oasis—with parched throats. Let me refill the glasses."

Nickelawn permitted that, even while showing

signs of impatience. Then he led Charity through a door and into the "guest" room. Once inside with the door closed, Nickelawn found himself impeded by the glass he was carrying. Charity was gratified when he gulped down the brandy before throwing the glass aside.

He now approached her, the lust she had expected aglow in his eyes. The moment had come, she realized. This was no time to resist or show reluctance, so she stood quite still, a fixed smile on her face while he went silently about the business of undressing her.

While he did so, she turned her attention to the room itself. The walls were of red velvet and upon one of them hung various instruments of torture, frightening in their very appearance. A collection of whips from a small, ten-inch lash to a long, heavy quirt studded with bits of metal. There were brightly polished rods no doubt useful as prods into the human body. A large leather bag with a rubber pipe attached suggested water torture; fluids forced into helpless victims.

The furniture was also functional. A satin-covered couch filled one corner of the room, evidently for less brutal lovemaking, while a table equipped with straps and rods for spreading the limbs suggested otherwise.

Charity was nude from the waist up now. The trousers of her suit had been loosened and Nickelawn was lowering them, savoring every inch of Charity's creamy-tinted body now revealed. She was not at this time required to act out a part because Nickelawn was completely occupied, paying her no attention other than as an impersonal ob-

ject of his lust, and Charity's thoughts went back
to the ordeal visited upon her by Orin Cade. This
was far different, however. Nickelawn approached violence by being skillfully gentle. With
his prey standing nude before him, he ran his
hands down her body, lifted them back to her
breasts and played the lovely brown nipples into
bulging prominence; then down her body, his fingers moving inward, teasing—inviting her thighs
to spread, rather than forcing them.

He glanced up at her face, and Charity was
frightened. It was as though she had not deceived
him in the least; as though he were silently telling her:

*You came here for reasons other than you gave
me. You are not what you claim to be, but I will
change that. I will make you into a creature to
my taste. Before I am through you will be begging for my attentions.*

Was that truth or was it only in her mind?

Either way, Charity found herself standing
with her feet spread wide, her body quivering
from Nickelawn's devilishly skillful touch as he
manipulated nerve-endings she had been unaware
she possessed. She had a valid reason for her cooperation, of course; that she must act the part
of the wanton to justify her presence there.

Still, the spreading of her limbs for Nickelawn's convenience had not needed that excuse.
And now there was an urge to help him by using
her own hands; to reach down to the delicate
flesh with which he played. The hot desire was
such as to shake her resolve. She looked across to
where she had left her purse and the knife she

320

planned to use, as a reminder of her primary reason for being there. Then she closed her eyes as Nickelawn leaned forward and she felt the maddening touch of his lips, his tongue. She reached downward to hold and direct his head, then restrained herself at the last moment.

Nickelawn drew back and came to his feet. His expression changed as his sadistic impulses came to the fore demanding that the gentleness end. He went to the wall of instruments and took a peculiar-looking object from the wall; a limp brown sack resembling a bladder. He turned and held it up for Charity's inspection.

"Do you know what we do with this?"

"I haven't the least idea," Nor did she.

"You hang by it."

"I don't understand."

"It is made of soft leather and can be easily pushed into you. Then we use this attached tube to blow it full of air. Once filled and inside of you, it holds firmly and cannot be withdrawn until it is deflated. Does that help you to understand?" His smile was thin and fixed as he watched for her reaction.

She said, "I can see that you blow it up inside of a girl but just what that achieves. . . ."

"This tube is very strong. When hung from the ceiling it supports the whole weight."

Charity now understood completely. She gasped. "You are saying that you hang a girl upside down from her. . . ."

His laugh cut in. "It is my own invention. My last guest was a haughty bitch. She screamed for

fifteen minutes against my sound-proof walls before she lost consciousness."

Reacting from instinct, Charity sensed that re-
vulsion would antagonize Nickelawn. So she
forced a smile and said, "It must have been exciting to watch her." Her first touch of real fear
came now, where previously there had been a
kind of excitement. She had not really believed
the stories of this maniac's cruelties. Now above
all, she had to keep that leather sack from being
thrust up into her. "You are fantastically inven-
tive."

The result of her praise was not what she had
hoped for. Nickelawn sneered. "You make me
sick!" He spat the words at her as he threw the
leather torture instrument aside and selected a
whip from the wall, a thin, six-foot thong with a
small metal tip.

He sneered, "A little target practice, bitch,"
and flicked the whip expertly. The metal tip
snapped like a live thing at Charity's left nipple.
Charity squalled in pain and surprise as she
snatched at her breast and turned away. That
was a mistake. The whip snaked out again to
touch her posterior with fire. She fell to her
knees, her legs spread for support, and now Nickelawn's aim found a mark dead center, on the
tenderest part of her body. She drew her knees
together, her back arched. Good God! would the
laudanum never work?

She cowered, waiting for the next bite of the
whip. It did not come. She peered fearfully over
her shoulder to see that perhaps her plea had
been answered. Nickelawn had dropped into a

chair, the whip hanging from his lax hand. There was a perturbed look on his face and he jerked his head back and forth as though trying to dispel mental cobwebs.

But he did not forget Charity. His sneer returned and he growled, "Over here, pig. Crawl to me."

With her nipple and most intimate part burning almost unbearably, Charity obeyed. She crawled until she was between his sprawled legs where she looked up pleadingly into his face. No mercy there. Only sneering contempt.

"Unbutton it," he said, thus demanding the utmost degradation of a woman; on her knees, taking his manhood unnaturally.

Charity obeyed, but with his semierect penis in her hand, she rebelled. *I won't! I won't!* Motivated by love it could be wildly exciting. Why was it so repulsive now?

She gave no outward sign of her rebellion, she only hesitated; until Nickelawn dug cruel fingers into her hair, holding her head rigid, and thrust his manhood against her lips. But then he seemed only to want the degrading symbolism of the act rather than the pleasure. After the vicious thrust, he turned again lax. Charity raised her eyes. The laudanum had done its work! At least partially, because his eyes had closed. He did not move as she twisted away and returned with the knife she had managed to hide under her pile of clothing. She raised it, but her arm froze. She sobbed in anger at herself. She had come to the triumphant finale of her plan and could not now drive the knife home and finish it.

"What is going on here?"

Charity froze, terror sweeping over her like a dash of ice water. There had been the sound of a door opening but the question came so quickly that she had only time to lower the knife. Acting instinctively, she thrust the weapon under Nickelawn's chair as she turned. She saw a tall, black-clad man, a stranger with a look of scowling alarm on his face. He rushed forward, his eyes only for Nickelawn, ignoring Charity completely, other than to push her roughly aside as though she were a sack of offal obstructing his path. She thought of flight but to run as she was, naked, into the street was impossible.

The man took Nickelawn by the shoulders and shook him. Nickelawn's head now hung limp. The man reviled him.

"You stupid fool! Carousing in this manner when you are due to face a blade almost within the hour. Is it suicide you want?"

Nickelawn mumbled an unintelligible reply. Evidently the man took it as a demand to know who he was.

"Devon, you idiot! Your second! I came as you requested to accompany you to the dueling ground."

Nickelawn muttered, "Devon—aye—good man...."

"You have Turkish coffee in the kitchen. I'll brew it thick and hot. Meantime, into the bath with you."

Devon now turned to Charity. He seized her by the hair and dragged her to where her clothing lay. He gathered it up and pushed her savagely

324

into the parlor where he flung it at her and snarled, "Get dressed and crawl back into your sewer, you slut!" Then he returned to the den and emerged with Nickelawn, the latter struggling along weakly as Devon steered him toward the bath.

However contemptuous Devon's treatment of her, Charity had to be grateful. It could have been far worse. Evidently the man Nickelawn had chosen as his second knew the roisterer's ways and saw Charity merely as a tool to amuse himself with.

She threw on her clothes and fled the odious house; back into the carriage where Wilferd had been patiently waiting. Fortunately he was on the outside, high on the driver's seat where he could not hear her when she burst into sobs. She had failed and it had been her own fault. There had been several times where she could have sent Nickelawn to his maker had she not been so timid; had she been willing to take even a small chance.

Thus she blamed herself bitterly while refusing to admit that she would have failed in any case; that she would not have been able to kill in cold blood.

That regardless of her determination, she would not have been able to drive a knife into a helpless victim. . . .

47.

Sean McDougal had selected Sibley as his second, and the latter met him on the cliff overlooking the hidden cove well before dawn. He had brought a horse for Sean and the two men rode slowly toward the dueling ground, Sibley in a morose mood.

"Man, you've no right to do this. So many of us depend upon you. Without you we would be at sea, the pun intended."

Sean laughed. No one could have told from his light manner that he looked forward to the duel with any fear whatsoever.

"You seem so sure, my friend, that I cannot best the fop."

"You know his skill. He went to that *salle* in Paris and reduced the proprietor, an absolute master, in a matter of minutes. In a serious duel he has never been even pinked."

"Ah, but you are not familiar with my skills."

"You know the saber well. You are an expert with pistols. But a rapier is a different matter. You have not the experience."

"Sibley, my eternal friend, I must say that you are most encouraging. With your display of confidence, what man could not go on to victory?"

"Sean, I'm truly sorry! I know that with the

duel now inevitable I should be mouthing praises of your skill, but. . . ."

"I know—I know. And let me say this. If by some ill fate Nickelawn does do away with me, I hereby appoint you my heir in all things. You will finish with the loading. You will take the cargo to Savannah where they will be awaiting its arrival."

"That's madness! I have never even been to sea," Sibley protested.

"Seamanship will not be needed. My first mate, Gordon Bridger, can handle a ship with the best of them. What will be needed is your intelligence, your loyalty. And by the way, did Dennis Wahl ever fix your roof?"

Sibley could not laugh but he managed a smile. "No. We could be drowned in a deluge before he would stir his stumps."

"And I vow you would choose such a death rather than fix it yourself."

"I will not be imposed on by such as he."

"I do not understand why you remain there. You are wealthy enough now to buy Camber itself if you choose."

"Hardly that rich, but caution keeps a man from gaol. The appearance of wealth would certainly interest the constable."

They arrived at the dueling ground to find that others were waiting. None were friends of Sean because the duel had not been noised about, Sean having instructed Sibley to say nothing about it. But several gentlemen from the Maidstone whist club had come, not necessarily as friends of Nickelawn; more as sporting gentlemen who enjoyed a spectacle. They kept to themselves in a group and did not approach Sean and Sibley who walked to the Dueling Oak, both contemplating the dawn rising in the east.

"Perhaps he will not come," Sibley said hopefully.

"And perhaps the sun will neglect to rise," Sean replied.

If a cowardly opponent had been Sibley's hope, it was now dashed as a closed carriage came over the rise and stopped close by. The door opened and a tall man in a black cape emerged. He was followed by Nickelawn. Under the second's arm was a black case. While Nickelawn waited by the carriage the second approached the tree where he addressed Sibley, ignoring Sean. He opened the case. "You may examine the blades," he said.

Sibley, unschooled in the decorum of dueling, glanced at Sean. The latter shook his head whereupon the second placed the case on the ground beside the tree and returned to the carriage. He took another case from the carriage and escorted Nickelawn to the dueling sward. Nickelawn remained rigidly formal, looking away from Sean and Sibley, apparently wrapped in his own thoughts.

The second said, "I am Dr. Devon, a physician, gentlemen. These are my instruments. Do you accept my services if they are needed?"

Again Sean nodded and Devon, sensing Sibley's inexperience, said, "It is required that a plea is made for reconciliation of differences. Is this possible?"

There was dead silence after which Devon offered Sean the weapon case. "They are of Italian steel," he said. "The very best obtainable."

Sean selected a rapier, tested its whip, and stepped back. Nickelawn took the other blade, still not looking at Sean, still maintaining his cold formality. Sean studied him. He seemed pale but otherwise composed.

There was one more formality. The doctor, as though reciting from rote, said, "The duel will continue until either adversary raises his free hand in surrender or falls to the ground unable to continue. No wound will be treated until one of those requirements is met." With that, he took a third blade from the case and offered it to Sibley. When the latter remained uncertain, the second said, "Then with your permission. . . ." and stepped to a position on the sward. Nickelawn and Sean stepped forward. The second raised his rapier and the adversaries crossed their weapons at its tip. Then the second stepped back. The duel was on.

Nickelawn attacked instantly, moving forward in a series of quick, graceful lunges reminiscent of ballet steps. Sean gave ground but parried the thrust without effort. They pressed face to face, their blades crossed at the hafts. A moment of this and Sean hurled Nickelawn back. Nickelawn staggered, righted himself, and each tested the other with short parries, seeking an advantage.

There followed a strenuous period of thrust and counterthrust, parry and defensive parry, and Sean became more puzzled as the contest proceeded. Nickelawn was functioning far below his reputation. Was it some sort of a trick? Sean did not think so because Nickelawn's face had gone ashy white, his eyes bloodshot and burning. Sean stepped back and lowered his blade and Nickelawn came to life, lunging forward with some semblance of a skilled swordsman. But only a semblance. Sean parried the attack which, he realized, the veriest fencing student could have avoided. As Nickelawn retreated, his blade half-lowered, Sean initiated his own attack. Nickelawn defended feebly, staggering as he fought from instinct. Amazed at the performance, Sean realized that he could easily have run the man through.

Nickelawn backed away to regain balance, then drew on his waning strength to lunge again. The attack ended disastrously with Nickelawn's blade down as he hung on Sean for support. Sean saw agony in Nickelawn's face and stepped back. Nickelawn slipped to one knee.

Stepping farther back and turning to the second, Sean said, "Take your man away, sir. He is ill. He is in no condition to continue."

Nickelawn was clutching his stomach in great pain as Devon came forward and lifted him to his feet.

"It is true," the doctor said. "I implored Mr. Nickelawn to ask for a postponement but he would not hear of it."

"His courage is not being questioned," Sean said.

"Then with your permission we will leave."

He escorted Nickelawn to the carriage while the group of watchers whispered among themselves. He returned to gather up the weapons.

"Mr. McDougal, will you grant my principal a continuance at a later date?"

"No," Sean replied. It was a perfectly honorable refusal, as Sean had come in good faith and stood prepared to go on.

"Then my gratitude for sparing his life," the doctor said. "The affair is ended."

He returned to the carriage and drove away. The witnesses followed, still whispering among themselves.

Alone with Sean on the field, Sibley asked, "What will happen now?"

"Nothing. As the second said, it is finished. Nickelawn should not have fought and I am sure now he would rather I'd run him through than let it end the way it did. Had the situation been reversed he would have shown no mercy. But the man has courage, no doubt about that. He expected to be killed."

"And you might better have accommodated him. He will be vengeful."

"I think not. On the dueling field he is a sportsman who plays by the rules. However, I don't quite see how he could have done anything else."

"I wonder what was wrong with him?"

"It really doesn't matter." Sean was unusually subdued.

Sibley smiled grimly. "I think your guardian angel put a spoiled fish in his pudding."

"Then I owe my guardian angel a favor. Let's go home. . . ."

48.

Charity waited in her rooms for she knew not what. Depressed by the failure of the plan she had so carefully worked out, the face of Borland Nickelawn leered at her in triumph from mental shadows. True, he was not in the best of shape when she left him, but she still conceded a high respect for his virility. A man who could retain his wits for so long, dosed as he was with the laudanum, would soon bounce back and be ready for his appointment at the Dueling Oak.

Time dragged by. Dawn came. The day brightened. Could Sean still be counted among the living? There was a tapping on her door and her heart jumped. Mrs. Dylan bringing tragic news?

Then the door opened and Sean walked in.

Charity stared, unable to move, unable to speak. Sean smiled and said, "Sweeting, I have come to apologize for last night. I did promise to come to you but I stopped for a bite downstairs and well. . . ." He paused to shrug ruefully. ". . . . I just forgot."

Charity went to pieces emotionally. Rushing into his arms she sobbed, "Sean—oh, darling. You are alive! That beast did not kill you. If he had I would have died."

Sean was obviously pleased by the show of affection but also amused. "Now, now, lass. Calm yourself. Have you that little faith in my ability?"

"But they said he could not be beaten. What happened? Did you win the duel?"

"After a fashion. The poor devil was sick as a poisoned dog. He collapsed during the match."

Charity drew back, her eyes wide. "Then I did help! He did not recover in time!"

"Recover? From what? You speak in riddles."

"I went to his house. I put laudanum in his brandy. He—oh, Sean. It doesn't matter now. You are safe."

She tried to go again into his arms but he held her away, a frown replacing his smile. "I fear it does matter. Tell me exactly what you had to do with this affair."

"As I said, I went to his house and..."

"You poisoned the man?" he asked incredulously.

"I've heard that laudanum has a strong effect upon the system and I poured a vial into his brandy. I know nothing about the drug—how to administer it."

Sean stepped back, his eyes blazing. Contempt twisted his lips as he lashed out with an open palm. His fingers only grazed Charity's cheek but the gesture was symbolic of his feelings.

"Am I to believe that! Am I to believe you sent a sick man to duel with me? Am I to believe that you would do such a vile thing?"

"Sean," Charity pleaded, "I went to his house to kill him and save you and Christopher. After all, I was to blame for your challenging him and putting your life in danger. I wanted to make amends."

"Indeed! I have no thanks for you nor will Christopher if he hears of what you did."

"I wanted only...."

"If you planned to kill him, why did you not do it, instead of passing him on to me? I might well have been the murderer."

The tongue-lashing stung Charity. Characteristically she was able to take so much, and Sean had gone too far. She cried, "Those are fine words coming from you! A freebooter! A felon in Spain and France who ruthlessly takes ships at sea and murders innocent people."

"I have never deliberately killed any living thing!"

"I wonder if those dead by your hand would agree?"

His rage remained at its peak. "Who asked you to intrude in the first place, my lass? And who are you to accuse others when you admit that you planned cold-blooded murder?"

Charity pounded him with doubled fists. "Get out of here you—you *pirate!* You *smuggler* You—you!"

She burst into tears and turned from him. She heard the door slam and he was gone.

Charity continued to rage as she reassured herself. *I don't care! Why should I care? He means nothing to me. Christopher will be here soon and I shall forget that Mr. Sean McDougal ever existed.*

With no one to hear, Charity stopped telling

herself how little she thought of the freebooter. But she remained completely miserable; doubly so when the stark truth cut its way through her internal tirade. *Would* Christopher be coming to Windward? No doubt, but perhaps in a box with the cut of Nickelawn's blade through his heart. For all her efforts, they would still meet on the dueling ground.

Charity! You coward; you weakling! You had a chance to save him and you threw it away. . . .

49.

On the day after Meg Wahl's funeral, Gaby Kirth hurried to London in pursuit of Christopher Leach, a question plaguing her all the way. Had that odious little colonial bitch given Christopher her version of the fight at the Camber picnic? It was possible that she had not. His brief stay at Windward Moors had been a time of mourning and the subject might not have come up.

Gaby had a plan for ingratiating herself with the Leaches. That would be most important, she thought—a first step in her conquest of Christopher—because without Clement's blessing, her chances were slim.

She had learned from Mrs. Dylan where Christopher was staying, so contacting him was a simple matter. She took a room at the Lincoln

Inn, left her card with a notation under his door, and he came to her immediately upon returning to the hotel.

Gaby, all softness and sympathy, seized his hand impulsively in hers and said, "Christopher—you poor darling! I have so wanted to again come to you and offer my condolences. And with your presence required in London I made so bold as to come here and leave word. . . ."

"Gaby, I need no explanation. I am delighted to see you. It has been so long. We must have dinner and talk of old times."

"Of course. And new times also. After all, I did mean something to you before you went to the Colonies."

She was a lovely thing, even more beautiful, Christopher thought, than he remembered her. And so gentle now, and understanding.

"Losing Meg so tragically was a terrible blow, Christopher. For all of us. We were warm friends. I loved her dearly."

Gaby spoke too of Clement and his wasted appearance. It was of great concern to her because she knew how dearly Christopher loved him. All in all, she sent Christopher away for the moment thoroughly enchanted. And when they met for dinner that evening in a private, candlelit dining room, she went expertly on with her seduction.

"That lovely little creature you brought with you from the Colonies," she said with a sad wistfulness in her voice.

"Charity."

"Yes, Charity. I so wanted to be her friend and make her welcome, but. . . ."

"I know," Christopher replied. "Clement was telling me. She attacked you at Meg's picnic."

"I don't know why. I must have angered her in some manner. Then I did not get a chance to apologize because when I had composed myself she had returned to Windward."

"Whatever it was, Charity is not one to stay in a temper. I am sure she is sorry and will apologize to you."

"That would hardly be necessary. But Christopher, I have had no chance to tell you how well you look. When I first set eyes upon you, you quite stole my heart all over again."

The enchantment remained. Gaby was wearing a rose-colored gown of satin. It caught the glow from the candles, making her look like a freshly picked blossom from a garden. Or at least that was how Christopher saw her.

"You said you would wait for me," he said softly.

"I know, darling. I was devastated when you left. I did not know that I loved you so much. Lord Kirth, bless him, was so understanding and I was lonely and—well, he asked nothing of me; he was such a fine old gentleman."

"I understand," Christopher said sincerely.

With so much understanding, Gaby was so greatly encouraged.

She said, "Christopher, I had an ulterior motive for seeking you out. I need your advice and your help."

"Whatever I can do, Gaby."

"It is Clement. I know he does not favor me. I am aware that he packed you off to the Colonies in order to separate us. That depressed me greatly and I am sure it had something to do with my marrying Lord Kirth. I was sure you were lost to me."

Christopher frowned and searched for the right words. "Gaby, darling. As a younger brother I put great store in Clement's wisdom. He had a great deal to do with guiding my life. He still does, for that matter, but four years in the Colonies changed me. In the plainest of terms, I am now more my own man."

"I am glad, Christopher, but I still want to be Clement's friend."

"I am sure you will have no difficulty in overcoming any prejudice he might have had."

"I hope that is true but I would like to demonstrate my friendship in a more tangible way. I noticed at the funeral that St. Jude's is badly run down."

Christopher had noted that also. It had seemed to him that the venerable old church and its illustrious pastor were going into decline together.

"The church *is* in lamentable shape," he admitted.

"That is what I wanted to ask you. If I made a donation, say five thousand pounds, would Clement accept it? Or would he feel it was impudence on my part—not being one of his congregation?"

"Gaby, one could hardly call such a generous gift an impudence. I'm sure Clement would accept it with thanks, and it would serve good purpose. It would shame the wealthy members of the congregation into taking more interest in St. Jude's."

"Then I shall give you a cheque for the amount if you will be so good as to present it for me."

"I will be glad to. And I am sure you will hear from Clement in short order."

"Christopher, you have made me so happy!"

Their destination was not necessarily a foregone conclusion but arriving at it was not difficult; the two legs of the journey—from the private dining room to Gaby's room and across that to the bed.

Their lovemaking was the bursting forth of long-pent-up desire. Body to naked body, they furiously made up for the time they had lost, and Gaby was surprised and, curiously, a little dismayed. Christopher had improved amazingly as a lover. She recalled other days when she'd had to furnish all the initiative with Christopher a fumbling, inept amateur. Now that was all changed. His hands, his mouth, his taking over with a self-confident skill, all his earlier inhibitions gone. Somewhere, he had acquired a knowledge that sent her quickly into sexual delight; the straining of splayed-out legs, a singing in her distended nipples and writhing torso that brought jealousy as well as ecstasy. Where had he learned the stunning new techniques? He had certainly been practicing on someone. That degenerate little half-Indian slut? God, how Gaby hated her! . . .

It was curious that the subject of the duel did not come up until they lay exhausted, seeking fresh vitality with which to continue.

"As you no doubt know, I have an appointment with Borland Nickelawn at Camber soon."

"Why, darling, that should not worry you," Gaby murmured.

"It doesn't," Christopher replied, and was quite proud of the truth in that statement. There had been no fear of Nickelawn from the very first moment, even though he had not deluded himself as to the gravity of the situation.

"I am sure he will not appear," Gaby was saying.

"Why should he not?"

"Haven't you heard? Even my coachman had the news as I drove in. Immediately you left Windward, Sean McDougal challenged Borland. They met at the Dueling Oak and Borland collapsed and begged for mercy."

"That is unbelievable! Nickelawn is no coward."

"But perhaps Sean McDougal was such a formidable opponent that Borland completely lost his courage."

"I still cannot believe it."

"Word of it has reached London. I am surprised you have not heard."

"I have been quite busy with the Prime Minister's people. What was the reason for the duel?"

"I did not hear. But Sean went to Borland's club and challenged him. Probably a dispute over some woman."

"Well, I shall appear, of course, even if Nickelawn does not."

Gaby shifted her position. "I think you have nothing to worry about." She pressed a hot breast

340

against Christopher's mouth. "Darling, forget those odious people. Make love to me. Thrill me again, sweetheart."

And a few moments later, "Oh, bite it, lover! Bite it *hard*!"

On her way home from London, Gaby stopped off in Maidstone to visit Nickelawn, bent upon getting a firsthand report of what had occurred. At first she thought the house deserted when he did not answer the bell. However, she had seen a curtain drawn aside and with typical stubborness she persisted until she was admitted.

"Borland, sweet! I have heard such rumors! They are not true, I am sure, but I had to come."

He was quite himself again physically, but mentally it was another matter. He said, "I suppose you heard that I am in disgrace."

"Something of the sort. Did you actually cringe before Sean McDougal?"

"So you too believe the rumors!"

"I only know that they are everywhere."

Nickelawn doubled his fist and slammed it against the wall of his parlor. "Lies! Stinking lies! I was ill, I was deathly ill—unable to raise my rapier. And I know why I was in such a condition."

"You were taken with a fever?" she asked sympathetically.

"I was poisoned by that little slut Charity Sturges—Christopher Leach's whore!"

Gaby stared in amazement. "Charity Sturges? What did she have to do with it?"

"She came here. . . ."

341

"Charity came *here*? To you?"

He took offense at that. "Why not? Am I such a reprehensible character that even gutter trash avoids me?"

"Borland—I did not mean it that way."

"No? Then how did you mean it?"

"I am just surprised that she would take the risk. You *do* know your reputation for using the whip on your women. And I am sure Meg told Charity. Meg did visit you on occasion, did she not?"

"That is neither here nor there. The Sturges bitch came here with the intent to do me mischief. She put a drug in my brandy that made me sick. Laudanum, I think."

"That innocent little...."

"Innocent? As a pit viper is innocent. She is the devil's child! She fooled me completely."

Gaby had a difficult time suppressing laughter. What a glorious tumbling of this conceited ass from his high place! No one she could think of deserved it more.

"Borland," she said, "I am so terribly sorry. Seeing a good friend humiliated is a terrible thing!"

"I am sure you don't mean that," he said cynically.

"But I do! We have always been friends. I *like* you, Borland. Even when you were whipping away at my bare bottom I had no hostility toward you."

"Then you will help me get level with that sneaky young whore?"

"Why, Borland! I am sure you can get your revenge without my help." The last thing she wanted was to get involved in one of Borland's vendettas.

"I need a go-between. You must invite her to Channel Light. I will be there. Send your servants away. . . ."

"It would be risky," Gaby protested, afraid she was getting into deep water.

"You said you were my friend."

"I am." She paused. Then, "What do you have in mind for her?"

"I haven't quite decided. But I promise you this. When I get through with her, Leach will have no further use for the slut."

Gaby admitted to herself that she would enjoy watching Charity's downfall. But she had her own interests to think of, and with the success she'd had in seducing Christopher she no longer saw Charity as a danger. Therefore she had no reason to risk trouble by intriguing against the little trollop.

She said, "I will try, Borland, but you must understand that we are not on the best of terms. I do not believe that Charity would accept an invitation from me."

"But you will try?" he persisted.

"Of course I will try," Gaby lied with a sincerity that convinced him. . . .

After Gaby left, Nickelawn continued to chew the bitter cud of his disgrace. It was the rumors that had done him in. Were the truth known, he would not have fallen so low in public esteem. Unable to use a blade because of sickness was not a thing to ruin a man. But people are prone to be-

343

lieve the juiciest rumors available, and the lie about his lack of courage was far more attractive to them than the truth. Also, Sean McDougal had scotched his chances of redeeming himself by refusing him a postponement, which it was his right to do. Now if Nickelawn challenged him he could refuse with contempt and honor.

But that little bitch would pay. Oh, how she would pay!...

50.

When Christopher Leach came home to Windward Moors, Charity met him in the driveway and fell into his arms. He gently disengaged her, his face indicating no pleasure at the reunion. Disappointment rather, as though she were an unruly child guilty of misbehaving.

He said nothing, remaining mildly aloof, as they climbed the stairs together. Then he asked, "Has Carton returned?"

"No. He has not been seen." Although Charity was desolated by his attitude, she said nothing.

"Strange that he would go off without a word. Now we have no hostler. Perhaps I should have tried to hire the coachman who brought me from London, although I am sure he prefers the city to dull country life."

"Christopher, I think I may be able to help.

There is a young man at Camber whom I met through one of the maids who was here. They were married and they now have a cottage at Camber. But I am sure they would like to come here and take over the stables."

"Excellent. Bring the man to me," Christopher said absently.

He left Charity at her door, saying, "I am tired from the drive and I need a bath. I will see you at dinner."

With that, he retired to his rooms without a backward glance.

Charity went crestfallen into her chambers. What a bitter disappointment! After her crushing confrontation with Sean McDougal, she had looked forward with yearning to Christopher's arrival. She had planned how it would be, the two of them finally alone with the time to renew that which they had shared on the *Hainaut* and afterwards in London.

But he was treating her like a stranger! What had happened? What had gone wrong?

Charity waited in desperate hope that there would be a knock on her door; that Christopher would come and explain that he had been preoccupied. He would apologize and then . . .

It did not come about. No tapping on her door. Only isolation like a guilty child sent to bed with no supper.

Charity could stand it just so long and then she surrendered to impulse. She left her chambers and entered those next door without knocking. She faced Christopher and demanded, "Darling, what is wrong? What have I done that you treat me this way?"

He had been standing with his hands clasped behind his back, looking out of the window. He turned, somewhat embarrassed by her precipitous entrance, then, as though to delay facing up to the main issue, he said, "I have some good news."

"*Good* news?" Charity replied as though it were difficult to believe.

"Yes. The Prime Minister has been very gracious. He has heard the story of your coming with me to England and he wants to meet you."

"You told him of me?" Charity felt a singing elation. Christopher had talked about her to the Prime Minister!

"Why, yes. During our talks he has grown quite friendly. In truth, he is quite a lonely man, cut off from the world by his high position."

Another thought struck her. "Is that why you have been upset? Because you do not want to present me to him?"

"Of course not, Charity!" Christopher protested instantly.

"Then why have you been so cold to me?"

Obviously this was difficult for him. It was a distasteful chore which had to be done.

"Charity," he said, "I am sure you will agree that your conduct while here at Windward has not been of the best."

Fear clawed at Charity's heart. What was Christopher saying? What had he learned? There had been Dennis Wahl; then Sean McDougal. But who could have known? Who could have told tales about her escapades?

346

"I have tried not to disgrace you," she said meekly.

"By attacking Lady Kirth at Camber?"

"Who told you about that?"

"Clement was quite upset. Word came to him even as far away as Bath. I was also most disturbed. And when I met Lady Kirth in London and she gave me the details. . . ."

Charity's relief at what she considered the least damaging accusation was overshadowed by rising anger. She struggled to hold it in check.

"And I'm sure the details were all in her favor—how I went berserk and attacked her with a meat cleaver for no reason whatever?"

"She was puzzled on that point, your hostility after she tried very hard to make you feel welcome."

"Christopher—you amaze me!"

"I see nothing amazing about concern for the Leach name. I do not wish to see it stained by scandal." His voice was unnaturally sharp.

"Let me understand what you have told me. You came home after a long absence to discuss my conduct with your brother. Then you meet Gaby Kirth in London and listen to her side of the story. All that without asking me, without hearing my side of the story. Now that I look back, it is obvious that the way you acted when you came home from the funeral showed that I was condemned from the first."

"Charity—that is unfair. . . ."

"I agree. As unfair as anything could be. In Virginia, the prisoner was always allowed to speak before they hung him. Here, it seems the accused must go to the gallows while still wondering what crime he committed." She spoke bitterly, trying to hold her anger in check.

"You exaggerate. I am speaking to you now. I am trying to get at the truth."

"Then you shall have it. Gaby Kirth came to that picnic with an intent to embarrass me and make me a laughing stock. I know her reason now, but I did not at the time. She insulted me openly, in front of all those people, and I fought back."

"With a meat cleaver? Wasn't that rather violent?"

Christopher infuriated her by his manner as well as his accusation. He was in no way hostile; distressed rather, as though he were a loving father trying to correct the ways of an errant daughter. Charity would have preferred a head-to-head battle. She had never backed away from a fight, and being patronized in this manner was frustrating as well as infuriating.

"Violent?" Charity said. "Yes, I suppose it was. But Gaby was scalped, not beheaded."

"I don't know what you mean by that, but I feel you should see my point of view."

"Oh, I do! I see it very clearly. I have been on trial here at Windward and have been found wanting, so I think I had better return to Virginia. I will leave Leach House as soon as possible."

But instead of rushing to her rooms to pack, Charity ran to the stables, tears of anger running down her cheeks. She had left Christopher stunned at her outburst, and he followed, but not in time to stop her. What he beheld was his angry ward astride a mare, her skirts and petticoats high on her thighs, revealing the lissome legs he had so much admired upon other occasions.

"Charity! Charity! Come back!" he cried.

He could as well have summoned the wind.

Rage still boiling within her, Charity rode south, wildly, to the danger of life and limb, and at the moment she could have gone over the cliff without greatly caring. She crossed the line between Windward and Channel Light and was brought back to reality only when a shabby-looking man on ahead pointed a flintlock at her and cried, "Hold up! Hold up! This is private property! You are trespassing."

Charity brought the mare onto her haunches. Good God! Was everyone in the world against her? Did no one have a kind word for a stranger in a strange land?

"Dismount," the guard called sternly.

"I'll do no such thing!"

With that, Charity put heels to the mare and rode the man down. In panic and terror, he threw his weapon to the side and followed in a desperate lunge, just avoiding the mare's flying hooves.

No friend to turn to! No sympathetic ear! Charity rode on feeling miserably sorry for herself, and though she did not realize it consciously, the need of a shoulder to cry on steered her toward Camber and the one person who had not yet criticized her.

Dennis Wahl was alone, puttering about a clump of rose bushes on the lawn. He straightened as Charity rode up, to throw herself off her horse, and literally into his arms.

"Dennis, oh, Dennis," she sobbed. "Don't scold me! I couldn't stand it!"

Greatly amazed, he held her and stroked her touseled hair. "Lass! Be easy. Why should I scold you?"

"Everyone else has. Christopher, Clement, that terrible Gaby Kirth. And when I came across her land a man pointed a gun at me."

"You were fired upon?"

"No, I rode him down and came here. Don't send me away, Dennis," she pleaded.

He held her off and looked into her eyes. "Charity, you have evidently been through a great deal. Now calm down and tell me about it."

"I'm sorry, Dennis. I have been acting like a child." The tears and the sobs were subsiding.

"Come. I have water boiling. We will make tea and talk."

He led her to the manor house and into a deep, cool kitchen. It was unlike the cold stone basement at Windward Moors. The manor house at Camber had been built of stout timbers. Great beams held up the ceiling and age had mellowed the walls and wooden floors.

A singing tea kettle hung on the hob in the fireplace over burning logs, and a table was set for tea.

"Your cook is away?" Charity asked.

"I have none. I have no one. I dismissed the domestics after Meg died and am here alone."

In observing him, Charity momentarily forgot her own troubles. He had changed. He was still

350

the shaggy, virile man she had first met, but now there was a difference. Charity found it subtle at first glance. Still, she sensed that some of his basic hostility was gone.

They were silent until the tea was made and they sat facing each other across the table.

Then Charity asked, "Durban has not returned?"

"Nay. I think we have seen the last of him," he answered gruffly.

"He was most devoted to Meg."

Dennis did not want to talk about that. "All right, lass. Tell me all about it."

"Dennis, I cannot return to Windward Moors," she said flatly.

"Is it that bad?"

"I made a mess of things. I think I do not even belong in England. Christopher should never have brought me across the ocean."

"I doubt if he would agree. You had a falling out with him?"

"He accused me of attacking Gaby Kirth without reason. He talked to her and got her side of it and that is what he believes."

"The fool!"

"You know he was in love with her before he went to the Colonies. I think he still is."

"Clement broke that off."

"Yes, but he is now old and sick. Perhaps his influence over Christopher is not as strong as it once was."

"Christopher seems to be doing well in London," Dennis said thoughtfully.

"From what he tells me. Dennis. . . ."

"Yes, lass? . . ."

"You miss Meg a great deal, don't you?"

"What makes you say that?"

"From what I see. You have dismissed your servants and are living like a hermit. But more than that. What I see in you."

He smiled. "You are very observant."

"It is no wonder how you feel. She was a wonderful person."

"It is tragic what fools we can be. How we can go through life trampling the blossoms—until the blossoms are no longer there."

"But you and Meg were happy. You understood each other and led the lives you wanted to lead."

"Did we now?"

"You were not jealous of what Meg did, and Meg did not resent the free manner in which you lived."

Dennis sat silent as Charity realized she had turned too abruptly into discussing a highly sensitive matter. But he made no objection. It seemed that he needed a shoulder as well as she.

"I suppose you refer to the women I knew."

"There were many, were there not?"

"And always the wrong ones."

"Dennis," Charity asked softly, "was I the wrong one?"

"You are a sweet little lass."

"Dennis—let me stay here!"

The plea was sudden, intense, as though all she had gone through had been a prelude to that.

"We could stay here together. We could help each other and let the stupid world pass us by.

You are a good, kind friend and I'll serve you in whatever way you ask."

Even as she spoke there were questions deep in her mind. *Is this what I want?* At the moment it looked so enticing. Retreat from the world she did not understand. Christopher said the Prime Minister wanted to meet her. Another carping critic ready to add complaints to the list of her shortcomings?

Dennis had arisen from the table and was eyeing her quizzically; as though he were silently seeking the answer to a question of his own.

"Lass, would you come with me without asking questions?"

My name is Mavourneen.

Charity lifted her eyes sharply to Dennis' face. Where had that come from? He had not said it. Why had it come so sharply into her mind?

She said, "Of course, Dennis. What do you wish?"

As an answer he took her by the hand and led her out of the kitchen, through the hall, and up the stairs to his bedroom on the next floor. There, he turned to her thoughtfully, and still not speaking, began to undress.

After a wide-eyed moment, Charity also began divesting herself of frock, petticoats, and the rest. They were curiously subdued as though each of them were occupied with their own private thoughts. When they were both naked, Dennis took her in his arms, put her on the bed and lay down beside her. After looking pensively into her eyes for a few moments, he kissed her gently.

353

Charity responded in kind, waiting for passion to arise.

It did, but there was no great surge of it. And when Dennis used a gentle finger to stir Charity, she responded obediently but her breath came no faster than before.

Dennis mounted her and she accepted him with the same automatic obedience. His penetration was gentle, even remote.

A strange mating indeed, as though they were there physically but their minds were off somewhere upon other pursuits.

Dennis worked in slow rhythm with Charity matching it, both of them waiting patiently for the rising of the blood. But even then, they were uncertain, Dennis finally asking, "Now, lass?"

She pressed her hips harder against him by way of response and they went on to the end, Charity crying out briefly and Dennis driving harder. . . .

Finally he rolled to her side and she went into the crook of his arm and sighed softly against his shoulder.

"See?" Dennis said, as though there had been some prior discussion. "It is no good."

Charity understood. "I wonder why?"

"I think the first time there was anger."

"Perhaps."

"We were two spirited beings, out to prove that each could best the other."

"At least we both tried."

He smiled and ran a quick finger across her lips. "And I think you won, lass. You had me against the wall."

354

"And I was quite proud of it."

"Yes," he said sharply, a new, vigorous tone in his voice. "You may stay here at Camber as long as you like. We will protect each other from the phantoms of our own making. You will be my housekeeper when snoops come inquiring, and let them think what they may."

Charity pressed closer, the gesture not unlike that at the roadside inn when she had sought comfort from the warmth of Christopher's body. And there was a contentment in her, knowing that she and this strange man were truly friends; that he would never again make physical claims upon her—nor would she want him to.

51.

"Hello, Chris."

Christopher had been loitering about the stables waiting for Charity to return. He was sure that when her temper tantrum subsided she would come back properly chastened and ask to be forgiven for her childish tantrum. He could not understand why she had accused him of not seeking her explanation of her conduct at Meg's picnic when he was doing that very thing.

With time on his hands he had been pondering the mysteries of human relationships. Why, he

asked himself, did he and Gabrielle Kirth understand each other so well when reaching and understanding Charity was the devil's own task? He
wondered about love. Could a man love two
women at the same time? It seemed so. Gabrielle
and Charity possessed far different qualities but
he was attracted to both of them, and if he were
to give up one for the other he would have been
hard pressed to make the decision.

It was all most confusing, and now he turned
to find that a shabbily clad poltroon had slipped
up behind him to smile and give a greeting. His
first thought was that this must be the new hostler Charity had suggested he hire. Then he recognized the man.

"Sean! Sean McDougal! Why are you gotten up
like that?"

Sean laughed. "Chris, old boy—I expected a
different reception from you, not an idle question.
A whack on the jaw, perhaps, and a demand to
know what I am doing here."

"Very well. What are you doing here?" Christopher fought to restrain his genuine affection
for his cousin.

"I came to give a beloved cousin the time of
day and hopefully take a spot of whiskey with
him."

"I have none of the Irish poison you no doubt
favor, so the drink is hardly possible. And it
would seem that you came a long way to say
hello. You were somewhere on the other side of
the world last I heard."

"The world is round and one has only to turn

about and roll the other way," Sean answered lightly.

Christopher continued his stroll around the stable, Sean keeping pace.

"And what made you roll in this direction?"

"A yearning to see old faces. By the by, I set up digs in one of your towers. Just temporary. I've cleared out now."

Christopher envied this wild cousin of his; the man's bold, uninhibited way of life; his colossal nerve.

"You might have waited for an invitation," he said sternly.

"I anticipated my welcome."

"And what now, Cousin Sean?"

"I thought I might be of assistance. Will you not need a second in your Dueling Oak set-to come tomorrow's dawn?"

"You know about that?"

"Who does not? It is the talk of the neighborhood and beyond."

"I was given an account of your duel with Borland Nickelawn. I was told he refused to fight and sneaked away like a whipped dog."

"More like a hurt dog. There is some doubt that he will turn up for your skirmish, but I would not count on it."

"I have not gotten around to finding a second," Christopher mused.

"Then it will not be necessary."

"Very well. I accept. I am grateful."

"Have you any idea of besting that dancing clown?" Sean asked after a moment.

"I have heard reports of his prowess but I have

had a few lessons myself." Christopher spoke with an assurance he did not truly feel.

"That's the spirit, Cousin. A ready blade and an eager spirit."

"You misunderstand. I am far from eager to engage Nickelawn, but I can hardly do otherwise." Then, to change the subject as they walked toward the house, Christopher said, "You did not tell me why you come here dressed as an impoverished tenant farmer. Is this a new fad of the freebooting brotherhood?"

"My tailor is on holiday and all my better clothing is with my pawnbroker."

"More likely you are clad for some scalawag project. What mischiefs *do* you plan while you are here?"

"I thought we might collaborate on a bit of smuggling, Cousin. Perhaps your friend the Prime Minister would like to buy some French silks at a discount."

Christopher knew Sean was trying to bait him and he resolved not to fall into the trap. Men of Sean's ilk amused themselves in strange ways. He said, "I hardly think so, but he might be interested in the purchase of a length of hemp for your neck."

Sean laughed and clapped Christopher on the shoulder, much to the latter's distaste. "Capital, Cousin, capital," he enthused. "You win the joust."

"A rather empty victory, I'm afraid."

"Are you planning to stay at the Moors permanently?" Sean asked, changing the subject.

"I must return to London in due time."

358

"I did not ask after your voyage across. Was it pleasant?"

"Moderately so. We were boarded by a pirate ship."

"No! Were many killed?" Sean's voice rang with shock.

"None were killed. The blacklegs stole some important papers I was carrying. I think their mission was financed by colonial malcontents."

"How cheeky!"

"As a matter of fact, Sean, I think it was a proposition which might well have interested you."

"Cousin Chris! You malign me! Do you think for a moment I would stir a finger to aid those rebels?"

Sean cared not a whit whether or not Christopher knew him to be the culprit, Charity might have told him. In fact Sean might well have done so himself if he had been in the proper mood. But from the way his cousin, spoke, he guessed Christopher was unaware, subtlety not being in him.

Sean stopped in his tracks. "I'll leave you here, Chris. Tomorrow at the Dueling Oak?"

"Very well."

"I shall meet you there." He gave Christopher a brilliant smile, placed a hand on his cousin's shoulder, and said, "Cousin, do you know what is wrong with you?"

Christopher smiled wryly. "I am sure you will delight in telling me."

"You are just too bloody honest for your own good. It is a sterling virtue which can be the death of you, so have a care."

With that, he was off afoot across the heather, leaving Christopher to stare moodily after him. . . .

After spending a restless night worrying about Charity, not allowing himself to think of what had happened to Meg, Christopher arrived next morning at the Dueling Oak to find Sean there ahead of him. They waited until the sun was well up, but Borland Nickelawn did not arrive.

Sean said, "I thought he might funk it. Still, I'm surprised."

"Something must have detained him," Christopher observed. "And I can't say that I am disappointed."

Something *had* detained Nickelawn. The doctor who attended him as second at the duel with Sean was called away on important medical business, or so he said. And with rumor more potent than fact, Nickelawn could find no peer who cared to second a rank coward.

All that little bitch's fault, of course. And she would pay. She would pay with her skin, flayed inch by inch from her body! Alone and abandoned, Nickelawn brooded over the injustice done him and planned Charity's downfall with the compulsive dedication of one whose mind was slipping and who lived only for vengeance. . . .

52.

Charity was up bright and early on that day and scurried to the kitchen where she prepared a tasty breakfast for the master of the house. She took it to his bedroom on a tray and bade him a gay good morning.

"Your housekeeper and servant, Master. Is there anything else you require?"

"A little more sleep, if you would have the consideration," Dennis grumbled.

"Oh, now—be not short-tempered. It is a beautiful day. The sun is shining and the birds are singing. Eat those fine eggs and stir yourself. We must make plans."

"Plans for what?"

"Milord, if I knew, we would not have to make plans, now would we?"

Dennis eyed the eggs on the plate before him, their edges darkly crisped, the yolks hard as enameled discs. "Just what have I inflicted upon myself by welcoming you to my bosom?" he muttered.

"Does your breakfast displease you?"

"No, child. We might frame it and hang it on the wall. Suppose you let me do the cooking until you get the hang of it."

Charity was not dismayed. "I shall learn

quickly. And by the way, would you object to Dorothy and Wilferd bettering themselves?"

"They may keep bettering themselves from morn 'til night with my blessing—whoever they are."

"The lovely young couple installed in that miserable hut of yours," she reminded him.

"Wilferd—oh, yes. I didn't know you knew them."

"I freed Dorothy from the clutches of that terrible hostler at Windward and now the post is vacant."

"What about a hostler for *my* stables?"

"I will take care of the animals. Besides, you said you wanted no one around but me."

"Did I say that?" He shrugged. "Oh, very well. Send them on their way. That Wilferd struck me as not having the experience for a good tenant farmer. Then too, I'll be doing no more farming."

Charity bestowed a light kiss on his cheek. "Dennis, you are just about the kindest man I've ever known! I'll go tell them."

She left her benefactor jabbing moodily at his breakfast and ran to the stables for a mount. She rode to the hut where Dorothy rushed forward to greet her effusively.

Charity gave them both the good news and was rewarded by their joy. "The Windward Moors stables," Dorothy marveled. "How wonderful!"

Wilferd was grateful also, but less articulate. He could only repeat his hope that someday they could repay Charity for her kindness.

Riding back to the manor house, Charity's spirits were at their highest. It was strange, she thought, how after that violent session in the hut, she and Dennis had lost all semblance of passion for each other. She so wanted now only to serve him in every way possible, as friend and companion. In the meantime she had found a home where critical eyes did not follow her every move, and a master who was hardly that; more of a kind, considerate friend.

Then, some ten minutes after she was back, there came a pounding on the front door. She opened it to find Christopher impatiently slapping his leg with a riding crop. When he set eyes upon her he came close to dropping the whip as he stared, frozen.

"Charity!" It came out as a gasp.

"Yes, Charity. How did you find out I was here?"

"I didn't. I only came to make inquiry, to ask if you had been seen. What is the meaning of this?"

Charity felt deliciously avenged. There was slyness in her smile that she could not hide as she replied demurely, "I wandered alone and rejected with no home and no place to lay my weary head. Then heaven was kind to me and I found this haven where my faults are overlooked and soft words are spoken...."

"Charity! Stop that nonsense! Why did you come here?"

Her burlesque ceased. "Why did *you* come? We have no need of you. We are doing just fine."

"*We?* To whom are you referring?"

"Why, the Duke of York, of course," she replied innocently.

"Charity! I'll not have you baiting me!"

Charity felt suddenly sorry for him. He was so genuinely naive. "Who would I be referring to? The fine gentleman who owns Camber."

"Very well. I shall thank him for taking you in. Now let's have an end to this. Put on your bonnet and come home."

"I wore no bonnet and this *is* my home. Mr. Wahl has engaged me as his housekeeper."

"Stop it! You cannot be serious."

"I am serious, Christopher. No one wanted me at Windward Moors. I was criticized and looked down upon. Everyone's word was taken against my own. I left because I refuse to be treated that way." She caught his thought, her eyes sparkling dangerously. "And don't tell me it was for my own good or I'll—I'll—oh, go away, Christopher, and leave me in peace!"

"You would humiliate me in this fashion?" Christopher could not believe that this was really happening.

"I am truly sorry if you are embarrassed, but you may as well know the truth. I shall never return to Windward."

"But the Prime Minister! I have a commitment to present you!"

Charity had been fighting her sense of guilt all along, trying to block out the memories of how much Christopher had done for her. Although his words now made it sound as though he were thinking only of his own interests, she knew that this was not true. Whatever his shortcomings, he had honestly tried to help her after his fashion.

Her mind began working against her when she remembered something she had heard from her tutor, Hicks, who tended to quote quite frequently. Mr. Shakespeare had written it. *Ingratitude more sharp than—more sharp than—*oh, something! She could not recall.

"I'll think about what you've said, Christopher. I truly will. But for now, just go away and leave me alone!"

She slammed the door, felt like crying, and refused to surrender to the impulse. Minutes later, when she peered around a curtain, Christopher had left.

And try as she would, she could not understand the empty feeling this brought on when she had ordered him to do exactly that.

But she clung to one resolution with unswerving determination.

I shall never go back to Leach House.

53.

Christopher paced the floor of Clement's parlor in the manse at St. Jude's. "I just do not understand it. Why she would leave comfortable quarters at Windward to move into that decaying pile of wormwood is beyond me."

Clement, reclining on his lounge, regarded his brother thoughtfully. Some strength had returned, but little of the old fire was left.

He said, "I think you do, Christopher. But you

refuse to admit it. There can be only one reason. You drove the girl away."

"*I* drove her away? How can you say that? I gave her a home, security, comfort."

"Yes, I suppose so. And now you say Lord North wishes to look the girl over."

"Clement, you make her sound like some slave property."

"Was she not a slave when you found her?"

"No. She was detained illegally, as I told you. And I only wish I could have remained in the Colonies long enough to bring down the bounders who imposed upon her so cruelly."

"Christopher, I think you care a great deal for the lass," Clement said thoughtfully.

"Frankly, I do. You must meet her, Clement."

He smiled wanly. "From what I've heard of her, I am probably not up to facing the whirlwind she seems to be."

Christopher may have noted the change in his brother's attitude. Clement did not seem to resent Charity as much as before. She now appeared to bring him more amusement than concern.

Clement now turned deeply thoughtful, saying, "North has never been known as a licentious man."

"Are you implying that he seeks Charity as a mistress?"

"I would doubt that. But we must be realistic. There is a possibilty that King George has heard of her and North seeks to ingratiate himself with the fat German."

Christopher was horrified. "Never! I plan to marry Charity!"

That brought surprise. "It has gone that far? I thought perhaps your romance with Lady Kirth had been revived. I understand she went to London to visit you there."

"Clement! How on earth do you learn these things hidden away here in your manse as you are?"

"I am kept in touch. My door is open to visitors, and there are many who still see me as having some power."

"Assuming then that mutual interest has been revived between Gaby and me, does that not anger you as it did before?" Christopher asked curiously.

"Anger, my dear brother, is a luxury I can now ill afford. It drains the system and I have little reserve. My interest now is in you and you alone. Your career. I am still with enough vanity to want the name of Leach kept banner-high in the affairs of this nation. You alone can keep it there, but I can no longer point you and push you forward as I once could."

"I shall be perfectly frank, Clement. I am still strongly attracted to Gaby Kirth but I now see her with your eyes. She would not do as the wife of a man striving in the affairs of state. Gaby is too much her own woman."

Clement's eyebrows lifted. "And this little tomahawk enthusiast is not?"

"I suspect that Gaby may have been more to blame than Charity."

"Christopher, from what you tell me, I suspect that you handled the affair rather badly, but there is another subject I wish to touch upon. The dueling challenge you issued and what came of it."

"Are you sure you do not already have the details?" Christopher asked with some wryness.

"Some of them, yes. I understand it did not take place."

"The man Nickelawn turned rank coward. He did not appear. I am sure his reputation is shattered."

"Perhaps, but were I you, I would not dismiss him too lightly. I have had reports on the man. I think it possible that he is not quite sane. He may seek redress through less honorable means than swords at dawn. He has disappeared from his usual haunts."

"I am sure he has crawled off like the whipped dog he is. Having lost public esteem there is little spine left in him. He displayed his soft mettle when he faced Sean McDougal. Then when I went to the Oak with Sean as my second. . . ."

Christopher enjoyed his brother's reaction. "Ah, something you did not know, brother Clement. I *am* surprised."

"I knew of McDougal's joust with Nickelawn, of course, but not of his seconding you at the Oak."

"We met and he made the offer. He is a wild scoundrel but he does have some good qualities."

"I daresay I would like to speak with Sean. Be so good as to send him to me if you two meet again."

"I shall be happy to."

"And now please leave me. My strength wanes quickly and I must nap through the day."

"I'll call again soon, brother," Christopher said gently.

"Please do. And remember what I said about Borland Nickelawn."

On his way back to Windward, Christopher gave Nickelawn scarcely a thought. His mind was filled with sadness at Clement's state. In memory, he returned to the time of Clement's greatness and could again hear his brother's sonorous voice ringing through the Commons, resounding against the buttresses of Canterbury as he exhorted his fellow Englishmen toward the paths of justice he felt they walked too rarely.

A great man, my brother, Christopher thought. *I depended upon him and now he depends upon me. I shall not disappoint him. . . .*

54.

Dennis watched pensively as Charity splashed about in the duck pond at Camber. She called out, "Come and swim with me, you dullard. Do not sit there on that log like a frog taking the sun."

He shook his head and continued to watch her. Charity was a remarkable swimmer, he had discovered, flashing in and out of the water like a mermaid born to the waves.

After a time, he called out, "Are you staying in

there forever, housekeeper? What about dinner for the master?"

"You did not appreciate my breakfast so you may starve, for all of me."

"Come out, I say, or I'll take a birch to you."

His opinion of Charity was quite simple. Enchanting. She was a child of many facets, each as intriguing as the next. There had been the aggressive wanton he'd known during that first encounter at the hut. Then, when their second attempt failed so miserably her attitude toward him changed diametrically to that of daughter; a gay, lighthearted daughter who began by bullying him, confiding in him, and giving him warm kisses utterly devoid of the earlier passion.

The change had its effect upon him. It made him realize, pointedly, the difference in their ages; eighteen against the mid-thirties, and touched him with guilt at having taken a comparative child. But there at the hut she had functioned as a complete adult, those false years only now having fallen away.

This sojourn at the duck pond had been the rarest of experiences for Dennis; to see Charity, on impulse, shed her clothing and plunge in without regard for modesty, as innocently as a young fawn sporting in the forest.

And now, as she emerged, her wet, sun-dusted skin glistening, his new attitude toward her was solidly cemented. He could admire her lovely body at a different level. Lewd thoughts would now have the quality of incest.

Charity stood before him and laughed as she shook water from her body, and Dennis could only wonder at his own acceptance of the new situation.

"You are shameless," he accused.

"I am wet," she replied.

"If you are hinting that I run back and get you a towel, put it out of your mind."

"I'll use my frock and carry it back to the house."

"Naked and brazen? Hardly. Put that frock on before someone comes visiting. Hurry now or you shall feel the palm of my hand on your bottom."

In another mercurial change, Charity sobered, held the dress about her, and said, "Dennis, I haven't disappointed you, have I?"

"You are no end of bother, I'll admit only that."

"I do wish it were different," she said wistfully.

"You wish no such thing—nor do I."

"Then I may stay with you forever? Here at Camber shut off from the hateful world?"

"If you go on as you do, I'll lock you in your room until you grow up into a proper young lady. Come now—before prying eyes find you and spread a scandal. . . ."

55.

Gaby Kirth slept restlessly that night. There were dreams; the channel cliffs loomed in her sleeping fancy. A phantom pursued her, and she was falling, falling. The jagged rocks below were much farther down than in reality.

Then there he was, the phantom, with a hand over her mouth to keep her from crying out.

But it was no dream—a true hand and the weight of an arm holding her hard to her bed.

"Quiet—quiet, I say! You will not be harmed."

She knew even as the intruder spoke, but it was hard to believe.

Borland Nickelawn!

He eased his grip carefully and now he withdrew his hand.

"I have come to hear what is being done since we talked in Maidstone."

Nothing had been done nor had Gaby ever expected to give Nickelawn an accounting. What could she say now that would satisfy him.

"I have tried but it has been most difficult. Charity left Windward Moors."

"I know that. She is living at Camber with that fool Wahl. Have you made any arrangements? Have you invited her here to Channel Light?"

372

Even in the dark Gaby could feel the heat of his madness. It was a fearsome thing to lie helpless under the power of a man beyond reason. There had been signs of it at Maidstone and she now bitterly regretted not having given them more heed.

"Borland—what have you been doing? How did you get here?"

He allowed the divergence. "I left Maidstone, where lies mean more than truth. I now live like a hog in an old miner's hut at the edge of Camber."

More like a skulking jackal, Gaby thought. "Why do you treat yourself so miserably, Borland?"

"Because it gives me freedom to stalk the one who brought me down."

"Charity? But Borland, in going on this way, you only destroy yourself. Revenge is futile unless it gains you something."

"It gains me what I seek most," he said harshly.

A waste of time, Gaby thought, talking reason to one no longer dwelling in those realms. Better she humor him and look to her own safety.

"I have watched," Nickelawn gloated. "I have seen the strumpet go naked while that lecher sat by the pond and slavered. . . ."

In God's name, what is he talking about? Gaby wondered, even while realizing that Nickelawn, in his madness, was reviling others for his own swinishness; trying unconsciously to move its weight off his own guilty shoulders to those of the innocent.

373

But only the immediate now mattered. Her own danger. "Borland, I will try again. . . ."

Wanting sympathy more than cooperation, he went on. "I go here and there like a shadow and they are not aware that they are at my mercy. But I wait and learn of this land. I wait for *her*—until fate puts her into my hands. It must not be quick and easy. Slow and painful when the time comes." He smiled a quick, sly smile and cocked his head in the telling birdlike gesture she'd seen once in Bedlam during a carefree evening when she and her friends went there with him to watch the loonies.

"Did you know there is a tunnel from Leach House reaching to the shore under the cliffs?" he asked conspiratorially.

"I didn't know."

"Of course not," he sneered. "You go about your silly affairs not knowing if your nose is on straight. You are disgusting!"

"Borland—please—I am your friend."

Even as she made the plea, Gaby realized that this madness was no sudden thing. The seed of it had been planted in Borland long before sanity finally left him.

"I am your friend," she repeated. "I will redouble my efforts."

"You lie! You have always lied to me."

Gaby felt that she lay balanced between life and death. Then providence took pity and there was a tapping on the door and a muffled query.

It was the old retainer she had inherited along with the Kirth fortune. "Milady, I thought I saw

374

a skulker by the vines under your window. Are you all right?"

Nickelawn drew away. "I will be back in due time," he snarled and was gone as he had come.

Gaby arose and hurried to the door, and the old servant was amazed at the reception she gave him. Going almost into his arms, she said, "I am quite all right, Quinton. Quite all right. It is good of you to be so watchful. I am sorry your sleep was interrupted. . . ."

The old man shuffled away mumbling in his confusion. "Strange. You expect a kick and get a blessing." Curious indeed, he marveled, were the ways of the gentry.

Gaby returned to bed and trembled, sleepless, for the rest of the night. What to do—what to do? Should she unmask that maniac and set the constable on his trail? A dangerous thing if the bumbling officials failed. Nickelawn would know immediately that she was responsible and come seeking her. Better she did nothing. It mattered not a whit what happened to Charity Sturges. Yes; better she locked her windows and her door and stepped lightly at all times. By its very nature, this nightmare would end and it behooved her to see that she remained a whole person until that finish came about.

56

"You wanted to see me, your Reverence," Sean McDougal said.

"Please do not call me that. I think it is more amusing to you than respectful."

"Please, Clement. You do me an injustice. I have always respected you."

"Sean—Sean! The gifts God bestowed upon you!"

Clement had come forth from the manse to sit in the arbor and enjoy the morning sun. The mark of respect Sean felt for him was indicated by the clothes he wore; not the serf garb Christopher had seen but breeches, hose, and weskit of subdued shades, as befitted a visitor to the manse.

"I am happy to see that your health has improved," he said.

"Somewhat. But there is too much to be done—far too much. And one grows weary."

"Belay that talk, Cousin. You need a bit of rest, no more. You are not an old man. Hardly in your forties."

"There is an illness, Sean. I think it is God's punishment for turning my back on Him to pursue my own ambitions."

Sean quietly marveled. Was this the old fire-eater who would have consigned him to perdition such a scant time ago? He said, "I think He directed you where He wished you to go."

"Perhaps, but enough of that. There are some matters I wish to speak of. First, my undying gratitude for saving Christopher's life."

"I am afraid I do not follow you."

"Have done with evasion, Sean. I do not know all the details but the coincidence was too great. Challenging Nickelawn. A man with whom you had no quarrel."

"Can you be so sure?"

"Sure enough. It is not your way to go about seeking trouble. You put yourself between that murderer and Christopher when you owed Chris nothing."

"Again, you surmise. But accepting your premise, must all favors be given in return for other favors?"

Clement regarded Sean thoughtfully. "I have always thought of you, Sean, as having a good heart. Perhaps the mistakes of the past were mine. Would we could turn back the years and begin anew."

"Clement! Be not so harsh with yourself!" This was one of the few times Sean felt at a loss. Clement was foisting the weight of misplaced guilt upon his own shoulders.

"The other matter," Clement went on, "your presence here in Kent. Why are you not off upon the trade lanes taking Spanish ships?"

"We all yearn at times for the hills of home."

"But this is not your home. Were that the reason, you would be in Ireland."

"My men—my crew. They are all of Kent."

377

"Oh, yes. That remarkable crew of yours. Would I'd had the skill to organize Parliament as you have had in bringing together your band of loyal yeomen."

"You give me too much credit."

"I doubt that, but I wanted to mention certain items—certain unrelated items." There was an inflection upon the *unrelated* that Sean did not miss.

"I would be interested."

"There is a word of thefts—disappearances—armaments and such purloined from various premises of the Crown. Have you heard?"

Sean kept his voice level. "I believe I have heard it mentioned."

"Opinions on the matter are divided. Some believe the thefts are of a casual nature and will subside as such waves of lawlessness do."

"And others? . . ."

"That the thefts are parts of a well-thought-out plan with a motive behind it."

"Armaments, you said. That would indicate thefts from armories and arms depots. In either case—casual thefts or by plan—I am sure the culprits, at least some of them, have been laid by the heels."

"Some of the goods have been found, I understand—a scattering of them. But not the thieves. What has been revealed is a lamentable laxity in protecting the King's stores. That of course will be corrected and no doubt some of the thieves apprehended." He paused to look directly into Sean's eyes. "Poor devils. It will mean the hangman's noose."

"Perhaps the thefts will cease before there is need for stern measures," Sean suggested.

"Mayhap. But one thing is certain. If the thefts are on an organized basis, the man behind them is a most remarkable person. The plan would be most daring and imaginative, the leader a skilled and fearless individual. Also, he would have to be cloaked in great loyalty by those who serve him."

"An able hypothesis, cousin, but could it not be the other way? That this mythical leader is more of a servant to his followers?"

Clement withheld his reply while he appeared to be considering the meaning of Sean's words. He then said, "Be that as it may, I wanted to bring the thefts to your attention as one loyal to the Crown. I am sure that if you come upon useful information you will inform the authorities."

"Have no doubt, cousin," Sean said firmly.

Clement extended a fragile hand. "And Sean— please visit me again—soon."

"I shall look forward to it. . . ."

Hard upon leaving the manse, Sean arrived at Sibley's hut. Sibley was on a ladder which reached its thatched roof.

Sean laughed. "So the stubbornest of mules can be brought around."

Sibley glowered at the handful of dried reeds he had just put into place. "Showers gather in the thatch and drip down through the dry spells. My wife spurned me for a lazy dullard and went to her sister's."

He climbed down the ladder and handed Sean a jug of ale resting in the doorway. "Did you bring news or did you come merely to laugh at my troubles?"

"Why don't you burn the place down and build your wife a decent abode?"

"That will come in due time," Sibley said impatiently.

"If we do not all hang first."

"There is some word?"

"My cousin, the Reverend Clement Leach, gave me a warning."

"Clement Leach *warned* you? Next you'll tell me he has deserted the church to become the freebooter's champion."

"Clement has changed. He now bends where he used to stand as rigid as the King's scepter. Also, he felt he owed me a favor for interfering in Christopher's duel."

"What did he tell you?"

"That the powers are upset. They suspect a plot."

Sibley sat down on the front steps and indulged himself from the jug. "Hmmm. We have not yet filled the ship. Would you consider taking off with what we have?"

Sean shook his head. "As nature abhors a vacuum, I detest an empty hold."

Sibley frowned. "If you were not so pickety as to quality! Those rebels should be happy with whatever they can get."

"Sibley, did you ever face an enemy with an exploding flintlock in your hands?"

"We will change our assembly point. Perhaps too many coffins have been moving about the country. If we continue that method, the authorities might start to wonder about all the dead people. Until they organize a check of road vehicles, we will use hay ricks and perhaps smaller loads carried overland at night, the stronger men functioning as mules." Sibley paused, then added, "Let's hope the weather holds, and go with what we have."

"We will secure a full cargo," Sean corrected with easy confidence.

"I wish I had your lack of good sense," Sibley sighed. "I would sleep better of nights. As I have told you before, I still worry over Carton's disappearance. The man is off somewhere. It was a mistake, my taking him on. He may even now be doing us in."

"In a project of this sort, there are risks that must be taken."

"And we certainly take them with leaps and bounds," Sibley grumbled.

"My dear fellow, you know this was the only way."

"And only a madman like you would have thought of it."

"The only way," Sean repeated. "None of the small European nations would sell me arms. I could not go to France or Spain, and the Prussians need all they have to defend their own borders. That left only Mother England to fill the bill."

"Gentle old Mother England," Sibley ruminated. "You will discover how gentle she is if we are turned up."

As Sean rode away, Sibley stared after him,

half-expecting to see a band of armed angels hovering over him. Otherwise, how had he lived so long?

57.

Charity dismounted at the Windward stables and threw up a defensive arm as Dorothy rushed forth to greet her.

"Easy, lass—easy," she murmured.

"Oh, Miss Charity. Being here is so wonderful! A lovely place to live and all these beautiful animals to care for!"

"I am sure they appreciate your loving attention, Dorothy, but now I have a chore for you."

"Oh, Miss Charity! I am so glad. Now I can do something for you!"

"You are to go into the house and tell Mrs. Dylan I want my cases packed. You will bring them out and have Wilferd cart them over to Camber. Is that clear?"

"Very clear, Miss Charity. Wilferd will bring them this very afternoon."

"You must be very careful with the gowns, Dorothy. They must not be rumpled or stained."

"Oh, I'll take care of them, you may be sure. . . ."

Dorothy was off to the house as though swift passage meant the salvation of her soul. Alone,

Charity considered what she had done. It *was* rather cowardly, sending Dorothy on a task she should have taken care of herself. But she had a reason that sufficed. Christopher would have confronted her and again tried to alter her decision and she feared he might succeed. That would never do, she'd told herself. A person who wavered back and forth like a reed in the wind could not be respected. She had made a decision with ample justification and it would stand.

Now her eyes turned toward the Moon Tower, her thoughts toward Sean McDougal. So bitter had been his attack upon her that moving to mend the breach was unthinkable; nor had he made any overtures himself. No, that affair was ended; but regardless, it would not have altered her determination to become Christopher's wife and pattern her life to his.

If her exodus from Leach House dimmed that possibility, Charity did not see it so. She had come to understand Christopher very well and she was sure that leaving Windward would gain her even more of his respect. A man could hardly love a girl who did not stand up for her rights. Remembering something she had forgotten, she went inside to leave a note:

> *Dorothy:*
> *Please tell Mr. Leach that I would like to speak to him, when convenient, at Camber.*

She read the note over and was struck by its peremptory tone. But instead of changing it, she smiled. The future wife of a high government official should conduct herself with some show of authority. Heaven forbid that she should turn into a mouse as had poor unfortunate Mercedes. Men like Justin were brutes. If Christopher ever moved in that direction she would certainly bring him up short in no uncertain terms.

On her return, she found Dennis standing by the Camber rose garden. As she approached, he bent to pull a weed, then threw it absently aside. He looked to be pensive of mood and it occurred to Charity that he had been more quiet of late as though thoroughly occupied with his own thoughts.

She said, "Dennis, I just ordered my clothes brought over from Windward."

"I am glad to hear that. Maybe there will be less of your running around naked. Didn't the Indians you lived with ever wear anything?"

"I did not live with Indians. Come, sit with me there on the bench. I have something to suggest."

She plucked a rose to take with her and when they were seated, she cupped the blossom in her fingers without actually seeing it. "Dennis," she said finally, "don't you think it's time you started thinking about the future?"

"Why? Are you afraid the provender will run out and you will be in danger of starving?"

"I have no fear of that. I am going to marry Christopher and be the mistress of Windward."

"Well, that's a sudden change. As I recall, you came here like a lost kitten begging for sanctuary. We were going to retire from the world, you and I."

384

"You didn't expect that mood to last, did you?" She raised her eyes from the flower and looked full into his.

"No, I suppose not. I should have known better, dealing as I am with an erratic female. You suggest I think of tomorrow. What do you propose I do with myself and these useless acres?"

"They are not useless and neither are you. As it happens, I have an idea."

He smiled in amusement. "Only one? I would expect you to come forth with at least a half-dozen."

As if she did not hear him, she went on, "I think you should turn Camber into a school for young gentlemen."

His quizzical look said that he did not quite comprehend. But he said nothing, waiting for Charity to continue.

"The location is excellent, here on the Channel shore—away from Maidstone and London, but not too far. You may not realize it yourself but you would make a fine headmaster. You would inspire confidence in your students, and parents in both Maidstone and London would be happy to send their sons to such a fine place."

He was smiling now, almost chuckling, regarding her with condescending amusement—much as though she were a small child who had suggested he sell sea water by the pail.

Charity rushed on. "The house is quite big enough to convert. One wing for classrooms and the other for student residence. You could ... "

He laid a restraining hand on her arm. Still

385

smiling, he said, "Easy, lass. You are off to the moon with cobweb wings."

"All right! Tell me what is wrong with the idea! I mean other than plain lack of ambition on your part."

He was enjoying her enthusiasm but he was still speaking to the impractical child. "Nothing, lass—nothing at all—if we could wave a magic wand and clear roads and paths and playing fields; if we could whisper to a good fairy and change the house as you suggest."

"Are you saying? . . ."

"That I am," he interrupted. "Money. The wherewithal to do these magical things."

"But I thought . . . "

"I am sure you did," he replied, shutting her off again. "I am sure you thought me as wealthy as the Leaches and Lady Kirth. Not true. Not true at all."

"But you have lived well. You had servants and horses."

"I did not say we were impoverished. We have always been able to keep up appearances. But that is far from being able to match pounds with the Leaches."

"But Meg *was* a Leach."

"She married me to get out from under the heel of Clement, who controls the family. I was much below their social level. My father made his money in trade and they saw him as an intruder when he bought this land. He improved only a small part—vegetables and such for our own use, and that was the way it has remained. The rest was used for hunting and fishing. It has gone to bush and bramble. The house is solid enough but the reconstruction which would be necessary . . ."

"Are you saying that Clement cut Meg off without a shilling?"

"He gave her an allowance and I have a small income." Dennis' smile was wry rather than bitter. Charity was sure that his thoughts were on the past, when Meg was alive—opportunities for happiness which were now lost forever.

"Dennis," Charity said quietly, "I can raise the funds."

Dennis stared. "You—you are incredible!"

"Not at all. I merely see opportunity where you see impossibility. The Leaches may be stiff people but I am sure they would recognize a good investment when they saw it."

"Charity," Dennis said with exaggerated concern, "go you and jump into the duck pond and cool your fevered brain."

"I have no such need. And by the way, Christopher is calling soon. I left a note at Windward telling him to."

"And I am sure he will ride the wind in his haste to get here." Dennis' tones were just on the near edge of irony. Then, as if by plan, Christopher hove in view riding a black stallion.

Charity could not resist a smug comment. "Not the wind. His stallion still brought him here ahead of my clothes."

"The man is a fool," Dennis snapped. "Did you put a ring through his nose?"

Christopher was, as usual, elegantly clad; shiny black boots, fawn-colored, skin-tight breeches, and a black riding jacket with an ascot at his throat. He looked every inch the prosperous country gentleman. There was no mark of his earlier fury as he dismounted and dropped his reins, the stallion obviously trained to stand.

He gave first attention to the master of Camber. "Dennis—good to see you, old chap."

"Nice of you to call," Dennis replied.

"I got a note from Charity. She has perhaps come to her senses?" Christopher spoke over Charity's head as if she were a child not to be included in grownups' talk. Charity masked the anger which rose within her.

Dennis said, "Perhaps, but I've seen no sign of it."

Christopher now turned to Charity, and fury boiled within her. She said, "I presume you are saying that I should return to Windward."

"I thought your note *was* perhaps indicative . . ."

"Hardly. And I thought, after you had calmed down, that I might more clearly explain my reasons for leaving." Her reason for the summons had been a nagging feeling that cutting herself off so completely from the man she planned to marry was not a brilliant tactic.

"I am quite calm now," Christopher replied with a touch of coldness.

"However," Charity went on, "something else has come up. We, Dennis and I, have been discussing the possibility of establishing a young gentleman's school here at Camber."

"*We?*" Dennis cut in. "Let's keep the matter straight, young lady. It was totally your idea."

Charity shrugged. "No matter. The point is,

the project would need financing. It could be a most profitable enterprise. Perhaps you would be interested."

Dennis' eyes blazed. "Charity—you go too far!" With that, he strode off in stark fury and vanished toward the stables.

Charity's reaction was honest surprise. Christopher stared after Dennis, then turned to her. In chiding tones, he said, "You should not have done that."

"Why? I don't understand."

"You hurt his pride," he said, feeling an unfamiliar sympathy for Dennis.

"His pride! The school is an honest project— and financial help is *honestly* needed."

"Charity, men like to handle their own affairs."

"And how do they offer other men profitable partnerships? Do they avert their eyes and whisper to each other around corners?"

"You are being ridiculous."

"Are you saying the idea is foolish?"

"Not at all," Christopher said quickly.

"Then you and perhaps Reverend Leach *might* be interested?"

Christopher eyed Charity quizzically. "You hang on like a terrier, my dear; on to matters, I might say, in which you should not be involved. You are too young—too inexperienced."

"Why, you smug—self-satisfied! . . ." Charity knew she should have controlled herself but found it impossible. Good Lord! Did a person have to be ancient—wrinkled and weak of limb—before an idea bore weight?

Christopher remained calm, no doubt feeling

himself in an advantageous position. He said, "My dear, there is no point in continuing this." There was the slyest of smiles. "We will continue the discussion when you have calmed down."

The beast! How sneakily he had reversed their positions! She watched as he mounted the stallion and rode away. She might have noticed that he paused at the far end of the drive to look thoughtfully about. His gaze covered a breadth of the wooded expanse, then turned back to study the manor house before he went out of sight. But if there was any purpose to his inspection, Charity was too upset to give it heed. . . .

Both Wilferd and Dorothy arrived a short time later. Wilferd walked ahead of the cart bearing Charity's cases, leading the horse rather than driving it so he could walk with Dorothy, who hand-carried the more delicate gowns, not trusting them to the cart.

Charity thanked them and offered payment for their services, but did not press when she saw that their pride was touched.

Pride! Everyone seemed to have an overstock of it regardless of how little else they possessed.

She watched them ride off together in the cart, envying them the joy of their simple, uncomplicated lives. Quickly, her mind played truant and she was walking hand in hand with Sean, the wind blowing her hair, the heather abloom all about.

Idle dreams—laid away as all such dreams should be to wither fragrantly like evening primrose petals in a memory book, finally to be forgotten.

Her prime determination remained as fixed as ever. Her destiny lay with Christopher. And if she had made mistakes while progressing along that path, those mistakes could be corrected. In truth, Sean McDougal had done her a favor by retiring from her life.

And now, she told herself, *I must find Dennis and smooth his ruffled feathers or I will find myself without a home. . . .*

He was at the stable looking to a mare whose time for foaling was nearing. Charity approached in silence and rubbed the mare's velvety nose.

When he did not speak, she said, "Dennis, I'm sorry I offended you. I was only trying to help. Do you criticize me for that?"

"I criticize you for being an impossible little busybody who snoops in other people's affairs without being asked."

"But Dennis," Charity insisted, "you know Camber is an ideal place for a young gentleman's school."

"I know nothing of the sort. But assuming so, it is not your place to goad grown men into doing your will."

"And I thought you were different!" Charity wailed. "I thought you were my friend!"

"Evidently your definition of a friend is someone who lets you lead him around by the nose."

"You are impossible! I think you *enjoy* hurting me!"

With that, she rushed off in tears—crocodile tears, to be sure, for her instincts told her they would soon bring Dennis to apologize. A nice reversal, done with talent and skill. . . .

58

Sibley, reporting to Sean McDougal in his cabin, where he sat working on a list of supplies, said, "There may be trouble."

"What sort of trouble?" Sean raised his head from the ledger.

"I am not sure, but there is a man who patrols Channel Light watching for poachers. At times he swings through Camber in search of possible lairs where they might hide themselves until nightfall."

"Is there no daylight poaching on the estates?"

Sibley was slow in answering. He was finding it difficult to capture Sean's whole attention. Sean seemed preoccupied and perhaps not too greatly interested.

"Yes, but at night the poachers flash a lantern in the eyes of the deer. The beasts freeze and are quite easily killed."

"I am familiar with poaching methods," Sean said mildly.

"But you asked ... "

"Sibley—go on with what you came to tell me!"

"This man went as far as the old iron-mine huts at the foot of Camber and saw an intruder skulking about."

"If he was looking for poachers, why is locating one so important to us?"

"He is a good man with good instincts and he said it was not a poacher. They would not set up a camp in such a barren area. The mines are too far from where the deer forage."

"Who is this guard? One of our men?"

"Aye, he serves us at shoreside when we load the cases. Therefore he is sensitive to our cause. That makes his warning worth noting."

"Then you think perhaps a constable's man is lurking there to spy on us?"

"That could well be."

Sean considered this for a moment, then said, "Unlikely—so far south."

"True, but it is a place whence he could move about and search the coves. There was Clement Leach's warning."

"Then see to it. Investigate the possibility. You do not need my permission."

"If we find such a man, should we kill him?"

"No. Bring him here, if he exists. Most of them have their price. So far none has died. Let us keep it so."

Sibley raised a hand in unconscious salute and as he opened the door to leave, Sean said, "Sibley, I have been staying away from Windward since Christopher Leach returned. I have been there but once since he got back. Has there been a change there?"

"None that I know of."

"I heard a rumor that the girl Christopher brought from Virginia is no longer there."

"Do you feel she is a threat to us?"

"No, no! I just like to keep abreast of things."

"I shall check and let you know if there is any truth to the rumor."

"Do that. And report whatever you find at the old mines...."

Alone in his cabin, Sean became restless. There was no mystery as to its cause. That delicious little vixen, Charity Sturges, kept intruding into his mind; into his dreams and his waking reveries. This was both surprising and annoying to a man who had sampled women around the world and back again, and Sean resented it. He'd had momentary infatuations but none that ever lasted past departures from this port or that when his affairs called him away. But this colonial minx had stirred something deeper within him; also he regretted his flash of anger at Windward. She had made a mess of things, true, but her intentions had been of the best and her act one of selfless bravery.

There was something else also; something far less clearly defined and hence more annoying. A sense of destiny? Even as he angrily rejected that, he had to admit there had been crises in his career which he had recognized as such; turning points where his path had forked. And his meeting with Charity Sturges—the manner in which it came about—seemed somehow of that nature.

Nonsense! He told himself that sharply as he paced his cabin. There was a clear reason for this unaccustomed mood. Boredom. Lack of activity. With little to do now but wait, it was quite natural that his thoughts should stray restlessly about. He would put a stop to it in a hurry by going out to inspect the operation and hurry it along. No matter how efficiently men worked, they could be goaded into greater effort.

But also, if the opportunity presented itself, he would apologize to the girl. There was no point in leaving her sad and crestfallen because of his show of temper.

Sibley returned the following day, but with nothing conclusive.

"We went over the huts and found one which had been lived in recently. The signs were unmistakable but whoever used it was gone."

"Then we have nothing more to go on than before."

"I am afraid not. But I think we can be sure that it was not a poacher, so our vigilance must be doubled."

"I agree with that, with a sharp eye to seizing anyone who comes close enough to discover the ship. If that happens, the man must be taken. He must not be allowed to escape."

"True. Every day the ship sits here, the chances of its being found are increased."

"You are right, but our luck will hold."

"Because it always has?" Sibley replied with worry in his tone.

"Let that be reason enough. And by the way, did you find out anything about that girl?"

"She has left Windward. She is living at Camber now, with Dennis Wahl."

"Hmmm. Meg Wahl's bereft widower."

"The word is that he has taken her on as his housekeeper."

"Interesting," Sean said, even as he tried to

evidence lack of concern. And changing the subject, he added, "You had better bring three or four men back to the ship for guard duty. I will go with you tonight to inspect the new routing you have laid out. . . ."

Sibley left and Sean wondered about Charity's reason for quitting Windward. But only briefly. In moments, he forced the elfin image from his mind and turned it to more important affairs.

But his efforts to show disinterest in Charity had not been successful so far as Sibley was concerned. It bothered him. As he entered the tunnel to rearrange some cargo which had been temporarily placed there, he lamented Sean's romantic preoccupation. That was what it was, pure and simple, definitely the cause of his abstracted mood of late. But Sean's promise to bestir himself and inspect the routing was encouraging. Sean was not one to sit alone and brood for very long. . . .

59.

Clement Leach's attendant entered his parlor wearing an uncertain frown.

Clement, his Bible open to *Proverbs*, waited, then asked, "What is it?"

"A young lady, your Reverence. She asks an audience."

396

"This young lady—does she have a name?"

"Charity Sturges, as she informed me."

"She made no prior request to see me?"

"No, your Reverence. That is why I have not admitted her. Shall I send her away?"

"No. Let her come in."

Charity had prepared carefully for her meeting with Clement, and without any fear at all that she would be refused an audience. She had dressed—with Dennis' grumbling assistance—in a fine, dark blue, watered silk costume, the required stays binding her waist almost beyond endurance. Her hat was a wide-brimmed, sedately flowered affair with a droop in its brim that forced her to peer out of the right side. She had seen the fine ladies at Meg's party walk about in such hats without bumping into trees and was now grateful to Christopher for having urged her to buy the hat in London although, at the time, she had never intended to wear it. But now, wishing to be entirely proper, the hat had come in handy.

"Miss Sturges," Clement greeted. "So gracious of you to call upon an old man. I will assert my prerogative of age and not rise to greet you."

"Please do not, your Reverence. I fear that I have imposed upon you by coming uninvited."

"I am glad you did. Please sit down and tell me the reason for your visit."

"I came to offer my condolences upon your great loss. Margaret was my good friend. She was one of the few who welcomed me when I came to Kent. I feel that I, too, have lost much by her passing."

Clement was in no hurry to further the conversation. He pushed what he considered his prerogatives to a point of boorishness by allowing Charity to sit in uncomfortable silence. So this was the lass Christopher had brought from Williamsburg. Hardly what Clement had expected; hardly a wild Indian, for all her appearance, and Clement had difficulty in visualizing her with the meat cleaver it was said she'd hurled at Lady Kirth. Unless appearances were totally deceiving, there seemed no reason for Christopher to be ashamed of the girl in high London circles. Still, appearances *could* be deceiving.

"I thank you for your sympathies, Miss Sturges," he said finally.

Again he fell silent, until Charity's smile turned a bit uncertain and she said, "Your Reverence does not make it easy...."

As if he had not heard her, or were thinking of other things, Clement interrupted her abruptly by asking, "Can you dance, Miss Sturges?"

Charity reacted as though she had not heard aright. "I beg your indulgence?..."

"Dance. Are you skilled in the social arts upon which society places such high value?"

"If you refer to the cotillion, the minuet, and currently popular English steps, I must say no. I have not had the opportunity to learn."

"There is much you would have to learn before you are able to live up to the social graces your exquisite toilette suggests."

"Please, your Reverence. You are confusing me. What is the point of this?"

"I am sorry, but I am inclined to get to matters

which are of special interest to me. But perhaps I do get ahead of myself. Has Christopher yet proposed marriage to you?"

Charity had the grace to blush. "No, he has not."

"He voiced that intent to me. So tell me—would you accept or refuse him?"

"Please—that is such a personal matter!"

"Young lady, I am an old man who might well pass into the next world at a moment's notice and my brother's welfare is of concern to me. Thus I do not have time for maidenly sensibilities. Would you accept Christopher or refuse him?"

"I—I would accept him, your Reverence."

"Well, we have gotten that far. Now, do you feel that you would make him a good wife, or is it your personal ambitions that motivate you?"

"That is not fair! You are calling me an opportunist and you've no right. I love Christopher and I would do my very best to make him happy."

"Unfortunately, personal happiness is not a goal Christopher should be seeking. He is destined to climb to high places in the government of England and he must be concerned with not falling short. In this respect, a wife can aid a husband or be a millstone around his neck. Which would you be, Miss Sturges, a help or a hindrance?"

"Do I look like a millstone?" Charity found the courage to ask.

Clement smiled. This lass was refreshing, to say the least. He could now see how she would attract Christopher; or any other man, for that matter.

"Miss Sturges, forgive me for being frank to the point of rudeness. But I have a reputation for rubbing the veneer off people through harshness."

"I see. Has my veneer rubbed off?"

"Not noticeably. In fact, you have taken on stature. Had you cringed or whimpered from my barbs, I would now think the less of you."

"I am grateful for your frankness."

"Now some advice, my lass. Go not into marriage with Christopher before learning to hold your own in the superficial society where he must make his mark. You have a spirit which gives me pause. It would be disastrous if you picked up a meat cleaver in Whitehall and hurled it at some poor unfortunate who displeased you."

Charity laughed and as she did, all fear and awe of this remarkable man fell away. She felt a warmth toward him and realized there was much about him that reminded her of Mother Mae. A feeling of confidence and love washed over her. She reached out to lay an impulsive hand on that of Clement but withdrew it quickly.

"Your Reverence, you remind me so much of my mother."

"Good heavens—how curious!" His eyebrows shot up.

"I mean—I mean—she was my foster mother. My parents were killed when I was a babe and Mother Mae took me in and protected me and loved me."

"I see, but I hardly qualify on those terms to . . ."

"I mean what you just told me was so like she would have said. You see, she insisted that I get some education when I would have preferred to waste my days in play with Indian children. She *believed* in education. She told me that without it, the wolves I encountered through life would eat me up." Emotionally charged by her own revelations, Charity shuddered. "And they almost did. That is why I am so grateful to Christopher. He rescued me and protected me and brought me here."

"Then perhaps it is gratitude rather than love that you feel for him," Clement suggested gently.

"No! That is not true. I love Christopher. But your Reverence, did you not just tell me that love is of less importance? . . ."

Clement held up a hand to stop her. The clever little vixen was trapping him with his own words! He said, "Your foster mother was certainly a fine woman. What was her calling?"

"What she did? They called her a witch woman. She made potions which she sold to the gentry."

"Pagan artifacts and powders? . . ."

"Oh, no. She had a knowledge of roots and berries and sold only things for physical well-being."

It was a tribute to Charity that Clement believed her, although she was confusing beyond measure. He said, "Perhaps you can tell me more at a later date. I must rest now. But let me say this. I think you would make a man the kind of wife you determined to be, regardless of your feeling toward him."

Charity took that as a commendation and arose from her chair. "Your Reverence, I shall take your advice. I shall learn the social graces and conduct myself with the utmost decorum on all occasions. Will that please you?"

"I will be most pleased."

Acting again on impulse, Charity bent down and kissed Clement's cheek. Then, abashed by her forwardness, she hurried from the room without a further goodbye, managing not to trip over her skirts. The male nurse accompanied her to her one-horse gig and placed the reins in her hands. He watched her off with marked interest. He'd listened at the door and was struck by the fact that the Reverend Leach had fairly come out of himself. Most remarkable. . . .

Left to his lonely lot, Clement conceded that the visit had been most refreshing. He could not remember when his interest had been so thoroughly stirred. A lovely young lass by all counts, and he could now sympathize with Christopher's strong attachment. As the day aged, his thoughts turned inward and he came as close to dreaming as his stern nature had ever allowed. Suppose, he asked, a young lady of Charity's qualities had come to him in his early years. Would she have turned him in other directions? And if she had would his life have brought him greater reward? Greater satisfaction? He sat now a tired old man rich in honors. They were gratifying, but did nothing to warm his lonely bed.

"Posh!" he said sharply, then picked up his Bible and continued with *Proverbs*, seeking what comfort the ancient words would bring. . . .

60.

"Dennis, you must teach me to dance."

Dennis looked up from the batter he was stirring as Charity rushed into the kitchen.

"Has Clement's health improved to that extent?"

"Silly! Of course not! But he gave me good advice."

"Then he did not throw you from the manse?"

"Of course he did not! He is a fine gentlemen," she answered stoutly.

"And he told you to learn how to dance?"

"Among other bits of advice. Can you do the cotillion and the minuet?"

"I am certainly not going to," he said, anticipating her request.

"I'm sure you will. Here, let me do that."

Dennis refused to yield up his dough. "Keep away. I want a decent meal for a change. Get you out of that gown before you ruin it beyond repair."

"I had Satan's own time getting into it." Her smile was sly. "You may help me out of it, if you wish."

"Not I. Let Satan help you now, too."

"Then I shall keep it on for the evening. I must get used to acting like a lady."

Charity flounced out of the kitchen and sought

a mirror before which to practice walking as she had seen proper ladies do.

Dennis continued to knead his dough. His anger at Charity having cooled, he had come to consider his situation at Camber since Meg's tragic death. Losing her had wracked him more deeply than he would have believed, but he'd known, even without Charity's nudging, that he could not vegetate. Life had to go on.

For all her irritating ways, Charity was a breath of fresh air in the decaying expanse of Camber. Truly a joy, and not without a head on her shoulders. *A boy's school.* The logic of it kept nagging him, his annoyance springing from the fact that the little gamine from the Colonies had thought of it. Why could he not have put his own brain to work without being prodded by a child a little more than half his age?

He shaped the dough into loaves, put them out to rise, and went out to look over the grounds with a new eye. First off, the road would have to be repaired. Then the real work would start.

If he could raise the capital. . . .

61.

Christopher, depressed, annoyed, and no end of frustrated, turned automatically to where he knew he would find sympathy. To Channel Light.

Gaby Kirth saw him coming and went quickly about the task of making herself as attractive as possible. She brushed her hair and allowed it to fall loosely over her shoulders. Slipping out of her frock and underthings, she put on a rose-colored robe, completely opaque, but as she moved, it moulded itself to her figure and was therefore totally revealing.

By that time, Christopher had been admitted and was waiting in the reception room. Gaby floated into the room on a fragrant cloud of French perfume and took his hands warmly into hers.

"Christopher! Such a pleasant surprise! I will not ask you why you came. It does not matter. You are here and that makes me very happy."

"I came on no particular matter," he replied. "I wanted to see you and that sufficed."

"You darling! Come up to my salon. We will be more comfortable there. You look tired. Would you like tea, or something stronger?"

"Nothing, thank you."

The room Gaby called her salon was comfortable and relaxing. It was done in gray and pale cream; the carpeting, the drapes, the comfortable chairs, and the amply-sized couch against one wall.

"Sit you down, here, Chris darling, and let me soothe you. You look so terribly tense."

She stepped behind his chair and began massaging the muscles of his shoulders and neck. He closed his eyes and surrendered to her touch.

"Your hands are strong for a woman," he murmured.

"We are not all hothouse plants. Relax, darling, your muscles are like iron. Ease yourself or I shall have to use a hammer to pound them soft."

"You could quickly put me to sleep."

She bent over and whispered into his ear. "Then let's to bed, sweet."

He needed no further urging and as Gaby lay in his arms, he thought of the swift changes which had come about; of Clement's rigid codes and the years he had lost in following them. Gaby went expertly about the business of stirring his passions and as the sweet struggle mounted, she whispered, "Oh, darling, I *do* love you."

A spark of memory ignited. Charity:
Christopher, I do love you.

Why, he wondered, was it necessary for both of them to emphasize the fact? Was he such a difficult person to love? Perhaps neither Charity nor Gabrielle had completely convinced *themselves*.

As Gaby's aggressive passions drove her to a climax she carried him with her to the ecstatic peak. Then she pressed hard into his arms and whispered again, "Yes—yes—I *do* love you!"

With passions spent, Christopher was overcome with a feeling of futility. The struggle to reach a peak always seemed to dissolve into nothing the moment one gained it. He had lately begun to feel that the solid gains and accomplishments in life could be more satisfying.

Gaby became aware of his preoccupation. It touched her vanity. "Have I not pleased you?"

Damnation! Why did each woman have to be a copy of the one before? Charity at that wayside inn across the sea. *I do not please you?* What did

406

they want? A crown of laurel leaves? He rose from the bed and quickly got into his clothes.

"Of course you please me, Gaby. I feel out of sorts today. I shall return when I am in less of a mood. . . ."

Gaby watched him ride away. Perhaps she had made no progress, but she felt that at least she had not lost ground.

For reasons he could not define. Christopher rode straight to Camber. There he found Dennis Wahl in the yard kicking pensively at the sod as he looked out across his acres.

Christopher dismounted. "The lord of the manor surveying his domain?" he said pleasantly.

"And a shabby enough domain it is," Dennis replied.

"A bit neglected, perhaps, but withal a fine estate. An excellent coastline and good depth of soil."

"Most gracious of you to say so."

"I bring you some news. Clement and I have discussed the school idea. We agree that it is well worth further investigation if you yourself look upon it favorably," Christopher said briskly.

"You must know from the start," Dennis replied. "It was not my idea. Charity suggested it."

"How surprising."

"Not when one gets to know her. The girl has a good mind."

"I would not dispute the point, but tell me, are you amenable to looking further into the matter?"

"I could hardly object. Have you considered the cost?"

"Several thousand pounds, I am sure."

"At the very least," Dennis agreed.

"But let us consider the advantages offered. The location for one thing. Far enough away to be exclusive, but close enough to London and Maidstone so that parents visiting their sons could make the trip comfortably."

"It is not a large estate," Dennis said, warming to the idea, "but when thinking in terms of a school, the size would be ideal. Room for athletic fields. Woods and strenuous surfaces for hiking and exercise."

Christopher turned to gaze at the manor house. "Would a great deal of restructuring be necessary?"

"I fear so. It would consist mainly of tearing out walls. The foundations and walls are solid enough, though. And the kitchen as it stands is large enough to feed an enrollment comfortably."

"Then we should discuss terms." Christopher looked around the grounds. "What would you offer in return for financial backing?"

"You will not find me difficult to deal with."

"Then let me make a suggestion. Let us assume that we have a gentleman's agreement. To hurry things along, you repair to London and engage a builder—I am sure you can find a competent man. Bring him here to make a survey. We can discuss costs then."

"I shall do that. And allow me to thank you for your interest. And please thank Clement for me. With both of you seeing a school here as a profitable investment, I am sure it will turn out so."

"Clement's interest is not financial," Christopher pointed out.

"I can believe that. There is a rumor that he rejected a sizeable offering from Gabrielle Kirth for the repair of St. Jude's."

"That is true, much to my surprise. I felt that he would accept it," Dennis observed.

"Gaby must have been disappointed."

"She was. But she took it graciously. She is not a member of his church—I would guess that's the reason for his rejection. But as to Camber, Clement sees it as a memorial to Meg." Christopher paused to scrutinize once more the adjacent area. He pointed. "Just there, perhaps. A pillar supporting a bronze plaque to read: *Leach College— In memory of Margaret Leach Wahl*. If we dedicated the school to Meg, Clement will not care if it makes money or not."

Also, Dennis thought wryly, if the Leach name remained for future generations to see. But he had no objections. For all Dennis cared, they could call the school *Bedlam on the Channel*. He looked forward only to its creation.

Christopher took his leave and when Charity came back from riding an hour later she found Dennis packing a case.

"You are losing your happy home," he said.

"But those are your clothes, not mine."

"Christopher was here. We are going to turn Camber into a school for young gentlemen."

Charity's eyes mirrored sudden joy. "A decision so soon? Then my persuasions were not wasted!"

"It would seem that they were not."

Charity attacked him in a fury of delight, rolling onto his bed and touseling his hair before she squealed and ran behind a chair to escape his counterattack.

"Oh, it's so exciting!" she gasped. "I could run all the way to St. Jude's and kiss that sweet old man!"

"That *sweet* old man? Hardly."

Suddenly serious, she said, "But why are you packing? We do not have to move out this very day, do we?"

"I am going to London to engage a builder."

"Good heavens! The Leaches are in a hurry, aren't they? How long will you be gone?"

"Perhaps several days."

"And leave me here all alone? I'm sure this house is full of ghosts waiting to pounce on me!"

"You will be quite safe. Camber ghosts sleep most of the time."

"Nevertheless I shan't like staying here alone."

"Perhaps it would be better if you were to go to Windward for the nights I am gone."

"I'll crouch in the attic with a flintlock, first!"

"I don't understand you," he said curiously. "Why do you continue to be so dead set against Windward?"

"Because this is my home. Does that satisfy you?"

"It will have to do. And now would you hitch up a rig while I finish packing?"

"Good Lord! You'd think I was a servant around these premises!" She flounced out but quickly returned, hesitantly serious. "Dennis, there is something we have never mentioned between us."

410

"I am sure I don't know what it is. I thought we'd mentioned everything under the sun."

"Money, funds."

"You are in need?"

"On the contrary. I have quite a few pounds of my own. Gold I brought from Virginia. Mother Mae's legacy to me."

"You are joking. I've seen no gold around."

"It is the truth. Gold sovereigns. Some I have under the mattress in my bedroom. The rest is buried at Windward."

He thought he had been exposed to all of Charity's surprises but here was a new one. He stopped packing and turned to stare.

"You possess gold which you *buried* at Windward Moors?"

"Yes. When we reached London, Christopher put my money in Barclay's Bank. But I know nothing about banks and do not trust them, so I went and got it out again. I did not tell him because I did not want to hurt his feelings. But neither did I want to be penniless if the people there lost the funds in some mad venture or other."

"My dear addlepate. Barclay's Bank does not indulge in mad ventures. Your money was as safe as though it were in the Bank of England."

"They told me it was safe and then tried to give me paper money when Christopher had given them gold."

"And you went into a frenzy and threatened to burn them out, I'll vow," he laughed.

"No, but I insisted in getting my gold back and took it with me to Windward."

"And buried it there."

"Burying your funds is the safest way. Mother Mae buried the gold by our hut. She was wise."

"Why did you not bring it with you from Windward. Don't you trust the soil of Camber?"

"To be perfectly honest, I forgot all about it until now—until it occurred to me that you might need some on your trip to London."

Dennis ran a slow hand over his jaw. Deeply touched, he reached forth and drew Charity into his arms, holding her close.

"My sweet little doe! You are something beyond all imagining. I do not need money but your offering it to me is so warming to my heart that I am without words."

Their communication had always been in terms of banter. This was Dennis' first display of deeper emotion and Charity reacted in embarrassment.

She said, "Good heavens! If this is the way you act when you don't need money, what would happen to me if you did? I'd be forced to run for my life or be smothered."

He let her go and whacked her trim backside. "Always the imp! Get to the stable with you!"

Charity was subdued as she stood in the driveway seeing Dennis off. She kissed his cheek before he climbed into the rig's seat, then looked up at him, her face solemn.

"You *have* missed Meg, haven't you?" she said.

He drove off without a reply. Charity watched, having voiced the only reason she could think of for the change she saw in him. Had he tarried, he might have explained that losing Meg was not the only reason, but he thought there had been enough soul-baring for one day. . . .

62

Charity opened her eyes, came fully awake, and froze, a dash of terror rocketing through her body.

She had enjoyed being alone in the house. It was small in comparison to the great castle at Windward but by other standards it was huge and she had roamed the halls and unused rooms with a sense of proprietorship. There were Meg's quarters, which had been left untouched. Charity visited them but left quickly, not relishing the somber mood they brought on.

When bedtime came she started to obey Dennis' orders concerning the doors and windows. Most of them in the unused part of the house were already locked, but as Charity threw the bolt in the kitchen, she rebelled. Why go to all that trouble? The door to the cabin off Ironbound Road had never been locked. She left everything as it was, and retired to a quick and dreamless sleep.

To awaken in terror.

Her panic died quickly, however, because the form silhouetted against the window could not be mistaken; slim, familiar—graceful, as the intruder crossed the room.

"Must you always sneak about and enter bedrooms in the dark?" she demanded.

The velvet chuckle of Sean McDougal touched her ears pleasantly but did not dispel her indignation.

"I come without fanfare, Mavourneen, not to disturb the master. Let him sleep."

"Well, you can leave as you came, and I hope you smash your silly head climbing back down that tree."

He sat down on the edge of the bed and reached forth with a hand she avoided. "But Mavourneen, my love. I have come to lay my heart at your feet. Trample it and you destroy me!"

"Trample it? If I but touched the flinty thing it would bruise my foot. Also, my name is not Mavourneen and I am not your love, so will you please leave?"

"But you would not send me away before hearing me out. My apologies; they must be made. And you must listen."

He could be so exasperating. The music of his words, that soft smile he would be wearing even in the dark; and above all, the tone of his voice—half-pleading, but with the touch of amusement which was ever there. It infuriated Charity. Was he serious or had he come to pass a pleasant night and then go on his way?

She did not dwell on whether or not she was being unfair because it did not matter. Whichever the truth, her dalliance with Sean McDougal was at an end and he must understand that.

Pitching her voice to as serious a tone as she could manage, she kept the anger out of it and said, "Sean—sit there—sit there quietly and listen to what I tell you. It is for me to apologize,

414

not you. If I have led you on and given you reason to think me in any way smitten with you, I am sorry. To be entirely truthful, I am not a very nice person. I am frivolous and flighty and often pursue things of the moment which have no lasting meaning."

Obeying her, Sean sat quietly listening.

"I think I did inform you of the truth upon occasion—when I told you that I intend to marry Christopher Leach and be a proper wife . . ." Charity cut off sharply and scowled in the dark.

"Will you stop *laughing!*"

Her decision to remain calm vanished in the explosion ignited by the soft sounds of his amusement. He was bending closer, in reach of Charity's fists, and she used them, beating on his chest in fury, until tears came.

She stopped fighting and as if she were a child, he held her in his arms, waiting for the storm to pass.

Given this respite, Charity fought desperately to get herself together. She succeeded to an extent, when an inner voice spoke:

If I surrender now it will be the end. If I allow him to take me he will be free to come again and again and I will be lost. I am committed to Christopher. I am committed at this moment as strongly as I will be when his ring is on my finger.

If Sean had pressed on rather than waiting, he might have won. But now it was too late. Charity's voice was steady when she spoke again.

"Let me go, Sean."

"My sweet colleen . . ."

"I said—let me go!"

415

With that, Charity drew back, her demeanor now more firm than ever. "I want you to leave. And if you are the gentleman I believe you to be, you will do so."

He arose and stood by the bed and she felt his eyes upon her there in the darkness, piercing the gloom as though he were some great cat.

"Sean, I do not love you," she said slowly and clearly.

Only silence followed. Sean stood motionless for a long moment while Charity waited for him to speak. He did not. Then he was moving away like a presence without form, and was gone into the silence of the night.

Charity wept but it was different now, not tears of distress; rather a sad farewell, so firm now were her feet set upon the path of her choice. Her tears were not unlike the falling leaves that herald the end of a lovely summer.

After a time, she slept.

63.

With Dennis' return, activity heightened at Camber. He brought with him a young man Charity thought too immature for the task of reconstructing the estate and turning it into a school for young gentlemen. Amos Peebles, however, had earned respect by his work in London, having remodeled a hopeless slum street near Whitehall into a row of neat redbrick flats—a philanthropic project of some worthy gentlemen who saw the profit they would make as a side issue, or so they claimed.

Peebles wore black hose and breeches and a black weskit at all times, possibly to make himself look older, and he seldom smiled. He looked the place over and decreed that outside work would first be necessary in order to make the road passable for heavy carts.

Meanwhile, there were trips to London for both Christopher and Dennis and need for Christopher to spend additional time at Camber.

Charity made the most of this, doing her very best to improve her image with Christopher. If she planned to marry him it was high time she implanted herself in his mind as a prospect for the altar, and she debated the best way of doing it.

She served tea when he was about and saw to his needs, but tried to do this more as a hostess than a serving girl. She suggested to Dennis that he hire a cook and a maidservant now that he no longer lived a hermit's life. In turn, he accused her of getting rid of his people by sending Dorothy and Wilferd off to live in the Windward stables. He added that if she felt she could not handle the simple little chores of Camber, to hire someone herself. She accused him of callous disregard for her and told him she would be no man's slavey and there the thing stood.

She was most meticulous about her dress and manner when Christopher was about, but by and large, he remained aloof in that he treated Charity with polite deference at all times, not again asking her to return to Windward or making suggestions as to how she should conduct herself. Nothing more was said about presenting Charity to the Prime Minister but neither was it cancelled. She could only surmise that she would meet the great man in due time.

But more important, it began to dawn on Charity that she did not know how a lady lured a gentleman into proposing marriage. She well knew how a gamine did it; undress and crawl into his bed and demonstrate her skills in that respect. However, that did not seem to be the procedure in the more rarified circles. In fact Charity had sometimes wondered how proper ladies got out of all that restricting attire before the gentlemen lost interest and went sound asleep.

She could only fall back on Clement Leach's advice and with this in mind, she harnessed a mare and drove to Windward where she found Dorothy as eager as ever to help in any way possible.

"Dorothy," she asked, "do you know how to dance?"

"Oh, certainly, Miss Charity. At home we used to jig to a point of madness. We also did polkas and . . . "

"I mean the more sophisticated dances—minuets and the kind where ladies and gentlemen promenade up and down and bow to each other."

"I've watched people dance that way. It looks very easy."

"Could you show me?"

The lessons began immediately, Dorothy or

Charity humming alternately. Dubious progress was made, but Charity's mind wandered. It occurred to her that she had not visited with her good friend Mrs. Dylan for quite some time. A cup of tea with the sweet old Irish housekeeper would be nice.

Perhaps she had seen Sean. . . .

Charity cut the thought off sharply. All that was past and done with. She did not care in the least about the man's whereabouts or his comings or goings—just so long as he stayed away from her! But that really had nothing to do with Mrs. Dylan so when the lesson ended and Charity promised to return soon for a second one, she went to the house and sought out her friend in the kitchen. Mrs. Dylan was not there, nor was the fat little cook.

Rather than begin searching the premises, Charity brewed herself a cup of tea and sat down to wait. Her eyes fell upon the strange door leading into the tunnel and that brought back thoughts of Sean McDougal.

This time, Charity handled them sensibly. There was no point in trying to ignore them; it was a childish thing to do. In fact, as she went on considering the situation, she decided it was downright cowardly to eliminate Sean from her circle of acquaintances. After all, she had been intimate with Dennis and they remained the best of friends. Mulling it over, she came to the conclusion that if she could not call upon Sean in the same manner she was now calling upon Mrs. Dylan, she would be wanting in strength of character. And finally, after plodding through that maze of self-serving logic, she finished her tea, took a flare from its bracket, lit it at the stove, and went through the door down into the tunnel.

A sense of excitement pervaded, which she attributed to the tunnel itself: its eeriness, and the feeling of being cut off from the world.

She moved forward, the torch above her head. She heard no footsteps, saw no shadow, as a hand from behind her was hooked savagely over her mouth, and an arm encircled her. The torch fell to the floor and was extinguished, and she was dragged backwards on her heels—backward and around a break in the tunnel wall, then thrown savagely against hard stone.

She cried out and collapsed to the floor. . . .

64.

Even if there had been no light in the crypt into which she had been dragged, Charity would have been able to identify her attacker. The voice that came from behind her was enough, purring its singsong into her ears.

"Come into my parlor, said the spider to the fly."

Borland Nickelawn, his face looking mad even in the dim half-light of the cave.

Charity tried to rise without success. She was pulled down as he yanked her frock at the neck and stripped her, camisole and all, to the waist.

Her natural instinct was to fight and not wasting breath on words, she ripped at him with clawed fingers. Only for a few moments did she unbalance him. Then he attacked her with a savagery she could not withstand. A fist smashed into her stomach doubling her over. She gasped for breath and moaned. A hand was entwined in her hair, almost tearing it from her head, and Nickelawn began slapping her viciously back and forth, on either side of her face, until her senses reeled. She was hurled to the floor and he knelt upon her stomach. She heard a ripping sound and a section of her frock was thrust into her mouth, painfully cutting off her cries.

With resistance brutalized out of her, he then began to punish her in a more leisurely fashion.

He squeezed her breast bringing the nipple upright and Charity felt the cold blade of a knife pressed against her flesh.

"I'll nip that off. The other one, too, and how odd you will look without them. As you destroyed me, so I shall destroy you, but much more painfully. Did you think you could escape me? Did you think I would let you walk free while I go about in disgrace?"

Charity tried to speak. She tried to beg but only pitiful animal sounds came through the gag.

"You will suffer," the demented Nickelawn promised, tossing the knife to the ground. "I read all the lurid tales of your Indian friends and what was done to their squaws. Inch by inch their skins were taken off with hunting knives to pay for what the redmen did to white women captives. Perhaps you witnessed some of the torment while you lived with those savages."

While he taunted her, Nickelawn put his hands upon her. Without removing her pantalettes, his clutch went beneath them, digging cruelly into her belly, then pulling her limbs wide apart to thrust fingers deep into tender flesh.

Then he snarled, "Once more before you die, you bitch!" and with that he laid her squarely on her back, bent her knees, and tore off her pantalettes. From a kneeling position he achieved leverage and thrust savagely until he literally tore his way into penetration.

Charity screamed through the gag. The pain brought her close to fainting, but she fought it even though it would have brought her the solace of unconsciousness. There was a grotesque fear that she would not awaken in time to die.

Nickelawn achieved his climax and rested for a few moments before Charity heard steel scrape on stone and knew he had picked up the knife. Where would he thrust it in? Had he forgotten his promise to cut off her breasts? Perhaps he had, because in his madness he was now fondling them with less viciousness, and seemed to be debating between torture and further satisfaction of his lust.

He laid the knife blade on her cheek, then turned it and drew the non-cutting edge down her face. He continued his torment by using that same edge against her nipple, simulating what he promised to do, before he dropped the knife and again drove his manhood into her body.

What followed happened so suddenly that it

blurred Charity's senses. There was a flash of light from a lantern and a man's face at the entrance to the crypt. Nickelawn's face—white, drawn, savage—blocked her vision as he clawed about the floor to retrieve his knife.

There was a roar of outrage from the intruder at what he beheld. The lantern fell to the floor and there was a rush of bodies in that narrow confine, and Charity felt Nickelawn being pulled away from her. But the maniac held on, making it difficult for her rescuer, whoever he was. Nickelawn, clutching at Charity's thighs, dragged her along with him, on her shoulders and back. In this position, with her head on the ground, in the center of the savage struggle, she received a shattering blow to the head from someone's boot—her rescuer or the murderous Nickelawn.

Dazed, barely conscious, Charity wondered why her savior had to be so violent. Then she understood. Nickelawn had gotten the knife back into his hand. Intent upon killing her above all else, he had come within inches of plunging it into her breast. . . .

65.

Charity opened her eyes.

Mrs. Dylan, tense and filled with concern, was looking down at her.

"Where am I?"

"It's all right, sweeting. You are safe in your bed."

"At Windward?" Charity asked, the room hazy in her sight.

"No, child. At Camber. You went through a terrible time and it is by the grace of God that you are still alive."

Charity struggled hard to remember. That nice Mr. Sibley, whom she had met but once before, coming out of Sean's cabin on the *Evening Primrose*, had rescued her from the madman Borland Nickelawn and told her that it would be best for her to say nothing about what had really happened in the tunnel. Surely he had his reasons, but the story he told her to tell was entirely different. "I was— I was. . . ."

Mrs. Dylan leaned close and helped. "You were driving back from Windward, sweet, and. . . ."

"Yes." Charity began reciting as though from rote. "I was driving back from Windward and my horse shied. I fell from the gig. My skirt got tangled in the hub of a wheel and I was dragged." Yes, that was it. That was what Sibley had told her to say in her own best interest. "I was dragged."

Mrs. Dylan, obviously relieved at what Charity had managed to recite, whispered, "Yes, pet. You will better understand it later. Mr. Leach brought me from Windward to watch over you, and Dennis has gone to the doctor. You must sleep now."

Charity closed her eyes. Nothing was very clear. Everything was muddled together, and she hurt so; ached as though her body had been

424

twisted into knots. Her head was splitting. To-morrow. Tomorrow it would all be explained. . . .

Sibley, reporting back to the *Evening Prim-rose*, was even then explaining it to Sean McDougal.

"That maniac was living down there in the tunnel. He was no doubt the one we almost caught at the old iron mines. I heard the scream and started hunting for the source and got there just in time. He tried to kill her as I entered the crypt and he kept right on trying to kill her."

Sibley paused to wipe his brow. "He died hard, that one. I thought the life would never go out of him. I vow that I'll now have dreams of him ris-ing from the sea where I threw his body, coming at me with that mad face all draped in seaweed."

Sean turned away to pour a brandy which he extended to Sibley. "Here, you need this." As Sib-ley seized it and gulped it down, Sean went on. "Faith, and you are wrought up with good rea-son, my friend. Now sit you down and give it to me again."

"It was the cargo stowed for packing in the tunnel. We could not have investigators potting about down there without time to move the goods."

"So you convinced the lass that an explanation leaving Nickelawn out of it was the best for her reputation."

"I told her the busybodies would rumor it about that she was there through choice—and that would have blackened her reputation." Sibley paused to judge Sean's reaction. "And it's true," he said defensively. "Not said as an injustice to the lass."

"I don't gainsay you. I seek only a clear picture; a clear picture of a job well done." He paused for a moment, then said, "You went to Mrs. Dylan for help. She is trustworthy, of course, but the fewer who know of this the better. Could you not have taken Charity to the gig yourself?"

"It did not seem to me so. Charity Sturges had to be in the house before entering the tunnel. Mrs. Dylan could well have seen her go in."

"She is a loyal lady, to Charity and to me."

"And for keeping the thing quiet, there was that young wife of the Windward hostler hovering at the gig waiting for Charity to return. She had to be lured away and Mrs. Dylan handled that—called her to the house while I carried the lass to the gig."

Sean's voice rang with relief. "You did well, Sibley."

"Another thing, Mrs. Dylan was taken immediately to Camber to tend the lass. So she will be there to see that she sticks to the tale."

"One thin spot," Sean said. "You coming along at the right moment there on the moor to stop the runaway horse."

"Coincidence, mayhap, but they'll have to swallow it. After all, did I not come in fact to the tunnel crypt to save her?"

Sean grinned and raised his glass. "Another brandy, my friend beyond price. I drink to you. If

426

heaven has blessed me at all, it is with good men like you to work in my causes. . . ."

Left alone with his thoughts, Sean found them most unsettling. He was a man of great enthusiasms, this by his very nature, and when the project of arming the colonial rebels had been put to him at Charleston, he had agreed without reservation. His sympathies for the Colonists were sincere and zeal in their behalf remained strong as he returned to England and got caught up in the excitement of the plan he evolved. It was daring, brilliant in concept, and catered to the pleasure he had always derived from skirting the near edge of danger.

In the beginning, he had been everywhere—shaping up the shadow organization he would need—expediting the movement of arms—stolen, purchased, acquired by any means possible. And the joy of it sprang mainly from his ability to hoodwink the English authorities. He saw this in no way traitorous because he considered himself an Irishman with no obligations to the Crown.

So things had gone well—until lately. For too many precious days, the project had bored him, had seemed somehow unimportant, and as a result he'd begun taking chances which had alarmed Sibley and caused his loyal cohorts much concern: dangerous, impudent pranks such as boldly revealing his presence in Kent to the Leaches—something he would have never done had his mind been put solely to the success of the project at hand. He had lolligagged about in fashion most uncharacteristic and foisted too much responsibility on Sibley.

There was of course a reason for this, but Sean McDougal was a stubborn man with a sublime belief in his guiding star, and was not inclined to accept warnings even from his inner self. But it is every man's instinct to hunt down the reason for basic changes in his pattern and Sean was no exception.

Still, he would not admit that his deviations began on the night he took over the *Hainaut* and casually raped a bonny little female who fought him tooth and claw and then surrendered, as had so many bonny lasses during his tempestuous career.

Finding her again in Kent he had begun risking his future by throwing caution to the winds and continuing the happy affair to a point of dalliance worthy of a callow youth involved with his first love.

Not only that, but when the opportunity to end it was presented and he had rejected Charity in her chambers at Windward, he'd crawled back to beg forgiveness at Camber and had been rejected in turn. An unheard-of defeat in the annals of Sean McDougal's conquests!

But did that bring him to his senses? No. He'd moped about and tried to tell himself that his unrest sprang from other sources, inventing them as he went along. And now, as things stood, the last place he should put in an appearance was Camber.

But regardless, he went through the tunnel to Windward, borrowed a mount, and set off for the Wahl estate. . . .

Part Four: *The Wedding Dress*

66

Word of Charity's misfortune came as a great relief to Gaby Kirth. She had been haunted by the fear of Borland Nickelawn returning to further his demand of cooperation in his plan, and she had nothing to tell him. But Charity having come to grief, a simple accident as it was explained, seemed too coincidental to accept. It was now far more likely that Nickelawn had somehow exacted his vengeance and would thus have no reason to come again to Channel Light with his demands.

It did seem strange that he would attack Charity in the open, on a public road, but madness left little room for logic, and she concentrated upon the favorable aspects so far as her own fortunes were concerned. With Charity lying abed, it behooved her to further the progress with Christopher which she had already made.

With this in mind she called for a gig and hurried to Camber, where she considered it a good omen when Christopher rather than some lackey met her and helped her down.

"Chris, darling, I heard what happened to your sweet little ward. Is it serious?"

431

"Rather more yes than no," he replied somberly.

"I am devastated at the distress you must feel and I so want to be of comfort."

As she spoke, Gaby used everything she had—the allure of her lush femininity, the promise in her eyes, and the touch of her hands—to add meaning to her words.

Christopher was not impervious. He smiled and did not draw immediately away. "You are most understanding, Gaby."

"You said her condition is serious." She carefully kept the note of hope out of her voice.

"We do not really know. She is hardly conscious. Mrs. Dylan is with her and we are awaiting the arrival of the doctor."

"Oh, Chris! I am so sorry. I feel for the poor child. And this is so unfair to you!" As his glance questioned, she went on. "You have been so good, so thoughtful and generous to the girl. You do not deserve the weight of concern this puts upon you."

"There are things over which we have no control."

"True, but I so want to be a comfort to you. And I am sure I could if there were time for you to let me." She lowered her eyes and her voice. "Darling, the hours at Channel Light are long and lonesome."

He smiled now, and said, "An hour or two of privacy would be welcome indeed."

Instinct told Gaby not to press further. The implication of his reply was enough. She drew back and said, "Under the circumstances I had better not intrude further. There will be time enough when the child's recovery has begun." Using the term *child* at every opportunity was not accidental on Gaby's part. It tended, or so she hoped, to lessen Charity's adult stature in Christopher's mind, though a poor substitute for the terms— *slut, bitch, trollop,* or worse—she would have liked to use.

Gaby said, "I got word of the tragedy through my hostler. But few details."

"Word of misfortune does travel fast here in Kent," Christopher replied. "There was immediate inquiry from Clement, and Sean McDougal, who scarcely knows Charity, came to offer his sympathy."

"Sean? That wild Irish lad? Has he been accepted back into the family?"

"He is not a bad sort, really. I think he has begun to regret his wild ways."

"I understand it was Dennis' man Sibley who found Charity and brought her here to Camber. What was the exact nature? . . ."

"Her horse apparently shied and she fell from the gig. Her skirt got entangled in the wheel and she was dragged."

"I see. As I recall, the child resented skirts and preferred to go about in male attire. Evidently lack of familiarity with genteel costuming did her in." Without giving Christopher time to reply, Gaby turned to her carriage. "I will go back now, darling, and take no more of your time for the present."

"It was so thoughtful of you to come."

Looking down at him from the seat into which

433

he had handed her, she smiled intimately and said, "It was little enough. I hope to do much more. . . ."

Driving back to Channel Light quite satisfied with her visit, Gaby did marvel at the high regard the little colonial half-savage had achieved since her arrival. Astonishing, but the majority of her well-wishers were men, and would thus be naturally attracted to the bold little creature.

So bereft was Gaby of conscience that she scarcely remembered her pact with Carton. The scoundrel seemed gone for good, and with her own safety no longer threatened, she was able to put the black deed out of her mind. She was now concerned with what might have been called the second phase of her campaign to win Christopher. She wanted him and had reason to believe that she was closer to her objective than ever.

Perhaps, she thought, Charity might well come forth a cripple if she recovered at all. The whole thing was most mysterious. Had Nickelawn actually been involved? Perhaps eventually, the truth would come out. . . .

Dennis arrived with a Maidstone doctor a short time later. He was a middle-aged man of serious mien, but lacked the pompousness displayed by some practitioners of the respected profession.

Dennis introduced him to Mrs. Dylan as Doctor Warner and then retired to await a diagnosis. The practitioner's examination was gentle. Mrs. Dylan had put Charity into a nightgown and he

434

asked, "Did she react with pain when you undressed her?"

"Not that I could tell, sir. She was hardly conscious but moaned softly at times."

He moved her arms and legs carefully in search of fractures and pressed her torso in places where internal organs might have been injured. There was no reaction. He seemed mainly interested in the abrasion and swelling on the back of her head.

"A hard blow," he commented.

"She is very warm," Mrs. Dylan said. "Perhaps you should bleed her."

"I have no faith in bleeding other than for certain infirmities, gout and the like." As he wiped his hands after washing them at the bowl, he asked, "Have you had experience in caring for the sick?"

"It is not my calling but I have tended many in my time. I know something of wounds—knife cuts and the like."

"You will stay close to the lass?"

"Aye. And I can administer medicines. Perhaps laudanum to keep her quiet until she heals?"

"It is the last thing we want. She is too quiet as it is."

Dennis and Christopher awaited him. He told them, "The head blow she received is of the most concern. The skull may be split with injury to the brain. In truth, she may never regain her consciousness. If not, she will remain in coma and pass from that into death."

"Hardly encouraging," Dennis muttered.

"I shall return in the morning but if she

changes from her present state, send for me immediately."

Christopher said, "I would prefer that you remain here at Camber. We can put you up."

"I have other patients and there would be no point. I could do nothing at present. Now I will speak again to Mrs. Dylan."

He gave final instructions to the latter. "Watch closely. When you rest, have someone at your side to remain awake. See that I am sent for if she comes out of the coma."

"I will not sleep," Mrs. Dylan replied. "You may be sure of that...."

67.

The hours passed with gloom lying like a black cloud over Camber. Mrs. Dylan maintained her vigil, watching Charity for signs of movement until her eyes ached. Dennis and Christopher tiptoed in to get the latest word and tiptoed out.

Christopher offered to relieve Mrs. Dylan and give her some rest but Mrs. Dylan refused to budge. She preferred to remain close to Charity rather than risk a crisis in her charge's condition. Finally, when exhaustion overcame her, she did doze off in the small hours, only to awaken to a sense of inner warning. She turned to her patient and cried out in sudden dismay.

Christopher, sleeping in a chair in the next room with the door open, heard the cry and ran in.

"The poor child is burning up!" Mrs. Dylan said. "She fairly radiates heat! Something must be done."

"I'll go for the doctor!"

"You may do that, but I'll not stand here and watch the poor pet turn to a cinder. She must be bathed."

Christopher roused Dennis who came in slippers and robe, his eyes heavy with the sleep he'd fought against.

Mrs. Dylan said, "You are to bring me water. Otherwise the child will set herself on fire!"

"I'll get it from the well."

"No—no! Tepid water from the kitchen. The cold well-water will shock her to death. Even tepid water will feel like ice on her skin. Please hie yourself!"

Dennis came back with a great pot of water and Mrs. Dylan, speaking like a mistress of the manor rather than a servant, said, "Now go about your affairs. I'll cool the child. And pray the doctor does not lag along the way."

Alone with her patient, she stripped the nightgown off and using towels for cloths began to bathe her.

The fever was awesome. The heat from Charity's body dried the moisture Mrs. Dylan applied and she resoaked the towels again and again.

The effect was gratifying after a fashion. It stirred Charity to life. She moaned and struggled weakly.

"Mother Mae—they hurt me."

Charity tried to rise from the bed. Mrs. Dylan restrained her and she fell back, her eyes flicking about like those of a trapped animal.

"You hurt Charley Short-Bow's finger but he didn't cry!"

"Easy, my pet! You are safe here and you will get well," Mrs. Dylan soothed.

"I'm so hot—so hot. Let me out, Mr. Cade!"

"Child. You *must* rest."

"I'll do anything you ask! I'm burning up!"

"Be calm, darling. They have gone for the doctor. Please, Miss Charity. I'll bathe you again."

She stiffened. Her eyes widened as though she saw savage phantoms advancing upon her.

"My name is Mavourneen!"

"Gently, sweeting. I am here with you. I will not leave you for an instant."

The minutes dragged like hours while Mrs. Dylan listened to incoherent babblings and prayed that this was not the beginning of the end.

The doctor arrived. Mrs. Dylan greeted him with pleading eyes. "Her mind has left her. Do something quickly before it is too late!"

"We must get the fever down," he said, and Mrs. Dylan cursed him in her heart. Jackanapes such as he came to strut and propound and collect their fees. Any fool would know that the fever was killing her.

With Mrs. Dylan to aid him, he wrapped Charity's flaming body in a sheet. "It must be kept wet," he said. "Pour the water gently but keep the cloth soaked." Then he stood back to observe.

"Some medicine to quiet the poor child?"

" 'Tis better not. We can only wait now. 'Tis her fight and she must win or lose it herself. . . ."

The dark hours wore on. The demons of delirium battled the defending forces in Charity's abused mind and body. She rambled aimlessly, speaking of things alien to an Irish lady who knew nothing of life in the savage land whence her sweet little patient had come. Chahalis? Who was he and what sort of a land could it be where devils hung prisoners head down over fires to cook their brains out?

In time, Charity wearied; she lapsed into silence and appeared to sleep, but the continued bathing did little to hold back the raging fever.

"There will be a crisis," the doctor said. "She will survive it or she will pass from this world."

Mrs. Dylan prayed—pleading with God to be merciful. . . .

68.

Christopher kept the night vigil in the anteroom, as close to Charity as he was allowed. Dennis, however, could not remain inactive. He prowled about the house and grounds and when dawn came, he was examining the gig in which Charity had ridden.

He was so occupied when Sibley rode up to inquire about the patient's progress. Dennis told him there was little to report, then turned his attention back to the vehicle.

He said, "I had little time to learn about the accident. On which side did she fall?"

"There—on the left."

"The mare went out of control?"

"She was running in panic when I came upon the accident."

"You caught the animal and calmed her and found Charity being dragged by the wheel."

"That was the size of it." Sibley silently wondered what Dennis was getting at.

"The material of her skirt wound around the wheel hub?"

"Aye. It was in tatters," Sibley said uneasily.

"But I find not a shred of the cloth caught in the hub. Does that not seem strange?"

"The bits probably fell away while I was driving the lass on here to Camber from where I found her."

"Sibley, I respect you. You are an honest man and your word has always been good with me. But I cannot now accept what you have told me. I want the truth."

Sibley tested his saddle for firmness as a means of gaining time while he debated within himself. Finally, he said, "I'll not tell you unless we make a pact; unless you swear to me that what I say stops here."

Dennis scowled. A man he saw as an underling speaking to him in such an arrogant manner. "I'll agree to no such thing! You'll tell me the truth in this matter."

Sibley realized that he had erred. He should

440

have stuck to the lie and brazened it through. Possibly his background as a subservient in the caste system had momentarily tripped him up. Regardless, the truth now had to be told.

"There was no accident on the road," he said slowly. "I came upon Borland Nickelawn attacking Charity in the tunnel under Leach House."

"And what was she doing there? And you too, for that matter?"

A look of fatigue reflected in Sibley's face; a weariness from the load he carried. This serving two masters was not easy. "There is a situation of which you are not aware," he said, fumbling the words out rather than speaking them with directness.

"What sort of a situation?"

"You might call it dangerous," he said, for want of a better word. "But it is under control."

A red flag suddenly began waving in Dennis' brain. A dangerous situation. *A scandal on the estates?*

Sean McDougal!

Do I want to know?

The question flashed suddenly, unbidden, as assessment of the over-all situation raced through his mind. The school. It had become a project of utmost importance to him, most dear to his heart. A scandal at this time on the estates would end all hope for the project. Questions still surfaced like bubbles on an evil-smelling stew. Charity. Had she been a victim or a principal? Gaby Kirth; vindictive, greedy, heartless; characteristics he had looked on with amusement when he'd been bedding her. How things had changed! How *he* had changed! How had he ever thought her enchanting?

Stay clear of it.

The directive flashed through his mind even before the reasoning behind it did. Knowledge of the intrigue would certainly constitute involvement in the minds of Clement and Christopher, and he would lose their confidence and their financial backing. The logic, wise or otherwise, followed swiftly, and Dennis' attitude changed with a speed which must have surprised Sibley.

"Perhaps," he mused casually, "Charity was in the tunnel out of curiosity. She is an adventurous lass."

"Oh, quite," Sibley murmured, unsure of what was expected of him.

The discussion was cut off abruptly when Mrs. Dylan came rushing from the house. "The fever has broken!" she cried.

Joy and relief washed over Dennis. He hurried to the woman and drew her warmly close. "It was your doing, Mrs. Dylan."

"God's doing. His mercy. The child sleeps now."

Sibley, momentarily forgotten, mounted his horse. But then Dennis turned and went to him. "Sibley," he said coldly. "You are dismissed from Camber. You will quit your cottage and move your wife elsewhere as soon as possible."

Sibley was not surprised. The dismissal was logical in view of Dennis' obvious decision to hide his head in the sand.

Sibley's reply was as curt. "No great hardship,

442

sir. It will be a pleasure to get out from under that leaking roof."

He then rode off to carry the news to Sean McDougal, meditating the while on the change in Dennis Wahl. From a man who could conceivably have made a fine smuggler, he had gone over to the enemy, so to speak—but still without the courage to do other than try to keep his own boots from being muddied.

69.

Life at Camber now returned to some semblance of normalcy, if the new activities could have been called normal; the surveyors were busy, and the architect, Amos Peebles, was shaping his plans.

The relationship between Dennis and Charity changed, but not so radically as to make Charity aware of it. Dennis decided that questioning her about possible involvement with Sean McDougal and whoever had attacked her would be unwise, at least for the time being. So while he remained pleasant and more or less attentive, he did draw away from her and she attributed this to his new responsibilities in regard to the school.

With the changes which had come about, Dennis expected Christopher to take Charity back to Windward Moors. At the moment, what with her post-crisis condition she was considered too weak to be moved and best left where she was. But she was young and vital and would recover quickly.

Dennis of course remained troubled. The intrigue from which he had divorced himself still hung like an invisible sword over his head. Would it break into a storm? If so, when? All remained calm but Dennis found himself worrying more and more about Gaby Kirth. After a single visit at the time of Charity's tragedy when she spoke only to Christopher, Dennis had not seen the Lady of Channel Light. Not too surprising, but what was she up to? Born for mischief, she worried Dennis more so than Sean McDougal. The freebooter was not to be trusted, but he usually knew what he was doing. At times Dennis' resolve to remain aloof weakened and he was tempted to seek Sean out and demand answers. He resisted those moments of weakness—but Gaby was another matter. The temptation to see what the minx was up to became stronger and stronger....

Ironically, Gaby Kirth's puzzlement over the situation was as great as that of Dennis. Her pieces of the over-all mystery were somewhat different but they left great gaps also. Though she did not relish the thought, perhaps Borland Nickelawn would again surface and add more pieces. As things were, back at Channel Light, she could only wait for a visit from Christopher. This she did with growing impatience until Christopher did arrive, bringing news of his own.

"I have made new arrangements," he said.

"You are bringing Charity back to Windward Moors?"

"On the contrary. I am leaving her at Camber."

"Will that not raise eyebrows? Your *agreeing* that she may stay there?"

"I think not. Dennis brought the subject up, so I have now asked Mrs. Dylan to take over as Charity's nurse and companion, and to remain at Camber. With Dennis' approval, of course. An additional staff will be hired and as I told him, I will be spending a great deal of my time at Camber also."

It seemed to Gaby that Christopher had lately turned somewhat pompous, what with his new stature in London, and what amounted to a taking over of Camber from its owner. But he had shown new unsuspected abilities for organization, and was perhaps entitled to a display of pride.

He said, "My reasons for leaving Charity at Camber should be obvious to you. I cannot keep coming here to Channel Light. That *would* raise eyebrows and start rumors."

"You are saying that I must come to Windward Moors?"

"My dear, it would be no great inconvenience to you."

Gaby turned away to hide her annoyance. *As much for me as for you.* She almost put the thought into words, then held back. There was no point in starting a quarrel at this stage.

She turned back and spoke mildly. "But here at least, my staff is trustworthy. They do not carry tales."

"With Mrs. Dylan and the young hostler's wife away, the same holds true at Windward," Christopher replied. "One housemaid left who is famous for holding her tongue. I will be taking only breakfasts there for the present." His smile and manner indicated that the matter was closed and it was time to get on with his visit. Christopher left no doubt as to what he had come for, leading Gaby firmly off to her bedroom where without preamble or by-your-leave, she found herself stripped and in his arms.

She could understand his need for release after the strain and tension he had been through; still she would have appreciated a little more finesse in his approach. But his newly developed skills at lovemaking were some compensation. This was still a novelty to her and she tried to classify the changes she had found in him. A boy suddenly grown into a man? That hardly defined it although Christopher had definitely matured. The gentleness in him remained, with perhaps a touch of smugness added. Yet, when passion-charged, he fairly devoured her, lifting her to heights she had never before experienced. His capacities were amazing. Only after carrying her into the rainbow realm of ecstasy three times did his manhood wilt and demand rest. . . .

Afterwards there was time for questions she had been waiting to ask. "You said Charity is doing well."

"Very well. Today she is sitting out in the sun."

"The accident, Chris. Was it not a strange one? Did you ever hear of a woman getting her skirt caught in the wheel of a gig?"

"No, although I wondered about that. However,

446

Charity lived under different circumstances in Virginia. She is not yet used to the more voluminous fashions worn by ladies here. And though she is learning quickly it is quite logical that a startled horse jerking the gig could cause her to lose control of her skirts."

Evidently that explanation satisfied him. Also, it indicated that he knew nothing about Charity's visit to Borland Nickelawn's house in Maidstone. This put Gaby in a dilemma. She could have aroused Christopher's suspicions concerning the accident by telling him what she knew, but she feared that this would react against her. It might bring questions as to her own relationship with Borland and lessen her chances with Christopher by outraging his moral principles. The fact that he had bettered his personal techniques of sex did not, in her opinion, lessen his sense of moral decorum. Men were that way, she had discovered. Those most lustful in the bedroom were the loudest in decrying moral laxity in others; particularly in the women upon whom they vented their lust.

So she could only accept Christopher's ridiculous explanation of the so-called accident and bide her time.

Later that week, she was thankful that she had held her tongue, when another visitor, Dennis Wahl, arrived at Channel Light.

Gaby watched his approach with surprise and mixed emotions. Their affair had ended abruptly after Meg's death; by mutual consent, really. Actually, it could hardly have been called an affair; neither had been even temporarily faithful to the other and Gaby had not been at all upset when Dennis withdrew because she would have terminated the relationship herself in order to give her whole attention to Christopher.

And now Dennis was returning—to pick up where they had left off? As the knock came upon the door, Gaby was torn. A good lover, Dennis, and perhaps with Christopher no longer coming to Channel Light something could be temporarily worked out. Would it now be too dangerous? She left the question hanging; one she quickly discarded when Dennis was ushered into her parlor. His frown quickly indicated that he had not come to discuss lovemaking.

He came directly to the reason for his visit. "Christopher Leach tells me, Gaby, that you have been questioning the circumstances of Charity's accident."

"Not questioning them. It just seemed an exceptional thing to happen."

"Are not all accidents exceptional?"

"I suppose so. But why do you attach such importance to what I thought was a private conversation?"

"I don't think Christopher meant to reveal any confidences. The point merely came up while we were talking."

"You have not answered my question."

"I'll get to that. It just occurs to me that you might have knowledge of Charity's affairs that could be dangerous to your welfare."

Gaby became wary. Hedging for time, she said, "I don't know how you expect me to reply to that."

"You were a close friend of Borland Nick-elawn, were you not?"

"I think that is my own business."

"I am forced to make it mine also. I have reason to believe that through Nickelawn you may have learned facts that are better kept quiet."

"You have reason to believe!" Gaby repeated scornfully. "What reason, may I ask?"

"Call it instinct. Anyhow, it is possible that Charity acted rashly and thus brought misery upon herself. However, her motives were of the best. If she did put herself into a perilous position it was to save the lives of those she held dear."

"I don't understand you! I don't understand your relationship with Charity. Why is she at Camber? Are you in love with her?"

He said, "That is none of your affair."

"Do you plan to marry her?"

Dennis studied her for a moment, then said, "You are still hopeful of becoming Christopher Leach's wife, aren't you?"

"Stop it! Stop all of this and leave my house! You are disgusting! You come snooping about for purposes of your own which I can't imagine . . ."

"Then let me make it clear, Lady Kirth. I am interested solely in Charity's welfare and so I have come to warn you—if you ever divulge anything you may know or suspect as to what may have preceded Charity's misfortune, a plague will fall upon your house such as you cannot dream. What has gone before is a closed book."

"Are you threatening me?" she asked boldly.

"If your lips remain sealed you have nothing to fear from me. But if you allow your hatred and

449

jealousy of Charity to surmount your better judgment you will make an enemy capable of reducing you to a miserable state."

The words were distressing enough, but added to them was the cold, resolute manner in which they were spoken. She had never imagined that Dennis Wahl, for all his shaggy appearance and coarse, cynical manner, could show such implacable resolution.

"The girl must have you in thrall!" she blurted. "Why do you come here to spew your frustration at me?"

He grimaced wearily, as though the task he had set himself was not an easy one. "I do not hate you, Gaby. Your affairs are of no concern to me. Marry Christopher Leach if you can. I do not care one way or the other. It is just of vital importance that we understand each other."

"I can tell no one anything because I know nothing whatever. Does that satisfy you?"

"It does. And now with your permission I will take my leave."

"Take it by all means! And please remember that you will never be welcome in this house again!"

Left to herself, Gaby broke down and wept. Why did she háve to be abused in this manner? Why could she not be let alone? She wished harm to no one!

She sobbed and yearned with all her heart that Christopher would come and take her tenderly into his arms. She had no one, while everyone crawled and catered to Charity Sturges as though she were some sort of goddess!

Gradually, Gaby took hold of herself as the tears dried. She stood up and looked at herself in the mirror. What she saw was impressive. A beautiful, highly desirable woman. Any time she could not outstrip a half-Indian savage who did not even know what to do with her skirts—well, that would be a sorry day indeed.

She pulled the bell rope, bawled an order for tea, and looked to the future. . . .

70.

"And how is my pet feeling?" Mrs. Dylan asked.

Charity smiled and looked up into her friend's kindly, Irish eyes. She had been dozing on the lawn after watching the road work which was now approaching completion.

She said, "I feel wonderful. The walk you made me take to the stables did me a world of good. I petted that lovely little newborn foal. Soon I shall be riding its mother."

"Not too fast, my dear. Strength returns slowly after the ordeal you went through."

Charity sobered. "I guess I nearly died."

"Why, heaven would not allow that to happen to a bonny lass like you!"

Mrs. Dylan had been busy all that morning in the kitchen. A new cook had arrived the day before and Mrs. Dylan had been schooling her in the preparation of her patient's food.

"Her name is Peggy Wales and she does seem competent," Mrs. Dylan informed her.

Charity squeezed her hand. "Mrs. Dylan, how can I ever tell you—how can I ever thank you. . . ."

"Now, now—enough of that. Before you know it everything will be just like the old days."

The old days. How quickly pleasures casually accepted could turn into precious memories!

Mrs. Dylan patted Charity's hand, bent down to kiss her cheek, and, finding all was well with her patient, returned to the house.

Charity was left alone with her thoughts. They were somehow muted, as though she could not quite get a grip on her mind; they floated across her consciousness like small clouds across the sky; thoughts she could share with no one.

The person she had once been no longer existed. Borland Nickelawn had destroyed the old Charity; the arrogant, pushy, dominating little opportunist who had come to England to conquer all opposition and shunt aside those who got in her way.

She remembered little past the moment a heavy boot crashed against her skull in the crypt and shattered her consciousness.

Up to that point it remained clear. When the torture and death Borland Nickelawn promised her had seemed inevitable, she'd known the taste, touch, and smell of pure terror, and it had left its mark.

Now, she wanted only peace and protection and safety.

She now cringed as she remembered the person she had been; flaring into anger at fancied wrongs; arbitrarily directing the lives of others, knowing better than they what was good for them. And it seemed ridiculous as she watched the road work progress, that sane, level-headed people like Christopher, Dennis, and Clement, could have taken an ubiquitous colonial upstart seriously.

But now she was divorced from all that, and high time, with but one of the old resolutions still bright and clear in her mind.

She would marry Christopher, make him a good wife, and sublimate her life to him. Peace, contentment, a gentle existence—those things would be her reward.

Still, some of the old Charity was left, and this became apparent a few nights later when Christopher walked with her toward the Channel cliffs with the sun dropping into late afternoon.

"We must not go too far," he said. "After such an ordeal as yours, strength comes back slowly."

"I have been fortunate," she replied. "I am almost myself again."

"Much to everyone's relief."

"Christopher, I suppose I am being very forward, but there is something I must ask you."

"Whatever you wish."

"When I visited your brother Clement, he asked me if I loved you."

"And your reply?"

"I assured him that I did."

"You make me very happy."

"He gave me to believe that marriage had been discussed between you, and that is what I must ask. Do you love me? Do you want me for your wife? If not, I wish to leave England and return to Virginia."

There was no passionate declaration. Christopher did not take Charity in his arms and assure her of his own passionate love. Still, his reply left no doubt. He put an arm around her shoulders and drew her tight against his side.

"Charity, darling, do you think for a moment I would allow you to do that? You belong where you are, here in England with me. Of course I plan to marry you. It has not been out of my mind for a moment since we reached these shores."

Charity pressed her face against his chest and murmured, "Now you will see me in another bad light. A proper girl does not propose marriage. She waits to be asked."

That appeared to disturb him. He frowned and asked, "You say *another* bad light. I don't understand. You imply that I have not approved of what I have seen in you."

"You have had every right. I have shamed you in many ways. Attacking Gabrielle Kirth as I did was unspeakable. Then I allowed my temper to rule me and resented being scolded."

"Charity, my dear, I did not look upon what I said to you as a scolding. Even then I was thinking of you in terms of marriage. It was not your fault that the life you lived in Virginia did not fit you for the modes and manners you found here in

454

England. That was my objective—to patiently direct and educate you in that direction."

"And you have been very patient and understanding," Charity said quietly. "I am grateful. I only hope you will believe me when I say I have tried and will continue to try in the future."

"My dear, you have been all that any man could expect what with the obstacles you had to overcome. I am very proud of you."

"That is all the reward I ask, Christopher."

"I have been gearing my affairs with our wedding in mind and I am now happy to tell you that it can be in the near future. A month hence, perhaps."

Charity was elated. "Oh, darling! Are you sure?"

"Quite sure. In fact I plan to speak to Clement tomorrow to set a date. As you know, I have been quite busy with the school project. The Leach interests must be protected, of course. But it goes well and will no longer require the bulk of my time. Also, there are my affairs in London. They must not be neglected because what transpires there is of vital importance to my future."

"To *our* future, darling," she reminded him.

"Of course. That applies without saying. I have been most fortunate in catching the eye of the Prime Minister and I have every reason to believe that he has plans for me."

"Christopher, I am so proud of you! One day you will be making decisions that will affect the future of the nation."

With all due modesty, he replied, "And I am

sure that when the time comes I shall be prepared for it."

Charity switched her train of thought.

"Christopher, you said that the Prime Minister showed some interest in meeting me. When will that come about?"

"Soon, I suspect. Perhaps he will come to the wedding."

"That would be wonderful."

"It would be a feather in my cap, no doubt about that. A man of Lord North's position taking time to attend my nuptials."

"Do you feel that you can really set a date?" she asked anxiously.

"I am sure of it. Clement will perform the ceremony, of course. At St. Jude's."

"St. Jude's," Charity mused dreamily. "I in my wedding dress. How lovely it will be."

"A London *modiste* will create the dress. The finest obtainable."

"I will be going to London?"

Christopher hesitated. "Only if absolutely necessary. The trip would be tiresome and we must look to your limited strength."

"You are very thoughtful," she replied primly.

"Also," he went on, "I must find a residence in London and see to purchasing it."

"We will not live at Windward?"

"Hardly. The estate will be maintained and we will retire to its privacy at times, but I will be based in London. I fancy that I will find a suitable house in Berkley Square. I would like you to be near Mercy. I am sure she is lonely there away from her family and you will be a comfort to her."

"I met her briefly at Meg's funeral and she seems a lovely person." The picture of Christopher's sister waving goodbye to her husband flashed across Charity's mind.

"Mercy lived up to Clement's hopes in every respect."

"You were never very close to Justin, I gather. He impressed me as being remote."

"He has always been that way. But with the building of the school his financial skills were needed and I have been consulting with him. He is a good sort, really, and I think we will be closer as time goes by."

"Oh, Christopher! It will all be so wonderful!" She pressed closer to him, her emotions finally surfacing. "And we will surely have a son—and perhaps. . . ."

"A family of course," he replied, gently disengaging her. "But now we must think of you. We have come quite far and it is time to return. Early to bed, my dear. That is the key to your complete recovery."

Charity felt quite strong. With her spirits high, she would have been able to walk with Christopher for hours. But his judgment was paramount and she would abide by his wishes. That, of course, was the first commandment in any good wife's decalogue. . . .

71.

Gaby Kirth's first reaction was to laugh. What Christopher told her was too unbelievable, particularly under the present circumstances. She was resting in his arms after they had joined so beautifully and with such mutual success on the great square couch in her salon.

He had been voracious in his lovemaking, moving her with his strength and hunger from one end of the couch to the other. His mouth had been on her breasts and body in the foreplay which was not play at all but a savage urging to match his own needs.

And then, while she lay in his arms and he held her most tenderly, he made the bald statement.

"Gaby, darling, I am going to marry Charity Sturges."

Gaby laughed and tugged playfully at his ear. "Sweeting, my hearing is not of the best today. I would swear that you said...."

"I did. I plan to marry Charity within the month."

The most infuriating part was his tenderness not abating in the least, his warmth still radiating out. His tone as gentle as though he were imparting a sweet secret.

But what he said was that he planned to marry *Charity!*

"Christopher, you are guying me. I think it is a poor joke."

"It is not a joke, my dear. And what I have told you is best for all of us."

She was up on her elbow glaring into his face. "Then if it is not a joke, it is an insult! You must be out of your mind! Are you saying that after what I have been to you—after what we have been to each other—you can turn from me and marry that gross little Indian from Virginia?"

"She is not an Indian, pet," Christopher replied.

"That really makes no difference. She could be a princess of the blood and I still would not allow it. You belong to me! I have worked too hard at pleasing you to be thrown aside like a mere tart!"

"You will understand in due time."

"I understand now—you—you libertine!"

With that she tore her arms away and pounded him in a frenzy of doubled fists.

"You can't do this to me. You *can't!*" she screamed.

Catching her wrists, he held her, but still with the same firm gentleness, almost as though she were a hysterical child.

Finding violence was of no avail, she tried tears, falling again into his arms and clinging to him.

"Christopher, I love you! I have always loved you. When you left me and went across the ocean you took a part of me with you! I waited and waited for you! When you returned my heart reached out to you as though you had never left!"

He did not destroy her fine fervor by stating the facts of the case; rather, he agreed with her, saying, "Yes, my love. My own thoughts remained with you over those desolate years. I longed for the sight of you each and every day."

"Then why, Christopher—why do you do this to me? Why do you desert me in this fashion?"

"I am not deserting you, darling. We shall remain close to each other as always."

"You are saying that I am to be. . . ." She could not believe what his words suggested.

"I will explain it to you, if you will lie quiet and listen."

She was not yet ready to do so, and said, "Christopher, do you truly know what that cheap little trollop is?"

Thus she came perilously close to telling Christopher the whole story. But even in her distraught state, the hard face and cold eyes of Dennis Wahl shaped in her fancy, almost as though he were there in person to warn her.

. . . a plague will fall upon your house such as you cannot dream.

Perhaps it was the height of cowardice to heed such a threat at this crucial moment but Wahl was a man dangerous to cross. Once the truth was out she would be so vulnerable. Also, there were other facets to that mystery that she did not understand. Where was Borland Nickelawn? Perhaps Wahl had spoken to him, and to have that maniac seek her out in the dark of some terrible night was too horrible to contemplate.

Something else helped her to hold her tongue. *Christopher might be fully aware of the truth;* of Charity's visit to Nickelawn's Maidstone house. Her purported purpose, that of saving his life and his honor, could be commendable in his eyes.

All that went quickly through Gaby's mind and she altered her attack. "A cheap little tart, truly, Christopher. She tried to kill me with a meat cleaver. Have you forgotten that? She flaunted herself in male clothing and has been the subject of scandalous gossip ever since she arrived in England."

"If you will only let me explain," Christopher repeated patiently.

"I am waiting!"

"Charity has changed greatly since her accident. What happened, I believe, was that it jarred her back into being what she is in truth—a quiet, docile little person who belongs where I shall put her; into a domestic situation where she will fit perfectly—a house in Berkley Square with a staff to supervise and a family, in due time. Gaby, my dear, a man must plan very carefully with a career at stake, and Charity as my wife, staying in the background as a wife should, will do much to burnish my public image."

"But you said it was best for all of us. Is it best for me to be discarded and shunted aside?"

"We will be closer than ever, Gaby. I shall set you up in Mayfair in a flat of your own...."

"I can afford my own flat!"

"But as my mistress that would not be proper."

She stared at him with new wonder. "You *have* planned your future out to the veriest detail."

"*Our* future, my darling. Do you not understand? I *do* love you. You *do* have my love. Charity running my home and giving me children has no bearing on that whatever. Also, it is no disgrace for a man to have a mistress. Even the King has one."

"Several, if the rumors are true," she murmured drily.

"But I shall have one—only you, and I want you gay and lovely—not burdened with the cares of family and household."

The frustration, the sense of loss, still remained, but Gaby had long ago learned how to accept defeat gracefully. *Just as well,* she told herself; *a wife's lot is not for me. Not for me waiting for the lord and master to bed me; to produce another brat. A mistress, now. . . .*

Yes! A mistress had only to look to her finery, to keep herself beautiful, to stir envy in other men, thus heightening her benefactor's stature as it kept his own interest in her alive.

Of course, the role of mistress was less permanent than that of wife. The man could tire of her. But that worked both ways. And as a financially secure widow she would not be bound to Christopher by need of support.

She realized that what she really wanted was the status in London's gay and glittering society, which was becoming more and more attractive. Love? The emotional attraction she had professed? Perhaps she had misinterpreted it. His rejection of her as a wife was certainly not tearing her apart.

Still, she was not going to fall weakly into his

arms in quick surrender. Let him worry for a time. Doubts would enhance her value in his eyes.

She arose from the bed, drew on a robe, and said, "I don't know, Christopher. This is too confusing. You spurn me and promise me fidelity at the same time. I must think it out. Leave me now. I will let you know as to my decision."

Completely unperturbed, he said, "I hope you will give me your decision soon because I have a favor to ask. I would like your good advice and counsel on Charity's wedding dress. I would like you to go to London with me to select a couturier. One of the best. I wish the wedding to be a glittering event and the bride's gown is of utmost importance. I have noticed in accounts of weddings in the society pages, it is the first thing to be described."

The arrogance of the man! Gaby stood speechless for a time. She was certainly seeing a new side of Christopher, but not one necessarily shocking. It was an aspect that could be of advantage to her. It reflected his determination to rise into higher circles and it followed that she would rise with him. And it did not detract in the least from his new skills as a lover, a talent she was coming to appreciate more and more.

"Very well," Gaby said, "I shall accommodate you in helping with the wedding dress, even though I reserve decision on the other matter."

"Thank you, my darling," Christopher replied, not knowing that it was his outrageous request that tipped the scales totally in his favor....

72.

The Reverend Clement Leach was troubled and was now voicing his concern to Christopher.

He said, "I have had some disquieting moments. . . ."

Christopher was quick to reply. "But I thought you felt the school to be a solid proposition."

"It is not that. I refer to you yourself, Chris." He studied his younger brother as though seeking a reassurance in his face that he could not find. "You have changed radically since returning to England."

"I realize that. What I have tried to do is what I assume you wanted of me—prepare myself in some small manner to take over where your health has forced you to slow your activities."

"Please do not misunderstand me," Clement hastened to say.

"Then I suggest you speak more plainly."

"I laud your new self-confidence, but is it soundly based?"

"I still misunderstand. The self-confidence you seem to decry in me was your own stock-in-trade, so to speak. You never doubted your own convictions."

"True, but I also depended upon myself and no one else."

"And where, pray tell, do I place my dependence?"

"Upon others, Chris. Let me put it this way. I always believed in what I thought to be right and fought for the reforms I advocated and I cared not what others thought. In short, I depended upon myself. You, however, are basing your hopes of betterment upon what others think of you; the Prime Minister, those who form his clique and those who must mirror his policies. And what is worse, you have no cause to support you in a time of adversity. You are looking only to better yourself and reap whatever benefits may accrue. Do I make myself clear?"

Christopher's respect for Clement was still a predominant factor, so he strove to control his temper. "You are being unfair, brother! I do believe in what Lord North stands for and join him with all enthusiasm and with no reservations."

"Most laudable. Do you *know* what he stands for?"

"Of course. A strong England. A ruling nation among the nations of the world."

"True, no doubt. We all stand strong for such—for power to grow greater, though methods of achieving that end change from man to man. Mine are somewhat different than those of North. However, I am not criticizing his administration. What I want to ask is this—if North topples and can no longer be of help to you, will you go scrambling like all the other sycophants for the favor of those who succeed him?"

"You have no right to call me by such a name!"

"My apologies. Being most zealous for your

465

welfare and your progress, I do become over-critical."

Christopher spoke bitterly. "Clement, I think I know what distresses you; that I no longer come to you for guidance on each little matter; that I have severed the strings with which you made me dance to your tune."

"My God, Christopher, did I give you that impression?"

Christopher, abashed by what his anger had made him say, reached forth and laid a penitent hand on Clement's arm. "Forgive me! I did not mean to speak so harshly. I still do treasure your advice, your guidance. But you would think the less of me if I did not finally become my own man."

Clement smiled. "Yes, I believe I would. Becoming your own man is inevitable with the Leach blood running in your veins. So we will say no more about it. You will forge ahead and reach high places."

"And we can only hope," Christopher murmured sullenly, "that Lord North will stay in favor long enough to get me there?"

"Please, Christopher, do accept my apologies."

"I am sorry, Clement. What I said was childish."

"And now tell me more about your marriage plans."

"My proposal was made and accepted and I would be desolated if you refused to officiate."

"What makes you think I would refuse? It is just that the lass is so young, so lacking in ex-

466

perience. The ordeal through which she passed must have shaken her to her foundations."

"I am sure it did, but I find there has been a favorable aspect. While wracking her viciously, the experience appears to have steadied her. She is no longer the erratic young lass I brought from Virginia."

Clement silently asked, *No longer the fascinating, vibrant young creature who would spontaneously kiss an awesome old prelate at first meeting?* The change in Charity had certainly been most radical.

And in Christopher also. Clement felt constrained to speak plainly in that regard.

"Christopher, I felt that upon your return you saw Charity as a ward rather than as a wife—that even then your affection for Lady Kirth still held."

Christopher felt a touch of inner alarm. Had Clement learned of his London meeting with Gaby? Had he been apprised of their carnal dalliance? He had ears everywhere.

Speaking with a hesitancy Clement must have noticed, he said, "Much has happened since I returned from the Colonies, Clement: recognition in London which required that I look carefully to my future. I still have a deep regard for Gabrielle, truly, but—well, how can I put it? Gaby, by her very nature, is spectacular."

Therefore, she would draw attention which you feel should be focused upon you alone?

Clement almost asked the question. But the answer was obvious and there was no point in embarrassing his brother.

"Most spectacular," Christopher went on, "while Charity, as she has become, will quietly and properly keep my home and mother my children."

"Does she love you, Christopher?"

"Clement, if I was as sure of all else as I am sure of Charity's love and unswerving devotion to me, I would be a fortunate man indeed."

"That is most encouraging. I would like to talk to the girl if I may. As a future brother-in-law, I should get to know her better. Do you agree?"

"Most certainly. I shall instruct her to come to you at the earliest possible date."

The reply did not cheer Clement. The wording. *I shall instruct*—Could he not have said, *I shall bring Charity to see you at her earliest convenience.*

Evidently not, and having been so harshly critical of Christopher and his new ways, Clement did not see fit to express further disapproval of his younger brother.

Charity came, as evidently instructed, on the next afternoon, to sit demurely beside Clement's lounge in the arbor of the manse.

"My dear," Clement said, "I wish to congratulate you on your coming nuptials."

"Thank you, your Reverence."

"Are you quite recovered now from your accident?"

"I feel much better. My strength has improved. I have even done some riding close about the premises."

"And now you will enter a new life as Christopher's wife. Does the thought daunt you?"

"Not at all. I look forward to it. I think it is what destiny, my good angel, meant for me from the beginning. The peace and the protection and the safety of Christopher's love."

"And you return that love?"

"With my whole heart. I owe him so much. He is such a special person; strong and yet gentle. It would be impossible not to love him."

No doubt the girl was sincere and Clement saw no reason to pursue the subject.

They chatted a bit longer, but after she left him, he was still troubled. Charity *had* changed. He would not go so far as to say the spirit had been taken out of her; not entirely. Perhaps she was still suffering from the effects of the accident.

Clement lay back and closed his eyes and turned his thoughts inward. He was clearly being arbitrary in his doubts about the marriage; and even the more so because he could not give himself a definite reason for his lack of enthusiasm.

No doubt it was simple petulance. He was probably piqued because Christopher had not come to him and asked for his permission and his blessing. Being consulted on matters of importance had been the way of things for so long that he now felt lonely and deserted—pushed aside as life moved past him while he should actually be grateful that the responsibility had been lifted from his shoulders.

73.

In order to appease Christopher's concern as to Charity's strength, Gaby suggested they work with measurements rather than fittings. Upon her directions, Christopher gave that task to Mrs. Dylan. An able couturier could easily work with a dress form—construct one to order, if necessary.

The couturier that Gaby selected was a prissy little gentleman, one of the best and certainly one of the most expensive in all London. Now that she had managed to readjust her sights relative to her status in Christopher's life she saw her role of selecting Charity's wedding dress as ironically amusing. Eventually, Charity would become aware of the situation; after she was so enmeshed in the trap of marriage that she could do nothing other than suffer the humiliation of knowing that Gaby had the pleasure of Christopher's company while she bore the suffering of childbirth and the boredom of wifehood back in the shadows. Gaby reveled in the fact that Christopher had left no doubt as to what Charity's status would be. Also, Gaby enjoyed the privilege of making the dress as expensive as she possibly could, thus hoping to bring Christopher some discomfort.

"This," she said, selecting a lovely cream satin

and holding it against her breast. "It will be perfect as the base material." Addressing the delighted couturier, she said, "I have a very clear picture in my mind of what we want. The body of the gown will be of this material. The neckline must be high as will befit a young and virginal bride, with a veil of your finest lace which I will choose from your samples. The train will lie gracefully over the bride's shoulders and be of a length and breadth which will require the services of two sweet little maids lest it trail in the dust. From the neckline to the waist, the gown will be of the simplest design but the skirt will require decoration. There must be loops of fine gold braid extending downward to the hem— strands of small, evenly sized pearls running the lengths of the braids. There will be curved stays over which the skirt will be gracefully extended on either side to give it a dignified width, these of course anchored at the waist. The bride's shoes will be of white satin, the skirt not quite touching the ground so that the toes of the slippers will be visible at each step. You have been given the bride's dimensions. Can you start to work on the gown immediately?"

"Oh, immediately, Madam!" The couturier was fairly bouncing with enthusiasm.

"The bride will not come here for a fitting. When fittings are needed, you will bring the gown personally to Camber on the Channel coast yourself because we are holding you responsible for the perfection we demand."

The trips back and forth had been suggested— even insisted upon—by Gaby, ostensibly in order to save Charity the fatigue of the long ride to and from London. But her true reason was to sky-rocket the cost.

This did not bother Christopher in the least. He was sincere in wanting Charity to have the very best without exception, to Gaby's disappointment. She had hoped, in piling on the expense, that Christopher would begrudge spending so much on the little tart he was marrying.

There was something else. Gaby would remember the wedding dress. Although she did not need money, having plenty of her own, Christopher would pay for her favors on the same basis.

She was going to be one of the most expensive mistresses in England. . . .

74.

With her strength coming back swiftly, Charity was now able to ride greater distances without tiring. She enjoyed getting off by herself away from the heightening activity of the school construction. The road finished, there was work on the house itself to start soon with the outdoor activity still continuing. Building the school had been a source of great satisfaction throughout the area. It meant employment and, for many, added prosperity.

One thing bothered Charity. She had expected

Christopher to take her back to Windward, but so far he had made no mention of it. She would have gone, of course, and it seemed the proper thing to do. But then again, perhaps staying at Camber was for the best. She had never felt at home in the vast, cold castle whereby the small house at Camber had a less forbidding atmosphere. Time enough to return when she had been made mistress of Leach House and could enter it with complete authority.

Also, there was Dennis to consider. At first he had been resentful of her coming marriage to Christopher. Perhaps there had been some jealousy although on the basis of the father-daughter relationship they had adopted, he really had no grounds. But that had changed. Completely occupied with the creation of the school, he thought of little else. It had become a source of pride to him and several times he had mentioned it as a memorial to Meg, Clement's reason for agreeing to the project. Charity thought it curious that with his seemingly casual regard for Meg while she lived, Dennis was now conducting himself as though they had been the closest of lovers and the marriage ideally made in heaven.

And now, as she rode pleasantly along and ruminated on things as they were, she became aware of a rider approaching.

A man. He was riding a bay stallion he had obviously borrowed from somewhere because Sean McDougal did not possess a mount of his own.

But he rode well and when he arrived at a gallop by Charity's side, he reined the horse up on its haunches.

There was no smile; no cheerful greeting. A scowl, rather, and Charity's attempt at a light approach fell quite flat as she said, "Sean! Sean McDougal. And not entering through a bedroom window this time."

"Charity. I have been trying to reach you!"

"Then why did you not come to Camber? I have not been inaccessible," she responded pleasantly.

"Because I might have lost my temper and made a scene. What is this I have been told? That you are going to marry Christopher Leach?"

"I *am* to marry him—very soon."

"Throw yourself away on him, you mean! What have they done to you? How could they have trapped you into making this terrible mistake." He fought to control his agitation.

"I am not trapped, Sean. Far from it. Why do you take on so? I love Christopher Leach. We will find happiness together, he and I."

"You will find misery! I am the one you love, as you very well know!"

This was a new Sean, coming as he had across the moor to intercept her and plead his case. Sean had never been one to plead; not the gay laughing buccaneer she had known, and the change saddened her. It was beneath his dignity to act in this manner. It lessened him as a man to beg a cause like a disappointed swain. Even Wilferd had shown more dignity when he came to ask for Dorothy's hand in marriage.

"What of our plans; what of our dreams?" Sean was saying.

"There were dreams, perhaps, but no plans.

474

You spoke of wild, impossible places that existed only in your mind. I never promised to follow you off into a life of madness. I told you from the beginning what I wanted; the security of a proper marriage with a proper man, not the wild existence of a sea rover not knowing of tomorrow, going whichever way the wind blew."

A curious change seemed to come over Sean. Holding a tight rein on his mount, he regarded Charity more calmly. The wind played with his black locks and a shadow of the smile Charity had known now returned. For a moment he did not speak.

Finally he said, "There was a lass named Mavourneen, do you remember?"

"Of course, Sean. I shall always remember."

"Where did she go? What became of her?"

"She went nowhere because she never existed. She was a dream, dear Sean. Can you not understand that? And dreams are for just that— dreaming, not living. That is where you fail yourself; not being able to tell one from the other."

"Yes," he replied more quietly. "I failed. I let Mavourneen go beyond my reach before she was strong enough to stand alone. I waited in my conceit for her to come to me. . . ."

"Sean, I must go. There is much to do."

"Yes, we both have much to do. A blessing on you, Charity Sturges. And a curse, Mavourneen, on those who destroyed you."

With that, he was off across the moor, not looking back.

Charity's eyes followed him with pity. How he

had wasted his life! If only he could have grown up with Clement and Christopher, what a different man he would have become.

75.

Things now began moving swiftly.

The following morning, Christopher took time out from his busy schedule to inform Charity, "We have been able to set the date for the wedding, my dear. Clement and I agree that it will be this day two weeks hence at high noon."

"How wonderful!" Charity kissed his cheek in a quick wave of happiness, then said, "The way you put that, dearest. Has the date some other significance?"

"How discerning of you! Yes, it has. It is the day Clement preached his first sermon. Many years ago, but it has always been a family date to remember."

"Will preparations be made in time?"

"They will have to be. I also have other news—great news! The Prime Minister has graciously consented to attend." Without waiting for Charity to express her joy, Christopher looked off into space as though visualizing the triumphs which would rise from the regard Lord North's presence indicated. He added, "I think I shall be entrusted with important responsibilities very soon now."

"I am so proud of you, Christopher."

"And I of you, my dear," he replied, cupping her chin in his hand and looking fondly into her face. "We have come a long way from the shores of Virginia in a very short time, have we not?"

"A very long way."

"Oh, yes. You must go to Windward this afternoon. The couturier will arrive there from London for a fitting of your wedding dress."

"Christopher! So soon?"

"Speed was demanded. They worked night and day and it is almost complete."

Charity turned thoughtful. It occurred to her to suggest that she remain at Windward until the wedding. To block the suggestion there came a vision of the vast, bleak castle, forbidding, almost macabre in her present mood, while there at Camber she had found warmth, friendship, and companionship. She did not see this reluctance as being disloyal to Christopher. Of course she would go back to Windward Moors—but as Christopher's wife, and with the man she loved at her side it would all be different. So she gave no further thought to leaving Camber for the time being.

The couturier bustled over from London on schedule. He remembered Lady Kirth's explicit instructions:

During your fittings you will make no reference whatever to me as having designed the dress. That is most important.

An odd directive but she did give him an explanation of sorts:

We wish my part to be a surprise to the bride-to-be after the wedding.

The couturier really did not care one way or another. He thought the whole arrangement queer but then the gentry, particularly the peerage, were people apart, their slightest whims absolute law.

In Charity's old room, that afternoon, Mrs. Dylan did the honors, seeing to her fresh, new underthings, camisole, pantalettes, and voluminous petticoats. Then she allowed the couturier to enter. She made it a festive occasion. She insisted that Charity close her eyes while the bodice was put in place. Then the hooped skirt was lowered over her head and the supporting band anchored.

Then Mrs. Dylan led Charity to the mirror. "You may look now, my precious."

Charity opened her eyes. She gasped. Who was that lovely creature she saw before her? Surely not the shabby little gamine who had come so far in such a short time!

"It fairly takes my breath away," Charity murmured. "How can I ever wear such a lovely thing!"

The couturier smiled at the compliment, and said modestly, "Madame's loveliness is worthy of my humble talents."

"When will we have the next fitting?" she asked.

"There will be no need. The gown fits almost perfectly. I will take it back to London for minor adjustments and it will be delivered in ample time for the wedding."

"Is that not exceptional?" Mrs. Dylan asked. "A single fitting?"

"With others of my profession, yes," the couturier replied with some pride. "But my shop is extensive. We have a fine supply of forms in store and so it was not difficult to select one with almost the identical measurements given."

He did not add that Lady Kirth had promised him a bonus for prompt delivery; also that returning the dress to London was not necessary other than to increase the final charge by the cost of one more trip.

Charity got out of the lovely gown with some reluctance. The couturier hastened off on his way, and Mrs. Dylan took Charity down to the kitchen for tea. Once there, she showed her concern.

"Are you quite well again, my pet? Has all your strength returned?"

"Oh, yes, that is also Christopher's concern. I assured him I have totally recovered. Otherwise he would not allow me to tax myself with even the trip here to Windward."

"And are you happy?"

"Gloriously happy, Mrs. Dylan. How could I not be? A fine man waiting to take me to the altar. A beautiful life awaiting me afterward. How could I not be?"

"Is it the thought of marriage which has sobered you?" the older woman asked suddenly.

"Sobered me? I do not understand."

"You were so gay before. A joy to my heart

each time I set eyes upon you." Before Charity could answer, she went on. "No, of course not. It was your terrible experience. It will take time ere those dark clouds are cleared from your mind."

"Have you seen Sean?" Charity asked, the question past her lips even before she realized that she'd asked it.

Mrs. Dylan frowned. "Oh, yes. That one is riding in a black mood for sure. He has come to wail in my ear several times."

"About what?" Charity asked.

"Nothing I can put a finger on. I think he has stayed too long in Kent. There was boredom, and now an intensity to be away."

Charity wondered if Mrs. Dylan was aware of his reason for being in Kent in the first place. But knowing of the guns in the Moon Tower, Mrs. Dylan would certainly know of Sean's plans. However, she did not mention it so Charity did not ask the question on the tip of her tongue. How soon would Sean complete his cargo and leave for the Colonies? The query would have been unimportant, merely a matter of personal curiosity.

"I must be getting back," Charity said. "I am afraid Christopher will worry if I tarry too long. He waits for me at Camber."

Mrs. Dylan said, "My dear, I had best stay here at Windward the night. There is so much still to be done. You do not mind?"

"Of course not. You must do as you think best. But see that you get your proper rest. You never seem to stop."

480

"I was wound up at birth and I'll keep going until God takes me. Come, I'll put you in the rig. Wilferd will be waiting."

76.

Mrs. Dylan was not the only one who worried over Sean McDougal's state of mind. Sibley also had a concern. Sean had quite suddenly taken over the operation in which a corps of good and loyal men were engaged. That was gratifying after a fashion. Sibley had decried Sean's earlier lack of interest. Now, however, it was completely the opposite. He had plunged in and was driving the men, acting the taskmaster, demanding increased effort when such capacities were already taxed to the utmost. There had been grumbling, murmurs of complaint; and that reaction, coming from a select squad motivated by respect and loyalty rather than the pressures of a tyrant, was a dangerous situation.

Sibley tried to make an end of it.

"Sean, the cargo is almost complete. Why take further chances? Call it sufficient and sail with what you have."

"Until we have a full cargo, we do not sail. We are miserably shy of bayonets for the muskets and flintlocks. In close combat such a lack is fatal and there are goodly supplies in the Pengallon Armory, as you well know."

"Well I do know, and also that obtaining them is perilous."

"Is there no one there who will take a bribe?"

"That is not the problem. It is the location of the armory. Only one roadway out, and the country around too rugged. The place was once a prison, you know."

"I know. And what you say is true. One roadway out. So what we must do is to carry the booty down that road."

"You ask too much, Sean. With patrols what they are, it is sure death." Sibley shook his head in protest.

"They will be on the watch for coffins, hay ricks, men lugging burdens."

"Or donkeys. Any logical means of conveyance."

"Even before the bayonets are missed?"

"The patrols have been posted, I tell you."

"It seems," Sean replied coldly, "that those in whom I place trust are long on courage but short on imagination."

"That is unfair, Sean!" Sibley cried.

He could be quick biting, and as swift with repentance. "I'm sorry. It *was* unfair, but my friend, there is a way. I have discovered it. A little time and we shall have the last of our cargo...."

Sibley found cause to be gratified. Sean's period of darkness seemed over. His old spirit was returning as the end of the arms project—

for better or for worse, success or failure—came in sight.

For ensuing days, he refused to discuss what he had in mind. It was a time of solitary operation; time during which he came and went alone. Then he again consulted with Sibley.

"The time has come," he said. "Your man inside the armory. You have kept in touch? He is satisfied with the offer you made?"

"We have never had a problem there. He is one of ours."

Sean laughed. "Then only one risk remains. Can I or can I not succeed as a clown. The Bentworth Circus performs in Williston tomorrow night. And Williston is but two short miles from Pengallon Armory." He clapped Sibley on the shoulder with all the zest of old, and the latter could not hold back the questions which had been in his mind.

"Sean," he said, "we are old friends and beyond finding offense in each other. So I must know."

"Know what?"

"The thing that haunted you which has now gone past. What was it? What put you in such low spirits."

"The danger of the project?" Sean replied glibly.

Sibley smiled. "You lie poorly."

"I must improve that technique. But to be honest, for a time I lost faith in myself."

"I was aware of that, but why?"

"You know. You have eyes."

"That girl, Charity Sturges. Her marriage to Christopher Leach?"

"I love the lass, Sibley. I love her more than my own soul. And for a time I thought I had lost her."

"Is the marriage off?"

"We are not speaking of that. We speak of faith in one's self. Lost her? Never! She will come to me. Never fear. No other possibility exists."

Sibley was greatly relieved. Not that he believed Sean would ever see Charity Sturges again. She was gone from him. But he understood that when a man like Sean fell truly in love, the experience would be intense, especially if he wooed her in vain. But Sean had survived the ordeal of losing the lass. His sublime self-confidence had brought him through. It would support him until this project was over, and once at sea, back in his element, he would forget the girl. Unless....

"Sean, you do not plan anything desperate, I hope."

"Such as?..."

"Perhaps kidnapping the girl?"

Sean laughed in joyful ridicule. "You fool, I said she would come to me. Have you lost all your faith?"

Sibley wished, as he had many times before, that he possessed the faith that had carried Sean along the razor edge of disaster for so long. It made for a charmed life and few men were so favored.

77.

Came the morning finally when Charity could awaken and whisper, "Tomorrow is my wedding day."

The waiting over, the quiet joy of it ran gently through her being. Come the morrow at high noon, she would be given body and soul to Christopher and the new life which she had crossed an ocean to find would open to her.

She lay for a time, savoring what the narrowing hours would bring. Then there were footsteps and a tapping on the door. Christopher, of course, coming with a good-morning kiss.

"Come in, darling."

Not Christopher. Mrs. Dylan instead, with a tray of tea and crumpets.

"Good morning, my pet. I came to bring the good news and could not resist bringing you your last breakfast as a maiden."

Charity laughed. "Mrs. Dylan. You make me feel like the condemned due at the gibbet. It is not my last breakfast, however. I plan to have one tomorrow."

"Oh, well, your last in this house. Take your tea while it is hot."

"You mentioned good news," Charity reminded her.

"Yes. That lovely wedding dress arrived at Windward late last night."

"Why did they not bring it here?"

"Mr. Leach has planned that you go early to-morrow morning to Windward where I will dress you and prepare you for the ceremony. Then we will drive to St. Jude's."

"Will we return to Windward after the wedding?"

"No, he plans that you go straight to London where your new home in Berkley Square is all furnished and waiting. Did he tell you? It is two doors from the home of his brother-in-law, Justin. His sister, Mercedes, will be that close. You will have happy times together."

"No," Charity said slowly. "He did not tell me."

Christopher meant well, of course; still it was a little disappointing not to be included in the preparations for her own wedding. Perhaps the protection and consideration she had yearned for would take a little getting used to.

Charity told herself that she was not going to mar the happiness Christopher so greatly deserved by taking him to task. Time enough after the wedding to gently remind him that she was not a fragile blossom needing shelter from the slightest breeze.

Mrs. Dylan stayed another hour and was then driven back to Windward where she would await Charity's arrival the following morning. Shortly before noon, Christopher was able to ease away from the tasks he had set for himself and spend a little time with Charity.

He kissed her, looked searchingly into her face, and said, "I am delighted, my dear. Every vestige of your perilous accident has vanished. You look radiant."

"Thank you, darling. I have made a special effort. I want you to be proud of me tomorrow at St. Jude's."

"I will be that, have no fear." Then he looked off to where three men were moving timbers out of a north wing window. "I wish I had more time for you, Charity, but one has to watch the work every minute. Dennis shows little talent for efficiency and I keep finding three and four men doing the work one or two should be able to accomplish. It is most frustrating."

"I understand, Christopher. Will the work go on through tomorrow?"

"No, we are declaring a holiday. It seems the proper thing to do."

Christopher bestowed another quick kiss and was off again to see that all the day's wages were fairly earned. Charity went to the stables to play with the frisky new foal and congratulate his mother for having such a fine son.

Her thoughts roamed on that lazy afternoon. It was mounting summer now, the lush land having fulfilled all the promise of the early spring when Charity arrived in England. Months swiftly flying by, with so many changes in what seemed so short a time. Christopher had changed, had broadened. No, perhaps not. Her memories of him in Virginia were of a man she had not really known. He had merely lived up to the potential which was always in him.

Have I changed? She asked herself the question and had no clear answer. She did not really seek one. Enough to say that she had weathered violence and come forth a better person.

Twilight came and she returned to the house to dine with Christopher, but there was a disappointment. He'd had to rush away on very important last-minute business. Nor was Dennis anywhere about to share her evening meal. This did not surprise her but it did make her a little sad. Dennis had withdrawn from her of late, become more remote. She suspected it was because of Christopher. Perhaps Dennis did not want to intrude. Did that mean that becoming Christopher's wife would require that she lose her friends? She hoped that would not be the case.

Charity ate sparingly, her appetite not at its best. Night fell and as she watched the moon peep up to begin its ride through a cloudless sky, she thought of the wedding dress. Such a beautiful creation. And how could the couturier be so sure it would fit properly? The more she thought about it the more certain she became that he had been too optimistic, and nothing, not even the smallest flaw, could be allowed to mar the perfection of the garment.

Charity became so resolute on the matter that she went back to the stables, harnessed a mare to a gig, and drove swiftly to Windward where she found Mrs. Dylan in the kitchen.

"Child, you should not be here!"

"I could not stay away, Mrs. Dylan. I want to try on the wedding dress."

"But that is not until morning!"

"I know, but how can we be sure it fits perfectly? What if we found something wrong? There would not be time to repair it. We *must* make sure tonight."

Mrs. Dylan sighed. "Very well, Charity. I guess there would be no harm. And if it would allow you to sleep better. . . ."

"You're a darling!"

"Come, child. The gown is in your old chambers. . . ."

78.

The Bentworth Circus performed in the town of Williston that afternoon but there was no evening show because of a commitment in another town the next day. As was customary, therefore, breaking down and loading began while the main performance was still in progress. It was well equipped for a small circus, with a bevy of clowns, four elephants, two tigers, half a dozen chattering monkeys, and the usual coterie of side shows.

With the audience in the main tent, the side attractions were broken down first, those wagons loaded. Then, when the performance was over and the audience dispersed, the main tent was struck in efficient fashion and in an amazingly short time, the circus was ready to move. In a matter of minutes, it was gone.

There had been a great deal of poaching in Williston County during that season, with a goodly number of men of the area to protect the King's hunting ground where the bulk of the game abounded, a supply of manpower that the Superintendent of the Pengallon Armory, one Cecil Boggs, had been able, through his influence, to draw upon.

Boggs had kept himself informed as to the thieving and pilfering of the King's stores at various armories and felt quite sure that Pengallon would not be overlooked. In fact he sincerely hoped that it would not be. He was convinced that an over-all plan lay behind the looting and if he were able to lay the leader by his heels it would be a great feather in his cap. The brigand was clever, no doubt about that; the leader had to be a man with an intensely loyal corps of blacklegs at his command and an incredibly smooth plan of operation. But if the shadowy leader struck at Pengallon he would be doomed. First, the geographical location of the armory with its single road and the roughest kind of country all about, constituted a trap. Secondly, Boggs was ever alert, and with extra men drawn from poaching duty to patrol the highway, there was little chance for escape.

Still, Boggs almost missed his quarry and saved himself only by taking an inventory, one which revealed that ordnance, a goodly supply of bayonets, had been pilfered in small lots.

Boggs went immediately into action, chasing

down his closest patrol on the highway, guessing correctly that the booty would have been moved to the southeast.

The patrol consisted of four men led by Tom Gibson, a veteran at his calling.

"Where have you been? What have you been doing?" Boggs demanded.

"Our duty, sir," Gibson answered, "faithfully following your orders."

"Excellent! Then you have our felons safely laid to—hidden perhaps somewhere in the forest?" Boggs added sourly.

"There has been no one by, sir, except three hay ricks which we checked thoroughly."

"No one else?"

"There was the circus, of course. On down the road several hours ago."

"You fools!" Boggs shouted. "That was it. It had to be!"

"Nay, sir. We were there. We watched as the encampment was broken down."

"And you saw nothing?"

"We saw the performance," one of the men blurted.

Gibson threw him a venomous glance. "What we saw, sir, was strictly in the line of duty."

"The line of duty!" Boggs repeated bitterly. "What you saw, or rather did not see, was contraband loaded right under your noses. The man we want so badly no doubt did the loading."

"Nay, sir. I watched carefully. One of the clowns handled that task."

"Imbeciles! Fools! You said the wagons are hours ahead?"

491

"They do have some start upon us," Gibson bleakly admitted.

"There may be time before dark," Boggs said, and filing the names of the patrol away in his mind for attention later, he rode off at high speed, heeling his mount viciously, with his three aides pounding along behind him. He could only hope now that there would be time before darkness set in.

He watched the road carefully until, miles later, he called a halt. "They stopped here. The wheel marks and the footprints show it." He peered closer. "They seem to have had the help of elephants."

"The circus did have elephants," one of his aides volunteered.

"How quaint," Boggs snarled, and looked off into the rugged forest slanting upward from the road.

"However, sir, elephants could not penetrate that jungle."

"His men, you idiot! On their backs! How heavy is a bayonet?"

"Then we are undone!"

"I agree that there is no point in following. It would gain us nothing. But we are not necessarily defeated."

"But what means could we use . . . ?"

"Our heads! Our brains! Look at this map. They selected this point with care. It leads southeast into a winding ravine which extends almost to the Channel coast. And another thing. . . ." Boggs paused in deep thought.

"You were saying, sir? . . ."

"This move was daring. Almost foolhardy. It signifies to me the end of the operation during which those scoundrels have gathered together veritable wagonloads of ordnance. Now the question is—what do they intend to do with it?"

"They certainly do not intend to go potting about with a parade of wagons."

"Of course not. And with no sign of internal revolution in the wind, the goods must be slated for export. A respectable shipload."

"Then we have them, sir—or do we?"

"They will move out swiftly now and there is one chance. Ride you on the nearest. . . ." He changed his mind. "No, I shall do it myself. We must get a gunboat into the Channel. If we succeed it will do the blackleg in for fair."

With that, Boggs was off, leaving his aides to fend for themselves as best they could. . . .

79.

The wedding gown was *so* beautiful.

Charity stood before the mirror in a trance. "All those lovely pearls. Where did they find so many?"

"With no expense spared there would be no trouble," Mrs. Dylan said, and smiled. "And they could not be worn by a sweeter lass."

"Be careful," Charity laughed, "or you will

turn my head completely." Charity circled the room, almost dancing.

"A crying shame," Mrs. Dylan said, "to wear such a gown but once."

"That is why I want to feel its softness as long as possible."

"But you must be getting back to Camber. . . ."

"Just a little while longer," Charity begged. "I will be so careful. I will not brush the skirt against anything or smudge an inch of it."

"Very well, my pet. But not too long. I *must* get back to the kitchen. There is much to be done. Your wedding cake. The other viands."

"Please come back in half an hour to help me."

"I shall do that."

Mrs. Dylan left. Charity began to dance, moving about the perimeter of the room. She posed haughtily and advanced as if to a partner, with dignity as befitted the lady she would soon become.

She laughed softly. "I wonder if anyone will be impressed." She hoped so, for Christopher's sake.

It was a warm evening and her dancing threatened to bring perspiration. Stain the dress? That would never do! If she opened a window perhaps she could catch a breeze. She crossed to the one at an angle to the wall separating her rooms from Christopher's.

Immediately, she heard a voice quite clearly. It seemed the corresponding window in his chamber was open also.

It was a woman's voice. Most curious. And even more so when she identified it. Gaby Kirth

494

was in there sounding out loud displeasure at something or other.

Charity soon learned exactly what it was.

"I say it is a pigsty, Christopher! It might as well be in Whitechapel. The flat is a disgrace to Mayfair!"

"I do not understand you, Gaby. You looked at the flat before I rented it for you. You liked it. You even complimented me on my choice."

"Your *choice*, yes. Always *you* and *yours*. Never *ours!*"

It would have been obvious to a listener who knew Gaby well, that she argued for the sake of argument. Logic had little to do with it.

"Even that prissy little bride-to-be. She is *yours*. You will take her to *your* London place where she will bear *your* children. One would think that the poor little tart had nothing to do with it."

"Gaby, I will not have you speaking of Charity in that manner. She deserves better from you."

"She deserves *nothing* from me!"

"Are you saying that the arrangement we agreed to is no longer to your liking?"

"Have I said that?"

"Not in so many words, perhaps. . . ."

"Then do not start putting *your* words into my mouth."

"Gaby, we must not quarrel this way! It bodes ill for our future together."

Gaby's strident tones diminished. "True, Christopher, but does a mistress really have a future with any man?"

"That is unworthy of you, Gaby, particularly

495

when you are obviously referring to me. What reason have you to doubt my fidelity? I am not a rounder. I do not womanize. And when I make a pact, I remain with it."

Gaby evidently decided that she had erupted enough for one session. Her voice softened further.

"Chris, darling. I'm so sorry. I think tomorrow's event is what set me off."

"I can understand that. But it will be over quickly. And my dear, if your flat is not to your liking I shall bow to your wishes in the matter."

Gaby was now fairly purring and she could be visualized as pressing close to Christopher, looking deeply into his eyes. "Forgive me, darling. They are beautiful rooms. But I do have a great favor to ask."

"Whatever I am able to do."

"On your wedding night—tomorrow—we will both be in London, and—oh, darling, I really cannot ask it."

"Please do."

"On your wedding night, will you come to me instead of going to your wife? . . ."

Charity's expression did not change a whit during her eavesdropping. Now she straightened, brushed at her skirt unconsciously, and quietly closed the window. There was no explosion of grief or indignation—nothing. She stared into space, seeing nothing, and as she stood there, a thought filtered unbidden through her mind:

He is so understanding, so patient. However unreasonable she becomes, he bows gracefully to her wishes. . . .

Then, after a long, timeless moment, she smiled. A small laugh followed. She moved toward the door, the wedding dress forgotten. She softly opened the door and paused to look back into the room.

"Thank you, Gaby," she whispered, "thank you—thank you!"

Then all the old verve and vitality of her being arose from the depths where those forces had been imprisoned. When she quitted the castle and crossed the moat ramp, her eyes were like glowing stars, and she was laughing joyously.

Wilferd and Dorothy awoke to the pounding on their door. Wilferd answered it and stood there, struck dumb by what he beheld in the moonlight. Miss Charity in her wedding dress, a look on her face as though she had just fallen heir to heaven and all it contained.

"Wilferd, I need you. Hitch a gig quickly. Faster if possible!"

"But Miss Charity. . . ."

"No dawdling," she replied, her voice sharp. "Smartly now or must I do it myself."

He began moving, his obedience springing from rote, his mind refusing to function with any clarity. However, he worked with such speed that by the time the gig was ready and he had helped Charity, wedding gown and all, into her seat, Dorothy had just arrived at the door, peering out in mute wonder at what she beheld.

Wilferd asked, "Back to Camber, Miss Charity?"

"No, Wilferd—off across the moor toward the

cliffs." She pointed. "In that direction. I'll guide you."

As they bounced along, the moon lighting their way, Charity asked herself why she had not thought to use the tunnel, then decided that the oversight was wise. Mrs. Dylan was in the kitchen and her coming through would have caused a great stir.

Finally Wilferd pulled up at the cliff, his eyes questioning. "And now?..." he asked.

Charity was already down from the gig. "There is a path just there."

"No, Miss Charity. You cannot mean it. I know that path. It is dangerous even in the daylight."

"I certainly cannot make it in this get-up. You must help me. Come! Unbutton me down the back." This was done with some fumbling on Wilferd's part, Charity said, "Now grasp the upper stays of the skirt and lift." While speaking, she cleared her arms of the gracefully puffed sleeves and lowered herself to her knees. A moment later, she emerged from the skirt as though it were a small tent in which she had been hiding.

"And now these ridiculous petticoats!" She stripped them off and stood finally in camisole and pantalettes to gaze fondly at the wedding gown that Wilferd still held, which looked as though it waited for her to jump back in.

"Goodbye, you lovely thing," she murmured, then raising her arms and voice simultaneously, she called out, "Goodbye, Windward—goodbye, Camber—goodbye, Dennis—goodbye, dear Mrs. Dylan." Then, seemingly as an afterthought, "Oh, yes—and goodbye, Christopher—tell Clement I love him!"

Fairly aglow now with excitement and joy, she kissed Wilferd. "Thank you, darling. You have been wonderful."

"Miss Charity!" he wailed. "What *will* I tell them?"

"Tell them nothing. Let them wonder. Let them guess."

"But Dorothy...."

"Yes, tell her—tell her I am happy—happy—happy! She will understand."

"I'll tell her."

"Oh, yes, one thing more—there is a bramble bush in the flat west of the Windward stable. Take a shovel and dig exactly three strides due south of it. You will find a reward of golden sovereigns. They are for you and Dorothy with my love."

He gaped at her. "Miss Charity!..."

"But see that you take them out sparingly," she went on, "as from a bank. Take them all at once, and those who feel we lesser beings should not have wealth may find a way to take them from you."

With that, she turned to the perilous path and started down. The idea of accident, injury, falling, was ridiculous. The gods would not allow it. And perhaps that was true. Perhaps they saved her for the shattering disappointment at the bottom.

When she reached the cove, the *Evening Primrose* was not there.

Sobbing her despair, Charity climbed over

rocks and ran down to the narrow strip of sand which formed the beach. If she feared seeing only watery solitude, that fear proved groundless, for to the south, just within sight, Charity saw a ship. The full moon was high in the still-cloudless sky, and with its help, and by squinting and peering, she found reason to believe it the *Evening Primrose*. This was of little consolation, however, so long as it had put to sea a fateful hour too soon.

But as she watched, there was more—the sound of cannon fire and explosion flashes beyond the ship from the south. The *Evening Primrose* was being fired upon.

Obviously aware of its peril, the beleaguered frigate now turned and began tacking back northward. Charity could only stand and watch as the slow naval drama unfolded there in the channel waters. She could now see the broad-beamed British gunship labor northward after its prey. Charity's spirit did rise somewhat when she was able to see that the frigate was indeed Sean McDougal's sleek vessel. His strategy was to tack a zigzag course, thus giving the pursuing gunboat a less stationary target. The comparative speed of the two vessels favored the *Evening Primrose*, but not by a great deal. The distance between them was widened at times when the gunboat yawed to bring its broadside cannon to bear. Their range and power were much greater than the more flexible deck cannon and when they blasted forth in sequence, the waters around the black frigate were churned up, the balls coming perilously close.

But after each such salvo the range was extended as the gunship straightened away. Charity could see the goal toward which Sean was struggling, a low-lying layer of fog to the north. If he could only make it before a lucky shot brought the *Evening Primrose* to bay—

Then Charity's spirits soared with hope and her heart pounded as she saw a possibility. Frantically, she estimated Sean's tacking path. If he maintained it as it was, he would angle in toward shore at a point not too far from where she stood. The *not too far* might have been optimistic but Charity did not think of it in those terms. It would be much closer than at present and that was something for which to be thankful.

There were estimates of logistics to be considered, the speed of the frigate after each tack; a careful judgment on the point of interception coupled with the progress she could make from the shore.

As she watched, she contained herself with difficulty, tempted to leave on the instant and trust to luck. She was able to resist the impulse and wait, to choose the right moment to the best of her ability.

Then she waded out through the breakers, threw herself forward, and began to swim.

It was an exhilarating experience, her fierce desire to reach her goal blotting out all sense of fear or doubt. The channel surface was choppy but the skill she had learned in the lakes and rivers of Virginia had not been lost. As she swam along with smooth, even strokes, she was even able to share in the excitement of the chase; the

501

black frigate swinging ably along with the fat gunship pursuing, broadsiding at times to blaze out its iron shot. It was a scene of conflict that stirred Charity's imagination—a kind of savage splendor about it, symbolizing the elemental conflicts that existed eternally in the human pattern.

Charity did not pause to contemplate the scene either physically or mentally. It was a sweep of sweet, fierce emotion that engulfed her rather than any philosophical aspect. Her highest elation sprang from the fact that she was finding physical strength over and above the norm; no sign of fatigue whatever. To the contrary, she felt that she could have swum forever if the need arose.

She was coming closer now, just as the black frigate prepared to yaw and the gunboat was again swinging about for a broadside—perhaps the last of them before the *Evening Primrose* went out of range. It would be well, she told herself, to be aboard ship before the cannonade was delivered. With this in mind, she increased her beat for a final sprint.

A problem she had anticipated solved itself. Would she be able to attract attention with all eyes riveted on the pursuing vessel? As things worked out it was not necessary to try. She came against the frigate's hull some feet past the prow where a line dangled as though it had been awaiting her arrival. She grasped it and climbed up the hull to drop over onto the forward deck.

A member of the crew stood by, his eyes on the gunboat as he crouched there listening for orders to be bawled from the after deck. He turned in time to see Charity arrive aboard.

He stood speechless. Only later would he recount the experience with fanciful embellishments.

Right out of the water she came, up over the side, naked as the day she was born—like a mermaid who lost her tail.

Most of it fallacious, of course. Charity was not naked. She was clad in the camisole and pantalettes. She was not a mermaid and had never possessed a tail.

The gunboat's cannonade boomed and Charity and the hand ducked instinctively, crouching behind the rail for protection. The Channel water frothed about them. The frigate rocked, then righted itself into the yaw.

Charity straightened. "The last one, I hope," she said cheerfully, then ran aft, turning astounded faces in her direction as she moved.

She climbed to the quarterdeck and stopped. It was her turn to be surprised. The ship's evasive action was being directed by a clown! A creature wearing a great crimson mouth, ridiculous baggy clothes, and a pointed dunce cap.

"My God!" Charity cried. "What are you got up for?"

Sean's eyes spoke. In a wordless language far beyond translation it told what was welling up in his heart. He then asked, "What kept you so long?" and turned his glass back on the gunboat.

"Well, that's a fine welcome indeed! Why didn't you wait for me?"

"And let the whole British navy gather about to welcome me out of the cove?"

"I thought for a while you were going down to meet them hand-to-hand."

"They popped out of nowhere. I had to turn tail and run." With the *Evening Primrose* practically out of range, Sean turned to her with a clown's smile. "Mavourneen," he said softly. "And whatever happened to that other maiden, Charity?"

She replied only, "Give me your glass."

He proffered it and she trained it on the cliff above the cove path, then handed it back to him. "Just there—what do you see?"

He peered, adjusted the glass and peered again. "A gaudily dressed tart without a head, being held up by a man."

"Nay, lover. That is Charity. Or what is left of her."

"Gad, lass," he said with high admiration as he lowered the glass, "you skinned out of your drawers."

Charity's mind had gone in another direction. "No," she said, "that isn't Charity up there. It is—oh, it is . . . " She frowned at not finding the right word. "A shell, a snail's. . . ."

"A chrysalis?" he suggested.

"Yes! Yes! My chrysalis. I lay in that shell as a great grub with naught but the yearning to be free. Then. . . ."

He drew her close. "Then the lovely butterfly emerged from the shell to break out and fly to the moon!"

Charity drew away. "Hardly that. But Mavourneen did come free."

"To follow where the wind blows," Sean laughed. "We will deliver cargo to the rebels and

504

then be off and down around the bottom of the world to the warm seas and the lovely brown sun children. To live out the rest of our days...."

"Not so fast, my bucko. You will have to marry me. I'll be no sailor's tart to lift my skirts at your pleasure."

"Then I'll break the most sacred law of the sailing man and wed you." He turned his attention to the wheelman. "Duty, man, duty. Watch the sea. Gape not like a hooked fish." Again to Charity. "It will be an odd splice for sure. A captain marrying a lass to the captain."

"It must be legal," Charity warned. "No shabby lie to delude the poor maiden."

Sean laughed. "Give thought to the poor captain. The maiden is well able to take care of herself."

The gunship now hurled its last barrage, gaining Sean's attention. While he was thus occupied, Charity had her own thoughts. *I have finally come to the man of my heart.* She was not confusing dreams with reality. She was well aware of the fragile stuff of which dreams are made and it did not matter. The south seas or the arctic snows. Any place so long as Sean was with her, his laughter in her ears, his lips upon her own.

Now he swept her up into his arms, whispering, "Any regrets, my love?"

"Yes," she replied. "I never met the Prime Minister and I never learned to dance."

"No mind. Lord North is a wooden man and the minuet is a bore. We shall dance on white beaches under a heartbreaking moon."

"Mayhap," she replied tartly, "but will you

stand here the whole night entertaining the crew in that outlandish garb?"

He kissed her, and then the clown carried the mermaid below....

THE END

Pinnacle Books wants to publish the type of books you enjoy. For this reason would you please fill out this questionnaire so that we can learn more about your reading tastes.

1. Are you _____ *female* _____ *male?*

2. What is your age?

_____ Under 15?
_____ 15 - 24?
_____ 25 - 34?
_____ 35 - 44?
_____ 45 - 54?
_____ 55 or over?

3. What is your level of education?

_____ Currently — Jr. High _____
_____ High School
_____ or College
_____ Some high school
_____ High school graduate
_____ Some college
_____ College graduate

4. Where did you buy this book?

_____ Bookstore
_____ Drugstore
_____ Chain
variety store
_____ Supermarket
_____ Department store
_____ Discount store
_____ Newsstand
_____ Bus or
train station
_____ Airport
_____ Other _____

(continued on next page)

5. *What types of books do you like best?*

——— Hardcover bestsellers when available in paperback
——— Historical romance
——— Gothics
——— Occult
——— Mystery and suspense
——— Science fiction
——— Cookbooks
——— Self-help and "How-to" books
——— Biography and autobiography
——— Nonfiction
——— Westerns
——— War
——— Action/adventure
——— Other ————————————————

6. *Why did you buy this book?*

————————————————————————

(Please give title)

(You may check more than one answer)

——— Recognized the title
——— Author's reputation
——— Friend's recommendation
——— The book's cover
——— Newspaper or magazine ad
——— Radio commercial
——— TV commercial
——— Free preview booklet

——— Saw author on TV, or heard him/her on radio
——— Subject matter
——— Price
——— Other ————————————————————

Name ————————————————————————

Address ————————————————————————

City————————————State————————Zip————————

Please return questionnaire to:

Pinnacle Books, Inc., Dept. LKB
One Century Plaza
2029 Century Park East
Los Angeles California 90067